Is This the Way explosive, jarring depiction of what unfolded in northern Uganda. The meticulously plotted story is totally mesmerizing, and a great resource to appreciate the inner details and effects of the two-decades long primordial conflict that traumatized the entire population. At the same time, it offers insightful lessons on how to handle the wounded, hurt, deprived, disadvantaged and traumatized persons. The author passionately manifests a combination of anguish, anger, desperation, empathy, and epitomizes all with exhibition of love. As usual in life, this kind of truth scathes the ears, but is a great blessing for the affected people's absolute recovery.

—Ojera James Latigo
Marcus Garvey Pan-Afrikan Institute (MPAI)

Is This the Way Home? is a poignant reflection on the psychological toll of war, the difficulty of reintegration, and the resilience of the human spirit in the face of unimaginable trauma. It's an exploration of the complexities of returning home, both physically and emotionally after a long period of violence and forced separation. The novel challenges readers to reflect on the idea of home and how one can rebuild a life that transcends the divisions of time, place, and culture.

—Phillip Odiambo
Chemist, Gulu, Uganda

IS THIS
THE WAY
HOME?

BCC PRESS

BY COMMON CONSENT PRESS is a non-profit publisher dedicated to producing affordable, high-quality books that help define and shape the Latter-day Saint experience. BCC Press publishes books that address all aspects of Mormon life. Our mission includes finding manuscripts that will contribute to the lives of thoughtful Latter-day Saints, mentoring authors and nurturing projects to completion, and distributing important books to the Mormon audience at the lowest possible cost.

JUDY DUSHKU

IS THIS THE WAY **HOME?**

Is This the Way Home?
Copyright © 2025 by Judy Dushku

All rights reserved. Printed in the United States of America. No part of this book may be used or reproduced in any manner whatsoever without written permission except in the case of brief quotations embodied in critical articles or reviews.

For information contact
By Common Consent Press
972 East Burnham Lane
Draper, Utah 84020

Cover design: D Christian Harrison
Book design: Andrew Heiss

www.bccpress.org
ISBN-13: 978-1-961471-19-1

10 9 8 7 6 5 4 3 2 1

This book is dedicated to Aol Lucy and Aber Rose,
and the other child mothers of the Beads of Hope sisterhood.
Your lives and your beads will always inspire.

and

To Kate Holbrook, who stirred me on as I wrote this book
with the words, "Remember, we are often honored to be
called to be caretakers of other people's legacies."

Foreword

By Ms. Dora Single Alal,
Director, THRIVE Gulu

I hail from Acholiland in northern Uganda, and inevitably witnessed the events that unfolded during the two decades of the Lord's Resistance Army (LRA) rebels' insurrections that pitted the government army, the Uganda People's Defense Force (UPDF) against the hapless population in a conflict that had long simmered below the surface. Deeply held animosities that seemed almost primordial led Joseph Kony's troops to commit shocking atrocities against whole families and villages from 1986 to 2006. This included the kidnapping of thousands of children and turning them into fighters. In a scorch-earth policy, a 48-hour ultimatum was issued by the UPDF in 1996 to the people of Acholiland to vacate their often-self-sufficient homesteads to a life of squalid existence in Internally Displaced People's (IDP) camps, an event that traumatized the entire population. The then UN Under-Secretary for Humanitarian Affairs, Jan Egaland described the situation as, "The most forgotten humanitarian crisis. A moral outrage. A human tragedy".

If captive children escaped from the LRA or from the IDP camps and found their way to a town, they were often paraded in the streets in the hope that someone would identify them. As a university graduate trained in Psychology, I was enjoined to become a mental health practitioner and to help reunite victims of LRA abductions with a host community. These engagements were expanded when "Operation Iron Fist" (2002-3) was launched allowing UPDF forces to infiltrate the LRA bases in South Sudan, a neighboring country. Many kidnapped girls who were victims of sexual slavery and had become child-mothers, were rescued by the UPDF, while others escaped, and were brought to a local non-governmental organization called Gulu Support the Children Organization (GUSCO), for rehabilitation and possible reintegration into the community. This reception center grew as it helped many formerly abducted children. While I worked there I saw many girls who had been forced to be mothers and had walked hundreds of miles with their babies tied on their backs. With swollen feet, malnourished babies, and some with fresh wounds from bomb shells, they poured in. Their suffering was heart-wrenching to behold; what I saw was the epitome of unspeakable human misery and pain.

In January 2012, I wanted to expand my work and was drawn to a new organization that began as an NGO that called itself THARCE Gulu (Trauma Healing and Reflection Centre) but soon expanded its operations and become Thrive-Gulu, currently one of the largest originally local NGOs in the region. It was then that I interfaced with Prof. Judy Dushku, who we fondly call 'Mama'. Judy led teams of like-minded professionals from the USA on several Solidarity visits to Gulu, to empathize with the suffering people and find ways to support them. To make a more permanent impact, they opted to become a Community Based Organization that invited the influence of people from Gulu. Driven by the motivational adage, 'from a survivor to a thriver', the organization meta morphed to Thrive-Gulu, an organization I am humbled to serve as a Country Director to date.

The unmatched passion and love that Mama Judy exhibited to the people of northern Uganda attracted many who joined her outlook and formed this thriving organization that is not only healing traumatized people but propelling them to self-sufficiency through various empowerment programs.

In the formative years, during her frequent visits to Gulu, Mama Judy, along with other friends and family, were enjoined to attentively listen to numerous stories from victims, and they conceived the theme; "*Your Story Matters*". The stories uniquely unveiled the resilience of African Women in northern Uganda, particularly those who'd survived the war.

In the most amazing way, Mama Judy integrates all these experiences in an imaginary story that she brilliantly shares in her book, "*Is This Way Home?*", for which I am extremely privileged to write this forward. In her book, she extols the stories of the teen moms reclaiming their lives after suffering the enormous invisible wounds. Reading this book, will provide every reader an opportunity to appreciate life the way it is here. Mama Judy walks the teen moms on their journeys as they are unleashing their potentials.

For all who wish to get vivid and clear insights into the two-decades conflict that unfolded in northern Uganda from a humanistic perspective, this book is a treasured reading. Thank you so much Mama Judy, for unreservedly sharing your passion, insights, and intellect in these pages. A must read.

Notes to help understand the language of the book

A NOTE ON NAMES I chose the names of characters in this book from among those most common among the Acholi. They are not intended to replicate anyone identically named that once lived, or who now lives in the North of Uganda. In fact, I repeat that I promised not to tell the story of any one person and name her. But until recently, most Acholi do not use surnames, and so a chosen "Christian" name combined with a traditional Acholi tribal name is common. I used Facebook to find names of characters I created, and they are from people I don't know. Most Acholi names of men begin with the letter O, while most names of women begin with A. Knowing that will help the reader remember the names here.

A NOTE ON LANGUAGE I count on the reader to follow this simple instruction while reading this book. With the names to identify which characters are Acholi, assume that whenever an Acholi is speaking to Acholi, they are speaking their common language. It is the common language of Northern Uganda. I wrote the conversations in English, as I did not want to confuse the readers. Just assume that what is written here in English is the best translation of what was said in Acholi. The national language of Uganda is English, the language mandated by the British during the colonial era, which is spoken all over the country, and in other African countries once part of the British Empire. It is ubiquitous. Except in the lowest grades, English is the language of schooling and business in Uganda, including in Gulu and other parts of the North where most of this book is set. While it is considered more in the British style of English in Uganda, there are enough Americans and American media that most adult Ugandans speak at least some English and the majority speak it well. Certainly, those who interact with tourists are English literate, so Agnes is not unusual in her proficiency.

A NOTE ON PLACE NAMES For any place that is famous enough to be commonly referred to in news or other histories, I have used the real name of the place. The city, the town, the region, the camp or the battlefield. For the purposes of making the story work, I have altered some descriptions of place to make it clearer to the reader. A few places, like the village where Agnes was born and lived until she was eleven, are invented to decrease speculation about what else may have happened there in the real world. Eve's Shelter is not real but is modeled on places closer to Kitgum and Palabek, that are real and huge and growing as the South Sudan wars continue.

An actual LRA camp called Aba Camp does not exist to my knowledge, but many LRA camps existed in that part of the Democratic Republic of Congo at that time near the end of the war.

A NOTE ON LOCAL ORGANIZATION OF THE MORMON CHURCH I simplified the otherwise quite complicated administrative organization as to do otherwise would unnecessarily interfere with the narrative. For example: there is no Gulu Ward in the real Mormon world. The description of the missionary program there is quite accurate, as is the description of the Mormon Temple in Johannesburg.

A NOTE ON DR. DENIS MUKWEGE'S CLINIC He is an actual Nobel Peace Prize recipient, and his Panzi Hospital is real and has inspired other similar clinics for women, but the Dungu clinic is not real, to my knowledge.

A NOTE ON INTERGENERATIONAL TRAUMA I am not a trained psychologist, but I have studied trauma for a lifetime, and know the field well. I know it well enough that as I have come to know the children of many child mothers in Gulu who brought infants out of the bush and have raised them in Gulu, and it is obvious even to observers like me, that there was no way to prevent some kinds of PTSD from being passed on to these thousands of children of this next generation. I expect them to be the ones who will publish their autobiographies and give this 20th Century epic tragedy the attention it is due. We can all look forward to reading their firsthand accounts.

Part I

Prologue

2005

Agnes swayed in the Ugandan heat, the weight of her fevered toddler, Grace, wrapped on her back and sapping the last of her strength. With bare feet blistered, a thousand memories could no longer drive the young mother onward: the sting of a man's fist, the blood-curdling threats, the two beloved sons she'd had to leave behind.

"Mama?" Beatrice cried out, sharp and urgent, begging for water. For food. For shade, as she clung to her mother's sagging arm.

Agnes meant to answer her seven-year-old's pleas, but no sound came from her sun-chapped lips. She'd already given the last of the water to her two daughters.

How long have we walked?

Past the Impenetrable Forest.

Past the place where they'd left behind the gumboots to conceal their escape.

Past the strange villages and languages that sounded nothing like her native Acholi.

Past the people who'd shooed the three of them away and flung insults: "Kony whore!"

Past more rivers than Agnes ever knew existed between the bush and Gulu, where Kony's men—soldiers in the Lord's Resistance Army (LRA)—had snatched her from school all those years ago, when she was just eleven.

How much farther? If she'd made a mistake in leaving the bush, it was too late now.

"Mama!" called Beatrice again, even more urgently as she tugged on Agnes's dusty arm. "Are we lost? Should we ask for help?"

Agnes had been commanded where to go and what to do since the day Kony's men had come for her at school. She had no practice with asking anything, much less for help.

Agnes blinked as her vision blurred. Her knees buckled, and she tumbled forward, her cheek hitting the hard, red earth.

Baby Grace began to wail as she struggled to free herself from the wrap.

Was that another voice in the distance? The rumble of a truck? *Let it not be a bad soldier.*

"Is this the way to Gulu?" Agnes said, barely above a whisper as Beatrice cried and cried for some helpful stranger to appear.

Agnes couldn't pry her eyes back open. Everything went black.

Is this the way home?

1

May 2014—Gulu, Northern Uganda

"Welcome to the Harmony Inn," said Agnes, smiling warmly from the reception desk as she greeted the new arrivals—six friendly Irish students. Smiling was part of her job, and here at work, she didn't mind. She'd gone half her life without smiling enough and saw no harm in it now. The gesture helped people feel glad to be in Gulu, doing whatever good things they had come to do. The influx of travelers, in turn, reminded her that the world was grander than the one she knew and that Uganda was not forgotten.

To not be forgotten, after all she had experienced in the bush, meant everything to Agnes.

She handed over the keys to the new guests. "Just leave them here when you go out."

"Thanks," said a cheery, sunburned girl in a purple T-shirt that read *You Never Walk Alone*. Another Christian group. Interfaith work. "Can we invite some friends from church back later? We could get to know them better here."

"Of course." Agnes was accustomed to this request. Since the war between Joseph Kony's Lord's Resistance Army (LRA) and his own Acholi people here in the North of Uganda, people from nearly everywhere, it seemed, had come to learn how people recover from ruin. "I guess that *is* the way to learn," some Ugandans acknowledged. "Come to Gulu and see how we live, how we do what we have to do." Other locals didn't care about helping the outsiders at all. They said, "Just give me a job."

The six young women from Cork rolled their suitcases away, their sweaty blonde ponytails swaying as they went. These travelers, at least, had not asked the usual questions yet—about the war, Kony, and Agnes's place in the story.

For the three years Agnes had been working the hotel's front desk, she'd thought it her duty to answer every question anyone asked about Gulu. She enjoyed talking with the guests, but some things made her uneasy. She'd recently told as much to her friend, Sunday, the owner of the Harmony Inn, restaurant, and bar.

"I want to be helpful to our guests, but it still hurts to talk about it," Agnes said. How could she possibly explain the way a string of three "husbands" had raped and beaten her, starting with Samson, who'd impregnated her at age twelve. The children she'd borne. The one she'd buried. The two older sons she'd left, and the two daughters she'd escaped with . . .

Though moments in the bush often returned to her in paralyzing flashes, it sometimes shocked Agnes how much she struggled to remember some details. But what was the point of reliving the memory anyway? It was better to smile. Make the guests feel welcome. Thank them for coming. Show them how to survive the worst.

Sunday considered her, his face soft with concern. "Of course it still hurts to talk about it."

Unlike Agnes, Sunday wasn't Acholi. A Muganda from the South, he had slightly lighter skin and a smaller forehead than Agnes's people. He'd been an army man, fighting for the Uganda Peoples's Defense Force (UPDF), but these days he laughed easily and loud, though never boisterously and never at someone else's expense. He understood what it meant to be an Acholi up here, to have the LRA be the town's claim to fame. Guidebooks said there was an old British fort north of Gulu where Arabs had once captured slaves before walking them all the way to Egypt, but no one really cared to see Baker's Fort. No, people came to see a 21st century tragedy: survivors of an unusually local and intimate war, fought by neighbor against neighbor, where in the same family people often ended up either on Kony's side or becoming his victims. Where children were commonly kidnapped and forced to attack their parents' own huts. Where these kids were forced to kill their loved ones. This was to make sure the children wouldn't try to run back home, so they would know that no one would ever welcome them back after committing such barbaric acts as Kony's child soldiers.

Sunday understood all this, even as a Ugandan from the South, even as part of the majority Baganda tribe that had dominated Uganda since Independence, even as part of the group that had been loyal to the long-time dictator, Museveni.

It was no secret that Museveni had stripped Idi Amin of power and promised to combat Joseph Kony and bring peace to Uganda once and for all. As promised, Museveni built a "great army" and called it The Uganda Peoples's Defense Force (UPDF). While the UPDF did indeed spend two decades pursuing the LRA, defeating them in battle, and capturing towns they'd dominated—eventually removing Kony from power as they'd set out to do—they also robbed the same villages and farms that Kony had pillaged to supply and feed his army.

Even worse, as the UPDF gained power, they didn't restore the war-torn communities. Instead, they replaced one abusive system with another as they raped the same abducted women and orphaned children Kony's men had left behind. For a good many Acholi people, the UPDF was almost as terrible as the LRA. They usually were better armed and had better uniforms, but they often caught escaped "wives" from Kony's camps and kept them for their own pleasure, leaving them pregnant and as broken as they'd found them.

The way Sunday told it to Agnes, he'd seen such horrors firsthand, while serving as an army man in the UPDF. There was no way to deny the truth, but he'd gone home to Kampala and found a way to get out of the army legally, so as not to be punished. Then he had two choices. He could become a high-rolling former military officer and get himself a beautiful wife, stock a shiny bar in his massive home with the best Jack Daniels and Tanqueray Gin (or the locally distilled Uganda Waragi) and become a raging alcoholic like so many soldiers who had turned to drink to drown their guilt. Or he could go back to Gulu as a rebuilder and a helper.

While he could not undo what destruction he might have contributed to, he believed he could do something useful for others. Maybe he could offer recompense to the victims of the UPDF, serving their community for the rest of his life. So, he took the money he was given when discharged, and he came to Gulu.

Here, he'd bought a small hostel with enough land around it to build out and up, and then he'd constructed the bigger, but still modest, Harmony Inn with a large kitchen, an informal restaurant, and a community room to hold the AA meetings that kept him sober.

He'd found his way.

Agnes had always known there was something special about Sunday Laroke. A Muganda she could trust.

"Is it honest," Agnes had asked Sunday that day, as a cheer from a cluster of men rose from the restaurant bar, "to pretend I wasn't a part of the war? Could I just shrug and say I never actually knew Kony, but that I knew others who had?"

"You could say that. Others do," Sunday said, watching her. "You can tell anyone as much or as little as you want, Agnes. You don't owe anyone your story."

"I suppose I don't hide my life because I don't want anyone to leave here thinking those atrocities didn't happen . . . or think that they were an exaggeration. The war was as bad as they've heard. Worse."

"And this is your way of doing your part?" asked Sunday.

"Maybe so."

Eventually, she'd learned how to answer in a way that felt honest but faraway, like a person she'd lost touch with. As if she were talking about something that had happened to someone else.

"Did you check in the Irish guests?" asked Sunday's wife, Molly, as she approached the reception desk with an armful of linens. "I need to put a towel in Room 3."

"You just missed them," Agnes said.

Molly offered a quick thanks before rushing off, in a kind of dance.

Agnes laughed to herself. She adored Molly, and they had become close over the years. Molly's friendship provided Agnes with a secure yet upbeat place to face her past and share the many difficult memories that she, for so long, had been unable to confront. She also hoped that one day she could be the "Molly" to someone's else's "Agnes." She'd learned so much from Molly, just by watching her curious, Western ways.

Molly Masters had first come to Gulu as a foreign aid worker—an English-born Brit with a Scottish father and a Ugandan mother who'd yearned to take her daughter "back home" all the days of her life. Molly promised her dying mother she would go home for her, but also to save herself from following in her drunken father's footsteps to nowhere. Her third week in Gulu, she slipped into one of Sunday's AA meetings, and before long, she and Sunday were business partners and spouses, co-running the newly renovated hotel together.

Still astonished by how they had all landed here together, Agnes felt acutely grateful for her job at the Harmony Inn. To work with people who cared about her and understood things she didn't have to explain—and who offered a salary, safety, a chance to use a computer—the couple had given her a life with such abundance that she had to remind herself it was real.

They'd taken her on after a recommendation from Pastor Emanuel, who'd previously employed Agnes at his Seed Store, and who still employed both her sons (the ones she'd had to leave), which still shocked her as such a stroke of good fortune that it confounded her. Jobs were hard to come by in Gulu. She had much to be thankful for: a church community that felt like a family, neighborhood friends who were kind, the knowledge that her sons were near and alive—even if her oldest, Moses, still refused to speak to her. All this was surely more than she deserved.

Did others wonder, as she did, why such blessings had been bestowed upon her? To be so extremely fortunate puzzled her, especially coming after those blurry years in the bush . . . and the languishing years that followed her escape.

Agnes rummaged through a few papers on the desk and forced the worries away.

∎∎∎∎∎∎

An hour later, the Irish Christians came to deposit the keys with Agnes before their outing. They were here to study child soldiers, they explained, and they'd also brought a large supply of children's books with them.

"Thank you for that," said Agnes. "The libraries will benefit from such a substantial donation."

"Is it true?" one of the bolder ones asked. "That Kony had been a Catholic altar boy?"

Agnes looked into the girl's astonished face. In the end, they always asked about Kony. About the war. About the role of God in all of it.

"Yes," Agnes said. "He grew up just 30 miles from here in a village called Odek." Agnes recited her usual speech, explaining how Kony joined his aunt's spiritual movement to "purify the people of his tribe." Then he formed a cruel group of soldiers, with aims to take over Uganda. He turned to abducting children, forcing youngsters to wage war.

"It happened all around us," Agnes ended.

"How could he claim he was a Christian?" asked a second young woman.

Agnes shrugged. For this, too, she had a practiced response. "He claimed he could hear the voice of God. And once he had built an army, he kept up those claims to save face. If he admitted his claims had been false, the people would have killed him." She recalled how fanatical Kony had become, how he'd hoped to 'cleanse' Uganda under his leadership. "He insisted he had been called by God."

"And people really believed this?" said a voice from the back.

Always the incredulous shock.

"Some people, yes," Agnes said, as neutrally as she could muster. "Too many."

Before they left, the Irish group organized a meeting at the restaurant bar that night. Agnes was explaining how they would stop serving food at 10 p.m. when her cellphone rang inside her sweater pocket behind the desk.

"Excuse me one moment," she said, swiveling around in the chair to answer a call from her youngest daughter, Grace, now thirteen.

"I've got it," said Molly, stepping in to retrieve the keys as the travelers left. Sunday followed, adjusting the A/C unit in the lobby.

"Mama!" Grace shrieked through the phone. "Mr. Carson, my teacher. He's . . . he's trying to hurt me. I'm locked in his bathroom."

From the other side of the call, Agnes heard a pounding sound and the rough voice of a man. "Open up the door, you little bitch!"

Everything seemed to slow to a stop as another scream come through the phone line.

Agnes's chest tightened. The corners of her vision blurred.

Grace.

She formed words in her mind, but none came out. Her whole body seized, her heart pounded. The phone slipped from her hand.

"It's happening again," Molly said with alarm, making Agnes sit down as she stroked her hair.

Sunday rushed to pick up the phone.

"Grace. Grace, are you there?" asked Sunday.

Agnes rocked back and forth, sobbing and trembling. Finally the words came. "Go!" Agnes shouted. "Go, Sunday. She's only thirteen."

She's only a child.

2

1990—In the bush

Life wasn't the same living with her mother, twelve-year-old Agnes learned quickly enough. With her grandmother, Agnes had *known* she was loved, had known she was the favorite. Everyone told her so. Her grandmother showed her in a hundred ways. The entire Lomora village seemed to admire her grandmother as much as Agnes did. And Agnes basked in her attention.

Then, one day, when Agnes was only eleven, that radiant beam of light was gone. Achieng Esther died, and Agnes had to go back to her mother Mabel's hut. A frail woman who, from what Agnes could tell, did not want her, nor even love her. Rumors suggested her heart belonged to children who'd died but whose spirits still clung to her. Villagers talked of Agnes's father's attempts to exorcize the evil spirits that plagued Mabel, but to no effect. Agnes could hardly wait for school each morning as she stepped out of Mabel's hut.

But now even teachers were distressed by bigger rumors of what every adult in Gulu was whispering about. A vicious and terrible war. A bad man named Kony, who lurked here in the North, burning huts and snatching children from their homes. People could talk of little else.

Agnes kicked a rock as she walked to school. She missed her grandmother, the mighty old woman who had made Agnes feel loved and safe.

Her school came into view. She liked her teachers, respected leaders here in Lomora. When her P-3 teacher greeted her, she did so with a smile. "Are you ready to learn some sums?"

Agnes took her seat. Children quietly whispered or laughed as they waited for class to begin.

Then Sister Prudence hurtled into the room, eyes wide and sweat on her brow. "They have guns! *Pangas*!"

Everyone froze at the mention of machetes and guns. All gazes locked on Sister Prudence.

"Spread the word!" the nun shrieked, moving on to the next classroom. "Run!"

The classroom became a whirlwind with fear on every face. Legs and books and arms were flying as everyone scattered.

Agnes gasped. She needed to run. But where? Her legs didn't wait for an answer. She grabbed her bag and raced for her mother Mabel's hut, following the lead of some bigger kids who were already sprinting ahead and stirring up dust in their tracks. She followed their path, zigzagging into the tall, golden grass across the red clay road from the huts.

"Shh, don't speak," one ordered as they crouched in the high grass.

Agnes held her breath, watching the rebels descend on the school. *Guns. In our village?* More men came, and a shot rang out somewhere in the distance. Agnes's whole body went rigid. Had a teacher been shot? A classmate? A friend?

Voices grew louder near her. She didn't think she could ever move from that spot. Shouting began. Agnes forced her eyes open as she looked closer at the soldiers.

They were not so old. They were . . . *boys!*

Boy soldiers who were now dragging two P-4 boys by the arm, hauling them away.

What would they want with these kids?

What could they want with her?

"Come out you stupid kids!" one man shouted as bullets hit the grass where Agnes hid with her peers. "If you don't come out, we'll keep shooting. Then we'll burn the grass. Do you want to be roasted alive?"

One of the older girls stood, hands up and lip quivering. "Please. Please let us live!" she shouted. At her feet, Agnes thought she recognized the girl's sister, a P-2 pupil. Safe for now, thanks only to her older sister's sacrifice.

Without needing a signal, the group of the hiding children crept deeper into the grass, away from the shooters. Then, they took off running. Back across the red road. To the huts.

Agnes was flying. Flying as fast as her little body could carry her down a back path between the brick huts with thatched roofs. From the corner of her eye, she saw her grandmother's hut, her old home. Empty.

She ran on. To Mama-Mabel's hut. To the only home she had left.

When she flew through the door, pulse galloping, this hut too stood empty. Her mother was not there.

Agnes was alone.

Not safe. Not protected.

She hid inside anyway. "Mama-Mabel?" she called. That small word might have given her away. Some soldiers were right outside. Agnes squeezed her eyes shut as she listened carefully to every sound—boots entering the hut nearby, her neighbor's mother pleading desperately with the soldiers to leave her son behind.

"Please," Agnes heard. Then, a bang so loud it shook her bones.

After a frozen minute, a bullet whizzed past her head, hitting the brick wall above her.

"Stop!" Agnes said, her voice wobbly. She mustered the courage of the P-4 girl, who'd stood up to the men in hopes of protecting her sister. "I'm coming out. I'm coming out!"

The soldiers dragged Agnes from the hut and shoved her into a clutch of children, many of them her schoolmates. Men in dusty army uniforms were tying all of them together with a long rope so that they would not be able to run away again. There could have been forty children. Maybe more. Most of them older, along with two teachers.

Agnes's mouth went dry as the rope tightened around her wrists. She couldn't run. Not now.

Where is my mother?

"March!" one soldier roared.

With the sound of his command, the group of captives were yanked forward in the intense heat and thick dust. The smallest children couldn't keep up the pace. Agnes kept her eyes on the road, willing herself not to trip, not to fall, as some did. Those who fell were hit by the soldiers, forced at gunpoint to right themselves. Some cried. She couldn't look at their faces. The world seemed to fade in, then out.

On they marched, and her stomach rumbled. If only she had eaten her breakfast—corn meal posho. When would she eat again? When could she speak again?

The rope burned her wrists. Her fingers tingled from the tightness. She stumbled, ashamed, and bit down on her tongue to avoid crying. She wasn't the youngest here. She needed to stay strong.

She *had* to stay strong.

To her right, a younger boy stumbled. Agnes reached for him, hoping to help him up before one of the soldiers noticed. But this time, instead of beating him, the soldier lifted his gun and shot the boy, right there next to Agnes.

Agnes's entire body shuddered. *Make it not real. This is all a dream. A nightmare. Mama-Mabel will come. Somebody will come. Make it not real.*

She should have looked away. But her eyes fixed on the boy, the twitching body, the way blood poured from his shirt.

She caught the gaze of a classmate. Their terrified understanding said it all. If they didn't stay quiet, if they didn't keep up, they would be next.

After hours and hours of walking, running, stumbling, Agnes's head pulsed from lack of food and water. Dirt covered her limbs. She forced herself to pay attention, to know they were headed north and east, away from Lomora, away from Gulutown.

She heard one bold boy ask what was going on.

"Haven't you heard of us?" one soldier mocked. He didn't look much older than a P-5 pupil. "We are the Lord's Resistance Army. Welcome to the LRA."

3

May 2014—Gulu

Beatrice was home at the compound, tapping a pencil against her schoolwork. At sixteen, she was a hard worker and a good pupil. It was important for Beatrice to excel at school, for her mother's sake and for her own. She remembered the years after their mother had fled the LRA camp with her and Grace. She remembered the tense ride to her mother's village where Mama-Agnes was beaten and shamed by the people she trusted. The three of them alone in that dark, hot hut. She remembered the years that followed, playing around her mother and the other child-mothers—girls who had been forced to bear their captors' children. These mothers sat for hours on the side of the road, inactive and inert, stunned by years of trauma—abduction, war, escape, and then being shamed and abused once they'd returned home.

Later Agnes had made some money by selling paper beads—beads the women made from tiny, balled up pieces of newspaper and shellac. Beatrice did not want to ever feel that hopeless and helpless again. She did not want Mama-Agnes to ever be so lost again. So, she worked hard and excelled in her classes, and now her science instructor saw fit to give her a challenge. Beatrice bit the end of her pencil, trying to focus, then looked up when she saw Mama-Agnes's incoming call.

"Mama?" she answered, grateful for the distraction from the equation she'd been struggling to solve, even if it meant another tense conversation with her mother. *Don't look at those boys staring at you. Did you walk home from school with a friend? Do not keep wearing the small uniform. Put on a longer dress next time.* The usual.

But this time, it wasn't her Mama's voice coming through the line. "Beatrice, it's Sunday."

She sat up immediately, holding the phone closer.

"Is Mama okay?"

"Yes. She's here with Molly. But, listen, it's Grace. I need your help."

Beatrice stood and paced, feeling her throat squeeze. Her baby sister, Grace. The one she'd spent her whole life protecting.

"Do you know where Mr. Carson lives?" Sunday asked. "The English teacher?"

Beatrice felt a knot form in her stomach. Yes, she knew. The British volunteer had a reputation. Beatrice had sternly rebuffed all his flirty attempts when he was her teacher for the Senior-1 literature class. She'd heard whispers of his charm from the other senior girls: invitations to his house, nice dinners, alcohol, racy movies.

How dare the disgusting brute go after her sister—anyone that young. In a flash moment, Beatrice remembered something her mother had said, expressing pride at how Grace, who'd always excelled at literature, had been invited among others to see a film of *Jane Eyre* with the teacher. He must have somehow singled her out, coercing her back to his place. Her sweet sister, so friendly and eager to make others laugh. She would not have suspected him.

Beatrice quickly gave Sunday the directions to the Bardege part of Gulu where better-paid aid workers rented apartments.

"That bastard Brit," Sunday spat.

"Should I get a *boda* and meet you?" Beatrice asked, forcing her voice to sound calm as she looked around for one of the many motorcycle taxis. People played roles in every family, and this had always been hers. Protect her mother and sister. Keep everyone stable and calm. Achieve high marks and find a way for all of them to build a better future.

"Come to the Inn to help your mother. I'll find Grace and beat shame into Carson."

••••••

Sunday had no trouble finding the place with Beatrice's careful instructions. He skidded his car to a stop outside the four-unit dwelling and yelled, a habit he was not used to since his days in the war.

"Carson! You *mzungu* foreign swine. Come out. Now. And bring the girl."

Sunday was pounding on the door when Carson finally appeared, holding a wide-eyed Grace by the arm with a look of contempt on his sallow face.

"Grace," Sunday said gently, offering his hand. "Are you okay?"

Carson huffed when Grace took it. "Why wouldn't she be?"

Sunday glowered. "How dare you prey on a child like this?"

Grace squeezed out of the doorway and hid behind Sunday.

Carson laughed. "She came because she wanted to, whatever lies she says."

Sunday felt his fist tighten. "You filthy son-of-a-bitch."

He led Grace down the steps and put her safely into the car. She smoothed down her dress and shrank from the window. To Sunday's relief, she didn't seem too disheveled. Her hair and clothes appeared okay, but it was too soon to know.

"Sunday," Grace said with a sudden panic. "I left my school bag inside."

Fool that Carson was, he hadn't closed the door. He stood there with a stupid smug smile. Like a man who'd never faced real consequences. Without invitation, Sunday stormed inside the apartment and retrieved the little bag. "Don't think anyone in Gulu is going to believe anything you say. We know your kind."

Carson laughed.

"You'll stop laughing when the police come."

"The police? Yeah, because they always come when they are called." He laughed again.

At this, big, strong Sunday Laroke punched Carson right in the jaw, knocking him over.

"If I ever hear of you so much as touching another youngster in this town, I'll beat you within an inch of your life, and I will find a way to have you disappear."

An old rage billowed up inside Sunday, but he channeled it into his words.

"You think we haven't seen men like you before? Come here to snatch up innocent girls, thinking they'll fling themselves at you on account of your white face and British money."

It wasn't hard to pick Carson up by the shoulders and fling him back into the apartment, knocking the man flat on his back.

Sunday stormed out without another glance. Some neighbors, overhearing the commotion, were leaning out their windows for a scene. He ignored them and joined Grace in the car, shutting the door and handing her the schoolbag.

She nodded with a deep sigh, tears in her eyes. "Thank you, Sunday. You came just in time."

"Good," he said with immense relief. He'd come to care for Agnes's daughters as family. Agnes had been the eighth survivor he and Molly had hired. Traumatized, all of them. Not all could keep the job or stick to a schedule. Some did better away from the front desk, working in the kitchen or as housekeepers. But there was something special about Agnes, a strength and humility. Her daughters had it too. Sunday would protect them with his life, and they seemed to know it.

Sunday's voice softened. "That man won't be bothering you, or anyone else, again."

When the curious neighbors stood in the road, he rolled down the window.

"If you ever see this bastard Brit with any other girls here, call on me at the Harmony Inn. He's the worst of the hyenas. Come to lunch on the broken bones of those who have been crushed by other forces. Stand up for our people!"

4

May 2014—Gulu

The weight of her fears crashed over Agnes. The threat of a man taking her vulnerable baby girl was too much for her to bear. She curled into her body as her mind was taken over by the past, when nobody had come to find her.

Agnes looked down, toes against the red dirt.

The soldiers formed a circle, cheering for one among them who was about to reap his promised reward for bravery in warfare and loyalty to his master, a prize for fighting the Ugandan government.

Agnes was twelve years old. She had been in the bush for months. Labwony—the name they called Joseph Kony—held her by her left wrist as he goaded on his frenzied men. His fingers dug into her skin.

"I offer this prize to one of God's chosen officers in the Lord's Resistance Army," he bellowed as Agnes stiff-

ened. "One righteous hero has earned a beautiful and fertile wife, with whom he can have sacred intercourse and make new citizens for the perfect nation we'll create."

He jerked her arm, causing her to stumble. Her ankle struck against a sharp stone. It hurt and bled, but she dared not whimper. She'd seen this before. Watched helplessly in moments like these when other girls had shown anything that might resemble reluctance. They were always punished. Ghastly, brutal punishments. To cry would mean to be cut with a panga, losing an arm or a hand, an ear, or another body part to the machete's sharp blade. Agnes once saw a small girl cut in two for not looking gratefully at her new husband when he tried to raise her right wrist high and claim her as his God-given wife.

Agnes sought out the faces of the other young brides before her. Girls like her who had now successfully menstruated for four carefully counted months—the sign that they were no longer children. Dread curled in her stomach. One wrong move and she'd bring down the wrath of this man who held her.

Samson stepped forward. Agnes forced herself to look at him.

She'd known Samson from a distance. Her marriage to him had been foretold. She knew she would soon graduate from being a lowly "ting-ting," an unmarried girl doing the grunt work for the full-blown wives. Some of the kinder women had warned her of this fate in hushed tones, offering Agnes advice on how to survive the pain of long nights with a rough, uncaring man.

"Take deep breaths if you can, and try to hold the tops of your legs a little together so he can't get too far into you."

"Relax and he won't be angry and hurt you more."

"Twist your body even a little, and it will keep his penis from penetrating too deep into your gut."

"Don't scream; it will enrage him."

"Beg him to be merciful, and tell him you might die if he is too rough."

"Sneak some shea oil into his hut before he comes at you, and smear it into yourself so he can slip more easily into you."

The harsher women piled on cruel taunts:

"Now you'll see what we've had to put up with while you were free of it."

Others just turned away to hide the pity they had for the girls about to begin their new role in the camp.

Agnes knew from one of those kind women that it was best if she could steal some clothes to take with her to stuff up against herself afterward, in case she bled. "The smell of your own blood all night long will make you ill." And she knew to pray that her new husband would get his fill quickly and fall asleep, so she could have time to recover in case he later wanted more. She tried to remember all this shared wisdom as she watched her ankle bleed into the dust.

After what seemed like hours of Samson's lewd gesturing in the circle, he dragged her to his hut and threw her inside. Other women had prepared the hut, leaving a bucket of water and cloths with which to bathe herself. She prolonged this ritual as long as she could and *then lay on a mat naked and in terror as Samson arrived, showing off his dark, hard male part—one that seemed bigger now than in her nightmarish imagination.*

Oh, how she loathed him.

Molly stroked Agnes's arm and rubbed her back. "Agnes, it's okay. Grace is all right. Sunday got there in time. She's safe."

Agnes heaved, coming back to the present with a gulp of air. *What had happened next with Samson? She couldn't remember...*

Molly pressed a cool cloth to her forehead. "Agnes, you are safe," she soothed. "You are here at the Inn. No one is hurting you. I'm here. Sunday has Grace, and Beatrice is on her way. Grace is okay. Beatrice is okay. Your girls are safe."

Fighting for steady breath, Agnes blinked away the tears and grounded herself again. She focused on the familiar taste of the air-conditioned air, the comforting scent of grilled fish wafting from the restaurant. Molly had pulled her into the small office behind the front desk. The door was open, revealing a few visitors shuffling in and out of the hotel.

"Oh Molly, I'm so sorry," Agnes said with a sob. "It happened again. These visions, these terrible, waking dreams—"

Molly took both her hands and looked Agnes in the eyes. "Never apologize. They happen rarely, and they are trying to tell you something."

"But the guests?"

"Are fine. Everyone is just fine."

A shudder ran through Agnes. *See? You too are fine. You are here. You are a grown woman now. They won't find you here. You're safe.*

At that moment, a guest came to get a map of Gulu. Molly attended to the request in her usual unfussy way and then returned to Agnes, studying her face.

"What if I can't stop the flashbacks?" Agnes said. "What if they get worse? How is it that I remember so little about the bush, and then so much all at once?"

Molly nodded and kept her attention on Agnes. Respected for being a good listener, Molly managed the AA meetings at the Inn, sharing their twenty copies of *The Big Book* with any who came to her for support. She and Sunday had tried to explain the program to Agnes before, and how people made an inventory of everything they'd done and experienced. Such a method seemed unfathomable to Agnes, who struggled with memory. AA was a mystery, but she saw people come and go all the time, thanking Molly and Sunday for their help, so it had to be good. But memories? Agnes's life seemed like a broken mirror. Shattered into a million fragments that stared blindly back at her and made no sense.

"You know," Molly began, still squeezing Agnes's hand, "there is so much we can't understand. Some things we cannot rush. We do as much as we can each day. Fix whatever we can fix. What we can't fix, we accept. I've told you about my father. His alcoholism. His . . . behavior."

"Yes, you have."

Molly leaned closer, making sure Agnes could hear her clearly. "It is difficult to escape the past. Maybe impossible. But there are ways forward. You're strong, Agnes. Each day, you always try again. And we are here to support you. We love you, and we believe in you."

"But how can I move ahead if I cannot bring myself to fully remember?" Agnes said. She still felt the loss and despair brought about by the flashback, but she clung to what Molly said. *You always try again. We are here to support you. We love you, and we believe in you.*

The front door of the Inn swung open. Grace and Beatrice rushed in, clutching one another as they hurried through the small lobby toward Agnes. The wave of fear retreated, and she opened her arms to embrace her beloved daughters. Her girls were safe. They were home.

・・・・・・

For days after Grace's near-assault by her predatorial literature teacher, Agnes insisted on walking the girls to and from school. One evening she finally agreed to leave them behind so she could go to the market. A jittery nervousness settled on her skin as she headed into town without them. A taxi horn blared. A boda revved its engine, making her jump. The sky had been dark and brooding all afternoon and as Agnes lengthened her stride, thunder rolled in the distance. By the time she reached the market, the clouds had burst into a downpour.

Agnes sheltered beneath an awning at one of the sidewalk stalls. As she wiped the rainwater out of her eyes she saw him, and he saw her. Unmistakably so.

Moses, her eldest son.

He stood across the street under a larger covered awning at the road's edge, a makeshift outdoor bar. The little boy she'd had to leave behind when she'd escaped Kony's camp, with no one to protect him from the world. Agnes had not had any choice at the time. She'd left both her boys behind in order to protect her girls. But she understood from people who knew Moses that he blamed her for abandoning him. He hadn't confronted her since his return to Gulu in 2007. He had, in fact, avoided her completely through those seven years here in town.

Agnes held eye contact with Moses and softened her face with a smile as she crossed the road to approach the bar area. Moses kept his arms folded tight in front of his chest. His eyes remained hard, as if he wondered how he might hurt her, as he believed she had hurt him.

"Moses," Agnes stretched her hands out to her son. Her smile twitched with nerves.

"If it isn't Adong Agnes, the fine mother of two well-fed girls," said Moses sarcastically. "I'm sure you're not here to drink with us bad boys. What do you want? I already helped build you that fancy house."

At the request of Pastor Emanuel, Moses had worked with her younger son, Dan, to help build Agnes a cement-block house. It had been built in Layibi, a neighborhood in Gulu, on a piece of land Agnes's father had left her when he died. Land that had been in their family for a few generations, passed via a childless uncle into Agnes's father's care. He had offered it to her, hoping to give her and her girls security and to atone for the cruelty he'd shown her when she'd first returned from the bush.

Despite Moses's involvement in the project, he'd kept his distance. Making it clear then, and all the other times Agnes had encountered him in Gulu, that he had no interest in healing his relationship with his mother.

She worked to keep her expression neutral. "I came here to get out of the rain," she said. "But seeing you here makes me think it was not an accident. It is always special for me to see my firstborn." To mask her inner turmoil, Agnes kept her voice steady and warm.

Moses's face darkened with anger. "Was your firstborn so 'special' to you when you left me and my brother behind to find your own safety with your daughters?" he spat. "Those years were the worst for us, so soon after your third husband beat that boy to death. That boy who was almost a little brother to me? Did it ever concern you what Okello Peter might do to us, your sons?"

Agnes nodded. "Yes. It tortured me," she said with resignation and sorrow. "And probably there are others here who had the same thing happen to them." She looked around the bar.

Some of the men got up to leave, eyeing Agnes with suspicion. No one appreciated conversations about what happened in the bush. In Gulu, so many people had lived through the long years of war, with jumbled complicated rememberings, that to bring up such a topic without warning violated an unspoken rule they all lived by. One never knew if a room contained people who had been perpetrators or victims of unfathomable atrocities. They all knew not to talk about it, but this had not stopped Moses from speaking the unspeakable.

Agnes had escaped the LRA in 2005. She had not seen either of her boys for almost two years when, on one of the endless days spent on the side of the road in Gulu, a passer-by had yelled to the women on the tarps. "The men are coming home from the war! Boys are out of the camps. They are walking into Gulu."

Hoping her boys would be among the group, Agnes had taken her girls and walked and walked through the streets of the city searching for the two sons she had birthed in the forest. She still yearned to hold them close to her heart after all those years. She did not allow her mind to even contemplate the possibility that they had not survived. "After all this, please God," she'd prayed, "Let these boys know to come home to me and make their home in Gulu. Guide them, dear God. Guide them home to me."

A short while later, Agnes had taken her girls to a field of dirt where she'd been told young men had gathered to play soccer. Half were shirtless, and their arms and chests glistened with sweat. She knew Moses was 17 by then and Dan was 14, but these soccer players looked like men. Much older than she'd pictured her sons being.

But then Agnes saw them. It was undeniable. Two of those young men were her own flesh and blood—her Moses, her Dan.

She pulled the girls closer to the game, and sat beside the field, hoping her boys would interrupt their game to run to her in a joyful reunion.

Instead, when they finally did approach, their faces revealed deep anger. They shouted vile words in Agnes's direction and spat out a nasty name for her. Then they laughed, mockingly, and ran back to the game.

Agnes had been devastated. They were Kony's soldiers. They were killers. That was all they knew. Reconnecting with her sons seemed hopeless, and she worried there was no escaping the war after all.

••••••

Agnes sighed as Moses fumed in front of her in the bar. In the seven years since her boys had come to Gulu, she had healed her relationship with Dan, but Moses would not forgive her. Now she tried once again to acknowledge his pain. "I am sorry for the pain I caused you." Her voice cracked. "If I could have brought you with me, I would have. Please know this."

Her son maintained a seething silence, and she knew he could and would maintain it through the night. She looked at the men who remained in the bar. Finally, she continued so all could hear, "I am not here to condemn any of you. I am one of you. I came home furious and eager for a warm welcome, and I, too, found neither. Consider our sameness. We have to leave the bush behind. I hope you will soon have peace of mind and a roof over your head."

Agnes reached out to touch Moses's cheek. "I hope we meet again, my son."

He flinched and pulled away. "I hope we never do."

"I know," Agnes said, holding her composure even as her heart broke.

She felt Moses's eyes on her as she made her way back to the soaking market to a sagging tarp where she purchased some potatoes, rice, and bananas. Then she went into the rain again and hailed a boda, which took her—once again—away from her son.

5

June 2014—Gulu

Four weeks passed and, despite their protests, Agnes still walked her girls to and from school. Each time she left the house, her heart hammered. That awful teacher had intended to rape Grace, and only the combination of Grace's call and Sunday's swift rescue had saved her from the fate of at least half the girls in Gulu. Of course, Mr. Carson would carry on. Men like him always do.

Agnes scanned the road, waiting for a good moment to cross.

"Never get into a man's van again," Agnes said to Grace. "Do you hear me? You must not be so friendly. Don't believe what men say: no movies, no nice meals, they all want the same thing."

Agnes was grateful there were many men in her girls' lives who were not this way. Sunday and Pastor Emmanuel. Bishop Okot too, from church. She knew the girls would quickly remind her of these esteemed exceptions. But that wasn't the point. Girls needed to be careful. Simple as that.

"Yes, Mama," muttered Grace. She had, Agnes observed, returned to her usual genial friendliness with everyone. No trace of fear lingered in her animated eyes. Grace had little sense of her maturing body, or how her yellow school uniform caught the attention of onlookers. Agnes knew from overhearing Grace's giggling conversations with her friends that there were many boys in her class who wanted her as a girlfriend.

"I have a gift from God that helps me know when a man is dangerous. I would have known if that man was evil, if I had met him before you went to his house," Agnes said.

"Mama, we hear you," Beatrice said with a slight edge to her voice. "You're doing it again."

Agnes stiffened. "Caring about my daughters, you mean?"

Beatrice sighed as the three of them darted across the road and turned the corner. The girls' school was in sight. "You've given Grace this same advice every day for weeks. She won't do that again," Beatrice paused. "Right, sister?" she said, addressing Grace.

"Of course," Grace nodded.

"She would be wise to remember it," Agnes said with a look at Beatrice that said: *You remember, do you not? You remember how bad it was in the bush? Please remember enough to protect Grace.*

Agnes presumed the girls both knew at least most of what she'd been through. What thousands of young women in their country and beyond had been through.

But she was not entirely certain how much they remembered of their shared past. Beatrice had been seven when they'd made their escape; Grace even younger. Agnes's first two husbands (Samson and George) were dead before the girls were born, and they'd only known their father, Peter, as very small children.

Now, Agnes watched protectively as her daughters walked through the gate into the dusty schoolyard. She waited until they were both at the front door, until Grace turned to give her a final wave.

Beatrice would graduate soon, and never swayed from her goals. Her natural confidence intimidated others, including boys. Even some men, Agnes guessed. Agnes considered Beatrice to be as much an ally as a daughter. They'd survived together, and Beatrice had already become more than Agnes had ever dreamed she would be when she birthed her in a camp in Sudan, after plodding back and forth across the border to be sheltered by the Khartoum army.

LRA camps in Sudan swarmed with a mix of soldiers from different armies. The thick underbrush surrounded the cleared area where their brigade settled, offering a perfect spot for any militia to leap out from behind the trees in a surprise attack. But once the newness of the place had worn off, women felt safer there and supplies from the Sudanese government included food deliveries.

Thankfully, and unusually, Beatrice had been a good-sized baby girl and fed well. Agnes had quickly forgotten that in her fear and worry about having another baby, she had hoped this child would die and feared that Peter would beat her because she'd had a girl.

They had not been alone in the Sudan camp. Someone had brought Agnes clean water to drink and then taken the infant, Beatrice, away to wash her. Agnes had appreciated having more help that time, and she was able to stay in the bigger hut for five days before returning to her third husband, Peter.

Agnes followed the road back to her house, thinking long and hard about Beatrice, and reflecting on her life as the girl's mother. With all the heartache and misery that had surrounded Beatrice's infancy and childhood, Agnes felt enormously grateful for this child who had, more than anything else, given Agnes the courage to run from the LRA. They had moved around a lot when Beatrice was tiny and it had been hard on Agnes, especially as she'd had to carry bags of rice on her head, as well as her child on her back. Moving miles and miles, day after day, as soon as she was old enough to walk had proven nearly impossible for young Beatrice, but she'd trudged along without complaint. To this day the two of them still maintained the same rhythm in their step, their strides perfectly matched, in sync. They even looked the same, though Beatrice had a fuller face and no scars, and she was decidedly beautiful.

Even as a baby Beatrice had carried a glow of dignity, but Agnes had feared giving her the appropriate Acholi name, 'Aber,' meaning 'beautiful and good girl.' It would have been dangerous to label the infant as the prettiest, as it would have brought unwanted attention from soldiers. Only later, much later, in moments of affection, did Agnes openly call her daughter by her real Acholi name. Agnes had worked hard and taken enormous risks to give Beatrice a better life than the one she'd had, but sometimes she wondered if her girls appreciated everything they had.

Agnes pushed through the curtain that hung over her front door and began to clear the remains of breakfast from the table. She'd have time to wash up and sweep the room before leaving for her shift at the Inn. Perhaps it was time she stopped walking the girls to school, time to stop warning them about the dangers they risked by being around men. But she'd never stop worrying altogether, and by denying herself the chance to voice her fears, Agnes tucked them away only for them to resurface in the long nights. She needed to protect her daughters in the ways she had not been able to protect herself.

Alone in the house, sweeping beneath the table with the hand broom, Agnes's thoughts turned once more to what could have happened to Grace. To the potential catastrophes that stemmed from women being the objects of men's desires. To the theft of their young bodies. To men's willingness to use force.

While both girls had learned to sleep through many of their mother's nightmares, Beatrice was especially alert when Agnes called out to the ghosts that haunted her dreams. After an especially bad night last night, Beatrice had suggested that Agnes call Bishop Okot. "You know it helps you when you talk to him, Mama."

This—as well as Grace's welfare—was something Beatrice and Agnes would always agree on. Agnes resolved to visit the bishop on her way to work that morning.

When Agnes arrived at the pharmacy, Bishop Okot James sat in a red plastic chair behind the counter, checking totals on a calculator and making small talk with his mother-in-law, Atim Lydia. Like all Mormon clergy, Bishop Okot gave his time to the church as a volunteer. To support his family, he worked at the pharmacy, which turned a modest profit. With his wife and her parents involved in the enterprise, he was able to spend some of his days at ministry. Work, Okot James frequently told Agnes, he had felt called to since he'd first converted to the Church of Jesus Christ of Latter-day Saints (LDS) a decade earlier.

Okot James often spoke to his congregation about his father who had underlined in his Bible the words from Proverbs 3: *Seek his will in all you do, and he will show you which path to take.*

Now, Okot James stood respectfully as Agnes entered the pharmacy. "Sister Agnes," he said, kindly. "You've been on my mind." He offered her his hand.

"You have God's ear, as Isaiah Odeki says," Agnes replied.

She knew the mention of Isaiah would make Okot James smile. The bishop was fond of the orphan, Isaiah, another member of the congregation who had become a surrogate son to Agnes after the war. He now lived in America, but their bond remained strong.

"Thank you for meeting with me, Bishop," Agnes said. "I'm struggling." She explained that she had not been the same since the incident with Grace's teacher, that old memories kept pestering her, and she needed to talk, maybe even receive a blessing.

Agnes had joined the LDS church in 2009, four years after she'd escaped from Kony's camp and walked halfway across Uganda to bring her daughters to safety. After her own father had rejected and abused her on her return, she and her daughters had squatted beside the dusty road, staring off into space with no idea where to go. It was during that in-between period that Agnes had found the church.

On a day when the wind had made it more difficult than usual to settle on one blue tarp and try to make another tarp stay attached to poles and cover them while they tried to sell tomatoes and paper beads, Agnes had been startled to notice two young men, very different from those who usually passed by. These young men had not come from the bush. These men were white, and they wore clean, white shirts and shiny, black shoes. They walked toward Agnes with purpose, their clothes ironed, their hair trimmed neatly. Not only were they headed for the tarp where women were selling vegetables, but they were headed straight for Agnes.

An older woman who sat near Agnes on the side of the road, told her that the smiling men in white shirts were called missionaries. "They're safe," she said. "They're called Mormons." She reached over and patted Agnes's knee. "They won't hurt you. They won't hurt the girls, either."

Eager to meet these safe foreigners, Agnes held out her hand to welcome them, offering them each a tomato as a gift.

The men declined, but offered Agnes a book which they described as "a new witness for Christ." Agnes had not been especially interested in the book, but the young men moved and spoke so gently, and their obvious foreignness suggested that they were in some way different from everything that was dangerous about Uganda. She liked them because they were not from Gulu. They had not been part of the war and Agnes believed they had not had blood on them. The young men's warmth had drawn Agnes in. She embraced each word they said, agreeing to meet them the next day at the LDS church. For short, they called it the Mormon church.

At the Mormon church Agnes met other Acholi people who had been shattered by the war. These locals had already joined this *mzungu*—white man's—church, and they told Grace that they had found peace and safety there. Among them were Okot James and his wife, Akumu Sarah. James and Sarah had made sure that Agnes, Beatrice, and Grace had felt welcome among the ninety-or-so church members in their local congregation. Through them and the Gulu Ward of the LDS Church, Agnes and her girls had gained brothers and sisters, aunties and uncles, and a warm community of friends. Very few things about this new church reminded Agnes of her past, which was precisely what she liked about it.

Leaving his mother-in-law to mind the shop for a while, the bishop guided Agnes to the office at the back of the pharmacy, where they could speak in private.

Agnes sat across from him and felt comforted by his presence. When he asked how he could help, she stared at her hands and gathered her thoughts.

"It's my father," she finally said. "Ever since what happened with Grace, he appears to me in my dreams.

He has been long-buried. Why is he coming to me now? I ask God, but I get no answer."

"I'm listening," Okot said, urging her on with compassion.

She exhaled. "I keep thinking I can protect Grace and Beatrice from everything I endured. From my father. From my past in the bush. But I cannot keep everything separate anymore. I see old men shouting at Grace, and I think they are trying to take her away from me. Even the missionaries, I fear, are trying to steal away my Grace. Beatrice is strong and wise. I don't worry about her as much. But Grace is younger, trusting."

"I know how difficult this is for you, Sister Agnes. But I think I understand why what happened to Grace might remind you of your own abduction—like ripping off a scab and watching the blood flow again. It's a terrible, terrible thing that happened to you, and scary to think about what might have happened to Grace. Please remember though that the church is strict with our missionaries. They are not allowed to flirt with anyone at all. They want to keep your daughters safe. I do, too."

"My past and my present are all jumbled up. I just want to be a good mother."

"And you are," Okot said.

Agnes winced. Being a good mother was her biggest worry. It was nice to hear this praise from the bishop, but also hard to believe it to be true.

"What is your father doing in these dreams?" Okot asked.

Agnes swallowed hard. "Beating me. Yelling at me. Just as he and Father Pius and my aunties did when the girls and I finally returned to Lomora."

Okot sighed heavily. "It happened to so many. They escaped the bush, returned to their families, only to be rejected again. Assaulted, by people they loved and trusted. It's the final blow, and it breaks many."

Agnes's eyes swam with tears. "I have told you about my father before," she said. "I'm sorry to take your time."

"I have time to hear some now, and then you can come to the church tonight after your shift at the Inn, and you can tell me more," he assured her. "A long walk in the sunlight might help you now."

She wasn't ready to leave, but she was embarrassed to linger.

"Notice familiar things around you on your walk to the Inn," said Okot James. "Name them out loud. Touch the ones close to you to remind you where you are. Say your favorite scriptures out loud. You will be fine."

●●●●●●

June 2014—Gulu

Having said the appropriate goodbyes to Bishop Okot and his mother-in-law, Agnes made her slow way to the Inn, thinking of one of her favorite scriptures, Psalm 119:105: "Your word is a lamp to my feet and a light to my path."

Bishop Okot had said that what her own father did to her was similar to the abuse Agnes had endured at the hands of the LRA. She had tried not to admit they were similar. After all this time, she was still trying to tell herself it was not so bad in her father's big hut when she and her daughters had finally returned to Lomora.

But the Bishop was right, and it was no wonder the two experiences got tangled together in her nightmares.

Just as she'd feared, images from that terrifying week with her father flooded Agnes's mind, and she wondered how she'd ever lived through it. She had thought she would be welcomed home, fed, even cuddled. Instead, she and her daughters had been beaten and insulted.

Now, as Agnes approached a post that held a traffic signal above the road, she grabbed it firmly. She needed something solid to ground herself, as she went back over what had been done to her and her girls by her own family.

Agnes clutched her knees and rocked back and forth in the darkness of her father's hut as she cried out for him.

"Listen to me!" she begged, into the blackness.

Beatrice sniffled, and Grace kept eerily silent. The oppressive heat had made her thoughts feverish as tears streaked her face.

After weeks of walking all those miles, and after enduring horrific dangers to escape and return home, this was their welcome?

Voices returned. Agnes flinched.

"No, please," she begged, the sweat rolling down her face and arms, which glistened with oil. The tormentors stoked the fire by the door, making the air even hotter, intent on suffocating the evil spirits they believed lurked within Agnes and her girls. It had to be done, they claimed. It was their job to purify her before she could live among them in her father's village again.

Did they care if she and her babies survived this purge? How long had she and the girls been kept here. Days? Weeks?

"Father," she cried again, feeling faint from the heat. The world shifted and seemed to tilt and fade. All went black.

When Agnes returned to consciousness, she was surrounded by a blur of faces. A drum throbbed like a heartbeat in the small space.

"Your spirit is inside the devil. He has swallowed your soul, and you are his captive," one of the faces shouted before hitting Agnes with a switch.

Brave little Beatrice grabbed Grace and stood back from the crowd.

"Father?" Agnes said, making out his familiar shape. All those long years in the bush she'd conjured his visage of love and joy, remembering him with such tenderness. His ringing laugh as they played. His strong hands. His pride in his daughter.

"Again," her father instructed, and the woman lifted the switch and brought it down on Agnes's back.

"Harder," Father Pius said. The priest, supporting her father's call for an exorcism, held Agnes down by the arms.

She saw her father reach for Grace, and she screamed from the deepest part of herself. "You cannot have her! She's done nothing wrong. We are innocent. All of us." Agnes fought to break free from the priest's grip, to stand and protect her little girls.

"You are impure," an auntie said, pushing Agnes down again. "A slut! Bearing those Kony babies."

Agnes could not believe these people thought she'd had any choice. Living as a captive. Forced to conceive and bear children with men she hated.

"We should give these daughters of killer-rebels to another woman. Someone who can discipline them and make them god-fearing," someone suggested.

"The older one is already evil. She refuses to eat or leave her mother's side."

Agnes howled with anger. "Never!" she grabbed Grace's foot, clawing her back from the woman.

Her father, the priest, and the other villages continued to try to make Agnes pure again in the only way they knew how, by exorcizing the evil they believed crouched within her, by beating the darkness away with cruel words and painful welts. All their efforts achieved was to erase every trace of love Agnes had once felt for her childhood village. The people and the place she'd immortalized throughout her terrible days in the bush, when she'd desperately needed to cling to hope.

Agnes steadied herself against the street sign, wondering if she had the strength to support herself if she let go of the pole. She was strong. She could do this. She knew that for all the people in the world who could hurt her, there were as many who would help.

After those terrifying days in her father's hut, Agnes's cousin had taken her and her girls, and dropped them on the side of that dusty road, where other child-mothers had gathered, their hopeless stares a constant reminder that they were the unwanted ones. The shamed. The shunned. The unloved.

Agnes had been careful to keep her head down, as she didn't want to pick a fight with anyone and risk being chased away, so she slept with Beatrice and Grace on the grass near a broken fence. One morning, a woman led them to a place where a hut had once stood. A ring of stones in the ground showed its boundaries. The woman had washed out some clothes and sheets and hung them to dry. "Someone died here a week ago," the woman explained. "You and your girls can stay here now."

It was the closest thing to a home they had, and Agnes was grateful. She thanked the woman and promised not to make any trouble.

Some people from an NGO came and taught Agnes and the other child-mothers to make beads out of newspapers and shellac. She had been excited to learn a new skill and gain some hope. The child-mothers worked hard to create necklaces, bracelets, woven placemats, and small handbags. Adopting a new identity as "Beads of Hope," these young women would sit on their blue tarps and hang their beads on wires between poles. Then, they would stop passers-by to purchase the items they had made.

And then, of course, the smiling missionaries had stopped to see Agnes's beads. For Adong Agnes, it was the Beads of Hope and the Mormons who had somehow brought an end to the war.

Another scripture came to Agnes's mind, one that a missionary had read at her baptism. Joshua 1:9: "Have not I commanded thee? Be strong and of good courage; be not afraid, neither be thou dismayed: for the Lord thy God is with thee whithersoever thou goest."

6

June 2014—Gulu

Agnes made it through her shift at work, knowing she could see Bishop Okot again. She even left early and hurried across town. Walking alone in the dark, she feared her thoughts from earlier would overtake her. Would she ever have peace in her head? She walked faster and faster, and finally saw the modest church building ahead, so grateful that a light shown from the office in the back. Okot unlocked the front doors, and let her in. Already she felt better. Unlike when she had come to her father's village and been so tormented and reviled, here she was welcomed and someone was ready to listen to her and believe her.

"May I offer you a blessing?" the bishop asked, leading her back to the church office.

Agnes nodded. She sat in another plastic chair and folded her arms in front of her, as Okot placed one hand on her head and prayed.

He asked Heavenly Father to bless "people around us, and indeed, people everywhere, that they will be more like God and treat each other with compassion." Then he put his other hand on Agnes's head, too, and beseeched the Lord. "Heavenly Father bless them that they will stop hurting one another, and especially in families, bless parents to stop hurting their children. Like Agnes's father, who hurt her so much, bless fathers to lift up their children and encourage them. Bless them that they can be more like Agnes and show love to their children and care for them with kindness."

This good man turned this chance to counsel Agnes into an opportunity to praise her and focus on what was good about how she acted as a mother and a neighbor and a friend to others. He didn't tell her to forget. Instead, he said, "When your father comes to mind again, and you remember what he did, just repeat to yourself: My father is dead and gone. And so is Father Pius. They can't ever hurt me again. I am here, but they are dead."

When he had finished, she looked into his eyes and smiled. "Thank you for being a great comfort," Agnes said.

Okot smiled. "And thank you for being an example of how healing is possible."

That night, for the first time in many weeks, Agnes slept peacefully. How sweet a blessing, but she questioned how long it would last. Then, on the seventh night, Agnes woke with a jolt again. Sweat dampened her face and, in a panic, she clawed into the dark. *No! You cannot have her. You can't have her!*

Not Samson. Not George. Not Peter.
Not Agnes's father.
Not Mr. Carson.
Not anyone who would do harm.
She would keep her daughters safe. She would.

Agnes rubbed her eyes as she rose and looked over at her daughters. Both were safe. Still hers and sound asleep. Her pulse slowed as she remembered Okot's words and blessing: *Your father is dead. He can never betray you again. He can never try to take your daughters either.*

Her father had had a choice. As a village elder, he could have welcomed them with love. He could have supported their healing. Whatever the war had taught him, whatever pains he bore, he had failed in what should have been his first duty: that of a loving parent.

The time spent in his dark hut, treated as an outcast, had happened nine long years ago. It was over, and far away. No longer her life. No longer a threat. The villagers had not succeeded in taking her girls, and Agnes was no longer helpless. She knew how to take care of her children and to be there for them when they most needed her. Now, if only she could let go of the past.

••••••

A few weeks later, while the girls were out, Agnes was preparing to do laundry when her son Dan appeared in the doorway of her hut. He was holding a tiny baby and, behind him, a young woman stood smiling.

"Mama," Dan said, holding the baby out to her. With no more words, Dan unwrapped the infant boy and showed Agnes his tiny feet, which were clubbed. Dan's eyes welled up, but he held back the tears.

Agnes took the infant in her arms and cuddled him, as she invited Dan and the woman to sit down. The story was told in a few moments: The newborn baby was Opolo Sam, named after that eight-year-old Sam who, as a new child recruit in Kony's army had been assigned to Moses and Dan for training. They had come to feel responsible for him, like older brothers. Sam had lost his cooking pot and, when Kony demanded that he be punished, Okello Peter, Agnes's third husband, had beaten the child so badly that he'd died in front of Dan and Moses. Now here was another broken Sam in Dan's charge, and Agnes could tell this latest blow had left Dan broken.

Agnes handed the baby back to his mother, who was introduced as Dora, and she took Dan in her arms. She had not held her son for years, but now he sobbed as though he might never stop.

Dora was patient and reassuring as she explained to Agnes how much she loved Dan and that she wished she could dry his tears forever.

Dan cried in Agnes's arms for a long time. Then, without words, he pulled away and fled from the hut alone.

While Agnes boiled some water on the cookfire for tea, she appraised her son's girlfriend. She was pleased to find Dora a tender, sturdy, and peaceful young woman, who returned Agnes's deep look of intelligent curiosity. The young mother did not fuss over her son's clubbed feet, but when Agnes unwrapped him again and had a chance to take a proper look, she could see that they were twisted inwards, in a way that promised a cruelly marginalized life in any Acholi community. He would be an outcast—never allowed to thrive.

Agnes asked Dora if they could pray together and then poured out her heart to the Lord. "Where should we turn, O Lord?"

Baby Sam opened his eyes and nudged around, looking to nurse. Dora took him to breast and fed him calmly. She was the mother Sam would need, and she was the partner Dan needed, too.

As Agnes watched the sweet face of her grandson, and held his folded feet in her hands, she had a vivid memory of a Mormon family from the US who had visited her church almost a year ago. The woman was Japanese and the man, half Norwegian and half Japanese. Both worked as surgeons, and the man specialized in orthopedics.

Agnes had asked God for ideas, and she was receiving one.

The family had been touring the north of Uganda and had come west from Mt. Elgon before heading to the game reserve at Murchison Falls. Agnes had been startled to notice that the man had a prosthesis on one leg. It started at the knee and ended inside a soft hiking boot. He had not seemed discomforted in any way, and from the family's description of their previous days climbing Mt. Elgon, it was clear that he was hardly disabled.

Agnes had not thought about the family for months, but now she recalled that Dr. Bjorn had told them he was teaching spinal surgery techniques at the medical school in Makerere. He and his wife, Dr. Aiko, would be working and teaching in Uganda for at least five years. Aiko was also a surgeon at Makerere, where she focused on girls' health, particularly those who became mothers before their bodies were physically prepared. Girls like Agnes.

Agnes tucked Sam's feet back into his wrap and stood to pour more tea for her and Dora. "I am not sure if this will help, but I have an idea." She was worried about speaking too soon, but the memory seemed like an answer to her prayer, that this is who God was sending to help them, and she felt she could trust Dora's calm sensibility.

Agnes called Bishop Okot. When she reached Dr. Bjorn Froyland by phone the next day, he was warm and took in the information about Sam's little feet.

"How old is he?" was Dr. Froyland's first question. "Has he seen a doctor in Gulu and what was recommended?"

One-week-old Sam had been seen by a doctor at Lacor Hospital when he was born, but Dan had not let the doctors put casts on his tiny feet until he could consult his mother. Dr. Froyland spoke to the doctor at Lacor who had recommended the casts, and they were in agreement about Sam's treatment. The Ponseti Method consisted of gradually turning the feet outward in the first eight months of life with a series of casts. Following that, a longer-term remedy with a brace set between Sam's legs.

The doctors reassured the young family that this method for treating clubfeet had been successful throughout

Africa. Sam could start treatment at Lacor and Dr. Froyland could oversee the progress from Kampala, where Dora and Dan took their little boy for regular checkups.

Dora and Dan had fastened their hearts to this remedy with such single-mindedness that Agnes knew it would succeed. And what a many-layered blessing the whole experience had turned out to be. It had led to Dan spending a lot of time at Lacor Hospital with his son, helping the medical team set and remove the casts of other children, as well. They gave him a white coat, so he looked like he belonged there.

Dan loved learning which bones heal most easily and which ones are easiest to break. He saw lots of heartache, but he also saw lots of good stories unfold, in addition to the story of Sam's little feet, which grew stronger every week. The little boy's malady and his treatment had made Sam special. They all called him by his Acholi name—Opolo—which means, "Sent from Heaven."

••••••

October 2014—Gulu

Months later, Agnes knelt in a patch of morning light on the bedroom floor and thanked her Father in Heaven for this safe place. It was still very early, but she decided to start her day and, leaving her girls asleep, she pushed through the curtain door and out into the compound.

The sun was not yet up, but it already cast the day's soft new light around their home. She waved at Justine, her friendly neighbor, and some of the other women who were already up and about.

At the time they'd come to Agnes for her help, Dan and Dora had been staying with Dora's parents, which was customary and appropriate for Acholi tradition, but little Sam's unique situation had made this a special case, and Agnes suggested that they move into her small brick hut, which was next to her cinderblock house.

This morning, Dora was also awake, sitting on a small stool outside the hut where she and Dan had been living throughout Sam's many visits to the hospital. The young woman looked up as Agnes emerged and greeted her with a warm smile. "The boys are still sleeping," she spoke quietly, gesturing to the door of their hut with a slight dip of her head. Her pregnant belly swelled against her dress, and she stood and arched her back.

Shortly after moving into the hut, Dora laughingly announced one day, "Now that we have our own hut, we intend to fill it with children." Dora was only a little older than Beatrice, but more curious about some things in life, and Agnes watched Beatrice take some of these qualities in and regard Dora as a role model. Dan and Dora's hut was close enough that Beatrice and Grace couldn't help but hear the joyful sounds of lovemaking that came from their hut on many nights. This was new to the two girls, and a cause for intense interest.

Agnes found it ominous in some deep way, but could find no respectable reason to criticize it, and decided it was simply the price she had to pay for having her enlarged family around her. Of course, she was a little curious herself. This loving, intimate thing that happened so near to her was unlike anything she had ever experienced.

A wonderful side-benefit of Sam's hospital visits was the relationship Agnes had developed with Aiko. A specialist in obstetrics and gynecology, the Japanese-American woman had arranged to teach at Makerere, as a department there concentrated on adolescent and pediatric gynecology. The prevalence of young mothers in Uganda after the war was epidemic, but with it came a shortage of doctors who had the knowledge and skills for working with young girls who had given birth or had high-risk pregnancies.

Aiko was a fierce but kind woman. She was very smart and spoke her mind. Agnes trusted her. She had come to church and spoken out on topics normally taboo to Mormons and had said wise things about how girls must be very careful not to get pregnant.

"Stand up for yourselves," Aiko had told them. This blunt, plainspoken advice had shocked the members, but they had listened. Agnes had also been shocked to begin with, but soon realized she liked Aiko's candor. She appreciated that Aiko told the boys it was their responsibility never to get a girl pregnant. She'd shaken her finger at them, commanding their attention. All this in a half hour at the church on the Sabbath. Aiko had captured her audience. She was an effective teacher as well as a respected doctor.

Her husband, Dr. Bjorn, was quieter and respectful of the sisters in the ward. He stood by and listened to his wife ask the local women about their lives. It seemed like a normal thing for the couple to do, but it wasn't normal in Gulu, so he'd made an impression.

When Agnes had told her friend that Dan and Dora intended to name their baby after her if it was a girl, Dr. Aiko was pleased and promised she would work to make the world a little safer for someone as special as this baby. "It is what I live for," she stated with conviction.

Dora took a sip of her tea and looked at Agnes over the rim of her cup. "Mama-Agnes, did Dan tell you his news?"

Agnes felt a knot build in her stomach. She should not have been thinking so much about how lucky she was, about having her family close by. She had to be careful not to be too happy or take anything for granted.

Her face must have changed because Dora frowned then laughed. "Don't worry so much, Mama-Agnes. It's good news."

Dora had not spent time outside of the Gulu area. She'd come from the villages in the opposite direction from where Agnes came from. Although her family had its own war history, Dora seemed to carry less fear in her body than most of the women in the compound. When watching her interact with Beatrice and Grace, Agnes saw a difference. She was glad she had rescued her girls from the bush and given them a legacy of freedom, but she could see she had also bequeathed to them a mantle of fear. An inheritance they carried from her. She was glad for Dora's lightness and hoped it would rub off on the girls, and on her.

Agnes breathed a sigh of relief at Dora's smiling face. "What is it?"

"Another part-time opening had come up at the clinic, and the technicians urged Dan to apply again."

For two years, Dan had been juggling his job at Pastor Emanuel's Seed Store, while doing most of the medical caring for Sam at the clinic where his son's casts were set and the braces had been attached. He was keenly observant of the work he'd watched the doctors at Lacor Hospital do when they changed Sam's casts. Each time an opening came up, Dan applied for the job. He didn't get it the first, nor the second, but he continued to apply, and here was another opportunity.

"And . . . ?"

"And he got the job!"

The two women's yells of celebration soon brought others rushing to see what all the noise was about. Filled with gratitude and joy for her son, the women shared the exciting news throughout the compound. Agnes's cup truly overflowed.

7

January 2014—Gulu

Before Dan began his new job making casts for the patients at Lacor Hospital, he wanted to officially resign from his job at the Seed Store and make sure Pastor Emanuel understood how thankful he was for all the opportunities Pastor had given him. Agnes was happy to accompany Dan and offer Pastor her gratitude for the interest he had taken in her family's lives.

As Agnes and Dan left the compound together, she took a moment to check the rows of vegetables that grew successfully along the boundary of her property. Especially the beans which had a special significance in Agnes's relationship with Pastor Emanuel.

"Did I ever tell you how Pastor Emanuel saved our lives?" Agnes asked Dan, bending down to pluck two green beans from a plant that had woven its way through the fence. She passed one of the beans to Dan and chewed on the other.

"Yes, many times," Dan said.

Agnes began anyway. "When I escaped with the girls, I thought we would be welcomed home with open arms. Instead, my father and aunties had a priest beat us and do an exorcism on us." Agnes shivered with the brutal memory of it. "It was almost as bad as all my years in the bush." She sighed.

Dan shook his head with empathy, encouraging her to continue.

"Three years later, when my father sent word that he was on his deathbed and wanted to see me, his last remaining child, I went, of course. There, he tried to atone for the cruel ways he had treated me after my escape. So, he gave me the deed for this property just before he died."

"An extremely rare gift," Dan said.

"Rare, indeed," Agnes acknowledged. "Gratefully, Beatrice, Grace, and I moved here. But we still had nothing. The land was full of squatters, but I had no heart to chase them away. After all, I had spent two years with my daughters, squatting on someone else's property, trying to survive on that blue tarp. Now, I had a deed to my own land, but I still had no way to grow anything on it, no money for food, and no skills to get a job. I was desperate to plant ourselves somewhere stable, so I prayed for patience. I waited on the Lord."

"And He provided," Dan said.

"Yes, but before we came to declare our spot and show the legal deed, the girls and I planted beans. While they did not grow, it was our first step towards making known our claim. Our failed beans drew neighbors to our aid and drew me to the Seed Store for the first time."

"And that's when you met the proprietor, Pastor Emanuel," Dan said, finishing her sentence with a laugh. "I know!"

Agnes nodded, but continued. "When he saw how quickly I counted out my own change—"

"Pastor Emanual spontaneously hired you, even though you were not a real bookkeeper. Please don't make me listen to the whole story again."

Agnes nudged her youngest son on the arm, happy to take the teasing. They continued in companionable silence as Agnes quietly thanked God for all the blessings she'd been given. Because of that job at the Seed Store, Agnes had been able to feed her daughters a bowl of posho every day on her small salary while saving enough to purchase bricks to build their first hut on her inherited plot of land. She had worked hard and made very few mistakes, and she'd found Pastor Emanuel to be a kind and fair boss.

She had been forced to quit this precious job in 2011 after two of her neighbors had spread ugly rumors around that Agnes snuck out at night to have sex with Pastor in exchange for the job. Beyond humiliated, Agnes had gone straight to the Seed Store to quit. Without the job, her dignity had been restored. She'd even felt triumphant, until she ran out of beans and oil and even rice and could no longer feed her daughters.

Agnes had cascaded into weeks of shame for overreacting in the face of wild rumors. After all, such talk was common. Now, she was really humiliated. Eyes were on her, and she looked foolish. She'd almost crawled back to the Seed Store to beg Pastor Emanuel for her job back, but when she'd arrived, Agnes was shocked to discover that Pastor had located her oldest son, Moses. He had been living out in an open field with equally vulnerable men beyond Gulu's town limits. Pastor was teaching Moses to drive and hired the young man to deliver fertilizer, bags of seed, and even some building materials to customers around Uganda. Soon after, Pastor had also employed Dan at the Seed Store.

On top of all that, Pastor helped Agnes get the job at the Inn. Now, Agnes and Dan stepped into the store and greeted Pastor warmly, sharing why they had come, as Dan described his new position at Lacor Hospital. "I will demonstrate to others what I have learned through helping Sam, and I'll receive training to expand my own skills. I will also be traveling to other clinics to demonstrate the Ponseti Method."

Pastor Emanuel was pleased for Dan and gave him his blessing, thanking him for the time he'd spent working at the Seed Store. When Dan had said his goodbyes and returned to Dora and little Sam at the compound, Pastor Emanuel asked Agnes to stay.

"What will people say if they see me alone with you, Pastor?" Agnes only half joked. She was aware of wagging tongues and did not want to be misrepresented in any way.

"We can sit outside if that eases your worries. I have something important to tell you."

Back then, Agnes was more curious about what Pastor Emanuel had to say than she was worried about her reputation, so she settled onto a stool at the counter of the Seed Store and encouraged him to continue.

Pastor took a deep breath and began. "I believe it is time I told you more about my past. I know you have been curious about why I was so quick to offer you a job, and why I chose to employ both of your sons. You once asked me if I knew you in the bush, and I told you I did not, though I told you I knew someone else who did."

Agnes leaned in, curious.

Pastor continued. "I thought telling you everything might be too distressing. I was afraid it would be hard for you to be around me."

Agnes tried to keep her mind steady. She wanted to hear what he had to say. "Yes, but I am a different person from the woman I was in those days. I am calmer, at least a little."

He rose to get them each a Coke, turning his back to her momentarily. This small action was all it took. Something shifted in her mind and two shards of mirror-memory came together. It was hot outside, and his shirt stuck to him more than usual, revealing the tense muscles in his back. Agnes observed the way those muscles wrapped around his ribs, and she was suddenly alarmed. Her mind flashed back twenty years to Samson's naked torso, and it was as though she saw that same back pulsing under the damp cotton. No denying . . . these were Samson's shoulders.

The realization hit her harder than almost anything Pastor could have told her. So many things about Samson and his body came rushing back to her. The two men looked so alike that Agnes was amazed she had not guessed this years ago. Had she perhaps known all along? Had she resisted acknowledging what now seemed an obvious truth? Why had she refused to recognize that this man—who often said he was "like family"—was truly family?

She drew back in shock, and her arms flew up as though she expected an attack. She gasped as it became hard for her to breathe. Closing her eyes, she folded her arms over her chest protectively. *Now what?*

Pastor paused halfway across the room, a Coke in each hand. "I'm sorry, Agnes. I didn't ever want to drive you away from the Seed Store. Many people say I look very much like my oldest brother, Samson, who made you his 'wife' in the bush and treated you so despicably."

Agnes breathed deeply because his voice was still Pastor's voice. Not Samson's. But now that Agnes knew who he was, it was so obvious. This man was a true uncle to Moses and Dan. No wonder he was glad to rescue Moses from the empty life he was living, to offer Dan a job in his store, to employ her so spontaneously the first time they'd ever met. As the urge to vomit overtook her, she excused herself to go to the bathroom, where she dampened a paper towel and pressed it to her forehead.

After a while, she came back out and took a few sips of Coke, with Pastor offering details about the way his family had been decimated when the two oldest sons voluntarily joined the LRA very early on. "It will not surprise you, Agnes, to hear that Samson forced another brother to kill our father, as so many of the boy soldiers were forced to do. He failed, but our father was left badly handicapped for the rest of his life. We lost touch with Samson during the war, but news would leak out occasionally. I knew some of the worst details—I heard what

Samson had done to hurry the death of his first young wife, before you were given to him as wife number two."

Agnes sighed and took a sip of Coke, relieved to have the drink as a distraction.

"I knew you had sons, and that two were alive when the war ended," Pastor continued. "But I feared they would never find their way home. As a penance for what my brother had done, I resolved to become a preacher and lift up the war-weary. I attended the Whole World Pentecostal School for Pastors in Lira, but unfortunately I lost my faith there. When I left, I had only the title, 'Pastor.' I took that with me when I came here."

Agnes tried to put all this together in her mind, filling out the portrait of this man who had shaped her life and her sons' lives in so many ways. "I remember the man Jonathan who came to see you the first time you left me alone at the Seed Store. He laughed about how he had become a pastor at that school but that he has never been called Pastor. And that you had not officially become a pastor, and yet you are the one who is called Pastor. He also said he was not Acholi, but was Langi."

"You remember correctly, Agnes," Pastor replied. "Jonathan is a teacher in Lira now, and he does not come to Gulu often. But he understood why I felt compelled to come to Gulu, as I was determined to find my nephews, your sons."

Agnes listened as he explained his determination to play a role in his cruel brother's family. To support and protect them after all they had endured.

"God works in unexpected ways to pull estranged parts of families together in the pattern of His own design," Pastor Emanuel said. "I hope you will forgive me for keeping my identity from you. And I hope you will allow me to continue to be a part of your family because I have something even more important I'd like to share with you."

Agnes sat back in her chair and rubbed her face. "I'm not sure I can take any more surprises."

"This is a good surprise," Pastor said. He stood to take a rolled piece of paper from a high shelf. He unrolled the paper to reveal a rough sketch of a building and a few hurried notes. "Agnes, how would you like to help me build a shelter? A place where women like you and men like Moses could go to recover from the devastating impact of the war?"

He stepped back and smiled as if he knew she would not be able to resist.

Agnes leaned over to get a better view.

······

Back at the Inn, noting the full email inbox and disorganized check-in forms for late arrivals, Agnes thought about her visit with Pastor. "Sunday, you know how just when you think that God is not watching over you, you find out He is? Well, it's kind of like that. Pastor Emanuel was looking out for Moses and Dan when boys from Kony's camps were coming home, and they didn't even know it. Now they have an uncle."

Sunday was not able to stop and talk, but he nodded to let her know he heard her.

"A busy evening," he said, passing back in a hurry as he made his way to the bar where a large crowd had gathered. Journalists, this time. As usual, they were here to do a story on the LRA. "Remember, Agnes. If anyone asks you questions you don't want to answer, you can direct them to me. You will be fine."

She nodded as two Germans approached the desk. One asked Agnes, "Have you seen a tall local man? A former LRA rebel? We scheduled an interview."

Agnes shook her head. At least someone else could talk about the LRA tonight.

"If an Okello Peter comes here, let him know we are in the restaurant," the other German said. "We reserved a room for him."

Okello Peter. Her third husband? Here?

Agnes's mouth went dry. Her heart started to pound. Why were all the men from the past resurrecting today? She went into the small office behind the front desk and closed the door.

Molly slipped in to check on her. And that was when Agnes heard it: Okello Peter's voice, introducing himself calmly to Sunday and asking where he could find the German guests. Her whole body tightened, and she waited for the wave of panic to wash through her.

But this time, it didn't come.

Something about Peter's voice had . . . changed. *Maybe he wasn't so dangerous anymore.*

Agnes leaned against the wall and took deep breaths. Her throat tightened, and she wiped the sweat from her palms on her dress. She usually felt safe at the Harmony Inn. She didn't know what to do. A part of her told her to flee. Another part stirred with a strange curiosity.

"He would know," Agnes said, softly, her chin firm

as she looked at Molly. "He would know the gaps in my story. The ones I can't remember."

Molly's brows pinched. "What do you want to do, Agnes? We are here to protect you, whatever you need."

Was it a need? To understand this lost part of her painful past? Could seeing her third 'bush husband' be another step toward healing?

She knew that Peter had returned to Gulu from Aba Camp on the border with the Democratic Republic of Congo (DRC) a few years after she did. Escorted by military officers, he would have followed a route similar to the one she had taken with the girls when she'd escaped in 2005. He would know how she was able to find her way home, and he would know what happened in the Kony camp after she'd fled with her daughters and left her two sons. But could she tolerate seeing Peter after all these years, and after refusing to take his many calls? Agnes hated Peter, but was her curiosity about her own past stronger than her hatred?

Maybe she could stand to see him here at Harmony Inn, where she was protected by people who loved her. Could finding answers help her to finally stop looking at every man with suspicion, help her to stop making her daughters roll their eyes about all her worries? She'd been home nine years, but still the old haunts followed her. Maybe this was her chance to clear the cloudiness out of her head, once and for all.

Agnes swallowed. "I need to speak with him." She could hardly believe the words coming out of her mouth, an almost desperate need to know things. To put the broken fragments together again.

8

January 2015—Gulu

"I need to do this," Agnes said, as Sunday searched her eyes.

She'd recognized Peter's voice before she saw him—a familiar, resonant voice from her past. The reminder made her shiver, as she often did when she encountered anyone she'd known in the bush. *It wasn't too late to turn back. Peter may be talking in a normal, polite sort of way, but he could be deceiving them all. Was this too much? To deliberately bring back memories? To dig into the blur of pain that marked her past? A past that still attacked her in the present.*

Agnes stood straight, then braced herself to enter the office behind the front counter. Sunday was beside her and Molly was seated at the desk.

"How are you, Agnes?" Peter asked in a way that felt different from how everyone asks that question. She heard the concern and maybe even—regret? Despite her hesitations, she didn't seem as upset as she'd imagined she might be, seeing him there again, like nothing had happened.

"I'm here," Agnes said. It was all she could say.

"Agnes, take a seat," said Sunday, offering her a chair. And so she did.

It was a wonder either had chosen to speak. Then again, there was sometimes the urge to know if what you remember really happened, or if you had imagined it all.

After a bit of small talk, Agnes was assured by Peter's respectful tone. Abruptly, she remembered the moments of calm that had once claimed Peter's face when he slept, the way his brow had smoothed out, how she had marveled that his meanness and desperation seemed to melt away in the light of dawn.

"Sunday," Agnes said. "Thank you. I think I will be okay from here."

"We'll be right at the desk," he said, leaving the door ajar as he and Molly made their way out.

"So, you work here now?" Peter asked, brightly. "They say they are grateful to work with you."

"It is a good place," Agnes said. "Sunday and Molly are very kind." How was it, Agnes thought, that they could slip into conversation like this? Like Peter was just an old friend who'd simply been away for a while? Not the man who had raped her, repeatedly, and beaten her anytime he pleased.

"What about you?" she asked.

"I repair buses. I live with my son and his mother behind a roadside market in Kampala. I support them," he said. Then, he took a deep breath. "My son's name is Sam."

Agnes closed her eyes. She could hear her sons' screams as Peter had beaten their little friend Sam to death in front of them. When she opened them again, Peter's face was soft. His eyes, full of remorse. She understood that he was telling her how much he regretted his actions, and that his son's name was a tribute to the young boy he had killed.

Agnes nodded. "I have a few questions to ask you," she said. "I have trouble remembering. Especially my escape." She took a deep breath. "I hoped you might have some answers since you had to follow the same route when the cease fire began."

Peter nodded. "Ask me anything."

They began by talking about what Agnes could remember, switching from English to the more intimate Acholi. "I escaped at the beginning of 2005," she said. "But those days are very mixed up in my mind. I know it was before the peace."

"At that time, we were camped near Aba, inside the forest," Okello Peter said. "How did you get from Garamba Forest all the way to Gulu?"

"I don't fully know," Agnes said, remembering her swollen feet, three-year-old Grace on her back, seven-year-old Beatrice tugging at her limp arm. *Would he dare to say they were his daughters? Surely he wouldn't dare make that claim, even though they were biologically his.*

"Thank heaven you escaped with your daughters. They might not have made it out otherwise." Peter's voice conveyed more than his words. He was telling her that he was glad she had saved their daughters, and he was also telling her that he would not claim them as his own. That he would give her the credit for bearing them, raising them, keeping them alive, saving them, and mothering them.

Her heart swelled with gratitude, and she raised her eyes to meet his. She was surprised to find that kindness there. The cruelty she had once seen was gone from him, along with his desperate fear. *How afraid we all were, even the soldiers. They were young too. Traumatized, too.*

She remembered, suddenly, a moment of kindness Peter had shown her in the bush. A few hours after Grace was born, he had come to see them. She had been afraid he might be disappointed she hadn't delivered a boy. Maybe he would even beat her, when he saw a daughter in her arms. But he had not hurt them. Instead, he had brought Agnes an extra portion of rice to help her recover from labor. And he had brought an extra portion of rice every day for three or four days, no small gesture in the camp.

Agnes shook her head a little to clear it, relying on the grounding exercise Molly had taught her. Slowly, she came back to the present, feeling her body in the plastic chair, her feet inside her shoes.

Together they looked at the large paper map that Molly had brought in earlier. "Uganda looks larger on this map than on a computer screen," Agnes said, remembering all the times she'd used the Inn's computer to try to track her escape. This map had more details, little roads. "Or maybe, this one just feels more true to how far it felt to walk."

"I imagine." Peter grunted with acknowledgement. Then he placed his finger on the map. "This is Aba Camp, just inside the DRC, across the Sudan border, in the direction of the Ugandan border. It is on the east side of the Garamba Forest, about 100 miles from a small city called Dungu which sits on the other side of the Forest. Kony picked this place on purpose. If we'd stayed in Uganda, the Americans might have come in and helped the Ugandan army crush Kony. He was safer over the border because the Congolese government would not allow Americans to fly over their country to make war." He paused. "Everyone was fearful when we went into the DRC, since we knew we were being taken farther from home—we knew we would be forgotten and that we would never get back to our families. But . . . we had no choice."

Agnes remembered that desperation, her throat tightening again in memory. The way some mothers smothered their babies to save them from such a horrific life. The way she'd risked everything to get her own daughters away from that place.

"Did you go north when you left Aba?" asked Peter. "Or did you head south toward the nearest Uganda border crossing—toward Arua?"

Together they traced Agnes's way out of the forest.

"A truck . . . I remember a truck stopped to pick us up. A bunch of rowdy women were in the back, but they were generous and fed us fruit. They picked us up soon after we'd headed north," she spoke in fragments, struggling to piece together her route. "We drove for a quite a while."

Peter said. "Oh good. A truck. You must have been driven across the Nile on the ferry back then. There's a ferry at Laropi. It takes you from the Sudanese side to the Uganda side. Then there's a real road."

Agnes smiles. She can remember the ferry.

"You were so lucky that the trucker took you all the way from Yei to Uganda because the only place to cross the Nile up there is at Laropi. People depended on that ferry going back and forth during the war and sometimes it was stopped by different armed groups. Some people waited for days on both sides of the river. Desperate people tried fishing boats, but it was dangerous as the river is broad. The ferry let vehicles on and kept people waiting because they couldn't pay. Trucks paid. I'm so glad you got across the Nile on that truck. Did it take you to Adjumani?

Agnes nods, confirming they'd been left in Adjumani.

"I'm so glad for you," said Peter, clearly relieved to know this bit of good fortune accompanied her. "You were driven 150 miles if you were dumped out in Adjumani. I'm happy it was a Ugandan city."

"Yes, but no one was speaking Acholi there, even though it was in Uganda." She doesn't tell him how the locals shooed her away, calling her a Kony whore. Agnes studied the map as faint memories began to rise.

"The rivers might have led you to Gulu," Peter said, showing how the waters all connected. He pointed out possible routes Agnes might have taken.

Some of the fog lifted as little fragments began to surface—leaving the gumboots behind, hoping the LRA wouldn't be able to track her. Emerging from the woods into open fields of grass where certain smells and birdsong reminded her of Gulu. Spotting the red dirt that looked like home. Finding water, being able to bathe her daughters. But then, the sound of unfamiliar languages.

She listened, hoping to hear her Acholi language. She was still too far from home. The memories rose quickly now, how she hid every time a vehicle with men rolled down the road. And a woman who offered fresh fruit to Grace. They ate bananas until they all felt ill.

"You were lucky that trucker brought you from Yei to Adjumani," Peter said, studying the map. "You saved at least 150 miles, crossing from the DRC into South Sudan, avoiding the armed forces there." Then, quietly, he said, "You started to go back along the trail we had walked from Kitgum, two years earlier."

"Yes." Agnes remembered, with pinched pain. She closed her eyes as the images came in flashes. Finding flip flops on the side of the road that someone had thrown out. Hoping to find some for each child. The infected blister on her foot. The constant cycle of hunger and thirst. Hiking up hills or outcrops of rock to get a better view as Beatrice guarded Grace. Lying down in the road, sleeping and hoping, those little girls always at her side. The way she tried to hide her tears when Beatrice asked how far they had to go. Beatrice, so strong. So young. Both girls, so loved.

Yes, and an illness that overtook Agnes, the day she lost consciousness. The first time.

The image shimmered, just out of reach. How many times had Agnes revisited this moment? A moment with a beginning but never an end:

There was a woman. A kind, old woman. Her dark eyes soft with concern. Hands open with a bowl of beans and rice. The feeling of a full belly, a safe shelter, the feeling of deep rest. A clean dress, one for Beatrice too.

How Beatrice had called the woman an angel. They rested for a day. Maybe even two. That dear angel of a woman wrapped her blistered feet, tending to the infection. Sitting on an upturned plastic bucket, she rocked Grace while Beatrice put her head in the old one's lap.

"This angel woman sent me on with clear directions to head south, to ask for Porongo first, then Gulu. A clear direction, though a long way still ahead." Agnes took a deep breath. "We started walking and we walked at least three hours before . . . a truck appeared on the road. It was filled with drunk Ugandan soldiers. They laughed as they passed, heading toward where we had come from. Where we'd been sheltered and fed. With the angel woman," Agnes recalled.

How I believed they would be kind.
That they were the "good" kind of soldiers.

"We turned around and followed the truck, hoping they would turn around for us and drive us to Porongo. We walked and walked going back to where we'd been. But then . . . we found . . . the angel woman . . . the soldiers had slit her throat. And raped her." Agnes's body shook. "I vomited. Then . . . I'm not sure."

The images blurred. Another truck, more soldiers. Different ones. Waking in that stiff hospital bed, the gray ceiling, her daughters somewhere out of reach. Asking, *Is this the way home?* Over and over and over. *Is this the way home?*

Suddenly Agnes stopped herself, coming back to the present. The four white walls. The door cracked open. At some point, Sunday and Molly had come in, hearing her words. They stood at the office door, listening with perfect love and silence. A balm.

"I think I know where you were," Peter said. "I'm amazed you found your way."

The image of the bloodied woman was now scalded in her mind. Agnes blinked, studying the map as Peter tapped the spot.

"These barracks here, Purongo Detach. They must have nursed you back to health." He sighed. "The Ugandan army, along with the LRA, did bad things. Terrible things. Like those soldiers who killed that woman for no reason." His voice was like a prayer. A prayer for the dead. "I am glad you got to the main road and could be picked up by some of the good men left in the army."

She could remember now. That large, low building with screens on the windows. How it was painted green. How there were few mosquitoes. The quiet. The beds around her, some filled with wounded men. The nurses who brought water, who helped her outside to squat and pee. How someone had wiped her face with a wet cloth, the comfort of that gesture. A nice man who took her pulse and smiled at her before leaving her bedside.

The absence of the tension that she'd felt every day in the Kony camps.

Was it God, all along, who'd helped me?

"I feel a little foolish," Agnes said, still returning to herself. How long had they been talking? Hours, at least. All these silly details with Okello Peter. Why did it matter to him? To her? To anyone, really? A familiar shame crept up. Agnes was not used to talking about herself in this way for so long.

Peter exhaled, knowingly. "I understand your quest for answers." He paused. "I think God helps us remember important things, so we know if they really happened to us or if we made them up. I know I did when I came out." His face fell, heavy with sorrow. "We have to be sure that our stories are real, even when others don't believe them. We say them out loud because we can't let others say we are lying."

The room was small. Twice she shook her head and closed her eyes. Molly brought water and gave Agnes a dampened towel to blot her forehead. And her eyes. Agnes remembered the cool comfort such a gesture had brought her in the barracks.

"Agnes," Peter said, "though your memory may feel fuzzy, it was able to take you from Kitgum to Garamba, then from Garamba to Yei in Sudan, then to Adjumani, on to the towns along the Nile and to Packwach. You found your way home by memory."

These words shifted her perspective. Suddenly, she felt proud. Rather than losing herself in her memories, she grew stronger because she had them. She wondered if she might tell her daughters about what they had achieved together. After all, it was their story too. And maybe she could tell Bishop Okot. And surely Pastor Emanuel. Maybe it would help him to believe in God again. Would not this story confirm there was a God and He was near?

"Is there anything else?" asked Peter.

Agnes was afraid to ask, but she forced the words out: "Can you tell me what happened to my sons when I left?"

What she did not ask: *Was it selfish of me to leave them? Was I a bad mother because I saved myself my girls by leaving Aba Camp?* For the first time that day, tears streamed down Agnes's cheeks. In the bush she had been told not to cry. Never. She had learned to cry silently, as it was a crime to sob out loud.

Peter's forehead creased with compassion. "You want to know if you could have possibly taken your sons with you?"

Agnes nodded.

"It would have been impossible," Peter said, gently. "They were expected to be Kony's next soldiers. Your sons were part of a group he kept in training, protected fiercely by him. When amnesty did finally come, he lost them, and they came home. But before that, up to the peace in 2006, it would have been impossible for anyone to free those boys. To do so would be a death sentence, for you and the rest of your family. I believe you did the right thing."

Agnes let herself sob with sorrow for what could not have been.

A little while later, Peter rose to leave. They shook hands before departing. Peter shook Molly and Sunday's hands too, as if they were making a treaty: Agnes and the LRA, the LRA and the UPDF, all here together in one room. Making peace with their pasts and with one another.

Molly and Sunday would stand as witnesses to the truth of what Agnes now could tell. If a guest asked if she had been in the LRA, she could say with full honesty, "Yes, but I escaped. I found my way home with my two brave daughters. Myself and my girls."

Part II

9

September 2015—Gulu

Agnes had enjoyed a long stretch of feeling grounded and sleeping well, when the nightmares came for her again.

On the third night, she woke screaming again, and Beatrice made her tea and rubbed her back, telling her again and again that everything was okay, that they were all safe, that it was 2015 and not 1991. Agnes didn't like that such a burden fell to her daughter. She wanted these flashbacks to stop. So she called Okot James and asked if he could meet her at church for another blessing. He agreed.

They met in the sanctuary, which was just a big square room with plastic chairs stacked, for the moment, against one wall. Okot had set up two chairs facing each other, and Agnes sank into one gratefully. He opened with a word of prayer, then turning his gentle gaze on Agnes, asked, "How can I help you today, Sister Agnes?"

She swallowed. "I need to confess something, Bishop Okot. It is very bad. From my time in the bush."

He nodded calmly. "I am listening. Begin when you are ready."

She closed her eyes, and the scenes from her nightmare came back to her.

She was fourteen years old, and baby Moses was strapped to her back. She and many of the child soldiers and child mothers stood in a circle, jeering. Three young people, a girl and two boys, all about fifteen or sixteen years old, were tied to a tree. They had not been allowed to eat or drink for several days, and Kony had ordered everyone in the camp to urinate on them and beat them during that time.

Kony stood by the tree and roared that the three of them had engaged in 'sinful sex'—sex outside the marriages he had ordered. They were to be punished.

Agnes shouted along with the crowd, lunging hurtful accusations at the three frightened teens in the center. "Whore!" they shouted at the girl, Madelyn, who lowered her head in disgrace. Then, Agnes followed the crowd to break off a sharp vine. And then she followed Kony's orders to run at the three teens and switch them with the vine, even as they were still tied to the tree.

She watched her strong length of vine bite into the flesh of Madelyn's leg, then tear off skin until the girl's body oozed with blood.

She did it again and again, her and the whole crowd, until Madelyn and the two boys, all three of them were dead. All three of them, beaten by the crowd, until they took their final breaths.

Agnes told Okot the whole story. How Madelyn had been a year ahead of her in school in Lomora. How Kony had insisted that Madelyn had seduced both young men for prohibited sex. And how she, Agnes, had taken part in their final punishment.

"I have been having nightmares about it, Bishop Okot," she whispered. "But the nightmares are all real. They're real and I can't escape them." She cried, watering the fabric of her dress with her tears. "I can hardly believe it was me there, doing those terrible, unforgivable things. I see myself there, but I feel like I am far above myself, looking down at what someone else is doing. How could that have been me? How can I live with this? I can't. I can't."

Okot sat with her and let her cry for a long time. He handed her a bottle of water and she drank. Then he said gently, "Agnes, what would have happened to you if you had not taken part in the punishment circle?"

Agnes shook her head. "They would have killed me, too," she whispered. "Me and Moses. We had to participate. We had no choice. We had to do it. They would have killed me and my baby."

"What would you tell a fellow member of our ward if you knew they had done this same thing?" Okot asked.

"I would—" Agnes shook her head and sighed. "Goodness, Bishop. It never occurred to me that this could be forgivable. Not this."

"When you take this to the feet of our Savior Jesus Christ, and ask Him to do what He has invited you to do, to ask for Him to take your sin upon Him, He will take it away. He will take it and will remember it no more. And then, of course, He will forgive you. You know Hebrews 8:12, Agnes. What does it say?"

Agnes took a deep breath and recited the familiar verse: "'*For I will be merciful to their unrighteousness, and their sins and their iniquities will I remember no more.*'"

"You see? When we take our sins to the feet of our Savior Jesus Christ and ask Him to do what He has invited us to do, He will take them and remember them no more. He will forgive us."

After a long exhale, Agnes explained, "I love that Scripture, but I thought this sin was too ugly. Too horrible. I thought I could keep it hidden, even from God. It has been buried deep, in my darkest self."

Okot gave her a gentle smile. "I am proud of you, Sister Agnes. I think you just came out of the darkness."

She sighed another shuddering sigh. "Thank you, Bishop. Thank you for not turning away from me. Even from this."

"You know, Agnes . . . this is about agency," Okot James said. "It is about choosing to take responsibility for what we have done. For what we have done wrong. And for what we have done right. It is part of recognizing in ourselves that we are not puppets. That we have choice and control of our next steps."

Agnes furrowed her brow. "I don't understand, Bishop. I was a puppet in the LRA, all those years. I had no control over anything."

"I know, Agnes. I know that you were watched over and punished for small things and forced to do many things you would never have chosen on your own. But I believe there might also have been a space within your circumstances where you could be free to use your agency to make intentional choices. Life is about the choices we make." He took a long drink of water and wiped some sweat from his brow. "Can you think of any times in the bush when you used your agency—maybe when you intentionally chose to help someone?"

"I remember the women with whom I shared rice," Agnes whispered. "And I remember who I chose to help when they were in labor." She hung her head. "And I also remember the ones whose labor I made worse. We . . . we did that to each other," she said, ashamed. "That's when we often took revenge on one another—during labor—because we were all so vulnerable. It was our only power."

Okot nodded. "Yes. So in the terrible circumstances you were in, you could use your agency to decide whom you would help and whom you would hurt. And those choices can affect our lives forever. But when else did you make a choice, a choice that gave you some control?"

Agnes suddenly sat up straight in recognition of what Okot was alluding to. "I decided to escape," she said. "That was using my agency."

"Of course, Agnes. Of course it was." He beamed at her.

"My girls are alive because I used my agency to escape. Can you say that, Agnes?"

Agnes shook her head and whispered, "Yes. They are."

"I want to hear you say it, Agnes. Tell me how you used your agency to save the lives of your daughters."

After a long, sob-induced pause, during which Agnes cried from the depths of her soul, she finally looked into Okot's kind eyes and said, "I used my agency to escape. I made a choice and took control and left the camp to save my daughters."

"Yes," Okot said, smiling. "Against all odds, you saved them. And you saved yourself. You're all still here today because you made that brave choice, Agnes. And you've made many other brave choices since you left that camp."

Agnes nodded, accepting Okot's hand as he said, "Let's pray."

Okot prayed again for Agnes. This time, he asked that she would be forgiven and also that she would learn to forgive, and that the Lord would release her sins and make her clean.

When they had both said "Amen," and she had lifted her head, Okot smiled at her once more. "And now," he said, "I have something to ask you."

"Yes?"

"The Kampala LDS Stake President asked me to select a woman from our congregation to travel to the nearest Mormon temple in South Africa. Some members find comfort and healing when they go there for a blessing, and I believe you could benefit. Would you be interested in traveling to visit the Mormon temple in South Africa?"

Agnes's jaw dropped open. "South Africa? Me?"

"Yes, you are a baptized and respected member of our church," Okot said. "I'll give you some 'family name cards' and you can fill one out for each of your grandmothers. That's usually what people do. You will get baptized again in their names in the temple. Would you be interested?"

After the missionaries had come to Agnes on the side of the road and invited them to join their church, she'd started going to every meeting the Mormons held.

One of her new sisters shared her orange plastic wash tub with Agnes, allowing her to wash their clothes and clean themselves. She'd taken English language classes and read some pages in the *Book of Mormon*. Okot James and Akumu Sarah had encouraged her to be baptized, even though Agnes had been baptized in her father's church as a baby.

Agnes remembered her LDS baptism and how she'd repeated the words from Joshua in the Bible: *"'Choose ye this day whom ye will serve.' Will it be the gods which your fathers served that were on the other side of the flood? No. 'For me and my house, we will serve the Lord.'"*

Agnes knew that the Bbishop and his wife had gone to South Africa several years earlier. Three young men who were called to be missionaries from their ward had also gone to the temple there, but few others had been given the chance. Now she, Agnes, might have the opportunity to follow the same calling and further serve the Lord.

Agnes lifted her hands to her face. She could not imagine traveling as far away as South Africa. Who would take care of her girls? She'd have to travel on a plane. How would she get to Kampala? To the airport? How much would the trip cost? The bishop's idea seemed impossible. Aside from her escape from the bush, she'd never traveled anywhere.

The bishop's voice was calm as he offered Agnes reassurance. "It's your decision, of course. We will look after Grace and Beatrice while you're gone. The church will sponsor the entire trip, which will take place in January. Some members find comfort and healing when they attend, and I believe you will benefit. Give it some thought?"

To Agnes's enormous joy and surprise, she said she'd consider it.

∙∙∙∙∙∙

A few weeks later, Agnes had given Bishop Okot her answer: she would travel to South Africa to visit the temple. She could hardly believe her good fortune.

The following week, two missionaries from church arrived at Agnes's compound. A red-faced young man explained that Bishop Okot had sent them to help Agnes prepare for her visit to the temple.

Agnes lifted the curtain that hung over her doorway and welcomed the missionaries inside. As impossible as it seemed that she, of all people, would travel somewhere as far as South Africa, to do something so wonderful, Agnes was curious about the opportunity, and honored. Bishop Okot had already done so much for her family.

The two men respectfully took off their shoes and shook her hand. Agnes seated them near her, making a circle with the white plastic chairs that were ubiquitous in Gulu. She had six, so plenty to offer guests. After a prayer invoking the Spirit, the men explained the purpose of their visit. Bishop Okot had explicitly told them that Agnes must be interviewed and found worthy. Only "worthy" members (according to a church Handbook carefully prepared back in Salt Lake City in America) could visit a Mormon temple, and their status needed to be guaranteed before anyone could undertake such an expensive journey.

The two young missionaries explained that Bishop Okot would need to grant her a "temple recommend"—a little printed card with the LDS church logo and a signed statement by the bishop testifying to Agnes's "worthiness."

"Good for three years," one of the young missionaries explained.

The two young men had recently arrived in Gulu for a three-month assignment. They'd gone through the temple for the first time themselves before they'd left their homes in California and Arizona. "The bishop will ask you fifteen questions, and we are here to prepare you for the interview," they said.

The conversation began smoothly. They asked Agnes about her knowledge of Jesus Christ and if she could give a testimony of her sureness of God's reality. She could and did. They then moved along to questions about the prophets. Joseph Smith was the first "latter-day prophet," who had seen angels and translated the Book of Mormon. The other prophets came after him. Agnes knew this.

Then, to Agnes's intense discomfort, the conversation turned to sex.

"Do you obey the law of chastity?" they asked. "Do you abstain from sex except with your husband?"

Too shocked to speak, Agnes looked away. She could not hold eye contact as they continued to elaborate. The more they spoke, the more Agnes's blood ran cold. These words could have been taken straight out of Joseph Kony's mouth. How dare these two men come into her house and ask her these questions? They were young enough to be her sons! What could they possibly know or understand about her past?

"God's will is that sex be a sacred experience between a man and wife," one of the missionaries explained.

Sex.

Husband.

Sacred.

Agnes's heart began to drum in her ears. She couldn't listen to another word. Agnes leapt to her feet, and ordered, "Get out of my home!" Her eyes narrowed to slits and her brows knitted, as she lifted the heavy brown cloth hanging from the pole above her doorway, signaling the missionaries to take an immediate exit.

Startled, the two young men tried to clarify their words, but Agnes assured them the problem was not the language barrier. Agnes understood only too well what they had been saying. She ushered them out the door. She could not entertain another second of this talk, and would not be satisfied until they fled.

Scrambling with their backpacks and Bibles, the boys tipped over chairs as they searched for their shoes—and were quickly removed from her presence.

The audacity! Agnes had a word or two for Bishop Okot.

••••••

Agnes went to see Bishop Okot at the church that night. "How could you not warn me?" Agnes said. "I trusted you to tell these boys what we went through."

Okot rubbed his forehead. It was clear from his worried expression that he had been anticipating her arrival. Agnes had made it clear to the American missionaries that they'd blundered in some big way, and she was sure the first place they came after leaving her home was to the bishop.

"Sister Agnes. I'm so sorry, let me—"

Before he could finish, Agnes began, "Sacred sex? Husband? Law of Chastity? Is this the church of Christ or the Lord's Resistance Army all over again?"

Okot stood and took a deep breath, "I can only imagine the insensitivity."

Agnes took a seat, her back rigid, her eyes flashing.

"I'm truly sorry, Sister Agnes. It hurts to see that this misunderstanding, which I am responsible for, has caused you fresh pain," he said. "May we pray? Invite a spirit of peace before we talk?"

And so, before unraveling the incident and discussing whether the temple was still something Agnes wanted to pursue, they prayed.

Trusting the Spirit as she did, Agnes began to breathe more slowly and steadily. Okot James knew of Agnes's catastrophic history with her three "husbands" in the bush. And even though she knew her first two husbands were dead, and that Peter was no longer a threat, Agnes felt terrified at the idea of someone forcing her to have "sacred sex" ever again. If that's what this trip to the temple was about, she wanted no part of it. None at all.

They each took deep breaths. She knew Peter wouldn't hurt her anymore, and she knew Okot knew that too; she had told him all about meeting him and reviewing her escape. She and Okot were good friends. Agnes trusted him.

"Tell me, Sister Agnes, what do you think when you hear the words 'sex' and 'husband' spoken?"

Agnes shuddered. Though other memories came in waves, she couldn't forget this part of her past. "When I was given to each of my husbands, I was told that my first responsibility was to never refuse them sex when they wanted it. It was my sacred wifely duty. God had chosen them for his army and me for their wife. I was told that was the reason I was born. If I didn't give that to them, I was useless. They would kill me. Three husbands, two now dead. And I can still recall how day after day I was reminded that letting them have me for sex was what God wanted. It was commanded."

"Sister Agnes," Okot James said gently. "You have been a member of this church for seven years and often talked to me about the healing our church has brought for you."

"Yes," Agnes said quietly. "But now I worry that there is something secret about this religion that I have not been told? Was I chosen to go to the Mormon temple to be the victim of more 'sacred sex'?"

Bishop Okot closed his eyes and seemed to offer a silent prayer before he continued. "Agnes," he said, "I hope God is with us now to do this difficult work, because we need to talk about this thing called 'sex.'"

Agnes felt herself blanch. She sat back in her seat, pulling away from Okot James, not sure she wanted to hear what he had to say.

He went on, "Sex between two loving people is something very different from what you experienced in the bush. Sex is what a free woman can decide to do with someone of her choosing. Sex can be for a woman's own pleasure. Or it can build a closer bond with a man. But it's always a woman's choice to engage in sex or not. In other words, what was done to you in the bush was not sex, Agnes. What happened to you was not your choice nor your decision. It was not sex. And it certainly was not sacred. It was *rape*."

It took all of Agnes's self-control to stay in her seat.

"You were raped, Agnes, and that was torture. Violence. The opposite of sacred. All those things that happened to you by men who called themselves 'husbands' and who considered you their property . . . that was rape. Sexual assault. It is important to remember that. To know there is something different. Everyone who has ever blamed you—your father, the priests, the people who hurled terrible words at you—they have all been wrong. In God's eyes, you are innocent."

Agnes sat completely still. She needed a moment to absorb his words. She did not cry or bury her face in her hands. She was surprised to discover a newfound strength in herself. A strength that straightened her back, lifted her face, and emboldened her. Agnes stood up, staring defiantly over Okot's head. Now that he had given her the language to frame her traumas, she had more to say. "I want to confront all those who wronged me, face to face. I want to name them and accuse them for what they did to me." She closed her eyes. "My three husbands. Samson. George. Peter. They tortured, assaulted, and raped me—each said it was his right because I was his wife." Emotions passed through her, but her voice was steady with resolution. She looked back at Okot. "You have given me these new words . . . for what these men did to me. These words have set me free."

A slow broad smile spread across Okot's face, "Sister Agnes, you still have a long journey ahead, but step by step, you're moving forward, healing your past and building a new future."

·······

After their long talk, Bishop Okot walked Agnes out of the church. The moon was full and high and although it was late, the streets were bright. Agnes walked confidently into the night. She would recommit herself to preparing for the temple, provided that the bishop led the preparations and not the missionaries.

10

September 2015—Gulu to Bunia

Moses gritted his teeth as the truck's engine sputtered then stalled. He cursed and thumped the steering wheel with the heel of his hand. The Seed Store's truck bed was filled with fertilizer and seed, and he was eager to make his deliveries. He twisted the key again in the ignition, and this time the truck rumbled to life. It wasn't only his impatience that had Moses on edge. Pastor Emanuel had gone too far in his chiding earlier that day. Moses could see that Pastor immediately felt sorry for comparing Moses to his bush father, but he'd crossed a line, and rather than talk it out, Moses did what he preferred to do. Leave.

No wonder his boss and mentor had not become a real 'Pastor,' Moses thought, peeling out of the Seed Store yard so fast he bumped the gate before tearing down the wide alleyway, sending people and dogs running out of his way. The truck flew down the crowded road toward his usual delivery route. He ignored the yells and honks as he gripped the steering wheel, trying to steady himself. Moses was tense. Then again, when was he ever *not* tense?

Once he'd turned onto the highway and settled into the rhythm of driving, something he always enjoyed, Moses began to regret leaving the way he did. He could have asked Pastor to explain the ways he behaved like his father. Then at least he'd be able to change those patterns. He could also have asked Pastor never to associate him with him again. Ever. He accelerated to overtake a car, kicking up dust as his back wheel slipped at the side of the road.

Would Pastor would fire him for taking off in such a rage? Would he be forbidden from making deliveries? At the thought he might have fewer chances to do what he loved, Moses really let loose, driving aggressively into the open road. Pastor was a good man—the best of men, really. After the war, it was Pastor who had brought Dan and Moses under his wing and given them reputable jobs with fair wages. He called himself "family" and put up with Moses's defensive behavior and discourtesy with customers, not embarrassing him when he pulled him aside to correct him. Moses could admit to himself that he soaked up Pastor's approval like a sponge, even if he only showed his gratitude by completing his responsibilities to the best of his ability. He hoped Pastor didn't think he was arrogant, when he was only showing off new skills he was learning from his boss. Moses didn't know how else to act.

Now, Moses thumped on the steering wheel again and again, until his hand began to sting. What if he'd blown it? What if Pastor wouldn't let him be in charge of driving the truck?

He'd been shocked and a bit suspicious when Pastor had gone to the trouble to find him and Dan in that barren field, and even more alarmed when he'd offered them jobs. And not just any old jobs, but the best jobs he could find. Moses had been dumbfounded since he'd begun the work at the Seed Store, waiting for his good luck to vanish. But seasons had passed, and—until today—he'd remained on solid footing with Pastor.

However, as Moses's appreciation for Pastor had grown through the years, so had his resentment for the other adults who'd failed to protect him through his traumatic childhood. And Moses showed that resentment. This is what had annoyed Pastor so much that morning. He did not approve of how Moses was so often rude and surly and quick to anger. Pastor had made it clear that he expected more from him. "Sometimes your behavior reminds me of Samson," Pastor had snapped.

Moses was also angry because Dan had resigned from the job Pastor had given him, accepting the job at the hospital as if it was a better job than the one Pastor had given them. His little brother, the one Moses had taken care of all those years in the bush—after their mother, Agnes, had abandoned them—thought he was a big man now. A man with a girlfriend and children and a fancy job in an important hospital. Moses knew he should be pleased for Dan's success, but instead he felt abandoned and jealous. He pressed down on the accelerator and let the truck whip through the traffic, the engine rumbling and grinding beneath him. Dan had forgiven Agnes for leaving them in the bush, and in doing so, Dan had chosen their mother over him. It wasn't fair. *Moses* was the one who had watched out for Dan all those years, not their mother.

"If *Mother* was what you could call her," Moses said out loud, a familiar twist of bitterness in his voice. Even before Agnes had abandoned them in the bush, Moses had never felt he had real parents. He knew that his mother had become Samson's wife at thirteen, and that when Samson died, she was then forced to marry that embarrassingly ugly officer, George. But what had that meant for Moses? No one cared. His mother's whole life had been occupied with keeping her husbands satisfied. Ugly George certainly had no interest in Agnes's boys from another man. Dan had felt no grief when George died, but then his mother's name was tied to yet another man—Okello Peter, a vicious soldier who was feared by children as well as adults.

Unlike George, who had ignored Dan and Moses, Peter had been openly hostile to the boys. It was God's way, people said. No man should raise another man's offspring. So, Moses and Dan knew no comfort in the bush, least of all from their mother. Where was she when Okello Peter killed their young friend, Sam? Where was she when they'd needed her most?

Bicycles blurred past the window, along with children playing in ditches. He felt the power emanating from the enormous engine—roaring, pounding energy—power Moses lacked in every other aspect of his life. He was only twenty-four. A young man oozing with unused energy and desire. An angry young man, who had found no decent outlets for all that angst. It was as if he'd been destined to always be searching, digging, yearning, and scrabbling for something, but he did not know what.

Gulu wasn't a big town, so Moses occasionally saw Agnes from afar, especially during the period when she'd helped Dan and Dora find that western doctor to fix baby Sam's feet. He'd been pleased for his brother's sake but had resented Agnes's involvement. He bristled to hear people praise Agnes for giving her hut to Dan and Dora and Sam. She deserved no credit. Her father had gifted her the land, Pastor had helped her build the hut, and he and Dan had helped build the cement-block house she lived in now. Moses had been proud to carry the heaviest bags of cement and hoist the longest logs for the framing of the roof. But he did not stay to admire the house and took no pleasure in knowing that his mother would live there more securely than she had in that shabby hut with his half-sisters. Moses had worked hard on that house, not for his mother but for Pastor. To impress his mentor. The only man who had ever been a decent father-figure in his life.

Moses spat out of the open window. He hated Agnes. And apart from the one time he'd seen her in the market on that rainy evening, he did his best never to acknowledge his mother to her face, preferring to nurse his resentment and to hurt her the way she had hurt him.

······

Moses continued to battle his memories and resentments as the road straightened and the day cooled with the sinking sun. He crossed the Albert Nile River and pressed on toward the western skyline and the border between Uganda and the DRC. The sun soon sank altogether and within moments, he was plunged into the night, in a part of the country where few lights diluted the inky darkness.

Moses flicked on the truck's headlights and comforted himself with the thought that at the rate he was traveling, he would see Mercy and her son, Moz, by tomorrow morning. The thought of Mercy's sweet face was the only thing that slowed Moses's pulse, though his foot on the gas pedal remained the same.

He hadn't intended to develop feelings for Mercy. Some truckers like him found comfort and companionship in the arms of equally lonely girls, who invited them into their beds for a small fee. They cried with them and shared stories of lost homes and lost parents and lost children. It was often a tender respite on their otherwise exhausting trips. But it wasn't so for Moses. For years, he went to those beds and hated those women, only wanting to use them. To hurt them if he could. He rarely visited the same place twice, but then there was Mercy.

Something about that woman made him want her again. What it was, he could not have told even himself. Was it her helplessness? Was it her fearfulness? Was it her hunger?

The last time he'd driven to the DRC for the Seed Store, he'd gone to see Mercy. She'd searched his eyes for something to indicate that he might care for her in some way. That she was special to Moses. Whatever she'd found there, she'd seemed disappointed.

Moses was used to that—disappointing everyone.

And yet, he did care for Mercy. She was special, as was her son. "Moz," she called him and the coincidence of their shared name had hooked Moses, who couldn't help but watch how Mercy mothered her six-year-old boy. The bottomless love she seemed to have for him, despite her difficult circumstances. What little she did have, she shared with the boy. And in doing so, Mercy had earned Moses's respect. She was the first woman with whom he'd shared his food. Before, he'd made his women sleep on the floor, hungry. He was not a good man, and he knew it, and yet when Mercy had begged Moses for permission to bring her boy to the room he rented and to feed him the remains of Moses's dinner, something about her love for Moz had made him soften. For that, and reasons beyond his understanding, Moses kept returning to that shabby room in Bunia, and to Mercy.

How many hours had passed? Moses's fury was taking longer than usual to subside. He ate a bag of groundnuts and chocolate, a poor substitute for dinner, and tried to drive himself into exhaustion. To a state where all feelings were numbed and even his rage loosened its steel grip on his insides. But the truck needed fuel.

He stopped at a roadside petrol station and left his truck just long enough to grab a couple bottles of soda from the back of the station's store. He hurriedly paid and was off again, but before he was even on the highway, Moses knew he was no longer alone.

He held his breath, waiting, knowing that there was a space just behind his seat for a person to crouch. When he found his courage, he slammed on the brakes and turned.

A hard-looking man pointed a gun at Moses's head. "Keep driving." He spoke with a Sudanese Dinka accent. "And don't slow down for an hour."

Moses's stomach turned and sweat trickled down his back. Was he a hostage in his own truck? No. Not his truck. *Pastor's* truck. Moses swallowed hard and gripped the steering wheel. Pastor had trusted him to deliver these supplies safely. He couldn't break that trust.

Seconds felt like hours; minutes, like years. Watching the barrel of the gun out the corner of his eye, Moses played out scenarios of how he could get control of the situation. How he might grab the man with his free hand. How he might slam the brakes and cause the man to tumble forward. But the man was careful to stay out of reach and stable, very comfortable with the gun. Occasional glances in the mirror allowed Moses to understand that the Dinka knew how to use it.

So, Moses drove on, trying to puzzle his way out of this. He knew no useful prayers. No God who'd ever cared about him. Maybe he could make a deal with the Dinka.

"What do you want from the truck?" Moses asked.

The Dinka snorted. "Everything, and we're taking the truck, too."

Moses laughed, more out of nerves and fear but also at the boldness of the hijacker.

The Dinka laughed too. "You think this is funny? You're the only thing that is laughable here, you fool."

Finally, the man ordered Moses to turn onto a smaller highway headed south.

"My shipment is due in two days. I need to get south of Butembo," Moses said, his words sounding pathetic and ineffective.

"Good," the Dinka said. "That means no one will miss you until then."

As they came over a low rise in the road, flashlights moved across their path and a dozen men waved them down.

Moses stepped hard on the pedal, hoping to run over them. But the Dinka hit him in the temple with his gun and jumped into the passenger seat, trying to steady the wheel while holding the gun in his free hand.

Moses saw only stars as the truck leaped over the roadside ditch, continuing for a short way at some speed before hitting an embankment perpendicular to the road. Both men were thrown into the windshield as the cab nearly overturned.

The Dinka was quicker to right himself, pressing the cold metal gun barrel against Moses's head. "Unlock the doors," he ordered.

Why the man hadn't already shot him, Moses didn't know. Every muscle in his body throbbed with pain, and his head swam in the murky haze of disorientation. But he managed to unlock the doors, as demanded. When one opened, Moses made out the sound of angry men. He felt arms grabbing him, dragging him out of the cab and then to the ground. He fought, but his arms felt weighed down. Everything became painful, slow.

The men in the ambush yelled and kicked, beating Moses with their flashlights as he remained on the ground. His face swelled as each knock sent him spiraling. His stomach clenched with the impulse to vomit.

They wouldn't stop.

An image of Peter Okello appeared in his mind. Looming over Sam at the camp. How the man had railed on Sam until the small boy had died.

Moses had seen too many people die. Some beaten to death by mobs just like this one.

White-hot pain. The crunch of bone. For a brief moment, the sight of Mercy's sweet face.

"Mercy," his voice was a whisper.

Blackness overtook him.

11

September 2015—Lomora

Walking down Jomo Kenyatta Road toward her childhood village of Lomora, Agnes felt far less burdened than the other times she had come this way.

Is this what it means to be carefree? Without cares? Agnes recalled her journey to Lomora in 2005, seated in a taxi between her father who looked stern and disappointed, and Father Pius, who looked even more stern and more disappointed. Agnes had expected cousins and old friends to be standing outside their huts with arms open. Her two young daughters were in the back seat, cleaned up and frightened, between two blank-faced aunties. The tall golden-green grasses looked even more wonderful than she had anticipated, waving past her window as if they were welcoming her home. But Agnes soon realized that only the grass was eager to embrace her. The few people who stood along the familiar red dirt road glared with contempt. "Where are the others?" she'd asked her father, but her loved ones had never appeared. These surly substitutes no longer saw this young woman as one of them. The one who'd been stolen as a child, now restored. What followed were days . . . weeks . . . she couldn't remember . . . of harrowing treatment. Treatment that Agnes now understood was abuse.

She'd left Lomora, and her father, with no intention of ever coming back. And she'd held that intention until four years later, when she'd finally found the courage to visit her father's deathbed. There, she'd felt obliged to confess that she had left the Catholic church and had been baptized, along with her daughters, into the LDS church. She'd been full of worry during that visit. Concerned that her father would damn her, as he had done so many others who had left his Catholic church. She'd started out with dark expectations, which had transformed into a miraculous experience when her ailing father had given her the deed—officially stamped and recorded—to the small plot of land in Layibi, where she could finally build her own hut. An honor and an advantage so few could ever expect, and one she would always be grateful for.

Her final visit to Lomora, a few months later, had been to offer homage to her father at his funeral. Back then, Agnes had made her way along the highway with the girls in tow, having instructed them to obey the commandment to "honor thy father," even if their grandfather was a man who had only shown the girls cruelty in their young lives.

Today Agnes enjoyed her lighter step, acknowledging that her unburdening was perhaps because she had learned to accept most people as neither totally awful or totally perfect, and to be relieved of the rigid judgments.

She committed to not think of those three futile occasions when she'd failed to find solace in Lomora. Today, Agnes was in search of names. The names of women who, she imagined, would undoubtedly have welcomed her home, had they not gone to be with Jesus years before her return from the bush. Once she'd gathered her ancestor's names and stories, she would take the "family name cards" to the Mormon temple in South Africa. There, she would be restored to them, joined forever as a joyful family.

Agnes passed rows of shops along Jomo Kenyatta Road, with cars, trucks, and bodas parked in front and plenty of people poking around with bundles, baskets, and "Ghana Must Go-bags," or Osuofia bags piled on their heads. The shoppers strode along the thoroughfare, where cyclists swerved in and out of traffic, skillfully avoiding the throngs of pedestrians. But mostly tall grass adorned the roadsides, especially on her left side. The Lomora side.

She turned off Jomo Kenyatta Road and onto the red dirt road that took her to the village. Along this stretch, Agnes took in the scent of the swaying reeds, with their familiar fresh smell, especially in spring and summer. It was well before midday, so the sun was not yet too oppressive. She carried a notebook and the blank cards Bishop Okot had given her with instructions to "gather the names of your ancestors, along with the dates of their births and deaths." With the bishop's help, Agnes had already secured a plane ticket to South Africa, as well as a fancy passport. Now, all she needed were her ancestors' stories.

As she drew closer to the beaten paths between huts in Lomora, a combination of nerves, excitement, and apprehension overtook her, reminding her of a saying Molly often said, "Life is a mix of things." Though Lomora was no longer home, Agnes longed to understand her beginnings and the many ancestors who had paved the way for her.

She carried herself as straight as she could and slowed to take in the details of the place she'd once called "home." The names and faces of the people who'd lived in the huts began to return to Agnes. She could picture them in her mind—the people she needed to speak with—but first she had to pay her respects to the elders. She prayed for God to guide her steps.

"Old Otito is expecting you," a girl on the road said, boldly. She had popped out to greet Agnes, clearly proud of her Batman shirt and perhaps braver because of it. "He knew you'd return."

What an encouraging surprise. A flock of children soon surrounded her, and skipped along as Agnes followed Batman girl. A younger girl took Agnes's hand and smiled up with a wide-open face and lively eyes. Her shirt was blue, her pants a darker purple. Her flip flops didn't match. One had a plastic chicken on the strap, which made Agnes smile.

Old Otito John, the oldest living man in the village, greeted Agnes as she approached his hut. It was freshly painted, and the roof was new and clean. He had set a chair for her to face him, as he clearly expected to tell some tales.

"You are the one I sought," Agnes said with reverence to his age, a man born in 1922. "I am in search of as many grandmothers as I can find, as my time away from here has all but erased my knowledge of the past."

"I knew your grandmother," Otito said, his voice clear but shaky. "I knew her when she was fifteen. Achieng Esther Oero was born before the first European war." He spoke of how that war touched their lives so harshly back then. How wars have continued to touch them since Uganda's independence in 1962.

Agnes felt a swell of tenderness. Of all her family, Grandma Achieng Esther was the woman she'd known best, the one who had raised her. Agnes grew up with her grandmother's singing, cooking, and on special occasions, drumming, dancing, and sharing advice to young mothers on how to raise their little ones. She'd listen to Agnes's complaints about school and then tell her over and over how blessed she was to have the opportunity to go to school. She'd always make Agnes promise to get the highest marks in her class.

It was Grandmother Esther that Agnes felt closest to in the bush as well. All those times she'd considered suicide. Others had done it, desperate to end the pain, to escape a life that was not worth living. How close she had come to ending it all, until, each time, she'd heard her grandmother's voice in the stillness of night. On some occasions, Grandmother Achieng Esther came to the forest when Agnes needed help, bringing with her another mother spirit she called Eve, both attending Agnes in her pit of loneliness.

"Achieng Esther was a hero," Otito John said. "You know the story? How she bravely got back land for her people after marrying a bad farmer-chief's son? She was young, but she behaved like Esther in the Bible. She volunteered to beg the bad farmer-chief working for the English to return the land he'd stolen from her people. She said she would marry his son if he granted it back, and he agreed."

Agnes remembered this story of her heroic grandmother, and smiled with pride.

"She was a good wife," Old Otito said thoughtfully. "However, her husband got sick and died before any children came. In death, he honored his promise and asked his father to honor his: to return the land that belonged to her people. It was a mighty feat for all our people. Those who had not already starved could live."

"I've come from the other side of Gulu to hear what you have to tell me," Agnes replied, struck by the shared sorrows across generations. Somehow, this story had given her a strange kind of strength. Old Otito was glad to have a listener, Agnes could tell. And she was a ready listener. He spoke not only of war, but of colonization and the early missionaries, first the Anglicans, and then the Italians who'd brought Catholicism. From Otito John, Agnes gathered as much as she could about her family's history. She also paid her respects to Mama-Barbara, then to Mama-Agata Anna Elizabeth, who worked at the Comboni Missionary School.

Mama-Agata was helpful, pulling out record books and school certificates. Here, Agnes learned about her great-grandmother, Akech.

"The name 'Akech' tells us she was born during a famine in 1890," Mama-Agata said. "The record says she was sometimes called Sister Evelyn. Although it was unlikely for an African woman to be educated in those days, she taught at the school and helped at Lacor Hospital—still the best in Gulu today! We have wondered what her record meant."

"Don't you wish we had pictures?" Agnes said.

Mama-Agata beamed. "Yes, yes, and what an incredible story is yours."

Agnes felt alive with the new information about these notable women in her family. Though she'd never known her great-grandmother, she did recall hearing her grandmother, Sister Evelyn's daughter, speak of her. It was from her that Agnes first learned about the spirit mother, Eve, insisting we could talk about her and celebrate her, despite what some Catholics say.

Mama-Agata's kindness prompted Agnes to ask something that had been nagging at her since she'd begun her journey to Lomora that morning. Memories of her father's funeral, when she'd tried to be an exemplary daughter despite her father's cruelty to her and her girls. Although it had not been the first time Agnes had been so internally split in her loyalties, it certainly was the hardest and she hoped on this visit to Lomora—with these people who knew her story, her origins, and her father—that she might find some peace.

"Mama-Agata, may I ask . . . do you believe in the Bible?" Agnes's voice was tentative, but her intention was strong.

"That's a big question," Mama-Agata said. "What's on your mind?"

A frown creased Agnes's brow. "What do you think about the Ten Commandments?"

"Well, my people have always been Christian and talk about the Bible all the time," Mama-Agata said warmly. "It is simply my opinion, but I think the commandments generally make sense."

"In the Bible it says to honor thy father and thy mother," Agnes said. "Recently, my youngest daughter, Grace, was put in a dangerous position by a teacher. Someone she trusted. Since that day, I keep asking God why He would put her in such danger." *And why He put me in such danger.* "My heart cries out to Him, Mama-Agata, and this week He let me know it is because I have sinned. I try to show my gratitude for Jesus, but I have not honored my father and mother. Especially my father."

A look of confusion crossed Mama-Agata's face. "Your father has been dead for some time now, Agnes."

"Yes, but before he died I did not honor him. When I read the commandments in the Bible, it says: *Honor thy father and thy mother*," Agnes said. "God directed me to read Ephesians 6:1–2, where it says: *Honor thy father and mother,* which is the first commandment. If we keep that commandment, Jesus promised that all will be well with us. It says we will live long. Ephesians 6:3 says: '*That it may be well with thee, and thou mayest live long on the earth.*'"

Mama-Agata nodded tenderly. "This is a commandment I know very well, as my mother hung it on the wall in our home. My father was not a gentle man and had a hand like a lion's paw, which he used to knock my mother around for years and years, and later used on me. My mother had the same question about the Ten Commandments that you do, but after she studied Ephesians 6, she told me so I would not forget that the commandment to honor your father and mother also tells fathers they have a commandment they must obey. This part she framed for the wall in my room, to let me know that because my father beat us, I was not obliged to honor him. Here, let's look it up." Mama-Agata paged through an old Bible on her desk. "Look, it says here: Ephesians 6:4, '*And, ye fathers, provoke not your children to wrath: but bring them up in the nurture and admonition of the Lord.*'"

Agnes followed the words across the page.

"In *nurture*, Agnes," Mama-Agata emphasized. "God commanded both my father and your father to bring us up in nurture! What does that mean?"

"It means that they were supposed to take care of us in a kind way, the way I am supposed to nurture my own children?" Agnes asked, so deeply relieved by this forgotten part of Ephesians. "So, both your father and my father broke their commandment?"

"Yes," Mama-Agata said. "I hope your father asked the Lord to forgive him for what he did to you before he died, but if he didn't, Agnes, I believe he is feeling very guilty about that now, wherever his spirit lives. He loved you, Agnes. When you were young, he was kind, but he was wrong to treat you the way he did when you returned from the bush. I do not believe you have any reason to feel bad about not honoring him."

But Agnes wasn't through. "At my father's funeral, I scolded my daughters for not honoring him. It was their first time back, and we had all suffered at the hands of my father. I told the girls to wail and throw flowers on his casket, which stood open at the bottom of the grave. He did not look so mean, lying there, but the girls refused to honor him. Their hurts were not healed. I squeezed their arms and pinched them. Still, they would not do what I asked."

"But, Agnes, they know he was very unkind to you all. You can't make that all go away."

"Do you think I was wrong to take them to his funeral? To make them stand by his grave? I even told them I was ashamed of how they'd behaved." Agnes shook her head, dismayed at her behavior that day.

Mama-Agata hummed under her breath. "Maybe this would be a good time to tell them a big truth, which is that most people are not always bad, or always good. We can all try to be better each day. Simply because you are struggling with this question, I can tell that you try. I do, and maybe your father did too. You must remember times when your father was good to you? Let the girls know that both are true. People tend to repeat only the best stories about people at their funerals. Everybody at a funeral understands that while there are still bad stories, they don't have to be reminded on that occasion."

Agnes nodded. The conversation with Mama-Agata had been reassuring and she was feeling much calmer, but still remorseful. "I treated my daughters very badly that day. I wanted all those people from my old village to think we were good people. That we weren't bad just because their father had been a rebel."

"Maybe you can tell them that, too," Mama-Agata suggested. "I'll bet they understand."

As Agnes began to retrace her steps to the main road, she felt a stirring of pride at her origin story, one that she could now proudly pass down to her own children. Also, she'd done what she'd gone there to do. Her little notebook was full of the names of family members, including the list of inspiring grandmothers she had come there to find. Agnes felt some peace about her father too, and the events that had unfolded at his funeral. A peace she felt would help her find peace with Beatrice and Grace.

She had so many thoughts, she almost didn't hear her phone ring. Fumbling to answer the call, Agnes was happy to see Pastor's name.

"My dear friend," Agnes said. "I have much to tell you." She was eager to tell him about her visit to Lomora. He, more than anyone, understood the life she'd come from. Now that she was healing, she began to share his dream of opening a shelter for women like her, women who were war refugees, women who needed safe spaces and compassionate listeners. Agnes couldn't really imagine how that might look in the real world, but now, filled with the stories of her strong and brave ancestors, she wondered if they could really bring this dream to life.

"Yes, we do need to talk," Pastor said, drawing her from her daydream.

Agnes's heart dropped in response to the urgency in his voice. She pulled the phone closer to her ear and nearly fainted when he said, "It's about Moses."

12

September 2015—Lacor Hospital, Gulu

Moses lay on a cot in a hospital room, trapped inside a white cast that covered his entire pelvis, both hips, and his right leg. His leg was elevated on a pulley to maintain blood flow, and he was tied down with restraints. Moses's entire body itched with frustration and pain, but he kept his eyes closed and pretended to sleep as the doctor stood at the foot of his cot and explained to Pastor Emanuel how the cast would be modified as Moses began to heal.

"Your boy is lucky to be alive," the doctor said. "The broken femur, known as a comminuted fracture, is the most serious wound, but he also has a badly bruised tibia and cracked ribs on both sides. I'm sorry to say, he may never walk again, and it's still not conclusive if any of his internal organs are injured. We'll keep an eye on things of course, but it might be worth considering how you'll manage his limited mobility when he gets home."

Moses struggled to keep his emotions in check. His broken ribs hurt as much as his crushed thigh. His face and arms were swollen, with green and yellow bruises blooming across his skin. And now this news about the seriousness of his injuries and his dire prognosis. He did not want to absorb what the doctor was saying. As if he hadn't suffered enough in his life already. His agitation grew, and his mood darkened. His body throbbed with rage. Pure rage!

"Moses," Pastor said, taking a seat beside the bed and gently squeezing Moses's fingers.

Moses kept his eyes closed and turned his head away. His shame was almost as deep as his pain. He did not want to have to explain what had happened, how he'd lost Pastor's truck and all the inventory. "I wish I'd died," he mumbled. "I heard what that doctor was saying, what my worthless future holds. Why survive all those years in the bush for a life like this?"

"You are already on a slow path to recovery, Moses. Even if it is against your will." Pastor made it clear he was not going to indulge Moses's self-pity.

"I mean it!" Moses said, his voice raspy. "I promised. I've always promised that I'd take good care of that truck."

"Moses, do you really think I, let alone your mother and brother, care more about that Seed Store truck than about your *life*?" Pastor sighed. "We can always get another truck. Things are replaceable. Even big, powerful things. You, Moses . . . your life . . . that's what matters."

Moses didn't respond. The lights overhead glared down. He could barely hold eye contact with Pastor. He'd always been so eager for Pastor's approval, to show his appreciation for the man's role in his life. Now, it was clear he'd need support while his body slowly healed. "There were so many of them." His voice broke.

"The mechanic in Bunia explained that this kind of attack happens quite frequently," Pastor said. "They work in teams."

Moses winced in pain. "What mechanic? When were you in Bunia?"

Pastor explained that he had brought Moses to Lacor Hospital after finding him at a petrol station north of Bunia, in the DRC. Moses had been under the watchful eye of a kind mechanic who had tended to him after he'd been found beaten on the side of a road. Stripped of all papers and cash and mostly unconscious, it was a mystery how Moses had managed to tell the mechanic where he was from and who to contact. Somehow, Pastor had been called and had made the twenty-hour round trip to pick up the injured Moses, bringing him home to Gulu.

Moses turned to look at him. "You went all that way? I thought you would be so mad at me."

"Moses," Pastor said with a heavy sigh and a smile. "You had a lot of help to make this a big disaster."

"Will they give me more pills? Something for the pain?" Moses cursed under his breath and tried not to moan.

"Moses," Pastor repeated, this time more firmly. "I'm sure they will, but first I have something important to say to you, so listen to me. You've been very hard on your mother since you came out of the bush a full decade ago. You blame her for what happened to you and your brother, Dan, and you are quick to tell anyone who will listen how much she wronged you."

Moses's eyes locked on Pastor, the fury apparent in his narrowed pupils.

"Listen to me," Pastor said, holding up a hand and speaking with his characteristic tender, toughness—a voice Moses trusted to bear truth. "You're twenty-four now, strong, and well-fed. Your papa was six years older than you are now when he joined up with Kony. After he killed his first young wife, your twelve-year-old mother was given to him, like a piece of property. *Twelve.* Kony called her his wife. Your mother was captured and held by a band of men your age and older, all with guns and pangas. She was one defenseless girl—twelve, thirteen, fourteen, fifteen, sixteen years old in the bush. Hungry. Overworked. Beaten. Another 'wife' to another brute. She was just trying to survive. Like all of you."

Moses kept still, but listened to what Pastor had to say.

"I won't mention this again, but I want you to think about your mother in this light when you think about what happened to you in the DRC—so many against one. I have told your mother what happened and where you are, and no doubt she will want to visit you here. Take some time with yourself, Moses. I'll see that you get some pills now."

Moses grunted his acknowledgment, but closed his eyes and turned his head away again.

"You're going to need constant care, perhaps for a long while. You have me, but you also have a mother who wants you in her life, even while you hold her at arm's length. For that, you are lucky."

As Pastor rose to leave, Moses said nothing. But saying nothing, instead of a string of rage-filled rants, was a start.

••••••

Dan, Beatrice, and Grace took turns visiting their older brother over the next several weeks while Moses was confined to his hospital bed. Dan readily passed on medical wisdom he had gained in his new job. The brothers put their heads together as Moses tried to accept his new reality as a 24-year-old man with a comminuted femoral fracture.

"The healing process will be long and painful and discouraging," Dan said. "You need to stay strong." He pointed first to his heart, "in here," and then to his head, "and here. But I will help you."

They discussed plans for when Moses was ready to leave the hospital. "Pastor will accommodate you in the back room at the Seed Store, until you are able to walk with a crutch. Then Agnes would like you to live in the compound. With the rest of the family."

"No, I cannot live on her property." Moses's voice was firm. He knew Dan would think it was because he was stubborn. That he could not let go of his old resentments against Agnes. But the truth was, Moses was ashamed. He could not ask this of his mother. After all the years he had not wanted anything to do with her, how could he expect her to take care of him now?

"You don't have to stay in the house with her, but you will need help," Dan said. "Dora and I have already discussed building a lean-to against our hut. You can sleep there until you are strong enough to manage on your own."

Moses began to shake his head in protest, but Dan raised his hand.

"Let's not argue. We will see how things are once it's time for you to leave the hospital."

Hearing about Moses's assault, Dr. Bjorn Froyland, who had been so instrumental in baby Sam's healing, offered his help. He'd approached the doctors at Lacor to inquire about their treatment plan and was soon an active consultant on Moses's femoral fracture care. Bones broken in auto and bus crashes were plentiful and the hospital was overburdened with cases, so Dr. Bjorn was welcomed. Even the very proud doctors who'd worked to repair Moses's broken bones admitted that the insight from Dr. Bjorn had given them hope Moses would walk again.

Dr. Bjorn and his wife, Dr. Aiko, were visiting one afternoon when Beatrice and Grace arrived with food for Moses, sent by their mother. Moses enjoyed the home-cooked meal and the busy chatter between his sisters and his doctors, who were also, he supposed, his friends. He forgot about his broken bones and found himself thinking about his sisters instead. Beatrice had been talking for ages about wanting to study medicine after school and he suddenly had an idea.

"Dr. Aiko." Moses called the Japanese doctor over to the side of his bed. "My sister wants to be a doctor. What kind of doctor do you think she should be?"

Aiko spoke directly to Beatrice. "Being a doctor is an exciting adventure, and you will know after you begin your studies what direction you should take to specialize."

Moses was glad to watch his little sister listen as Dr. Aiko offered Beatrice advice. For the first time in his life, Moses began to see how family worked. How they all supported and cared for one another. When all his visitors went home, Moses wept silently into his pillow, touched by the care offered to him by his family and friends and the growing evidence that, even as he found it hard to value himself, there were people in every area of his life who valued him.

October 2015

Moses continued to make steady progress, and after one particularly challenging morning of physical therapy, he arrived back in his room to find Pastor waiting for him.

"I have some news for you," Pastor said. He seemed both excited and nervous, as he helped Moses swing his legs up onto the bed.

"Good news, I hope." Moses did not need any surprises.

"I think so." Pastor made himself comfortable and leaned forward.

"Well, spit it out. You're making me worried."

"As I closed the Seed Store earlier today, preparing to come over to visit you, I found a young woman waiting at the front door." He paused and watched Moses's face as if hoping for a reaction.

Moses was tired and hungry and not in the mood for any games. "And . . . ?" He indicated with a flick of his hand that Pastor should continue.

"She did not look like our typical customers. Her clothes were more worn, and she was very thin. She held the hand of a dust-covered child, no older than six by the looks of him. I asked if she needed help, and she asked me if I knew a delivery man named Moses?"

Moses felt the breath leave him. A woman and a child looking for him? There was a part of him that hoped, but another that was afraid.

Pastor leaned over and put his hand on Moses's. "She came all the way from Bunia. She told me she saw the truck drive up to the carpark beside the bar where she works, but of course when she went to greet you, she found different men coming into the bar."

Pastor pulled papers from his satchel and held them up for Moses to read. "The bill of lading," he said. "She snuck into the truck and found the papers, then traced the Seed Store from the address listed. Somehow, she managed to travel 366 km with the small boy in tow. She must have taken some serious risks to find her way to you, Moses. This is no ordinary woman." Pastor nodded with respect.

"Mercy?" Moses whispered her name, afraid if he said it out loud he might be disappointed. A young woman with a small boy. Moz. Traveling all that way on their own. He thought of her gentle face. The face he'd held in his mind all through the attack.

Pastor nodded, "I couldn't help but think she has the perfect name. *Mercy*. Just what you need, Moses."

Moses squeezed his eyes against the tears that threatened. Mercy had made a brave decision to come all this way to find him. She must have been seriously impeded by her language. She was a Hema from a part of the DRC to the north, making her a refugee in Bunia in the first place. Her second language was French, which she could rely on in the DRC but hardly here in Gulu. She spoke some Swahili and Lingala, and enough English to get along, as did Moz. Yet here was Pastor, sitting in front of him, reporting that Mercy was here in town. Moses understood only too well, that when you are alone in the world, you devise remarkable strategies to survive.

"There's more," Pastor said. "She is carrying a child in her belly. She says it's yours."

Moses's heart lifted. He felt a renewed purpose to heal and to return to work, to build a home for Mercy, Moz, and their unborn child. "Where is she now?"

Pastor shifted in the chair and pinched his lips. "I'm not sure you're going to like this part, Moses."

"Tell me. Did she leave? Is she still in town?" Moses felt the dream of the little family he'd just been gifted drift away like smoke.

"She's staying with your mother."

⦁⦁⦁⦁⦁⦁

In the days after Pastor's visit, as Moses lay helpless for hours at a time in the hospital, he reviewed the circumstances of his life. Despite his accident and the long recovery ahead, Moses was able to find silver linings. Most of these had to do with the fact that he had people in his life who cared for him, who wanted him healthy, happy, and safe, and who wanted him in their lives too.

On one of these occasions, his thoughts were interrupted by a quiet knock. Moses opened his eyes to find Agnes in the doorway. He lifted a hand and waved her into the room. She was carrying a parcel that smelled of matoke, posho, and roasted peanuts. His mouth began to water.

"I thought you might like more homecooked food," Agnes said.

"Thank you." Moses felt foolish. He had rejected his mother, deliberately and publicly for so many years, but so much had changed during the past few months. He'd had time to consider Pastor's words and his role in his family. With all his energy focused on healing, the rage had finally left him.

"I met Mercy," Agnes said, putting the food on the bedside table. "She and Moz are staying with us in the compound and will be waiting for you when you are ready to come home."

Home. She said the word like a promise. Moses fought the emotion that threatened to betray him.

"You are a lucky man, my son," Agnes continued. "Mercy is very brave, and she seems kind." She straightened the bed linens and opened a window.

Moses nodded as his mother moved around the room.

"Anyway, I just wanted to bring you some food. I hope you are healing quickly. I will be back again tomorrow." Agnes patted his arm through the covers. They looked at one another. Moses wanted to say something to her, and he could tell she wanted to hear from him, but he was unable to speak. Agnes turned and was gone.

"Thank you," Moses said into the empty room.

•••••••

When Mercy walked into Moses's hospital room with Moz the following week, it was as though a light shone around her. If not confined to a bed, Moses would have kneeled before her and thanked her for liberating him. After her harrowing escape with the lading documents that identified Pastor as the truck's owner in Gulu, and her successful scheme to find a safe driver going from Bunia to Gulu where she and Moz could get a lift, there was no question in Moses's mind about her loyalty and concern for him, and it touched him. Deeply. There was something about this little boy, also named Moses, that reached into the softest spot in Moses's heart.

Mercy did all the talking, while Moses wept.

"What's the matter with Moses?" Moz asked his mother in Hema. "Why is he crying?"

"He was hurt in a terrible accident and many parts of him are wounded. Some we can see and some we cannot. He needs to get well before he can get out of here. I think he wants to come home when the baby is born. Wouldn't that be nice, Moz?"

Putting his hand on Mercy's belly and nodding vigorously, Moz asked, "When Moses gets out, is he going to come live with us? Where the good people are?"

"We don't know yet, but Moses is listening for God to help him decide."

And Moses did hear the voice of God inside him. He asked Mercy to stay where Pastor was building a hut in Agnes's compound. "I can join you there soon," Moses said. He wiped his eyes on his sheet and reached for Mercy's hand. In it, he found hope.

●●●●●●

When Moses was released from the hospital, Pastor provided a cot in a backroom at the Seed Store, exactly as promised. Once again, this devoted uncle had remained true to his commitment, caring for Moses's needs and offering him companionship each day. He urged Moses to talk openly about his past, and of his hopes for his future. While he avoided the subject of Agnes, Moses was beginning to turn everything around and around in his head as he learned more about the useful art of self-reflection.

"I can see you will emerge from this disaster a wiser man," Pastor said during one of his many visits with Moses. "A man capable of being a decent husband as well as a more than decent father to Moz and to the infant in Mercy's belly. That is a big step."

Then Pastor announced that he and Agnes were moving forward with plans to build a refugee shelter and that he would be traveling for a few days to search for the ideal piece of land. Moses would be transferred to Agnes's plot where a lean-to had been built against Dan and Dora's hut. There, his brother and some church members could help meet his daily needs while Pastor was traveling.

As promised, Moses became the favored beneficiary of two intensive months of compassionate care and companionship. Meanwhile, Pastor and Dan had built a second hut at the furthermost end of Agnes's plot, where Mercy and Moz were now staying, and where Moses would move once his full body cast was replaced with something less limiting.

13

November 2015—Gulu

At the Inn on Thursday evening, Agnes forced a smile as a group of tourists arrived, looking shell-shocked after their long travel from Europe. Having finished her tasks for the evening, she opened her email to find a new message from America, a letter from Isaiah, the young man she'd considered a third son.

> Dear Mama-Agnes,
>
> You are the best mama I could ever ask for and I am always grateful for you for saving me when you did. I pray that your sons and daughters are well.
>
> My sister-in-law Rita is friends with a professor at the University of Washington, here in Seattle, and this professor invited me to speak to her Storytelling and Leadership class. I decided to talk about my experience growing up in the Awach IDP camp. I thought you would like to see it. <u>Here is a video of the talk.</u>
>
> Blessings,
> Isaiah

"Molly, Molly!" Agnes called, excitement pitching her voice high as Molly came to see what was wrong. "I need to watch this video. Will you show me how to play it?"

"Of course." Molly leaned over Agnes's shoulder, showing her where to click. "Who is this Isaiah Odeki again?"

"Isaiah? Oh," said Agnes. *How to describe Isaiah?* "He's like my adopted son. Before Moses and Dan came home to me, Isaiah was the only son I had. He is the same age as my firstborn." *All grown up now*, she had to remind herself. "He's so full of love for everyone, one of the young men who helped build our hut. An orphan."

"Oh." Molly's face darkened. "What happened to him? Where did he go?"

"He found his place with our church and went on a mission to Ghana. When he came back to Gulu, he met Peggy." Agnes smiled.

"American?"

"Yes. She was here with an NGO. They fell in love, married, and moved to the US together."

Agnes opened an attached photo and leaned close to the computer screen. "See, that's Peggy and Isaiah, and their little ones. Winnie, short for Winston, is a year and a half. And baby Agnes is just a few months old. There's a baby in America named for me." Agnes laughed. "They call her Aggie. Can you believe it?"

On screen, Isaiah stood in front of a classroom, wearing a blue button-down shirt tucked into black slacks as the video played. Agnes and Molly listened as he shared his story:

When I was six years old, my parents, my older sister, and I were sent to the Awach IDP camp. IDP stands for "Internally Displaced People." The Ugandan government told us that the camp would protect us from the LRA. But, in reality, the camps brought nothing but suffering. They were like concentration camps, and we were trapped.

My parents were allowed to 'choose' which camp we would go to. My mother heard that a good teacher who lived near us in Gulu was going to Awach, so they decided to settle our family there. They erected a temporary hut, and my sister and I ran around the camp looking for the teacher. We found her teaching a group of kids their letters and songs.

We all shared two books, and after a year or so we had no pencils or paper left. My mother would wait for hours to get bad water from a borehole. I was always hungry.

After three years, our teacher's energy waned. She was teaching dozens of kids, then a hundred or more, all on her own. Kids started fighting to get close enough to hear her teach. The camp had grown overcrowded and was becoming lawless. But it was she that taught me to read as a child. It is hard to grow up and not know how to read. In that awful place, she taught me.

One dreadful day, my sister accidentally set our hut afire from the cooking stove. It was all my parents and their close neighbors could do to contain it. I believe the family fire took the last spark of vitality out of my parents. My sister died from her burns.

I barely remember how they bore her body to the site where my mother had promised to bury her—out-

side of the fence that surrounded the camp. I wish I could remember her face better.

More time went by. My parents fought more and more, and my father left our hut to be with another woman. We ran out of things to say to one another. Our days were filled with boredom and apprehension. And then one day my mother told me she had to leave the camp to look for food, as she knew we were starving.

She had an uncle outside, she told me, who could help find food for us. She would be back, she promised, as she walked away that morning.

Just like that, she walked away. I never saw her again.

Later, when the war ended when I was sixteen, I went back to Gulu, but I didn't know anyone. I was looking for my mother. I didn't know where to look. Some Mormons took me in and fed me, and that's where I met my surrogate mother, Adong Agnes.

When I was eighteen, the Mormons raised money to send me on a mission to Ghana. It was very modern there, and I learned how to use a computer. When I returned to Gulu, I met my wife, Peggy, who was in Uganda working with an American NGO. We married and I came here to the US with her. Here, I was able to use my knowledge of computers to get a degree.

But sometimes I wonder . . . why me? Why did I have the good fortune of meeting the Mormons and being sent on a mission and marrying an American woman, which gave me so much opportunity? I don't know, but I am determined to make the most of the opportunities I've been given.

The video ended there, and Agnes blinked back tears. She had known Isaiah's story, but it was still so terribly sad to watch him retell it, the pain still evident in his movements and voice.

Molly squeezed her shoulder, and Agnes looked up to see Molly's eyes were wet, too.

"The first time he told me," Agnes said, swallowing against the thickness in her throat, "I was surprised. I had thought no one had as hard a time as the children who were abducted."

Molly nodded. "Of course. We are all shaped by our own experiences, Agnes. But your compassion does you credit."

14

December 2015—Gulu

This wasn't the first time Beatrice thought she loved a missionary. Since her baptism six years ago, at least one elder a year came to Gulu that she wanted to marry. *How could she help it?* Searching for a word to describe them one night on the computer at the Inn, she lit on "decent" and ever after that she would attach that word to each new missionary she met. They all looked so good, too, and their optimism never faded. They didn't ignore the sad circumstances they saw in Gulu, but they didn't get gloomy and hopeless like local folks did. Some elders even looked like singers she saw on TV at the Inn.

It embarrassed her to feel the way she did, so she told no one. After all, Beatrice had a reputation for being level-headed, and she didn't want to be like the silly girls in her ward who flirted and hovered around the missionaries.

At first, she was only drawn to South African missionaries. They had such confidence, and, in her eyes, they were more mature than other men their age. But those missionaries weren't respectful of her brothers, so she stopped begging Mama-Agnes to have them visit.

Next there was the handsome one from Ghana. But he was too foolish for her.

Then she'd met an elder from California who wanted to be a doctor like she did, and that prompted her imagination to go a little wild. She imagined marrying him, working together in the same hospital somewhere. But he had girlfriend back home. Then he was gone.

Of course, all these dreams were only possible because her adopted brother, Isaiah, had married a white American. Isaiah and Peggy stood as proof that it was not a bad path to marry someone from so far away. Curious about how that might work, Beatrice asked Agnes what it would be like for a Black person to be married to a white person. Agnes said it didn't matter as long as both people were good people. So, Beatrice identified more candidates.

The missionaries were never allowed to be alone with a girl, since they were in Gulu to do God's sacred work. But Beatrice couldn't ignore them completely. They were not only handsome. They wore nice clothes and always kept themselves clean. And they often had chewing gum and candy bars. Best of all, they made girls feel safe. "I don't feel afraid around them," Beatrice said to Grace.

She had been afraid of Moses and Dan at first, especially when Moses had first come to live at their compound, so angry and sad about his injuries. But now her lack of fear was a gift she gave them. She knew what it was like to be born in the bush, after all. No matter how good she was at many things, she would always carry the stigma of being a "bush-girl." She was proud to be her brothers' defender.

"Mama hopes I don't ever get married," Beatrice told Grace. "Though she wants me to be as happy as Dan and Dora someday, I think it scares her. We both know that one reason they are so happy is that they love having sex."

"Mama would be so upset if she knew we were even thinking about sex," Grace teased. "Certainly, she would tear her hair out if she knew her prim Beatrice thought about it at church!"

They roared with laughter. Although, truly, Beatrice did not think about it so much on Sundays since she always had important things to do at church. But the two nights when she taught literacy class with the missionaries had become her favorite part of the week. And even though she liked teaching, she also liked being the prettiest girl there and having the missionaries watch her as she taught English. After dark, when the class was over, they would lock the doors and windows of the church and joke around a little before the elders would either walk all of them to their homes, or pay for each of them to take a boda. Sometimes they even drove them home in the church van. Mama-Agnes was very nervous when she knew Beatrice had been in a car with a missionary, even though her daughter had never disobeyed any rules.

● ● ● ● ● ●

After church one Sabbath morning, as the sisters walked home, Beatrice said to Grace, "I really like the two missionaries assigned here now. Don't you? At first I thought Elder Busakwe from South Africa was the cutest and I didn't even notice Elder Murdock since he is just another white American. Then two weeks ago, at the night class, I really looked Elder Murdock in the eyes. He is very beautiful, and right away I liked him more than Busakwe. He is smart and serious but also funny. And tonight, Busakwe teased him about liking me. Maybe Elder Murdock likes me as much as I like him. Maybe he talks about me. Do you think so, Grace?"

"Well, I'm sure nobody discourages Murdock if he does. The elders that are here now are pretty casual. I'll bet if they weren't missionaries, they would be a lot of fun," Grace observed, laughing.

"That's for sure," said Beatrice, always checking herself for excessive frivolity. "I worry if he talks too much, Mama might hear about it and not let me go to the class anymore." Beatrice daydreamed for a moment about what it would be like for Elder Murdock to kiss her on the lips. "Elder Murdock always puts fewer chairs in a circle than the others do, so we all get to sit closer together. It's nicer that way," explained Beatrice, thinking of the previous week's classes when Elder Murdock was there, watching her. She had become alternately embarrassed and excited when she'd caught him staring. She'd tried to stop her heart from beating fast, as the two played their own game to see who could not look at each other the longest.

The next Sunday, Beatrice had something else to tell her sister. "Did you see me talking to Elder Murdock?" They skipped a few yards along the road, laughing together. The weather was beautiful, as it usually was.

"Of course, I saw," Grace said, hoping Beatrice had something exciting to share.

"He told me that I was exactly like the woman he hoped to marry! When I asked what he meant by that, he said, 'Think about it—who in all the world is exactly like you?' I think that means he likes me enough to marry me."

"He said that?" Grace asked.

"I can't believe it, but, yes, he did," Beatrice said, squealing uncharacteristically. "But don't tell Mama. She'll blame me for doing something bad. You know I didn't do anything bad. You were there. You saw us."

Grace nodded reassuringly, but both girls sobered up at the thought of what their mother would say or do if she knew about any of this.

Beatrice thought she noticed her mother looking at her more often in the days that followed, but she cradled her secret and tried to keep a straight face. While Elder Murdock and his companion from South Africa were scheduled to leave next week for a new assignment, Beatrice prayed that Heavenly Father would keep Elder Murdock in Gulu. Surely it was His will that they be together.

And so she felt vindicated when she arrived home and, trying to speak with no sign of emotion at all, announced, "Elder Murdock and his companion were supposed to be transferred to Kitgum today, but another elder here got sick and left. So, now they have to extend their stay here."

What she didn't tell Agnes was that that Murdock had also told Beatrice that he was not disappointed to stay in Gulu. "Certain people here have made this my favorite ward in Uganda," he'd said, lifting Beatrice's hopes that he might mean her.

The following week Beatrice was careful not to break any missionary rules that might result in Elder Murdock being sent away. They talked in class and Beatrice was delighted to learn that his first name was David. "What a beautiful name," she said.

In response, David told Beatrice he liked the way she had braided her hair. (That was probably not allowed, but he said it softly.)

Then Beatrice told David that her name meant 'like a saint,' but he said *beatific* is almost like Beatrice and it means 'bestowing bliss.' He said that fit her even better. Bliss. A word that meant joyful.

Beatrice wondered if others knew what David and she were feeling inside. They had never gone out of the room or talked in private together. They had never held hands, and they were careful not to call attention to their growing affections.

That night, David drove them home in the church van, and Beatrice let Akiki Betsy ride in the front next to him. But even from the back seat, she could tell he was watching her by some magical means, and she was sending secret messages back to him and he knew it.

Maybe God was helping them tell each other how they felt. *I wonder if Mama will believe me if I tell her that our Heavenly Father approves of David and me. Probably not yet.*

While Beatrice thought about Elder Murdock every minute for the rest of the week, imagining passionate escapades with the handsome David, she wondered if it would be this fun when their secret was out in the open. What if having a secret love, a forbidden love, was more exciting than having a partner everyone knew about?

She needed to pull herself together and prepare for what might happen next. She had long had a blueprint for how her life would unfold: attend medical school and then move back to Gulu to practice medicine. Marrying David Murdock was not on that blueprint. But now she wanted to make a new one that did.

15

January 2016—Kampala & Entebbe

Bishop Okot James escorted Agnes on the six-hour bus ride from Gulu to Kampala, the raucous, buzzing capital city she'd heard so much about. Stepping off the bus, she was keenly aware she'd stepped into a much bigger world. From here, she and a small group would travel to South Africa to visit the Mormon temple. When she and Okot arrived at the crowded market in Kampala, she ate grilled meat-on-a-stick and roasted maize while carrying a small suitcase she'd borrowed from Bishop Okot's wife, Sarah.

After enjoying a quick lunch, Bishop Okot brought Agnes to the home of the stake president, Simeon Muwanga, and his wife Priscilla. Their pink stucco, two-story home felt grander than anything Agnes had ever seen in person. Simeon and Priscilla would host Agnes here for two days. Then, she would meet up with the rest of the group at the airport.

Simeon exuded a gentle confidence, and Priscilla had a sophisticated air, with elegant clothes and heels. Agnes thought this glamorous woman would get along well with Molly.

Priscilla and Simeon were Baganda, not Acholi, but for Simeon, this was simply a characteristic accidentally acquired at birth with no particular implications. He acknowledged that it gave him some privilege in Ugandan society, but he was almost apologetic about that and never wore it as a badge of entitlement. He was humbled, in fact, when asked about his tribe by foreigners. Priscilla, on the other hand, proudly wore her identity as a Muganda. Her faith in the Lord Jesus Christ had shaved off part of this pride, and she prayed to be more like her good husband and to discard her ethnic arrogance. And, to be fair, at middle age, and with serious effort on her part to learn humility, she had become far more than tolerant of others. She was more and more active in modeling inclusion.

Agnes was not the first Acholi she had generously welcomed to her home.

On Sunday, Simeon and Priscilla brought Agnes with them to church where they graciously invited Agnes to share some of her life story with the congregation. Agnes felt a strange surge of energy as she was able to articulate the challenges of her life. Without getting too graphic, she talked about her meetings with Bishop Okot and the question that had been nagging her, "What does it mean to be worthy?" She surprised herself by sharing all the ways she hadn't felt clean, even after baptism—that she had still felt defiled by what the rebel men had done, and how she was healing. She saw now that these were sins done by others. Rape had been committed against her. Agnes shared what the Savior's Atonement meant to her on her healing journey, closing with a scripture from Jacob Chapter 2 from the *Book of Mormon*:

> For behold, I, the Lord, have seen the sorrow, and heard the mourning of the daughters of my people in the land of Jerusalem, yea, and in all the lands of my people, because of the wickedness and abominations of their husbands. And I will not suffer, saith the Lord of Hosts, that the cries of the fair daughters of this people, which I have led out of the land of Jerusalem, shall come up unto me against the men of my people, saith the Lord of Hosts.

The scriptures went on to condemn the bad husbands in the story, then ended:

> Ye have broken the hearts of your tender wives, and lost the confidence of your children, because of your bad examples before them; and the sobbing of their hearts ascend up to God against you. And because of the strictness of the word of God, which cometh down against you, many hearts died, pierced with deep wounds.

Agnes had gripped the pulpit, looking into the eyes of people in the congregation. She'd amazed herself at what she was sharing so publicly. She concluded with her hope. "It is clear, I think, that men are not allowed to defile women and girls, and if they do, they will be punished by God with a sore curse." She paused. "When I read this, after study and prayer, I learned I was clean of any nasty thing that any evil man had done to me. I learned that I was worthy to visit the temple after all."

There had been, Agnes noticed during the service, a white man in the audience who had bristled at her talk—especially when she talked about the abusive men in her life who had caused her harm. *An abuser*, Agnes sensed immediately. She could always tell.

After church the man's wife approached Agnes in the foyer. With American earnestness, she introduced herself as Marian Mortenson and thanked Agnes for her words. "You keep telling the truth," Marian said with conviction.

When her husband approached, Agnes stiffened. She could tell by his posture, by his mean expression, by the way Marian shrank when he came near, that he was dangerous—an abuser. Agnes stepped back. Marian introduced him as her husband, Martin.

He surveyed Agnes with disdain and said, "I haven't heard many people speak so vividly in a sacred meeting about the 'nasty things men do to women.'"

Agnes flinched and walked away, into the bathroom, without saying anything. *Should she not have spoken up? Was she in danger now?* She took some deep breaths and tried—as she'd practiced for so many years now—to not feel it was all her fault.

She regretted nothing, she decided. She'd spoken a deep truth in her heart. The heat of it still glowed inside her. The meeting had been a success, and she was safe. Agnes felt a swell of confidence in not just herself, but for the trip to come. She felt so capable, like she was doing the right thing, no matter how daunted she'd originally felt about leaving her family at home. Moses was healing better than the doctors expected. Though conversation between him and Agnes was never comfortable, it was at least cordial now. Mercy, who would be Moses's wife before the baby arrived, had helped soften some of the harshness between them.

After church the Muwangas' driver took Agnes to a hotel in Entebbe, to be closer to the airport. Simeon and Priscilla had to go back to Kampala to sort out visa issues for another member of the traveling party. Simeon assured Agnes that the hotel was very safe and that should she have a need, to call them.

Agnes checked in at the desk, charmed by the sprawling hotel with its rooms designed to look like huts with faux grass roofs. The front desk attendant handed her a key stamped with a 9 and gave her directions to her own little hut. She found it easily, the number 9 stenciled on the door, and stepped inside, slipping off her shoes and feeling the cool tile beneath her feet. She flipped on the light and tested out the A/C, then noted the modern TV.

A room of her own.

Agnes sat on the bed. It was so soft. She'd made beds like this at the Inn, but never slept in one. She noted all the ways this room looked different from the Harmony Inn back home: the sofas, lamps, and glossy magazines. Plus, a very fancy-looking shower. But apart from the details, it was a startlingly different experience because for the first time in her life, she was a guest instead of an employee.

She called home to hear Grace and Beatrice's voices. They celebrated these luxuries with her, laughing when she told them the room number.

"We don't need to hear *every* detail," Grace teased.

"Just enjoy yourself," Beatrice said. "We're fine here, Mama."

And as she hung up, a sudden sense of expansive opportunity filled her. She was in a hotel alone for the first time in her life. She had no responsibilities here, and no one required her care or attention.

She thought more about her upcoming visit to the temple. Who could have known that she would travel to Kampala—then stay in this beautiful hotel on the shores of Lake Victoria? Who could ever have guessed, in all the years she'd spent captive in the bush, that she would fly on an airplane to South Africa?

She thought back to the missionaries who had talked to her about "sacred sex," and how upset and angry she had been. She thought of Okot explaining to her that she had never, in fact, had "sex." She thought of the passionate and joyful sounds that spilled from her son's hut every night. *Love making. What would that be like?*

And then a new thought occurred to her, and before she could talk herself out of it, she picked up her phone and called Peter Okello.

••••••

An hour later, as the sun began to set outside the widow, Agnes felt her phone vibrate. Okello Peter's number appeared on the screen.

What am I doing? Agnes asked herself. *He was a brute in the bush.*

She thought of what Bishop Okot had taught her about the difference between rape and sex. She thought of how she'd never experienced what people referred to as "love making." She thought of Dora's ecstatic sighs coming from the hut next to her house. And she wanted to live that life. She wanted, in some bold and curious way, to experience sex. Besides, she was still technically "married" to Peter, so it wouldn't compromise her "worthiness."

Agnes answered the phone.

"Is this the right hotel?" Peter asked. His voice seemed familiar, yet distant. He sounded surprised, perhaps because he knew how nice the accommodation was. Or maybe he was just baffled by her request to meet her there.

Agnes assured him it was the right hotel. "Room number 9," she said before hanging up and taking a deep breath.

It was awkward at first, even after the customary greetings. Of course, it would be. It was a much more intimate space than the tiny office in the Inn where they'd talked for hours. Peter stood in the doorway, seeming desperate for direction. He looked confused. Anxious. Maybe even frightened.

"Have you eaten yet?" she asked. Agnes found that she liked being in control. This was her room, her space, and she was inviting him to stay the night.

She offered Peter a seat on a small, cushioned chair beside the desk, then poured him water. She handed him an orange from the market, and took a seat across from him, perched on the bed.

He ate, telling her a bit about his trip to get there. She asked about his living situation near town. Small talk. "You look weary," Agnes said with concern. She was surprised by how much she cared. She really had healed and grown in ways she could never fully measure since the day she'd left the bush.

"I work hard," he said with a shrug. "I repair buses. It's enough to feed a small son."

Agnes nodded. "And how is he doing?" Agnes was keenly aware this boy was a half-sibling to her daughters, that Peter was Beatrice and Grace's biological father.

At this, Peter seemed to relax. "He is learning." He beamed. "I'm gentle with him." His beam faded into a shadow of regret, but he pressed on. "I pay his school fees. He is such a good little reader."

"I'm happy for you," Agnes said with honesty.

"Tell me more about your children," Peter said with equal kindness as he cracked open the orange. The sweet, citrus smell clung to the humid air.

She still appreciated that he called them "your children" and not "our children." He would never be a full father to them, and they both understood that. Agnes told him about Beatrice's plans to become a doctor. About Grace and her studies. She told him about Moses's accident, and the strange way they'd slipped into reluctant speaking terms as a result. Also, about how Mercy had found him, the child she would soon have. And about Dan and Dora and little Sam.

She had much to be grateful for.

As Peter's large hands clumsily peeled the final bit of the orange, Agnes noticed a tear run quietly down his face, tracing the path of an old, familiar scar. He sucked his breath to stop another from falling.

Even she knew they had too much between them to speak aloud. She took Peter's hand and squeezed, saying nothing. Silence was a comfort. Even if the silence was filled with bitterness for the lost years, the pain of the war, the almost too-sweet joy that life could go on, with such audacious beauty reflected in the eyes of the children. The next generation.

"I'm sorry," Peter finally managed to whisper.

He was. Agnes knew he was. For years, he'd tried to say as much when he called her. But here, sitting in his presence—a hotel room that looked nothing like the huts they'd shared in the bush—she felt it and *knew* he meant it. That sorry extended far, but especially, maybe most especially, to this.

To the ways he'd used her body, the ways he'd failed to see her.

"I am not at peace," he said quietly.

Agnes leaned her head forward and touched his cheek with the scar. It was warm and soft.

"I'm nervous," Peter said, looking up to meet her in the eye. Finally, they addressed the matter they'd discussed. The reason for his visit.

"Did you bring a condom?" Agnes asked, surprised at the confidence in her voice.

"I did." His voice was reluctant.

She explained, again, what she had said to him on the phone: She needed to know what it was like to be a woman with agency, a woman who'd experienced sex with a husband and not just rape. She wanted to, *needed to,* feel the difference. But the words alone in trying to describe her motivations, she sensed, were not enough.

"You're sure?" he said.

"Of course. Are we clear on the terms?"

Peter nodded. They planned to never see each other again like this after tonight. It would be too messy, too complicated—especially with the children. He could never be a father to Beatrice and Grace the way he was a father to his new son. Besides, Moses would strangle Peter if he knew where he lived. The bush might feel far away right now, but it had still happened. They would never forget that.

No. Agnes and Peter lived their own lives apart now. This would be more than enough. They could leave here with mutual respect, as friends. Without fear.

Agnes turned off the lamp and slipped off her clothes, savoring this moment of need, of power, of whatever wisdom in her had initiated this strange request.

Peter washed himself at the bathroom sink. Leaving that light on, he came back toward the bed, naked and apprehensive, which was as it should be. He was not in charge.

He slipped beside her into the cool, white sheets, where he lay perfectly still, that same look of fear in his eyes, like he might make a wrong move, or another mistake.

Their arms barely touched, as tension brewed.

The minutes felt like hours. Maybe they were hours, all that silence. Time passed in different rhythms.

Agnes closed her eyes, listening to her body. She felt jittery, but not upset. Not angry. And still grounded in the present as she slid her leg against his, reached toward him, and ran her fingers across his naked chest. She had heard so many tales of what women do to excite their men, but she was clearly a novice. Still, this was not about pleasing him, and she felt no need to impress him or show off.

Peter took a deep breath as she moved closer. She felt his skin against hers, felt him grow hard against her thigh. When he paused to put on a condom, her pulse raced.

Suddenly, that weakness she'd seen in Peter washed away. He drew two fingers down the little dip at the bottom of her throat, then down to her breasts, drawing a tightening in her core. Apprehension fought with growing need, but need was winning.

She wondered about this need. Was its only requirement safety, and agency?

Slowly, Peter touched her. And that was different too—his slowness. All the other times, with him and her other "husbands," they had rushed. She flinched at first, then, just as slowly as his fingers moving on her skin, she relaxed.

They did this for a long time, Peter tracing her arm, then down her leg.

With equal patience, Agnes traced the fine muscles along his shoulder . . . his ribs . . . stomach. When he placed a hand between her legs, she startled.

"Agnes," Peter said. "I'm a different man from the one you knew before. I am new. I will not hurt you. And I will stop if you ask me to."

"I know," Agnes said. She opened her legs, searching for him with her hand. To her surprise, the hardness of him did not feel dangerous. She placed her lips against his lips, then pulled him into her.

No pain. Only urgency.

Her *own* urgency.

Together, they fell into a passion, drawing out the moments and leaning in with the waves of their bodies.

How would she explain this to anyone? Then she realized: *I will never have to. This is what it means to have agency*

After sex, Agnes showered and took delight in wrapping one of the huge, soft towels around herself and stepping back into the room. When Peter showered and used the second towel, it seemed another affirmation of this choice she'd made. Before returning to the bed, she let the towel drop to the floor as she looked into a mirror at her own naked self. Agnes had never seen her whole naked body before. She liked the way her breasts looked.

They dozed a little on toward morning, making love a second time before Peter took his third and last shower. When he returned, Agnes sat on the bed with her feet on the floor and offered him her open hands. Peter knelt in front of her and kissed her fingertips before burying his face in her upturned palms. Then he cried out the remnants of his guilty anguish.

Exhausted now, they lay together for a morning sleep, until woken by the sounds of birds and of waiters delivering breakfast to the families next door. Agnes ordered two full meals to be delivered to room #9. As she and Peter looked deeply into each other's faces, they saw each other fully for the first time. Here, in the light of day.

16

January 2016—Entebbe to Johannesburg

On Tuesday morning Agnes settled into a gray, squishy seat on the airplane, relieved that she had not been placed near the window and would not have to see the ground move beneath them. She sat still, waiting for instructions as passengers fumbled down the aisle with their scowls and heavy packages. Her stomach jumped with nervousness.

They were headed to Johannesburg.

I can't wait to tell Molly about this, Agnes thought, trying to push down the anxiety at the prospect of this big hunk of metal sailing into the air. When guests arrived at the Harmony Inn, Agnes always asked, part out of courtesy, part out of curiosity, "How was your flight?"

But no secondhand details could have prepared her for this fascinating experience. The intense A/C. The screen bolted into the back of the chair in front of her. The fashionably red-dressed attendants helping people stow their bags.

Once again, Agnes was a guest and not a worker. She leaned back and felt a flutter rise in her chest, thinking of the night before, when Peter had come to room number 9.

She closed her eyes, remembering every detail: three empty condom wrappers on the nightstand. Peter kissing her in the early morning light before he headed to the shower. The way she held her own gaze in the mirror across from the bed—a chance to look at herself, wrapped in nothing but a sheet.

I have become a woman, she had thought. And then: *No, I am a woman. And I look good. Strong.* She felt it too, seeing herself, at last. She felt no need to justify herself, no need to tell anyone. Last night was for her.

"I'm sitting next to you!" came a cheery voice to Agnes's left, interrupting her train of thought.

"My good luck," Agnes said, returning a smile and coming back to herself as she greeted Diana Nielsen, an American missionary who had been serving in Kampala. Diana and her husband, President Nielsen, managed all the Mormon missionaries in Uganda. Diana was in her sixties and would be acting as a personal guide for Agnes. Her blue eyes were as kind as her voice.

Diana settled into the window seat, as the attendants told them to fasten their seatbelts. Agnes's heart raced.

Diana patted Agnes's hand and said, "Don't worry. Air travel is much safer than car travel." She kept the light conversation going without fail, exuding calmness, and allowing Agnes a sense of peace.

And then they were off.

Once air bound, Agnes peered out at the passing clouds as the attendants served bottles of water and little packages of pretzels. Diana and Agnes fell into easy conversation. Agnes surprised herself by talking about her father, her conversations with Bishop Okot that had prepared her for the temple, and how her nightmares had started to abate.

"And where is your mother?" Diana asked.

Agnes caught her breath and looked away. She hadn't even made a name card for her mother. Next time she would bring a family name card, be baptized for her, and bring her back into the family.

"I'm sorry," Diana said, her face falling. "I didn't mean to talk about something hard for you."

"No, it's okay," Agnes said. Diana Nielsen did not seem like a meddling sort of person. Her curiosity was humane, her intentions genuine. Agnes trusted her. "I rarely speak of her. Not even to my own children."

But Agnes felt a nudge from God, telling her that it was time to open up this wound. Could she even remember what her mother looked like? Her round face and dark, deep-set eyes, a short woman with a blue skirt. Agnes remembered pressing her little face against her mother's legs, the smell of bitter herbs and the smoke of the cooking fire. How her mother used to shoo her away. How she and her sisters had needed their mother.

It was always Grandma Achieng Esther she ran to for comfort. Her soothing singing. The way she rubbed Agnes's back and told her stories or calmed her in the night. Agnes still remembered her grandmother's tender fingers on her forehead when she had a fever, or how she nodded along and asked questions whenever Agnes read to her from her primary school workbooks.

Oh, how Agnes missed her grandmother. How she'd wept at her funeral when she'd died the year before Agnes was abducted. "All throughout my captivity in the bush, I raged at my mother," Agnes said. "The rebels took me from my mother's hut because she wasn't there to protect me. My heart never forgave her." Agnes's fingers smoothed the pretzel wrapper. "Even when I returned to my village to collect names of my ancestors for this temple trip, I avoided asking about my mother. Her name was Aber Mabel. All I know is that she died during the Kony war years, while I was . . . away."

"I'm sorry," Diana said.

Agnes shook her head. "She was only sixteen when she married my father."

Having said this herself, Agnes allowed her mind to consider the age of her mother for the first time. Sixteen was still so young to become a wife and mother—younger than Beatrice.

Agnes knew something about being thrust into a situation too young.

"She immediately started having children," Agnes said, wondering how much Diana might know about how common it was for people in Uganda to lose their children to death. "I didn't really know my surviving siblings, though I heard that my oldest brother died in the war. As a child I was told I had a twin named Opiyo Monica." Agnes caught her breath. She hadn't allowed herself to think of these things in so long. "She died when we were infants. My name, 'Adong' Agnes, means survivor."

"That's very fitting," Diana said with a look of thoughtfulness as they passed out of a cloud and into bright sunlight.

"My grandmother raised me. I only visited my mother a few times a year," Agnes said. "Even though her hut was close by. I hardly thought about her, and I believe my father ignored her, too. He saw his mother and me every day, and never let us forget that we were the most special ones in the family. When we walked to mass on the sabbath, my father and his mother and I led the way. The rest of the family tried to keep up with us." Agnes could almost feel the contempt she had for her mother, when she looked burdened or ill. Surely her mother yearned to hold her daughter's hand, and walk beside her distinguished husband. "I moved to Mama-Mabel's hut when I was eleven, after Grandma Esther's death. After a lifetime of disregard for how she felt, how could I blame her for not making me the center of her life when I moved to live with her? I made it very clear that I did not need her." She paused, the flashes of her banishment after walking home from the bush a blur across her heart. "Perhaps I have judged them all too harshly."

Even my mother.

Agnes felt a deep grief stirred up. Not just for her grandmother, but for her lonely mother, too. In the bush, Agnes had called out to her grandmothers, who felt present and near, even when she was alone and afraid. She'd felt their love, their spirits near her when she was in captivity. This, in part, was what had interested her most about the temple. The chance to think about these women, to carry their names with her as she underwent this spiritual rite to bring them back—close to her again.

She paused and thought about her mother almost for the first time. Perhaps in the temple she could embrace the memory of her long-lost mother.

17

January 2016—Johannesburg

On Wednesday morning, when they drove up to the temple, Agnes stared in amazement at the sand-colored stone edifice. She studied the six white spires surrounded by lush green grass, and a long row of arches that lined each side of the building. The temple seemed much larger than what she'd seen in pictures, and the sight made Agnes dizzy.

This is it, she said to herself, feeling her pocket for her name cards. Attending the temple for the first time, she would perform a ritual for herself, and then similar rituals on behalf of each ancestor. As she walked through the temple door, she hoped her daughters would get to visit the temple one day too.

A beautiful African man dressed all in white—right down to his shoes—greeted them at the entrance. Even his hair was white like the clouds she had seen from the plane. He radiated an assurance of safety and peace, and she understood this sanctuary was set apart from normal turmoil. Fear left her, as she linked elbows with Diana and was swept away. She could almost hear Bishop Okot James's advice: *Just bring your full heart.*

Agnes was instructed to change into a white dress provided by the temple. People from at least a dozen countries shuffled into a large room, then sat on cushioned chairs that folded down. All dressed in white, the men sat on one side and the women on the other. The lights dimmed and the music started. For a moment, Agnes felt bored. Or maybe disappointed. Was the temple like a fancy movie theater? She looked at Diana and shrugged.

But then, Eve came onto the screen. She stood tall, stared down a trickster kind of man called Satan, then scanned the heavens and asked God if there was a way that she could not just see the beautiful world, but could understand it and make good choices about how to live happily in it, and even help other humans come to earth and understand what is right and wrong, too. The man said all she had to do was eat a strange little fruit.

Eve asked, "Is there no other way?"

Agnes's head swam with stars. She would know that voice anywhere—Eve's voice. The voice of her own grandmother. Each time Eve spoke on screen, Agnes *heard* her grandmother's voice. Then, she saw in Eve's sweet face, her grandmother's eyes. The vision lasted just long enough for Agnes to know she was in the right place. Eve had become a wise Acholi grandmother, and the room felt holy. Her grandmother Achieng Esther was near. Agnes looked sidelong at Diana.

Did Diana hear her speak?
Did she recognize her deep voice?
She must tell Diana about this powerful woman spirit. This Mother Eve who consoles us when we need her.

To remind us we are not alone in this world. Was this not exactly whom Agnes had summoned all those years in the bush? The secret companion closest to her heart, her solace that oppressive men could never take from her?

Agnes closed her eyes tight. She could sense the world of the bush, so far away, but always there, pressing against the back of her mind. She could see herself at a distance, holding her bony knees and biting her fists to keep from crying, hiding her pain to avoid another beating. She could see Nancy, her one true friend in the bush, and Nancy's smile the morning before she had been killed.

Through it all, Agnes had kept this secret—this voice from deep inside herself. The same voice of that spirit woman, who had reminded her that life was still a precious thing. That there was more coming in her future life, if she could just hang on.

I hear you, Mama Eve. I hear you, my good mother. Stay beside me, I pray.

──────

Isaiah had told Agnes there were many temples, and they were almost alike. She thought of people, dressed in white like she was, doing what she was doing in other places around the world. Maybe at the same time.

Agnes was glad to have Diana by her side, telling her softly what to do next.

At last, they entered a spacious room. At the center stood a marble pool, an elevated round structure filled with clear blue water. This basin, called the font, was perched on the back of twelve carved statues of buffalo, just like the Ankole long-horned cattle in western Uganda.

"We Ugandans love cattle," Agnes whispered to Diana.

"They represent the twelve tribes of ancient Israel," Diana said.

Agnes knew her Acholi people had descended from an ancient tribe of Israel—once part of the vast Luo people with a history spanning back to Egypt hundreds if not thousands of years. These great beasts of marble were so familiar, so noble, so beautiful and dignified.

While her group participated in baptisms, going up a staircase and then into the big marble pool as their name cards were read, Agnes kept her eye on the font. She studied the cattle, tracing in her mind's eye the animals' muscles, their noses, their eyes. Even though it was only in her imagination, Agnes could hear them breathe.

Feelings without language came to Agnes: an admiration for the grandmothers before her. She thought of Beatrice and Grace. She had always told them, "Don't ever let anyone tell you that you are just the bush daughters of evil rebels. You are descendants of noble people who came from Egypt, led here by God." She felt that same sense of destiny here in this chamber.

Then it was her turn to be baptized for each person on her family name cards. At the baptismal font, Agnes gave the gatekeeper her stack of name cards, with Grandmother Esther's name on top. She would honor them all today. She thought of herself as a kind of shepherd, gathering up her relatives and family, so they might be together in heaven.

After her baptism she stood in her wet dress and studied the cattle. Such reliable animals, constant and predictable. She had often walked behind them as a child, mimicking their gait. Unfaltering was what they were. Moving together in one great steady movement onward, refusing to give up or turn aside.

In this sacred room, Agnes was surprised to sense a different presence. She felt a rush of love as a voice spoke to her heart. *I am your mother, Mabel. I loved you always, and I am always near you. I understand what it is to lose children. I promise you, I will protect you from losing another child.*

With that, the air seemed to change around her. She was alone again.

When Diana came back to see if she needed help, Agnes said, "Diana, my mother has come home. She is always near me. I know her better now."

18

January 2016—Gulu

When Agnes arrived home on Saturday, Beatrice and Grace hugged her at the door and immediately bustled around to attend to her. Grace unpacked the small, borrowed suitcase and put away her mother's things. Beatrice brought Agnes a meal. They each asked dozens of questions about the hotel, the flight, and the temple. Agnes smiled when she thought of Peter but would not reveal that secret to her girls. When Grace went out to the borehole for water, Agnes said, "Beatrice, do you ever think of your father?" She hadn't planned to mention him, but the words had slipped out.

"No," Beatrice said. "I don't remember anything about him." A shadow passed over her face. "You are all the family I need, Mama." She came and sat in the chair next to Agnes, who put an arm around her.

"He lives in Kampala now," Agnes said. "If you want, you could meet him when you move there for medical school."

Beatrice stiffened a little in Agnes's embrace.

"I hear he is a changed man, Aber Beatrice." *Beautiful Beatrice.*

•••••••

The next day was a big day on the compound, as Pastor was taking Moses to Lacor to have his body cast removed. Pastor arrived early in the morning, and he and Dan helped maneuver Moses into the truck. When Grace and Beatrice went to school, Mercy, Dora, and Agnes pulled down the lean-to behind Agnes's house so Moses could move into the hut with Mercy and Moz. They burned the nets, which smelled terrible after Moses's long convalescence, and Mercy prepared her hut for Moses's return.

When Pastor's truck rumbled toward the compound at the end of the day, a crowd of children swarmed it, excited to see Moses cast-free. Agnes stood watching by her house. Although Moses was slowly warming to her, she was careful not to be overbearing. Pastor got out and hurried around to help Moses down from the other side of the truck, now with a full-leg cast. Agnes could tell that something was wrong.

The swarm of children asked questions and badgered them until Pastor shooed them away. Grace stepped next to Agnes and said in a low voice, "Pastor says the bone didn't set correctly. They had to rebreak something. He needs to wear this new cast for another month or two." And then in a lower voice still, "Moses is crushed."

Agnes could see her son's disappointment in the set of his head. Still, she thought, even extreme disappointment was good progress. Just a few months ago this setback would have been met by Moses with rage. Agnes went back to the house to stir the fire under the beans and rice.

"Mama?"

Agnes was surprised to find Moses in her doorway.

"May I speak with you?"

"Of course." Agnes motioned for him to come in, and Moses swung into the house on his crutches. She watched him arrange his body to be more comfortable, leaning the crutches against the table.

Agnes sat down across from her son and waited for him to say more. She marveled at how far he had come in just a few months.

"I have to wear this for at least another month." He paused, and then with tears in his eyes, added, "You have been so generous. But . . . I have to ask . . . can we stay here longer?"

Agnes gave him a small smile, reserving her exuberance. "Of course, Moses. I would be honored if you would stay."

He nodded.

She sat, knowing this could not be the end of what he had to tell her.

"Mama," he began again. "I thought a lot in the hospital about how I have made a big mistake. I know you had no way to control what you went through in the bush and what my father did to you that kept you from me. I know you would have made it different if you could have, and that you have always loved me. I feel the same for you."

With that, he pulled himself up to his full height with his crutches and clumsily reached out his arms. Agnes rose to hug him, and Moses held her close to his chest. Together they shed copious tears.

■■■■■■

Still, things were not quite smooth sailing yet. There were rumblings on the compound about Mercy.

Agnes had been preoccupied with preparing her trip to the temple, but now that she was home and Moses needed less care, she began to notice her neighbors' reactions to her growing family.

She heard familiar voices insisting that the compound was not a place for a foreign refugee. "Who is to say that Mercy's baby, due in just a few weeks, is really Moses's baby?" Agnes had the sense that her neighbors were watching for an excuse to throw them out of the compound, and she wondered how she could turn the tide.

Moz had recovered from malnourishment and was growing closer to the size of an average 8-year-old. He spoke Hema and three other languages from eastern DRC tribes, plus French. He spoke little English but no Acholi. Although Agnes made sure he'd started school, he was struggling.

One afternoon Grace brought a sobbing Moz to Agnes's house after school. From what they could piece together, his teacher had humiliated him because his English was so poor. He had run away and four of his new friends from the compound had run after him to keep him safe. When Grace met them on the road, she thanked his heroic schoolmates.

Grace rounded up a bunch of the kids in the compound and started pointing at different things, saying their names in English. Elders Murdock and Busakwe, who had been dropping off food for Moses and helping him to bathe, joined in the game and soon started coming to the compound regularly to help Moz and the other children practice their English.

Several of the normally critical parents started praising Grace for her natural teaching abilities, and they even began to say supportive things about sweet Moz.

In the end, it was Moz who saved the day, assisted by Grace. They played word games where older children challenged younger ones. Moz was so happy to be playing with so many friends that he took losing in stride, and nobody argued. Everybody else got to win.

Since Justine's hut was the closest to Mercy's hut, she heard Mercy cry out when she went into labor. And when she went to her, the previously shy and quiet Mercy blurted out her unlucky history with childbirth. She had already endured two stillbirths plus two live births in which the babies did not live. Justine spread this sad story and stirred up neighbors throughout the compound, as Agnes, Beatrice, and Dora rushed to attend to Mercy.

Soon all twelve women from the compound were gathered outside Mercy's hut to advise and to participate in her baby's arrival. It was a bad labor. And this soft-spoken stranger who had come among them, was no longer quiet. At about the five-hour mark, Agnes sent for Pastor to drive Moses home from work at the Seed Store and take Mercy to a hospital. But by now, the women were insisting that a newer clinic called Village Birth International was close by and had the best reputation for skilled midwives. One strong-willed neighbor's daughter worked there. "Come, I'll take you there. Don't let this sister suffer so," she said, jostling the others for a seat in Pastor's truck so she could show the way. To avoid conflict, Pastor followed the neighbor's insistence.

Several women from the compound patted Mercy on the back as they helped her into the vehicle. She was no longer an outsider, but was now known for her fervid faith in Jesus, the Good Shepherd, whose name she cried out over and over. Off they went.

Mercy had told Agnes just the preceding week, that she had been visited by the same spirits that came to her when Moz, her one strong and healthy child, had been born. These spirits were caring servants in God's kingdom: Mary, the Blessed Virgin, of course, but also Mary of Bethany who had washed the feet of Jesus with her tears, and the kindly disciple, Barnabas the Cypriot. The presence of these holy ones made her feel confident, Mercy said, that this baby would come into the world with the strength to live. The baby would, in fact, be a peacemaker and a healer. This baby's birth would heal Moses's wounded leg.

While Pastor drove Mercy and the neighbor to the clinic, the rest of the family, including Moses followed on foot. Once there, they stood outside and sang intermittently.

Seven hours later, their beautiful, healthy baby girl was born. Mercy and Moses named their daughter Peace.

Less than three weeks later, Moses's cast was *finally* removed. He began driving short distances for Pastor again and helped at the Seed Store. Determined to reach a full recovery, he walked and walked.

Soon, with his newly healed leg, Moses took his first long, slow walk into the city with Moz at his side, and Pastor drove Agnes, Mercy, and Peace there to prepare for the baby's christening at St. Barnabas Church where Father Luke would give the Mass in French and another in English.

Part III

19

January 2017—Gulu

Beatrice had told her mother that Elder Murdock would be visiting them to say goodbye. He was leaving Gulu to go to Kampala for the final few weeks of his mission, and then he would go home to Utah. Her heart clenched at the thought. *All those miles between us.* She would no longer see him every Wednesday at literacy class and every Sunday at church. *Plus all the times he came to the compound to help care for Moses.*

She had not told her mother the *real* reason for his visit, that they hoped to be married sometime next year, with her blessing. They couldn't be officially engaged until his mission was over, so for now, it was just a hope instead of a plan. But it was hard to tell the difference. Beatrice and David Murdock had goals, steps, and a shared vision for how things would proceed. *Beatrice Murdock. It had a nice ring to it.*

Yes, Beatrice thought as she helped her mother prepare tea, it was all happening quickly. This might seem sudden to others, especially since the couple had never once been alone. But she was in *love*. Just like when Isaiah had met Peggy in their ward a few years ago. They'd fallen in love immediately, and Isaiah had gone to live in America, and they were terribly happy together.

Beatrice had no intention to move to America. She had been accepted to medical school in Kampala and was due to move there in a few weeks for the start of classes at Makerere University. After graduation, she would practice medicine in Uganda and heal people. David was on board with this plan and had agreed to move to Uganda.

When Beatrice caught sight of David through the doorway of their house, her heart leaped. Then it fell, just as quickly. *How were they supposed to have a private conversation if Elder Busakwe had come with him?* David was not allowed to go *anywhere* without his companion—a strictly enforced rule of his mission—but she had hoped tonight would be an exception.

Agnes greeted the two men at the door, but Beatrice found it all so unsettling. As if in a dream, she sat next to David in the same white plastic chair she always sat in, but this time he nudged her foot with his under the table. Her mother sat across from them pouring tea into plastic cups.

Elder Busakwe had stayed outside with Grace, playing with Moz and the other children. Beatrice breathed a sigh of relief and blessed his discretion. She let herself slip into another dizzying daydream: she imagined running out of the house with David to make love in a field of blue flowers like she had seen on TV at the Inn.

She shook her head and tried to focus as David was telling Mama-Agnes about his travel plans. When he finished, he took a sip of tea and went silent. His hand twitched as if he wanted to take hers, but he was not allowed to hold hands with anyone (although they'd broken that rule once.)

Beatrice had told him that she must be the one to break the news to her mother. "Mama," she said, before taking another sip of tea. She swallowed hard and cleared her throat. "Mama, we have something to tell you."

Agnes's eyes narrowed as she studied the two sitting next to each other.

"We are in love," Beatrice said bluntly, her heart hammering in her chest now. She wondered if Grace could overhear their conversation from outside, and that increased her feeling of being onstage. The moment called for drama! "We are in love, and we plan to be married once David's mission is over. We would like your permission."

Her mother stood up so quickly that she bumped the plastic table causing tea to slop over the edges of each cup. She swirled around and began clattering with the cooking pot, although the evening meal was already prepared.

"Sister Agnes," David said quietly. "Beatrice and I have not broken any rules. I will be good to her. I love her, and I want her to marry me."

Beatrice shifted a little uncomfortably. They *had* held hands one time after English class at their ward. And he had called her a few times when he'd been in Kampala for missionary training, and they'd had a few long talks, which were strictly forbidden. He had told her about his abusive dad, and the verbal nastiness that characterized his family. Beatrice had told him what little she knew about her father and how she sometimes felt stifled by her mother's overprotectiveness. They understood each other, like best friends. They understood complication, ambition, companionship, and security. They shared the same values. He seemed to have everything Beatrice had ever wanted in a partner, never suspecting she'd find it in a white boy from Utah. He was perfect. Their plan was perfect. Surely Mama-Agnes would be delighted.

But when Mama-Agnes turned around, her eyes were wild, looking at Beatrice. "I should have protected you better!" She glared at David. "Men cannot be trusted."

Beatrice rolled her eyes before she could help it. And she saw that this small gesture of disrespect shocked her mother deeply. With the one exception at her grandfather's funeral, Beatrice had only ever shown her mother deference, obedience, and respect. "Mama," she said in clipped tones. "David and I have intentions. We have dreams. We plan to be married, and we would like you to support us."

Agnes recovered some of her composure. "Elder Murdock, you are not welcome here right now," she said. "Please leave so I may talk to my daughter privately."

David stood immediately. "As you wish, Sister Agnes."

As he walked to the door, Mama-Agnes burst out, "This is inappropriate, for the two of you to tell me your intentions! The groom's family is meant to visit me to discuss a possible marriage."

Beatrice sighed. "I will be back in a moment, Mama." She followed David out the door and walked with him and Elder Busakwe to where they could catch a boda. The conversation had gone worse than she'd feared, and she knew that her mother would scold her terribly for the infraction of leaving the house without permission.

The conversation was over.

······

Later that night Agnes dialed Aiko's number, now her pulse pounding in her ears. *Please, Heavenly Father, let Aiko pick up the phone.*

"Agnes!" Her friend answered. "How are you?"

Agnes let out a wail that surprised even herself.

"What's wrong? Is everyone okay? Are the girls safe?"

Agnes poured out the whole story: how her daughter Beatrice had sat calmly at their table with Elder Murdock and told her that they intended to be *married!* Agnes wailed into the phone. "This is not how a young girl should behave!"

"I hear you, Agnes," Aiko said. "Beatrice's plans for medical school are all set. She and I spoke about the arrangements just a few weeks ago. She's not planning to move to America with him, is she?"

Aiko had mentored Bea through the application process to Makerere.

"No," Agnes said, brushing tears from her cheeks. *Why was she going to pieces like this?* "No, they spoke of Beatrice going to school as planned. David will return home when his mission is complete, as required, and then he will come back and get a job in Kampala and they will get married."

"Well, that's a relief," Aiko said. "She's not running away from her plans and ambitions, Agnes. That's a good thing."

"This is not the way things are done here," Agnes said. "I have failed her." *I should have kept her far away from all these missionaries. These men do not understand us.*

"Their plan does sound . . . a bit American," Aiko admitted. "The kids calling the shots, I mean."

"Exactly." Agnes nodded vigorously. "His family has not sat down with me. There should be a bride price. Or *something!*"

"Well, I wonder if his family would talk to you on the phone," Aiko said. "Might be worth floating the idea with Beatrice and David. Would that make you feel better?"

"I don't know if it would. I feel . . . like I'm losing my daughter." Agnes felt her voice thicken again.

"It's a big change to adjust to," Aiko said gently. "Especially since you are already anticipating her leaving for Kampala. But Beatrice has a good head on her shoulders."

Agnes's heart swelled a little. Beatrice did indeed have a good head on her shoulders. As Beatrice's mother, she must have done something right.

"Now, how is little Sam?" Aiko asked. "Bjorn will never forgive me if I don't have a full update to give him when he gets home."

●●●●●●

Agnes was very short with Beatrice over the next several weeks, perhaps unreasonably so. After all, Beatrice had always been such a good girl, so smart, so respectful. But now she was risking everything for some foreign missionary she barely knew.

She felt slightly better knowing David had flown home to Utah, even though Beatrice now spent an hour each evening talking to him on the phone.

Agnes doubled down on watching both her daughters' every move, even asking Mercy or Justine to check on them when she was working at the Inn in the evenings. Grace didn't seem to mind, but Beatrice had grown more and more frustrated with her mother's constant supervision.

A few weeks later, on a Friday afternoon, Okot James stopped by Agnes's house, his brow furrowed with worry.

"I have had a call from President Nielsen, the mission president in Kampala," he said. "Elder David Murdock's parents are flying to Uganda as we speak."

Agnes sat stunned.

Okot cleared his throat, shifting in his seat uncomfortably. "Apparently Mr. Murdock is quite angry about David and Beatrice's . . . intentions. I want you to be prepared. Mr. Murdock used quite inappropriate language. He repeated over and over that under no circumstances will he 'allow his son to ruin his future for some starving African beauty.'"

Agnes stared at him, affronted on Beatrice's behalf. "She would never—she's not—"

"No," said Okot. "Of course, she's not." He sighed. "Mr. and Mrs. Murdock will attend our church on Sunday, and they wish to meet you and Beatrice."

"Very well," said Agnes, straightening her spine. "We will be prepared to receive them for dinner."

••••••

Agnes could tell that Beatrice was worried about meeting David's parents, too. Even David had said his father was something of a bully, and now this aggressive man was coming to Gulu. "He's angry as hell," David told Beatrice.

Agnes did not tell Beatrice what Mr. Murdock had said about her. Beatrice could make up her own mind about this man who could one day become her father-in-law.

As Beatrice left the house to fetch water, Grace set to peeling bananas for matoke. Agnes was proud of how responsible her daughters were. And she couldn't erase the words Beatrice had told her recently, that she was too strict, that she was destroying their happiness.

Nothing mattered more to Agnes than her children's happiness, so now she had been rethinking her attitude toward Beatrice's . . . boyfriend? Fiancé? Maybe Beatrice was right. Maybe Agnes had reacted badly. Maybe Beatrice needed to support this young man and protect him from his mean father. But what should be Agnes's role in this? In an effort to please Beatrice, she would make the most of the Murdocks' visit. She would protect who needed it most. She was good at that.

Sunday morning dawned sunny and clear, as it so often did in Uganda. Agnes and the girls left for church, and she considered what it might be like to have them marry, listing in her mind the qualities she hoped their husbands would exemplify. Bringing Elder David Murdock into focus, she imagined what she would expect of him should he become Beatrice's husband. They were both committed to living good lives before God, and he had gone out of his way to support Moses, helping him bathe in his cast and even teaching him to write better English. Still, Beatrice and David were both very young. It was too early for them to be thinking of marriage. Hopefully the Murdocks would agree, and then the young couple could remain friends for a few years while Beatrice completed med school.

But she was infuriated by what Mr. Murdock had reportedly said to Bishop Okot about Beatrice. Starving African beauty? Ha. Won't he be surprised! Once he met Beatrice, he'd probably beg her to marry his son.

······

At church, Beatrice and Grace were assigned to welcome people at the door. Agnes could tell Beatrice was nervous, but when the service began, David's family had still not arrived. The girls took their usual seats beside their mother.

About halfway through the service, just before the bread was broken for the sacrament, a loud, male, American voice called out from the doorway. "This place sure is hard to find!"

A missionary sitting at the back rose to greet the visitors with a quiet welcome.

As the Murdocks took their seats, their jostling and rustling echoed loudly across the quiet space. When all were settled, the men at the sacrament table knelt to bless the bread and pour bottled water into tiny cups. The mic was not working, so they prayed in strong voices as Beatrice shifted uncomfortably in her seat for the entire service.

After a missionary played the postlude on the keyboard, people milled about greeting one another. Agnes gathered both of her daughters and walked directly to the back of the room.

Bill Murdock was as large a man as his wife, Sandy, was a diminutive woman. Right away Agnes sensed that Bill was trouble. It was in the meanness of his narrow eyes, in the aggressive way he held his body, and in the way Sandy shrank from him. In that moment, Agnes knew that she could shrink from him too, or she could stand up to him with strength. Her daughters' hands in hers, she pulled her shoulders back and marched directly up to him.

"Hello Brother and Sister Murdock. I am Sister Adong Agnes." Agnes held out her hand. Sandy took hers right away with a limp grip. Bill's eyes narrowed but he did, after an awkward pause, shake Agnes's hand too. "These are my daughters, Beatrice and Grace. We are pleased you have come to visit Gulu."

"It's a good thing you introduced yourselves," Bill said, sharply. "Davey told us what you looked like, but to tell you the truth, everyone up here looks alike to us. Right Honey?"

Sandy's face flushed, but she said nothing.

"Everyone in this ward knows Elder Murdock," Agnes said. "And many of us were deeply touched by his mission here."

Bill looked Beatrice up and down.

Sandy said in a thin voice, "That is very nice of you to say."

"I do not say it to be nice," Agnes said stoutly. "I say it because it is the truth." She smiled warmly at Sandy. "We would be pleased to welcome you to our home to share a meal together."

Agnes invited the Murdocks to walk with them, but they insisted they would drive Agnes and the girls home. Agnes explained they preferred to walk, which seemed to annoy Bill. He asked if people in Gulu always walk, and Agnes replied that yes, of course they did, as very few people in Gulu had cars. But Bill was determined to drive them, so they got into the back seat of the big SUV and told him where to go. He drove too fast, like politicians from Kampala did when they visited before elections. Then he was upset that he could not park right beside the house, even though it was only a few steps into their compound.

Sandy asked questions about the huts, which did not surprise Agnes. Most foreigners were curious about them. But Bill began cracking jokes about how only backward people lived in huts.

Beatrice and Agnes exchanged a wordless glance.

Bill also laughed mockingly about the chickens that roved the compound, pecking at the dirt for morsels of corn. When he saw the pot of soup on the fire grate beside the door, he laughed about that too, though Agnes told him it was very safe, as their neighbors were near to check on it and keep animals away.

The Murdocks came in and sat in the chairs around the table. Agnes gave each of them a banana, and Bill said that he was glad he knew what a banana was since he was a little nervous about what was in the cook pot outside.

Sandy said a couple of nice things about her son, "Davey," emphasizing how much he had loved being on a mission here and how proud she was of him.

Beatrice warmed to the subject, telling a story about the English class they'd taught together.

Sandy nodded and smiled, but then began talking about how Davey was very young and hadn't had many serious relationships in his life, and how it might not be the smartest thing for such a young and inexperienced boy to make the most important decisions of his life so soon after he had been away from his home for two long years.

Agnes, who had been planning to direct the conversation in much the same direction as Sandy was, found herself angry with the insinuation that Beatrice somehow wasn't good enough for David. She couldn't quite pin down what Sandy had said to make that point, but she knew somehow that it had been made—implying that if Davey had more time at home, he'd have found someone better than Beatrice.

She busied herself by bringing the hot pot of bean soup inside and setting it on the white plastic table while Grace, on cue, put plastic bowls in front of each person along with a big spoon. Agnes ladled out some soup into each bowl. Then she bowed her head and prayed, "Bless this food that it might nourish and strengthen our bodies."

When the prayer concluded, she gestured to everyone to begin eating. Grace and Beatrice did so with gusto, being hungry after the long day of excitement. Sandy pushed her bowl away, saying she was nauseated after the long car ride from Kampala. And Bill poked the soup with his spoon a few times without taking a bite, then pushed his bowl away, as well. He leaned back and looked at Beatrice, whose smile had disappeared.

Bill boomed in his loud voice, "So Beatrice, it seems you are quite the popular young lady up here. Seems like you were looking for a good boyfriend from America, and maybe you think our son could be that. Is that right?"

Beatrice shrank a little under Bill's intense gaze and said, "No, no, I was not looking for a boyfriend. I am going to medical school in a few weeks. Elder Murdock and I became friends, and we . . . we thought we could become engaged after his mission."

Bill laughed. "He's not ready to be engaged. He's only twenty-one."

"I'm only eighteen," Beatrice pointed out.

"But you girls in Africa have babies and marry young," Bill said.

Agnes, Beatrice, and Grace looked at each other. Agnes thought of herself, given to a "husband" in the bush and raped repeatedly as a young girl. And while many women did choose to have babies or marry young, Agnes filled with fury as this man degraded her daughter, as he also degraded all African girls.

Bill threw his big body around in the plastic chair so that the legs of the chair began to bend. "Davey has a bright future ahead of him," he said. "He's going to college, then getting a good job." He pointed a thick finger at Beatrice. "You will not stand in the way of that." He let out a big, mean laugh, turned his attention to Grace, and asked, "So do you, too, have your eyes on an American missionary?"

Jarred by this sudden remark, Grace stood up quickly, but Bill grabbed her arm. As she wiggled away, he reached out and smacked her across her bottom with his other hand. "I'm just joking," he said, his grin huge. Then his face got serious. "But this is also a warning. Don't you girls get big ideas about catching a Mormon missionary and tricking him into rescuing you."

Agnes moved between Bill and Grace. "How dare you," she said, pitching her voice low. Bullies, she knew, responded to strength. "Get out of my house right now. You have defiled my innocent daughter, and you are not welcome here any longer."

Beatrice moved behind Agnes and took Grace in her arms.

Sandy laughed nervously. "He was just joking around," she said. "Please, Sister Agnes. He didn't mean any harm."

Agnes turned her head slowly to look at this small American woman, David's mother. "Don't you know that a man who would do *this* in front of mothers will do worse things when alone with a child?" Agnes said. "Wouldn't you protect your daughter if such a man had handled her? He's acting no better than a common rebel warlord."

Sandy dropped her head in shame, gathered her bag, and stood to leave.

"No," Bill boomed. "I won't be kicked out of—"

"Out! Now!" Agnes said. "I don't allow any violence in my home—ever! Not from anyone, no matter whose father you are!" At that moment she felt like a startled animal, but she knew that if she did not stand up to this man, he would do what he did to Grace with other young women, in Gulu or in America. Agnes stood by the door, and Beatrice stood by her side like the loyal lieutenant she had learned to be.

Bill stormed through the compound, kicking a chicken as he went.

"I'm sorry," whispered Sandy, then followed her husband at a distance.

·······

The first thing Agnes did for her daughters was to help them feel safe. She brought out two blankets from the bedroom, and the three of them huddled together. Grace cried. Beatrice cried. Agnes did not cry, but she held a girl on either side of her and rocked with them.

Then she said, "Let's pray."

They shifted into a kneeling position, and Agnes called down the legions of angels and their loving Father in Heaven to calm their hearts and keep them free of men like Bill forever. Then each girl prayed her needs, as was their custom, and then they held one another for a long time, until their knees needed a break.

Agnes asked them, right then and each day after, how they were feeling. Grace was scared, then sad, then scared again. Beatrice was mostly angry, and a little . . . *wary*.

A few days later, when Grace was playing with Moz and the children, Agnes gathered Beatrice in her thin, strong arms and pulled her close again. She had something to say, but it was slow in coming. Finally, she spoke. "Beatrice, my daughter, did you know that David had such a father?"

"I did not," Beatrice admitted. "David told me his father was abusive, but I thought it was mostly with words. And I didn't expect him to act that way to us, whom he had just met . . . at church."

"Well, this visit has brought about a change in my heart. I am left with two possible directions, and I will seek counsel. One, I am very concerned that a child raised by a bad and violent father often mimics his parent and replicates his behavior in the next generation. We see it all the time. Elder Murdock could have the seeds of such adulthood in him right now, ready to be released one day when he is the head of his household. That concern makes me want to keep you from him. I want you to find another man more worthy of you."

Beatrice's head dropped low in despair.

"But the opposite can also be true," Agnes continued. "While some men follow the model of their abusive fathers, it is possible that Elder Murdock will see the gravity of his father's bad behavior and will vigorously turn away from his example, making himself into the warmest and most gentle husband to his wife and father to his children. And, dear Beatrice, any son who has been treated viciously by a father such as his, could benefit greatly from having a more loving home to be part of . . . a home like ours, Beatrice. Maybe David needs to be part of our family."

"Mama, Mama, do you mean it?" Beatrice nearly screamed with joy. "Could you find room for my good husband under your wings like you do so many around us?"

"Wait, Beatrice," Agnes warned. "I was very clear. I said wait until I pray more and listen for the voice of the Lord before I decide. This is important."

"Whatever you say, Mama," said Beatrice, suddenly the humble supplicant.

Of course, in voicing the idea of David becoming part of their family, Agnes had already made her decision. She would help save this good man from his father.

20

January 2017—Gulu to Kampala

Just a week after the Murdocks' disastrous visit, Beatrice boarded the bus to go study in Kampala.

Agnes's anxiety had been allayed somewhat because she was able to arrange temporary accommodation for Beatrice in the home of the Stake President, Simeon Muwanga and his wife, Priscilla, before Beatrice would move into a dormitory at Makerere.

"They are Ugandan, Beatrice," Agnes said. "They can tell you things about being a Ugandan in Kampala that most people from America do not know. And they have a kind, protective driver who knows the city."

At the bus stop, saying their final good-byes, Agnes pushed a piece of paper into Beatrice's palm. On it, she'd written a phone number.

Beatrice raised her eyebrows, questioning the importance of the number. She already had the Muwangas' details and Dr. Bjorn and Dr. Aiko's contact information in Kampala, all carefully written in neat handwriting in her notebook.

"It's Okello Peter's number," Agnes explained. "Now that you are a student living in a new city, it might be the right time for you to meet with your father. But only if you feel ready."

Beatrice balled the paper into the pocket of her sweater. She hated to admit how much bustling Kampala and its nearly three million people intimidated her, and it was strangely comforting to think this man, essentially a stranger but also her father, was close by and contactable. Being in Kampala was the start of a grown-up life chapter for herself. She had her spring classes selected and would move to the university housing soon. But for now, she was a little girl from Gulu, moving to an unfamiliar place to launch her big new life.

After a proper greeting from the Muwangas, Beatrice was left alone in a guest room to settle in for the night. The room was far nicer than any she'd seen at the Harmony Inn, though perhaps a little too quiet. The tile shone like glass, as she took in the surroundings with as much enthusiasm as a child. What would it be like to have her own apartment someday? Her medical books spread across the table? David's novels on the shelf? Their own plates and glasses, maybe some art on the walls? Their own habits and everyday routines? Their own rules! She got a tingly feeling just thinking about it.

Over the next few days, Priscilla Muwanga took Beatrice around the whole city, leaving her with a sense of the layout. With its vast urban sprawl, known for traffic jams and accidents, Beatrice might have avoided Kampala for years had Sister Muwanga not given her this tour, demonstrating that it would not be impossible for Beatrice to manage on her own someday. With its nearly three million people concentrated around the bus station, and fanning out in all directions, Beatrice was surprised to learn that only 10% of the city's residents had access to the sewage system and clean water. There was much to learn. Before her stay with the family ended, Beatrice felt like she could soon call Kampala her city, and no longer be an outsider.

Priscilla bought Beatrice a few skirts, sweaters, and boots since more people wore shoes in Kampala than in Gulu. When it was time for Beatrice to move to the medical school, Priscilla insisted that she visit them at least twice each term and to call with any questions, including where it was safe to go at night. Then the Muwangas helped to set her up in her residence hall.

With Beatrice settled in Kampala, and David attending classes back in Utah, the couple planned to use this year apart as effectively as possible. They had officially become "engaged," and Beatrice would fly to Salt Lake City for their temple wedding in January. Then, they would return to Kampala as newlyweds in time for her to start the next semester. David would leave university after this, his junior year, and get a job in Kampala. His ambition was to support Beatrice and he wanted them to start their life together with him working as an English language tutor, much like he'd done on his mission.

In the meantime, she would arrange for their apartment so they could move right in on their return.

It is all happening, Beatrice thought, and smiled.

Beatrice had never entered a new community where people knew nothing about her. Acholi people did not traditionally have last names, but here she listed her own as Beatrice Murdock, and she liked the sound of that. She told anyone who asked that she'd grown up peacefully in Gulu. She'd gone to school there like any other child. If pressed she'd add that she'd always dreamed of being a doctor and that she'd been swept off her feet by a wonderful man from America, to whom she was now engaged to be married. She had earned a scholarship to Makerere that covered tuition, and her soon-to-be mother-in-law was paying the rest of her expenses. Her dreams were coming true.

Beatrice did not add complicated pieces to her story, as she liked the tidy simplicity of this revised autobiography. Yes, she had parents and a sister, and two married brothers, and they were all doing well and a happy part of her life. Full stop. She seemed so clear about all these features of her story, that few challenged her for additional details. Since her family lived far away, they did not visit, but she had family friends in Kampala who were supportive. "The Muwanga family lives on the other side of Kampala and their daughters went to local universities," she would say. "I also have close friends who are doctors on the faculty at Makerere, and their daughter is my friend."

She didn't need other friends and didn't reach out to fellow students. If she was approached by anyone looking to connect, she politely demurred, offering her busy schedule as the reason.

If it ever crossed Beatrice's mind that she was hiding something or not being completely honest with herself about the enviable simplicity of the successful life she presented to others, she pushed the thought away. Something deep inside told her to hang on to this self-portrait until she was safely married to David. Then maybe she could comfortably explore her inner reaches. Beatrice understood herself well enough to know that she could not become a doctor, marry an American, and look in the mirror at the same time. To explore any complexities in her life now might lead to her own unraveling.

So, she did not tell anyone she had been born in the bush, or that her mother had been one of the child mothers kidnapped by the LRA. She plodded along and showed up as a model student, and with every extra breath she tried to plan her wedding.

──────

One breezy day, Beatrice grabbed the sweater she had worn on the bus ride to Kampala and retrieved the balled-up piece of paper she'd dropped into her pocket at the bus stop with her mother. She smoothed it out to reveal the phone number scrawled in faded pencil in her mother's hand. It was time to contact her father.

Just two days later, she found herself standing inside a restaurant, looking for a man she didn't know. Would he have her smile? Grace's dimples? A familiar rhythm to his stride? Beatrice wiped her palms on her dress and took deep breaths. She shouldn't be this nervous. She wasn't doing anything wrong. Her mother had encouraged her to meet up with Okello Peter once she was in the capital. Mama-Agnes had even given her his phone number!

The restaurant was busy and noisy as she found a table. Would her father be proud of her achievements? Happy that she had been accepted to Makerere to study medicine? Would he be curious? Apologetic? Or would he be menacing?

Although Beatrice didn't suffer from nightmares as badly as her mother, she'd had some lately about Okello Peter. They were filled with her running away and of being hidden by strange shadows. Were these her mother's dreams, transferred into her mind through the years like osmosis? Shaped and deepened by the tales of cruelty Moses and Dan had told of Peter's unforgivable behavior in the bush? Though no one told her directly, she'd overheard the stories about a boy called Sam. She'd watched the shadow cross Moses's face if ever the name Peter came up, no matter how casually.

Beatrice felt for the reassuring shape of her phone in her pocket. She'd told the Muwangas' family driver to pick her up again in an hour and that she would call if she needed him to come earlier.

The door to the cafe swung open, and there he was. Her father.

Beatrice swallowed, frozen for a moment. How had she known it was him? Would he recognize her? He was a big man, disheveled. His eyes scanned the busy room, then fell on her. He smiled, an apprehensive smile that reminded Beatrice of Grace. She responded, signaling . . . a little wave that said, "*It's me, over here.*"

He joined her at the table. "I'm sorry I'm late," Peter wiped his brow on the sleeve of what looked like a once-nice shirt. "I'm so glad you asked to meet me."

For a moment, they said nothing. Then Beatrice smiled and said, "That's okay."

Peter continued to apologize. "I'm sorry we had to meet at this busy cafe." They could barely hear over the conversations and orders. "I work from noon until ten at night as a mechanic at the Kampala station. Then I take my shift as the morning guard for the people like me and Doreen who live at the market, where we work."

Instead of sleeping, Peter had come to meet her instead. Beatrice wasn't sure if she felt moved or guilty.

As if reading her thoughts, Peter responded. "Don't misunderstand. I'm glad to be here. A welcome break," he said. "I am excited to see you."

They placed their breakfast orders. Peter's phone rang, and he picked up, stepping away from the table and speaking about schedules. Beatrice studied his tone: firm but mild. Something she could trust. She had learned that from her mother. He had a strong body, from what she assumed were years of working with his hands and outdoors.

"You work hard," Beatrice said.

He laughed. "True. Though I am glad for the work. It allows me to provide for Doreen and my son, Sam."

"Oh. You have a family in Kampala?" She tried to hide her surprise. She vaguely remembered her mother mentioning that possibility, but until this moment, she'd forgotten. Maybe allowed herself to forget. She also vaguely remembered hearing terrible tales of Peter killing a boy named Sam in the bush. She shook her head to clear it. "I'm sorry if it's inappropriate for me to ask about your family," Beatrice added. "I don't want to be intrusive."

They spoke of Peter's life: alluding to the evil he had done as a member of Kony's forces and what he'd done since being granted amnesty and immunity from prosecution for crimes committed during the war. Peter was quick to show his deep remorse that the real victims of the war were not so rewarded. When he'd first come to Kampala, he'd spent his time and his freedom foolishly, on bad living with women coming in and out of his life. When he met Doreen, he'd recognized her as a good woman. He called her his wife.

Beatrice found the conversation with her father comforting in its commonness. This could be almost any man's story, and he was not such an exceptionally horrible man or a mean father. She asked more questions and was pleasantly surprised when Peter answered them with equal comfort. He was not boastful but seemed humble about his meager achievements, and said he guessed God was with him even after the evil he had done as a younger man.

Although Peter responded to all of Beatrice's questions, it was clear that he wanted to hear more about her. What was bringing her to study at Makerere University, such a prestigious place? Beatrice told him about medical school and also about David. She tried not to brag about her accomplishments and opportunities, ones that he and perhaps his son would never have.

Their hour flew by too quickly, and Beatrice soon excused herself to meet the Muwangas' driver as arranged.

As the car merged into the traffic, Beatrice reflected on the experience. *Would the memory of that hour with her father give her peace, or would it leave her longing for more?*

21

May 2017—Kampala

It seemed to Beatrice that every part of planning a wedding took thought and effort. No matter how many decisions she made, still there seemed to be more. Luckily, Dr. Aiko and Dr. Bjorn's daughter Adela was very interested in weddings.

Beatrice had always thought Adela was shallow and uninteresting, but now she found herself relying on Adela's knowledge about American weddings. Beatrice juggled wedding planning along with her schoolwork, and still managed to talk to David each day.

On Sundays after church, while Aiko was cooking, Beatrice and Adela would flip through fashion magazines and scroll through social media on Adela's phone. Beatrice took note of the leading popstars in the US and found herself looking up Drake and Taylor Swift, playing their music on her laptop while she studied. She also listened to Beyoncé and dared to admit she liked Nicki

Minaj. There was something Beatrice found appealing in the angry lyrics of defiant women.

Beatrice enjoyed giggling over online photos of celebrities and other outrageous people decked out in wedding attire, and sometimes she imagined herself in the sexier styles depicted in these pages, but she would soon back off from those ideas and go back to something more acceptably beautiful and demure. She would be wearing the dress in the temple, after all.

She knew she had not done enough to involve her mother and toyed with the idea of inviting Agnes to Kampala to help find a dress, but it seemed too exhausting an undertaking. Her mother would not mind. After all, what did either of them know about Utah wedding receptions?

One Sunday afternoon, Beatrice was studying when Adela asked, "So when are you sending out wedding invitations?"

Beatrice fidgeted. "The wedding isn't until January. I read that you aren't supposed to send invitations until two months before."

"Yeah," Adela said. "You're right. But you can start writing them now and choosing your stationery."

Beatrice felt a flare of annoyance. She was studying for a big Applied Anatomy exam.

"Don't worry," Adela said. "I'll look up some templates and you just tell me when you're done studying."

Half an hour later Beatrice felt confident in her grasp of the material and closed her books.

Adela wiggled closer on the bed and angled her laptop screen so Beatrice could see the choices. "You know, just because David's parents are getting divorced doesn't mean they both can't be on the invitation. But the more important question is how you'll list *your* parents."

"What do you mean?" Beatrice already felt out of her depth. The drowning sense of being overwhelmed rose in her chest.

"Well, are you going to say like, 'Adong Agnes invites you to the marriage of her daughter Aber Beatrice'? Or would your father's name be there too? Like, 'Adong Agnes and Okello Peter invite you to the marriage of their daughter'?"

"I can't possibly say Okello Peter's name on the invitation," said Beatrice. "My mother would be devastated. No, Adela, that won't work."

"I'm just looking at the different ways you can handle these delicate issues. This website has all kinds of options."

"They probably don't have an option for my situation," Beatrice muttered.

"What do you mean?" Adela kept scrolling through the wedding website.

Beatrice was silent, and finally Adela looked up. "You mean because you didn't grow up with your father?"

"I mean because he raped my mother!" Beatrice burst out. She got up and paced the room. She didn't like talking about this.

Adela's mouth was hanging open. "What? He raped your mother to get her pregnant and that's how you were born? And Grace? Did he rape her again to get Grace?"

Beatrice sighed and sat down on the bed. "Yes." But then she sat up a little. "But you know, maybe it's like David's father. He has been abusive, but now that he and

Sandy are getting divorced, David swears his father is behaving better and trying to make amends. My father is like that too," she said, a little desperately. "He's reformed."

Adela's eyes were still very wide and suddenly Beatrice wanted to prove to her that her life wasn't totally messed up. "It was just because of the war. It happened to lots of people. Anyway, let's look at some different options. Could we put their names on different lines?"

"You can do anything you want. It's your wedding." Adela went on with a smile and a click of her fingers, "The bride is the boss!"

"I'd need to talk to David about this too." Beatrice wondered how she could honor her newly repentant father. Was he entitled to be there beside Adong Agnes as Beatrice's parent? Maybe if she honored him, he might step up to an expanded role in her life. Finally become a "real" father to her and Grace.

She texted David about the matter, but even as she scrolled through the wedding planning website, Beatrice was coming up with different scenarios. All arriving at the same notion: Okello Peter should be on the invitation. But by morning, Beatrice could see that doing so would dredge up too many painful tales from Agnes's past. At worst, it might even cause her mother to have a flashback and fall apart. That would be a disaster and people might blame Beatrice for causing it. She lay in bed with that hard fist of worry building in her chest. Worry about doing the wrong thing, about having to accommodate everyone else's wishes and concerns, instead of being able to please herself. She was the bride after all, and as

Adela had said: "You can do anything you want. It's your wedding." Beatrice found herself resenting her mother's pain and how it always took center stage in their lives.

·······

One day, on impulse, Beatrice called Okello Peter and asked him to meet with her again. He responded immediately, and Beatrice was surprised at the calming influence he had on her. All the anxiety she'd dredged up over the past few days drifted away, as she basked in her father's delight in his daughter.

They began by perusing the menu and discussing their favorite Acholi dishes. Did she make matoke? Of course she did. What kind of peanut sauce tasted best? The minutes flew, then the hour. When it was almost time to say goodbye, Beatrice felt the true reason for this visit burble up in her chest. She had to ask him. It was time.

"I am getting married," Beatrice said, startling him with her abrupt declaration. "To the American boy I mentioned last time we met."

Peter's eyes widened.

"I was wondering if I could put your name on the invitation. As my father?"

Time ground to a stop, and she felt as if all the hustle and bustle of the restaurant dimmed. She couldn't read all the expressions that flicked across his face: honor, shock, surprise, remorse. It was so dramatic she glanced around to see if the people next to them felt it. Regret. Peter's eyes shone with tears.

"I am sorry, but I must decline, Beatrice. I have not been a father to you. It would be an insult to your mother to name me alongside her like that."

Beatrice thought she might cry, but she was too stunned. This was not the response she had imagined. She'd expected him to be honored and immediately willing.

Okello Peter's eyes flicked across her face as she tried to get hold of her emotions. He shifted his shoulders back slightly. "Please try to understand, to accept this would be the meanest blow I could give to your mother," he said. "She may have told you some of what I did to her when she was given to me in the bush, but she may not have revealed to you all the terrible details of how I harmed her."

Beatrice nodded, hoping he wouldn't say more.

But he continued. "And yet, she rescued you, and escaped from my hold on her. Since then she has lifted herself up, and I admire her courage and persistence. Now that I have witnessed what she has done for you and your sister, I cannot claim to be your parent in this very public way."

She wiped a tear, wishing she hadn't let him see her cry.

He reached across the table and took her hands in his. "You are who you are because of something special in you, Beatrice, but also because of who your mother is. You are not the fine young woman that you have become because of me. It would be hypocritical of me to arrive at this time of celebration to claim an honorable role. I offer you best wishes, but please do not put my name there as your parent. I am honored enough to be called your father with the two of us here."

"But, Father," Beatrice attempted to interrupt him, afraid to acknowledge the certainty in his voice, which suggested that he would not be moved. She'd thought he would welcome this chance to be invited back into their Gulu family in this way. She had presumed that almost nothing would have pleased him more, but she was mistaken. "Can't you see that by standing beside me as my father, you would have some of your respectability restored?"

"Try to understand," he said. "For most of my life, I was a truly bad man. I did almost nothing that I can look back on with pride. When I decided to make myself into a different kind of man, it was hard, but I believe I have done that. I am not a perfect man, Beatrice, and not by any measure am I exceptional, but if I stood beside your mother as your other parent, and suggested in any way that I was equal to her in the ways she raised her children, I would be doing the kinds of things I did as a younger, selfish man. I would be putting my own pleasure above the joy of your mother. I would diminish the respectability of your family. I would be so ashamed, as if I'd stolen something that was not mine."

For a moment, words failed her. On one hand, Beatrice was disappointed that she had not succeeded in getting what she wanted. But on the other hand, she had a rush of pride in what she felt her efforts had accomplished. She had shown that she could bravely retrieve her errant father from the exile that had been imposed on him. She had shown that she was above bitterness.

In return, Okello Peter had given her something better than what she had offered him—dignity and humility.

"If only there was a way to take things back, to erase the things we did when our worst selves overtook us," he quickly said. "If only I could make up to Agnes, to you and to Grace, to your brothers and their friend Sam, and to the many others I hurt during those days at war. I would do anything to make it not true what I did. I am so sorry. What can I do for you, Beatrice, to show my contrition for what I have done?"

Beatrice shook her head, "Thank you, but I didn't come here to ask for anything else from you." The driver waited outside the window, so Beatrice stood up to leave. "I am glad to have met you once more," she said, trying not to think about what her brother Moses might say. "Perhaps I could meet Doreen and your son someday? Grace, I'm sure, would also like to meet you—she is so clever and pretty and spirited. And though you will not be on the invitation, may I send you one?"

Peter started to shake his head but before he could outright refuse, Beatrice blurted out, noticing the note of desperation in her voice, "Would you consider coming to our . . . our first wedding, in Gulu?" Having never even considered the possibility of what she was now presenting to her father, Beatrice continued before she came to her senses. "Although I will be marrying David in a temple wedding in Utah, we will also have a smaller Gulu wedding. I'm not sure exactly when, but could you, I mean, would you come to Gulu for that?"

In her desperation to get her own way, Beatrice had invented an entire celebration. In Gulu. Between now and January. How on earth was she going to explain this to her family? Or pull it off?

Okello Peter grinned widely. "I would be honored." He offered her his arms and they parted with a hug. Almost like a real daughter and father. Then he held the door for her as she checked to make sure she had her phone. She crossed the street toward the car, and as soon as the car door closed behind her, Beatrice sunk her face into her hands. *What have I done? I can't put my brothers through this. What about Mama? She will fall to pieces. I have gone too far. But I also can't take it back, or my father would be hurt.*

She lifted her head, resolved to push forward no matter the cost. *I will have a wedding celebration in Gulu that my father can attend.* Adela's words rang in her head, "The bride's the boss!"

●●●●●●

Unsurprisingly, Agnes put up a fight, expressing how deeply disappointed she was that Beatrice could not see her side of things. But Beatrice gave her few alternatives, and to ensure the unity of the family, Agnes accepted this shocking demand.

"I'm glad I have no actual fear of Okello Peter anymore," Agnes said, when Beatrice called her to discuss her plans. "You should know, however, that it is difficult for me to accept the interjection of such a troubling figure from our past into this celebration. A celebration I am already struggling to accept as God's will for you, Beatrice, since you have chosen to marry a man who is not

Acholi. I wonder if you've considered your brothers in all of this?"

Beatrice had considered her brothers and felt confident she could bring them around to her way of thinking. Why anyone would imagine Adong Agnes would raise a daughter who was anything but resolute, was hard to imagine. She had graduated from S6 with the highest grades in her school. She had led the literacy group at church as the best teacher. She had earned scholarships to study medicine at Makerere University where she expected to be first in her class, and she would marry the unlikely man of her dreams in a temple in the United States. An event that would bring together parts of an impressive intercontinental family. Why not add to these lofty goals and bring home a prodigal son of Gulu? One Okello Peter, an infamous killer from the LRA, who was the sworn enemy of her now-returned and increasingly successful brothers?

Against the advice of nearly everyone she cared for, and at the risk of alienating her brothers, Beatrice dug in her heels and announced she would have her first wedding party in Gulu, thus finding a way to honor her father.

······

Now that she had secured her mother's acquiescence, Beatrice was eager to proceed with her new cause: the Gulu "First Wedding." She took her plans and the final invitation wording back to Aiko and Adela, excited to go over the details and filling each step with high drama. Sitting at the dining room table, while Aiko worked nearby on her computer, Beatrice took Adela through the invitation debate and explained the important role she imagined for her father. "It will culminate in the two of us performing a formal father-of-the-bride waltz. We'll make this Gulu wedding an event to remember!"

Aiko closed her computer with a snap, causing both girls to stop their chatter and look up. Her face did not reflect any of the excitement Beatrice was feeling.

"I'm sorry to interrupt you, Beatrice, but I can no longer listen to this and not say my piece." She held her hands up in a gesture of openness. "Please accept my apologies if I am being culturally insensitive, but I have a real concern that you are making choices that are more about you being the star in what sounds like some Hollywood-inspired awards ceremony! A ceremony which does not take into account the feelings of others who love you, especially your mother."

"Mom!" Adela looked horrified at her mother's intrusion.

Aiko continued with a calm but firm voice. "Beatrice, you know that you are like a daughter in our home. You assigned me the role of mother *locum tenens* when you moved to Kampala, a role I am honored and happy to play, as I revere your mother. You have been a good friend to Adela, who could afford to take life more seriously," she raised her eyebrows in her daughter's direction, "and now I feel I need to step into my role and offer you a few hard truths. There have been times these last few months when I have wanted to take you by the shoulders and shake you back to your senses."

It had been a long time since Beatrice had been spoken to like this. The well-raised, respectful child in Beatrice knew to sit back and listen to what Aiko had to say, a woman of good standing whom Beatrice respected. But the Boss Bride in her, the girl who had become used to getting her own way, immediately defended herself. She regaled Aiko with her tale of the great injustice that had been committed against her by her not being allowed to have her noble father play a part in her life, "because my mother will not properly forgive him."

"I don't believe that is what is happening here at all," Aiko said.

"Well, I am going to make up for it in Gulu, showing off my reformed parent as a model for how others should forgive and move forward." Beatrice went on to describe how she'd read up on some traditional Acholi weddings and was considering how she could get Peter to offer a bride price to her mother, then enact a faux kidnapping, with David stealing Beatrice from her father in the style of very traditional Acholi weddings that had been more common long ago.

Aiko held her hands up again. This time with a clear indication for Beatrice to stop talking. "Can you consider how this would make your mother feel? She really *was* kidnapped and forced to marry, as a young girl. Why would you want that scene to be part of this celebration?"

Beatrice's eyes widen. "I . . . I've never thought of it that way."

"It is a mistake to keep pressing this issue of Peter's involvement, a mistake that you may find embarrasses you in the end. It's time to grow up, Beatrice." Aiko said this sternly, making clear the debate was over.

Beatrice deflated back into her seat, knowing at last it was smarter to listen.

"You and Adela should understand that this is not a game. Family structures, traditions, and cultures hold serious weight at events like weddings, and to violate the rules of these can bring disgrace. What you are planning will be perceived as a mockery rather than an honor. If you insist on this 'first wedding' in Gulu," she put air quotes around the words, "and since you have already given your mother no choice but to concede to your iron will, then I suggest a muted affair with a toned-down role for Peter. A role I will be happy to explain to him if you are unable."

Beatrice began to reply but Aiko silenced her with a firm shake of her head and stood up from her chair, coming around to Beatrice and Adela's side of the table to review the invitation on the open laptop.

"It should absolutely not be called a wedding, but rather a celebration to honor the marriage. Your mother is the matriarch. It is her place to honor you. You cannot play the matriarch. You will usurp her position and embarrass her. Which in turn will embarrass you. Can you see this?"

Beatrice nodded, but Aiko was not finished.

"Furthermore, Beatrice, if this is to be an opportunity for reconciliation, give some thought to how your brothers feel? You have repeatedly said that Moses will be seriously troubled if Peter comes to Gulu, especially if you're expecting your family to honor your dad. Moses was particularly harmed by Peter, a man who beat his eight-year-old friend to death. Right? All this on top of

Moses's terrible accident and spending six months in a cast unable to walk. You have mentioned that Moses has promised to kill Peter if he sees him again. All are huge obstacles. Right?"

"Yes, yes," Beatrice said. "You are right. I was trying to point the way for our family—"

Aiko stopped her. "You know very well, Beatrice, that no one can direct the healing for another person. We can watch for clues as to when another is ready for help, and then offer to move ahead with them."

Beatrice complied with Aiko's direction for how to properly word the invitation, and Adong Agnes was placed back in her proper singular role as matriarch. Aiko suggested a few more changes and Adela's skilled fingers flew across the keys until the Gulu invite reflected the respectful tone of the event.

When they were done, the doctor stood back and folded her arms across her chest. "I also strongly suggest that you take this idea to Bishop Okot as soon as possible. He not only knows Acholi customs and respects them, but he will also understand how to bend them in deference to Agnes, as well as to your family's religion as Latter-day Saints."

Aiko then sat with the girls and together they did a search on Acholi marriage customs, listing some modest modifications Beatrice could gently pose to her mother and Bishop Okot.

After a productive evening, Beatrice was left with the clear understanding that it is the parent who is the host of a wedding celebration, which is conducted on the bride's behalf. Aiko also made it clear that Beatrice's attitude from now on toward her mother should be one of gratitude and cooperation.

Compared to Ugandan mothers, Beatrice had always believed North American mothers to be relaxed and liberal, but she was learning that when push comes to shove, they could also be ramrod strong. Aiko hadn't made it this far by being a pushover, and Beatrice was left with no doubt about how it was that Dr. Aiko Shamada had accomplished so much in a career that spanned two continents. Beatrice had also witnessed something powerful, the collaboration of two strong women who stood up for one another.

●●●●●●

Beatrice's wings had been clipped. She felt embarrassed and knew her overstepping had not been thoughtful or considerate. She dutifully called Bishop Okot and told him the things Aiko had said, and he offered to talk to Agnes. He agreed to officiate as a master of ceremonies, rather than a clergyman. Sunday and Molly offered Agnes the use of the Inn for the party and even offered to provide the food. Pastor Emanuel also offered support. The community would ensure that, for a poor woman from a small village, who had endured captivity in the LRA and was now rebuilding her life, this would be a respectable occasion. The actual wedding would come afterwards in Salt Lake City.

Beatrice took on the responsibility of talking to Okello Peter, and with an attitude of slightly resentful humility, she did precisely as Aiko told her and invited him as a guest of her mother to the celebration in Gulu. She thought a lot about what Aiko meant by "grow up." She'd heard that said by many Americans. A Google search revealed this phrase was meant as a true condemnation for someone who is irresponsible, silly, careless, and self-centered. In other words, Beatrice was being childish. She didn't like that Aiko had felt compelled to say this to her, but it made the point. Beatrice could still indulge herself in talking with David about the small details of their wedding over the nine thousand miles between them, but in public, she would rectify herself. Aiko had done her a great service by reining her in after this unbound half-year vacation from her mother's strict household.

More and more, Beatrice—or Bea, as David now called her—looked forward to talking with her Chosen on the phone in the evenings. She was living in the dorm, and had solitude in abundance, and a clean, simple living space that took no effort to keep tidy. Each night she would dial up her fiancé, and they would talk, like a long-distance cuddle, while they wound down from their days. When Beatrice told David about the conversation with Aiko, he lightened the load by saying how grateful he was that they had such a sensitive consultant in Aiko. He was glad that there were people on this side of the Atlantic willing to help his overstressed fiancée.

This also sealed the question of whether David would fly to Uganda beforehand. He would come for the Gulu celebration, then steward Agnes, Beatrice, and Grace on the journey back to Utah.

22

November 2017—Gulu

Agnes had put aside the embarrassment she felt in her own community after Beatrice had rejected all the Gulu seamstresses who had offered to sew her wedding dress because, her daughter replied, "the dressmakers in the capital are better." She'd put aside the hurt that Beatrice had not called her once to ask advice on any aspect of the American wedding. And the rejection when Agnes called Beatrice only to have her call sent to voicemail and then receive no return call from her daughter. All of which left Agnes with her mouth full of unexpressed words.

She'd struggled to keep up with all the complexities around international air travel arrangements. She'd found a way to send a photocopy of her passport to the airlines. To make sure that Grace received her new passport in time, and she'd navigated the airline website, indicating her and Grace's preference for a window or an aisle seat, on the six separate flights they would be taking to Salt Lake City, and back.

Beatrice was her child, and Agnes was willing to do anything for her. She put no conditions on her commitment to do what Beatrice might need her to do. She did not ask to understand this child's peculiar demands. Beatrice could always rely on her mother to be there in any hour of need, but now that child wanted to bring Okello Peter to Gulu and expected her mother to graciously play host?

It was one thing for Agnes to have seen Peter privately in Room 9, protected from public glare, but quite another for Agnes to stand by and honor him as her daughters' father in this public ceremony. Agnes had to call this request from Beatrice what it felt like to her—a betrayal—and asked herself over and over why her beloved daughter, of all people, would put her through this?

After much debate and without any consulting of Agnes at all, Beatrice had finally settled on wording for the invitation:

Adong Agnes

Invites you to a Reception

to Honor the

Marriage of Her Daughter

Aber Beatrice

To David Backman Murdock

*Son of Sandy Sorensen Murdock
and William Wilkinson Murdock*

*At the Harmony Inn in Gulu
January 6, 2018
At 6:00 PM
Dinner and Dancing*

*The Marriage will be solemnized
in the Holy Temple*

of the Church of Jesus Christ of Latter-day Saints

*in Salt Lake City, Utah, USA
January 11, 2018*

Agnes sat with complete stillness. Things were as they were. That's all. The day she gave birth to Beatrice, she had contemplated letting her die, as so many mothers did under those impossible circumstances. Instead, she had intentionally decided to save her, to care for her the best she could, and to defend her against the cruelties of life.

She had made that choice and been at peace with it, so now, she focused on holding herself together, not so much from the bursts of fear and helplessness that came from the traumas of her past, but from fear that the tight, stable life she had constructed for herself and her girls, and now her sons, might be unraveling. Once upon a time, she'd worried about bringing them together, and now she worried that one by one, they might peel away. That she simply was not capable of holding all the strands together.

The night before, Agnes had dreamed she was tied by a length of rope to all four of her children who followed one behind the other. In the dream, she was ordered to lead her family across a raging river on a log. There was no safety net to catch them if she, or any of the children fell off the log. They would hit the water and be carried away. The rope connecting them was all they had. Agnes had watched this happen in the bush, and now it was those she loved most that were lined up behind her, clinging to the log and the rope. She'd almost reached the far side when one by one, her children began to fall.

"Catch them, catch them!" Agnes cried out.

"I'm right here, Mama," Grace had said, patting Agnes's arm in the darkness. "The best part of that dream is that we are all together. Right?"

It was so like Grace to look for the light.

"Mama," Grace went on, "Inviting Okello Peter here, may not be so bad. It is better he comes here where we are all together. I want to meet him with you nearby. Or with Dan or even Moses near me. We are a strong family here."

Agnes did go back to sleep, more soundly than before. She dreamed again about the rope that tied them together. This time the family climbed up the other side of the river together, and no one got lost.

Grace didn't seem to miss Beatrice as much as she had at first, and she had become accustomed to being her mother's only daughter. Agnes began to recognize strengths in Grace that seemed to blossom out of her sister's shadow. She was a survivor, too. She had escaped Kony, though she had no memory of him, and rather than feel shame for her family's origins, Grace felt proud. "Why run away from rumors that surround everyone who'd escaped from the bush?" she asked her mother. "I am not ashamed." Grace's new confidence continued to grow in the empty place Beatrice had been, and Agnes's nightmare did not come back.

Agnes needed Grace. There was a freshness to the way she spoke of old problems. On days when Agnes sat with a pot of half-peeled bananas between her knees, unable to finish the task of preparing matoke, her mind drifting toward worries about how this marriage would affect her family, Grace knew to pray with her and implore the Savior to calm her mother's mind. She even knew to ask the Lord to especially bless Agnes and Moses, to not let Peter disturb the tranquility that each of them worked so hard to preserve.

"Let his visit be as a wind in the trees, not a storm that tears the branches off the trunk," Grace asked humbly. Since she was eager to meet her father, she asked that he come and go in peace, leaving no new wounds behind.

Moses had argued bitterly against Peter's visit, letting his mother, his sisters, his brother, and Pastor know that he and his family would not appear at this event, under any circumstances. But Agnes began to see this event as an opportunity for Grace's new gifts to shine and for Moses to face some of his demons. She turned her attention to him, again, knowing that he had the most to overcome.

Privately she thanked God again for the time she had chosen to see Peter at the Inn and again in room 9.

She would have been incapable of facing him for the first time at the celebration. She was proud of her foresight. Choosing to see him had not been an error for which God was about to punish her.

■■■■■■

January 2018

The morning before the Gulu celebration, Okello Peter, his partner, Doreen, and their son Sam arrived on a crowded, dusty bus from Kampala, which was late, as usual. They were slow to get off as they had been at the back. Agnes spotted them making their way down the center aisle together. She watched Grace's eyes flick from face to face as travelers left the bus, trying to find her father's face in the crowd. Beatrice walked ahead to greet Peter with a brief hug, but Grace stayed back to watch as he helped some elderly people unload their bundles.

When his family had claimed their belongings, Peter turned. Perhaps it was because Grace looked conspicuously ripe with anticipation, but he immediately picked her out as his other daughter, which Agnes could tell, by the light in her face, pleased her. He reached for Grace's hands, and then looked into her eyes and said her name.

Grace had rehearsed what she would say when she saw him, but when faced with the reality of her father, she stood silent. Agnes could tell that he was ready to hug his daughter, but he seemed to understand that she was not ready for that. He simply said, "Let's find a time to talk a little about your life, Grace. I hope you have lots to tell me."

Only then did he greet Agnes before walking away with Beatrice and David.

Grace pressed herself against Agnes's side. "Everything I thought I wanted to tell him, no longer matters."

Agnes squeezed her child's hand.

"It was very good to see him, Mama, but maybe that is enough for now."

"Maybe," Agnes agreed. She wondered if Peter had noticed that Moses and Dan were not there.

Peter and family stayed at the Inn which was familiar and safe. Sunday's presence guaranteed that nothing dangerous would happen. Grace would arrange to meet her father alone the next day, within earshot of Sunday. While others worried over the food and other preparations, Agnes knew that Grace's mind and heart was focused on her father. When Peter arrived at the party, he behaved appropriately, as a humble guest. He was cautious and reticent and his whole body seemed to beg forgiveness.

Grace gripped Agnes's hand when Peter crossed to their table to offer his congratulations and compliments on the event, but the agitation Agnes had anticipated was largely absent. After the main event in the AA room, people pushed back their chairs and danced and played drums and sang. It became the happy occasion no one had quite dared to hope for.

Agnes sat and slipped her shoes off under the table, grateful for the fact that they had enjoyed a calm, unexceptional occasion, with no outbursts or tears. Beatrice looked beautiful in her bright white American wedding dress, which she had haughtily told her mother was a "mermaid style." David was not a stranger to many, but he was strange enough in his tuxedo and with his hair neatly combed with water that people studied how he ate, drank, and tossed a few toddlers in the air while they giggled. They got used to him quickly. Dan had greeted Okello Peter and now sat watching Peter's son Sam play with his son Sam.

Pastor joined her at the table with a large plate of food. "You've done a wonderful job, Agnes. Beatrice has much to be happy about, and I have some exciting news that will make you happy too. I have found the perfect piece of land for our shelter. It is in Kitgum, a few hours north of here. An ideal location to serve refugees from Palabek."

Agnes sat in wonder for a long time. "I never thought this would happen, Pastor," she said. "I thought it was simply a dream."

Pastor smiled. "We still have a long way to go, Agnes. It will not be ready for development for another year or two."

Agnes felt overwhelmed at the very thought of it, but Pastor squeezed her hand, as if he understood it was a lot to process. "Enjoy the party," he said. "Do not think of this for some time yet."

Grace arrived with a plate of food just as Pastor returned to the buffet, and the day dipped into the evening. "Can I help with anything, Mama?"

"No, dear Grace," Agnes said. "I am at peace. Nothing is amiss."

Grace fidgeted and did not look at her mother.

"Did you speak to your father?" Agnes asked calmly.

"I did," Grace replied. "I told him there was too much going on this weekend, and it would be better if we met again another time. I said that sometimes there is wisdom in having few expectations, so that we are not disappointed. He laughed, Mama, but not at me. He said he understood and called me wise. He said I had learned good things from my mother."

Agnes gave her daughter's hand a squeeze. "I'm proud of you, Grace. You handled this all very well."

"I don't feel any anger toward him, but I did want to show loyalty to Moses."

"You have become an adult," Agnes said, beaming with pride.

⬤⬤⬤⬤⬤⬤

As the sky outside darkened to indigo, and the stars came out to shine on their celebration, the energy of the gathering began to lull. Agnes stood with the mic and asked Jesus' blessing on all gathered together in love and called out many by name with thanks. She invited Grace to pray and said one last good wish for David and Beatrice.

Okot James wished Agnes good night with a peaceful smile, and labeled the evening "dignified."

When Beatrice told her mother that she planned to stay with David at the Inn, Agnes strongly disapproved, but she quickly recognized that she had lost that battle. She seemed to be losing many with her eldest daughter lately. She snuggled into bed next to Grace and slept soundly.

23

January 2018—Salt Lake City

Agnes entered the lavishly decorated ballroom at a place called Pierpont Place. Thank goodness Sandy had recently called Agnes in Gulu to tell her what to expect in Salt Lake City. Unfortunately, Beatrice had told Agnes very little, even though the reception had been planned for months.

Sandy had tried to fill in the gaps, even offering suggestions on what Agnes and Grace should wear, but when Agnes confessed she had not even seen the invitation yet, Sandy expressed deep disappointment in her son and immediately emailed a copy, apologizing that Agnes had been ignored.

Thank Heavens for Sandy, thought Agnes, as she'd printed a copy of the invitation to show Grace. The invitation read:

Adong Agnes

Announces the Marriage of Her Daughter

Aber Beatrice

To David Backman Murdock

*Son of Sandy Sorensen Murdock
and William Wilkinson Murdock*

*In the Salt Lake City Temple
Of the Church of Jesus Christ of Latter-day Saints
On January 11, 2018*

And invites you to a reception in their honor at

*Pierpont Place,
163 W Pierpont Avenue,
Salt Lake City, Utah.*

*On January 13, 2018
7:00 pm
Dinner and Dancing
8:00 pm*

RSVP by December 1, 2017

Now, she and Grace joined at least two hundred people at Pierpont Place for Beatrice's Utah wedding reception, and Agnes couldn't quite believe she was there at last. After all the planning and worrying, the flights to Utah had been relatively easy and the experience less daunting than she had anticipated. But meeting Elder Murdock's expansive family and then putting on big heavy coats to face the snow, and then getting into the right cars to go to the homes where they would stay . . . it had all been perplexing. And exhausting.

The private marriage ceremony had been disappointing, too, even though it was at the fabled temple she had seen in so many pictures. Grace hadn't been invited inside, and Agnes had a hard time concentrating. Even Beatrice and David almost slept through the tedious service. Sandy had not been allowed in the temple either since she had left Mormonism, so she'd kindly waited outside with Grace. David's father had not been invited to witness the wedding ceremony either because he had been excommunicated from the church for his well-publicized infidelities. As they'd all left the temple that afternoon, Agnes was not surprised that Beatrice and David went in the opposite direction. They were staying with Bill, who had surprised everyone by being so nice.

After such a boring wedding ceremony, Agnes was glad there was something more to look forward to with the reception. Surprisingly, the most interesting part of the trip so far had been an unexpected exchange with strangers in the Dallas Fort Worth airport on their way from New York City to Salt Lake, three days earlier. She and Grace had been waiting at the boarding lounge for quite a while due to weather delays. Waiting for the same flight was a big group of healthy, affable young men who were attending a wedding in Utah, too. They were very outgoing, and one of them told Agnes and Grace that the wedding was "a gay wedding!" The two grooms were accompanied by their two young sons, Emmanuel and Romeo, and Agnes commented on how well-behaved the boys were.

"We've heard about your 'kill the gays' law in Uganda," one of the men said, asking Agnes about the policy.

"I don't know too much about it," Agnes explained, telling them how Molly and Sunday had warned a few guests to be discreet in public, acknowledging the real dangers they could face in Uganda for being gay. But this was Agnes's first time to see so many gay men who were not discreet at all. In fact, they acted almost like Beatrice and David had acted on the plane, flirting in front of people, and holding hands right out in the open.

"Why are there so many gay men here in Texas?" Agnes asked.

"Oh, honey. There are this many gay men everywhere," the man replied. "Some say that up to a fifth of all people in the world are gay. We just can't all show it because of laws like yours in Uganda."

"You mean 20% of all people in Uganda are secretly gay?" Grace asked.

"Yep," said the man. "Think about it. I'm sure you know lots of men who just don't feel romantic about women."

"I do," said Agnes, thinking immediately of another Emanuel back in Gulu. "Do you think they want to marry other men?"

"Wouldn't you?" asked the man with a smile, as he beckoned the little boys' fathers over for Agnes to meet the grooms.

She and Grace congratulated the happy couple on their upcoming marriage.

"Maybe people will change in our country," said Grace. "Maybe someday we will have gay marriages there, too."

The little American Emanuel showed Agnes something on his electronic tablet and endeared himself to her. She would tell Pastor Emanuel about him when she got home. She had been wondering about Pastor for a while now. Maybe, this explains why he had never married. Maybe Pastor was gay.

Someone dropped a glass across the room and snapped Agnes back to the here and now, all dressed up at this gorgeous reception, with so many people she didn't know. As she looked around the room, she wondered how the gay wedding had gone and figured it hadn't been half as boring as the temple ceremony had been.

Isaiah Odeki's four-year-old son, Winnie, was making a beeline for Agnes through the crowd as Isaiah chased him. Despite her wedding attire, Agnes stooped down and swept Winnie off his feet, kissing him on both cheeks.

"He's just as eager to wrap you in a hug as I am," Isaiah said, lifting Winnie out of Agnes's arms and setting the boy on the floor. "Just seeing your face makes me feel like we're home in Gulu." He held Agnes's hands and backed away from the embrace, taking her in.

"Thank you for coming," Agnes beamed. It was always a delight to see this young man, whom she considered a son. They both teared up a little.

"It's a much shorter flight from Seattle than from Kampala! We wouldn't have missed it for the world."

"We miss you in Gulu," Agnes said.

Isaiah sighed and a shadow flickered across his eyes. Agnes wondered whether all the familiar Ugandan faces had brought back hard memories for him. She was only too familiar with how memories could be triggered by the most unrelated events, often in unexpected ways. "Is it a comfort to see us?"

Isaiah gave her a small smile. "Of course. But you know how it is, Mama-Agnes. I just didn't anticipate how an American wedding reception could bring it all up again. Suddenly, I'm reliving the day I was expelled from the IDP camp. One minute I'm here in America, the next I'm wandering down a muddy red road looking for Gulu!"

They shared a small smile of quiet understanding and surveyed the room. Was it the sheer number of guests moving *en masse* from one place to another? Or was it the sense they and so many survivors shared, that even though they'd found a place that was safe and welcoming, normal life still managed to feel alien to them?

"Sometimes I wonder if I'll always feel like a stranger, no matter where I go," Isaiah said.

Agnes gave his hands an understanding squeeze, and then gestured to where Beatrice and David were emerging from a garland of fragrant flowers, trailed by a photographer. In all directions, guests drifted from the generous *hors d'oeuvres* tables toward the assigned dinner tables, each one set with fine linens and silver. Beatrice wore her mermaid-style wedding gown, and her smile made her whole face glow. Such a pretty scene.

"This is beautiful, Mama-Agnes. You must be very proud," Isaiah said. "Our wedding after-party was a more modest affair in rural Idaho."

Together they looked around at the women in dazzling clothes and the men with colorful silk ties. Priscilla

Muwanga might fit in here, but Agnes was not sure she did. Waiters bustled about refreshing drinks and removing any used plates, glasses, and napkins. Grace was already seated at one of the beautiful tables, chatting with David's sisters. Winnie had made his way over to her and was repeating some words in Grace's Ugandan accent, making them all laugh.

Grace waved warmly to Isaiah when he caught her eye.

"How are Moses and Dan?" he asked.

Agnes shook her head with a sigh and described the conflict about Okello Peter that still stood between her children. "Moses was hurt not to be invited to America," she said. "But I doubt he would have come anyway. Dan didn't expect to be invited, and he seems fine with that. They don't go to our church, so they didn't know David very well."

Isaiah expressed his sadness at the news. He and Moses were agemates and had lived parallel lives in many respects, even though Isaiah had grown up in an IDP camp and Moses in LRA camps in the bush. He whipped around as Winnie skidded past. "I need to keep my eye on that boy every minute."

"Daddy, can I see the princess?" Isaiah's little daughter, Aggie, who was two and a half, was pulling on his hand.

Agnes kneeled to eye-level with the little girl, her namesake. "You are the only princess here tonight, sweet girl." She was pleased that Beatrice's wedding would be Aggie's introduction to her African heritage. She wanted endless pictures of this night for her family's history. It was unlikely she'd see her adoptive granddaughter very often, and Agnes wanted to have a framed portrait of the two of them at home.

Aggie pressed herself to her father's leg with a shy look as Isaiah took the child's hand, "Sure, Daddy's darling girl. Let's find Mommy and tell her I'm taking you to meet Beatrice."

"Find us when you're done," Agnes called over her shoulder to Isaiah as Sandy Murdock tugged on her arm, indicating the table at the front of the room where the parents of the bride and groom were to be seated. "Bring Peggy and the children with you."

"Of course," Isaiah replied and went to find his American wife.

Agnes was led to a table on a raised platform with flowers all about them. She was grateful to be spared the task of further mingling and trying to remember names and faces, but she was also discomforted to find she was to be seated between Bill and Sandy. Perhaps trying to make up for the terrible way he'd acted in Uganda, Bill now fawned over her so lavishly that she did not know how to react.

Winnie and Aggie seemed happy to visit Agnes in her place of honor, but their real interest was in the bride's stunning gown, smooth pearls, and sparkly jewelry. Beatrice's magnificent hair also merited careful examination by their curious little fingers. And Beatrice was regal. She held each child for a moment and snuggled them in her arms, while her husband looked on adoringly. She expressed delight to discover that Isaiah had taught his daughter to pronounce her name, "Bee-Ah-Trice." They played name games for a moment before Beatrice was reminded that she had hundreds more guests to meet and charm.

●●●●●●

"I hope my words were okay," Agnes whispered to Bill as she finished the last of the parents' remarks. "I wanted people to know we appreciate how friendly everyone is to us here. And I wanted them to know a little bit about our lives back home."

"You were perfect," Bill purred. "Most people don't know much about the war and about Beatrice's background."

After dinner, there was dancing. Agnes was standing at the edge of the dance floor, watching Winnie and Aggie dance with Isaiah Odeki, when Sandy approached her with a few friends. "We are so looking forward to your talk tomorrow, Agnes," Sandy said.

A few weeks before Agnes had left Uganda, Sandy had invited her to give a talk to a group of Utah women. The speaking event had been announced to several wards in the vicinity because Sandy wanted to call attention to physical and emotional abuse in the home. Sandy had endured this with Bill and had watched Agnes call him out during their Gulu visit. Since their divorce proceedings had begun, she wanted to shine a spotlight on abuse.

Agnes shifted her weight uncomfortably. She wasn't sure it was appropriate to discuss this at the wedding. She was also having second thoughts about what she could offer. "What do any ladies around here want to hear from a poor mother from Gulu?" Agnes said.

Sandy leaned in. "I know that women around here often have money and economic security. They have a roof over their heads and can take care of their children. However, many are still battered by their husbands, fathers, or sons. It's awful, but it's invisible. It is kept behind big, heavy locked doors."

Agnes nodded and tried to change the subject, but Sandy seemed to want to keep talking about it.

"There are women who need to hear your story," Sandy said, "and to know that women all around the world suffer from men's abuse. Only by admitting it and reaching out to others, can they reach a point where they can take their lives in their own hands and get healed."

"It just looks so different here," Agnes protested. "People are well fed and clothed and look content with polite-looking husbands." She gestured to the room. "Are any of the men here really abusing their wives?"

Sandy lifted a brow. "You'd be surprised."

At that moment Beatrice and David cut across the room. They held hands, clearly smitten with each other. "We're about ready to cut the cake," David announced, moving on to find his father.

"Things look very serious over here. What are you talking about?" Beatrice eyed her mother and Sandy skeptically.

Sandy took Beatrice's hand. "Your mother has agreed to the most wonderful thing," she gushed, and before Agnes could intervene, Sandy began to tell Beatrice all about tomorrow's "fireside chat," at which she'd invited Agnes to speak to dozens of congregations about abusive men.

Few people would have noticed the way Beatrice's radiant smile fell just a little. The way her dark eyes narrowed slightly. The anger that flashed in them. But Agnes knew her daughter well. Beatrice had hardly spoken to her mother since they'd left Entebbe, but she sure had something to say now.

"Thank you all so much for coming," she addressed the group that stood around Agnes and Sandy. "I hope you are enjoying *my* wedding." The emphasis on the word was imperceptible to anyone else but the snap came through loud and clear to her mother. She walked around the table and leaned down to kiss Agnes on the cheek, while speaking quietly so only Agnes could hear. "Why do you have to make everything about you?"

24

January 2018—Salt Lake City

The next night Agnes looked at herself in the bathroom mirror at one of the huge LDS ward buildings in a city called Bountiful, north of Salt Lake City. The name of the place is perfect, she thought. People here look like they have everything in abundance.

Sandy knocked on the door and called, "Agnes, are you ready? We start in ten minutes."

Agnes leaned her hands on the counter, and nodded slightly but firmly before opening the door to Sandy's eager face. "Are you sure these American women will understand me?" Agnes didn't only mean her accent. She wondered if Sandy's American friends could possibly relate to anything she would have to say.

"Maybe it was selfish of me to spring this on you, Agnes. The day after the wedding. But knowing the stakes for so many women in the area, I couldn't imagine not asking. You being here is such an opportunity."

"Everyone speaks of such a happy life here: bicycles and skis, vacations and cars. I've only been in this country a few days, but I can't imagine a richer place. And this city is even richer looking than where you live."

Sandy nodded, then placed a hand on Agnes's shoulder. "No matter what the outside looks like, some things are universal."

Agnes took a deep breath and remembered how much other people's stories had helped her heal. Would she have ever made it this far if she'd thought she was the only one struggling? Maybe she really could help another woman by sharing her story of survival.

"You have important things to say, Agnes. And these women have important things to learn from you," Sandy prompted. "But . . . you can back out if— "

"No," Agnes said with conviction. "I want to do this."

As they entered the foyer, a small kerfuffle broke out in the corner where a man grabbed a woman on the upper arm, and she flinched.

"I know that woman," Agnes said, eyes wide with recognition. "I saw them once. In Kampala, after a talk I gave." She paused. "The husband wasn't pleased with my remarks about the violence I suffered. I don't think he'll be pleased with what I have to say tonight."

Sandy's eyes flicked from Agnes to the arguing couple, then back to Agnes.

"That's the Mortensons," Sandy said, her teeth gritted. "I'm glad to see Marian is here, but I can't imagine why her brute of a husband is here."

At this, Agnes stood up a little taller, holding her chin high.

The two women watched as Marian Mortenson shot her husband a glare, then tore away, taking a seat in the pew at the back of the chapel, leaving her husband to storm out alone.

Moments later, Sandy stood at the podium and adjusted the mic, waiting for the room to settle. She made some opening remarks and welcomed the attendees before introducing Agnes.

"Ever since I first heard Agnes talk about how men in the rebel army acted, I have been unable to ignore the parallels to my own life and my own marriage. For years I made excuses to rationalize my husband's behavior: *Bill has a bad temper. His bark is worse than his bite. He'll get over it; he's really a big teddy bear.* But abuse, all forms of abuse, deserve to be called what they are. Only by accepting this could I be free. It also set my husband free. By naming the poison between us, we were able to move ahead with our individual healing." Sandy paused and looked out at the audience.

Agnes understood the courage it took for Sandy to stand up in front of all these women and name her own husband as her abuser. Sandy had explained that there were many women in their community who suffered from various layers of abuse, but that it was hidden behind silence and the image of a perfect home-sweet-home. That false image to be preserved at all costs.

"I hoped that if Agnes—my son's mother-in-law, a woman I so deeply admire—could speak to you all today, that her spirit could touch our hearts and give us all the courage to improve our situations at home, or to support a friend or a neighbor in need. You'll see when you meet her that this is a woman with an aura about her. Something special, despite all she has survived."

The audience applauded as Agnes and Sandy hugged and Agnes took the mic. Her knees did not tremble as they had in the past when she spoke about her experience. She gripped the podium and stared out at the sea of faces.

You can do this, Agnes told herself.

When she began with her own story, the audience sat spellbound.

"What made things worse for the girls in Uganda was that our abuse was denied. It took a few years after the war for women to speak out and tell our stories. We refused to be ignored, and women began listening to one another. We acknowledged what had happened and we condemned it and supported the victims. Of course, this did not make the assaults go away—although we believe there are fewer now—but women can once again hold our heads high. We made it clear that what happened to women who were beaten was not our fault. Our stories have spread all over the world now. We've learned that when the brutality is over, survivors must be encouraged to speak out and be heard. We must not be shamed because of what happened to us, as we are not responsible for other people's cruel behaviors. Remembering that and reminding one another of that, is important for healing to begin and continue."

Agnes spoke about the violence against girls and women in Utah she'd heard about recently. "We don't suffer less in Uganda because we 'got used to it.' And you don't suffer less here in Utah because you keep it wrapped in secrecy. What happened to any woman yesterday, does not make it easier to take the abuse today."

She spoke of many other kinds of abuse, the layers to an abusive mindset, and how the victim can feel worthless—as Agnes herself had felt for so long.

As the minutes went by, Agnes grew even bolder. The audience nodded, intent and listening. She hoped that Marian was still there, somewhere in the back row, gaining courage to change her life.

"I think there is a reason so many of you showed up tonight, to hear about this subject. Whatever brought you here, I hope we can all be part of the solution to this problem." She paused. "And if the victim is you, and you aren't sure where to turn, please be brave. Your story matters. *You* matter. The first step is to be aware and name what is happening to you, to know that it is not acceptable in the eyes of God. Use the senses that our Lord and Savior Jesus Christ has fine-tuned for us to use on behalf of one another. All women deserve respect and kindness. *You* deserve respect and kindness."

She closed her presentation by pleading with the audience to "Hear our fellow sisters as God hears us. He wants us to hear one another."

What happened next was a blur. Sandy rose to give her a hug. Women and men flocked into the foyer to shake her hand and ask what she was doing now. "Are you writing a book?" "Would you be interested in talking to so-and-so?" "Will you visit again soon?"

Agnes felt a strange surge of pride, a pleasant jittery sensation in knowing that she had spoken truth, that God had spoken truth through her. She pulsed with the heat of it. A sense of meaning and rightness. She walked around the gatherers in a daze, not seeing Marian Mortenson, but wondering where she might be.

The next morning, when Sandy shook Agnes awake in the guest bed of her home, Agnes knew something was terribly wrong.

"Remember Marian?" Sandy's voice shook.

Agnes felt her heart pound. "What is it?"

"Come see," Sandy said, leading her to one of their many TVs. "She is speaking directly to the news."

Downstairs they both sat down on one of the high stools around Sandy's marble kitchen counter. Sandy's eyes were red. "Apparently when she got home last night, Martin Mortenson started beating her," she said. "I heard it from one of the women in my ward very early this morning. And he bashed her over the head with a heavy candlestick." Sandy's voice thickened. "He nearly killed her." The kitchen TV was replaying the headlines, showing Martin being put in a police cruiser—handcuffed.

Sandy switched channels, and there Marian Mortenson stood in front of the Church Office Building not far from the temple in Salt Lake City, her head wrapped in a big white bandage. "I am making a statement by my own choice, supported by my four daughters. They know how much abuse I have suffered at the hands of my husband, Martin Mortenson, their father. Last night he tried to kill me, and he would have succeeded if I had not called the police and if they had not reached me in time. My husband has held a high-level job in the Missionary Department of the LDS Church for two decades, despite the fact that many people there know he is a dangerous man. I also want to accuse countless bishops who, over years in Bountiful, have listened to my reports of abuse. My daughters and I expressed deep fears with them, many times, but they only offered to counsel our abuser to repent. They did nothing to protect us nor to report his crimes. Instead, they allow him to continue his work as a leader in the church. The LDS church has failed my daughters and me. I call them to account."

25

January 2018—Gulu

So Beatrice could begin spring semester on time, the newlyweds left Utah right after the festivities, which made Isaiah's offer to visit Gulu with his son and accompany Mama-Agnes and Grace home, a relief. And while they brought gifts for Moses's children, Moses himself was quite guarded when his mother and sister arrived, full of exciting stories from a trip on which he had not been invited. Also, Moses had just recently identified as Agnes's son, and had even more recently begun to embrace the role, thus he was not so pleased to have another man who had long been called his mother's adopted son, resume his place. And Isaiah now lived in America in, from what Moses could tell, extreme wealth. This was underscored when little Winnie blurted out, "Daddy, how come Mama Agnes doesn't have a real sink?" and "I'm glad we sleep on real beds at the Inn instead of on the mats in the huts."

Isaiah relieved the tension by spending most of the time when Moses was home, visiting other places in Gulu, but after a week, Isaiah stayed closer to Agnes, and talked more about what his experience had been coming back. And he began to plan his departure, discussing travel logistics with Agnes. Then quite abruptly, Isaiah asked if Moses would make the trip to Kampala with him and Winnie when it was time for them to fly home. "I know you like to come with me," Isaiah said, a little shyly. "The SUV I rented is very comfortable. Would you like to ride with us?"

When Moses accepted the offer, it was hard to tell who was more surprised: Isaiah, Agnes, or Moses himself.

Moses and Isaiah were roughly the same age, and both had been parented to some extent by Agnes, but they had experienced dissimilar childhoods. Apart from their age, national origin, and shared ethnicity, they had little in common. Driving the rental back to Kampala together would either be an opportunity to get to know each other better as adults, or it would drive a wider wedge between them.

Making too steep a turn right after they left Gulu, Isaiah had shown what they already knew—he was unfamiliar with this place where people drove on the left side of the road. This was just the first example of how their lives had become completely different. Five-year-old Winnie—asleep in an elaborate car seat in the back—had a pile of books beside him, while Moses could barely read. The trunk of the SUV was stuffed with gifts Isaiah would take home to his family in their eleven room, two-and-a-half story house in Lake Union/Seattle, while Moses lived humbly in a one room hut on his mother's land. His wife had no kitchen but cooked each meal over a grid set on bricks around a fire beside the doorway to their hut. They rinsed the plastic dishes in a bucket of water that she or her son hand pumped from a deep well they shared with the eleven other families who lived in a circle of nearly identical huts around them. Agnes owned one of only two larger three-room houses. A house that had a front room with a sofa, six plastic chairs, and a large plastic table around which they ate family meals. In Moses's hut, his small family ate their meals either standing or squatting, with one hand picking the food and the other holding a bowl of whatever was being served that night. Moses was pretty sure that no one ate standing up in Isaiah's modern kitchen. Isaiah worked for his wife's brother as a highly respected software engineer in a successful technology company where he managed twelve employees, while Moses worked as a driver for Pastor's Seed Store. As unpretentious Isaiah seemed, he had, quite frankly, everything. Moses had next to nothing.

Moses respected that Isaiah made every effort not to call attention to these differences, but the boy, Winnie, didn't know the rules to that game. When they stopped to get a soda and pee, Isaiah helped Winnie use the hole in the floor of a small shed in the pit latrine. He sang out cheerfully, "Daddy, why can't we just use a real toilet?" and then "How come everybody here likes dirty bathrooms?"

The imbalance provoked Moses. "Why don't we just dispose of the questions that point out all the things we don't have here, and talk about something else?" he snarled.

"Fine. You ask the next question," Isaiah said.

Moses did not know a good way to start a new conversation. Maybe there was no good way to pass the time. Nearly two hours passed, and traffic was threatening five hours to Kampala.

Moses looked across at the petrol gauge. "We need to stop. The traffic is a mess anyway."

Isaiah turned into the next petrol station. As Isaiah checked on Winnie, Moses got out and slammed the door before going for a piss.

Why did I agree to come with him? Moses asked himself. *Why did I think we would become friends if we traveled together?*

Isaiah took Winnie behind the men's toilet building which had empty gallon jugs to scoop water from barrels to wash around the holes in the cement floor.

Moses seethed as he imagined Isaiah's disgust and Winnie's questions. *Why did he bother coming home if he could not embrace his roots?* He finished fueling up the car and saw Isaiah head toward the store to pay. Across the forecourt, a truck driver was trying to force a young woman into his truck. An image of Mercy working at the truck stops sprang into Moses's mind. Already irritated and looking for a fight, Moses saw red. Despite his injuries, he flew over to the large truck and grabbed the man by the back of his shirt and threw him to the ground. Moses yelled insults, then grabbed the arm of the young woman, and told her to go to the rented SUV.

Isaiah ran over with Winnie in his arms. "Come on, Moses," he called out, as the truck driver's friends gathered around. But Moses would not be stopped.

Moses's deep well of anger buried inside of him for some time now, rose to the surface with dangerous results. He braced himself for a brawl as Isaiah tried again to disengage him.

The girl began backing toward the SUV.

"Who is your friend here?" Isaiah asked the trucker. "Does she need a ride somewhere?" With Winnie still in his arms, Isaiah stepped even closer to offer Moses his body as a shield. "Hey, Moses, let's get on to Kampala."

Seeing the child, the men started to back away.

Moses looked as though he might smack the driver again, but relented to Isaiah's urging and pushed past him, heading toward the SUV.

The young woman looked mildly relieved but also curious. She followed Moses who stormed away, his ears still ringing with his fury.

"Do I know you?" the girl asked. "What do you want?"

"I want to get you out of here. Do you want a ride home?" Moses asked.

"No. My father sells me to get money for drink. If I go home, I will get sold back to the fucking truck driver and he's a violent rapist pig!"

Moses and Isaiah exchanged glances. Since Moses had made such a scene about rescuing the girl, they could hardly leave her now. Isaiah gave a short nod and Moses said they would take her to Kampala. Moses drove and she sat up front, while Isaiah sat beside Winnie in his car seat, and read him books for an hour. Being in the driver's seat calmed Moses down. After almost an hour and not yet close to Kampala, the woman asked

Moses to drop her off. As directed, he pulled over where she wanted, and she left them.

Isaiah gave Winnie more cookies and moved back up front. "Moses, if you didn't know the woman, why on earth did you decide to rescue her?"

"I'm not sure," Moses said. "I was already mad, and when I saw the guy grab her it reminded me of Mercy, of so many men I've known and of how I used to be. I lost my temper."

"What were you already mad about?" Isaiah asked.

"I don't know. I was mad before we stopped," he said, trying to explain what had really bothered him all day. "I wanted to be the hero, the good guy, someone who counted for something. You know it is hard to be that kind of man, when you don't have expensive stuff to show off to prove you're a hero?"

"I get it, Moses," Isaiah offered, but his voice sounded tentative. "I'm sorry it feels that way."

"Do you really get it, Isaiah?" Moses could not keep the edge out of his voice. "I mean, look at us. Here we are—two Gulu men—who started life at the same time, and you have it all, and I have so little. Moses held up his finger and thumb to demonstrate 'so little.' I was embarrassed to be with you and not show up equal. So, I decided to knock that bastard around and have people look up to me back there. Then you step in with your fancy clothes and fancy shoes. You made me look like an idiot."

"I didn't want you to get hurt. You've barely gotten over your injuries."

They drove along the Gulu-Kampala Highway, with their elbows out the windows and the warm air blowing into the car.

"You don't know how it feels to always be behind. You're from Gulu. How did you manage to escape the rut the rest of us are in? How come you weren't in the bush with us? And how come you were able to find an American woman and get out of this place? Most of us in Gulu have the fucking war churning inside our bellies for the rest of our fucking lives!" Moses pounded the steering wheel with both hands at once.

Isaiah checked over his shoulder as Winnie slept in the back seat, a half-eaten cookie in each hand.

"You're right. I was never abducted. I was never forced to become a soldier, like you and Dan were. I carry a lot of guilt, Moses. I have real compassion for those who survived the bush, and, of course, for those who did not survive. I understand that so many returned with severe wounds—emotional and physical."

Moses sighed. It wasn't pity he wanted.

"I wanted to come home and be of some service to those I really do think of as my people," Isaiah continued. "And I wanted my son to know what it is to be Acholi."

"If you cared so much, why did you run away?" Moses demanded.

"I didn't run away, Moses. I fell in love with my wife. It was a surprise to both of us. Still, I know I haven't paid my share for what other people suffered. I think about that a lot. I wish there was something I could do for the people in Gulu, especially those I think of as family."

Moses seemed to chew on every word. It was not just jealousy he felt for Isaiah. He didn't just want things Isaiah had. He wanted to know that Isaiah had suffered. He wanted some evidence that this man next to him knew pain—that he had not avoided all life's hardships and could therefore genuinely respect a man like himself for whom life was a constant struggle. Without some evidence of having survived a refining fire of loss and want, Moses could not accept Isaiah as a peer. Certainly not as a friend or a brother.

"Do you resent me for thinking of you as my family?" asked Isaiah.

It was a question that had hung over the whole visit, and Moses did not respond for a good five minutes. "I do," he finally said. "Our whole family has been affected by the war. We all came close to dying in it. We've had to work to stand up to insults made to those who were in the bush. We carry the war in us, and it's often so heavy. But you managed to avoid ending up in an LRA camp, yet you still get to be part of our family. Yeah, it makes me mad. It's not fair. Okay? I'm angry."

"I'm sorry, Moses. I'm sorry you had to go through what you did. You are right. Although we are the same age, you were born in the bush, while I was sent to an IDP camp. I had no control over any of that. I was six years old. It was awful, but I carry tremendous guilt for those of you who suffered worse fates."

Moses listened but guilt was not what he hoped to find in this companion. And Isaiah was not finding the bond he sought either.

A long silence moved between them.

Isaiah tried to say more. "I know I am an outsider in your family, Moses. But your mother was very kind to me when I came to Gulu. I was an orphan at sixteen and totally alone. She was very lonely for you and Dan. And I longed to have a mother. Somehow, we filled that space in one another's lives."

"Yeah, I know my mother thinks of you as another son," Moses responded with more irritation. "Did you lose your parents in the war?"

"I lost everything and everyone in the war," Isaiah replied. When we went to the camp, we left our belongings behind, except for a pot to cook in and 2 books. My mother was a reader before the war.

Moses was pleased to hear Isaiah's experience. Maybe he did know what it was like to be beaten down and have to pull yourself up. It was the honesty he hoped for. "Which one were you in?"

"It was north of Gulu-town at Awach," Isaiah said.

Moses nodded, "I know where Awach is. I heard it was a mess up there. Still is."

"I was born in 1992. My family was forced into the camp in 1998. From all I know of what happened to my family, my parents had me and one daughter with them when we left. But I think another one had died before. The one with us, my older sister, died in the camp when our hut burned down. My father left after that but was somewhere in the camp. Just not with us. My mother left the camp a few years later. Everyone in the camp was starving, and she said she was going to leave to find us food. She never came back. I was alone for a few years. There was nothing to do. Then one day soldiers came and said the war was over and for us to get out of the camp. I thought I should find my mother, but I had no idea where to start looking. I knew I was from Gulu, so I made my way here. I never found her."

"So, you were never out of that camp? For all the war years?" Moses asked.

"Never. We were warned that we would be killed if we left at all, and we knew of people who did leave and word came of their murders. It was unbearably crowded and violent, but we were stuck there. But we had the sense that nothing important really happened for all those years, so we had few stories to tell. And I knew that many resented anyone who had not been abducted or had not been a child soldier, so while I was just a child refugee, I knew it was not a popular story to tell to people like you. People who had been in worst places," Isaiah went on. "I never lied and said I'd been in the bush, but if someone assumed that about me, I wouldn't correct them. I thought it was more respectable than being in an IDP camp."

"It is weird that being a kid born in an LRA camp kind of became a badge of honor, when for us it was hell," Moses said.

They both nodded. It was strangely true.

"When I came back to Gulu, I was so hungry. I had to have a job," Isaiah explained. "The one good thing that happened to me at Awach was that there was a teacher there the first five years who taught a bunch of us kids to read. But she died and one of the kids stole the books. But I could read. So, I tried to become an assistant to a teacher in a Catholic school. They didn't hire me, of course, so I volunteered just to have a place to sleep. I read to little kids for a few months, but the priest and nuns were not kind, so I went to other churches. That is when I found the Mormon people and . . . your mother."

Moses nodded, a new understanding building between them.

"Then something quite amazing happened," Isaiah continued. "The Mormons sent me on a mission to Ghana. I became a missionary. I had something to do. I felt needed and loved. I also learned to use a computer in Accra."

"You're like me," said Moses. "I have learned to use the computer a little by working for Pastor at the Seed Store. That and to drive the truck." Suddenly they had some things in common.

Before dozing off, Isaiah smiled warmly. To Moses he said, "All I can say is I hope you know that I deeply admire you and the life you have made for yourself. I wish you were my actual brother."

To which Moses replied, "I am glad you told me all this, Isaiah. I like you better now."

• • • • • •

As planned, the next morning Moses, Isaiah, and Winnie visited David and Beatrice, who had since returned from America, and David made breakfast for everyone. Beatrice made a big fuss over Moses, which was the right thing to do. After all, he had not killed her father at the pre-wedding party in Gulu!

After breakfast they drove around and shopped for more gifts for Isaiah to take home to friends and family in the States. "I would be so happy to buy something for each person in your family back in Gulu," Isaiah said. "But I respect you if you say no. I will understand."

Moses did find it difficult to be with someone who had more money than he did, and yet, having spent a few days with Isaiah, he now understood that having more money did not mean Isaiah felt he was a better man than Moses was. He wandered through the market for a while to give Isaiah's offer some thought, then came back smiling and said he'd like to have gifts for them all. Together they picked out some things for Dan, Dora, and their children, as well as for Mercy, Moz, and Peace.

"Do you know that Mercy had an operation after Peace was born? And we won't be able to have any more children?" This was another sadness for Moses, but he didn't feel he needed to keep it from Isaiah. He no longer felt that they were in competition with one another, with Moses always on the losing end.

"Yes, she told me last week," Isaiah said. "I'm so sorry."

Moses grew thoughtful as he counted out the gifts he would take to each child. "Each week at St. Barnabas, we say together *Psalm 106: Praise ye the LORD. O give thanks unto the LORD; for he is good: for his mercy endureth forever.* We say it together in our home and it helps me accept what I have with a full heart."

"Your family is blessed to have you as their father," Isaiah said. "You are a good man. We do something similar in our church. Sometimes we recite that verse, and sometimes another. Like you, the Psalms inspire me."

"Mercy understands me," Moses said. "She chose St. Barnabas church, since Father Luke speaks French and English, so sometimes he gives Mass in her language. He said he would say special prayers for her to have more children. Mercy asked him if I should have another wife so I could be a father to many, and he said we should pray about it. Would you have a second wife if your wife could not have more children?"

He worried Isaiah might be appalled by the idea since he'd married a white woman and lived in North America. Although it was fairly common for men in Uganda and the DRC to have more than one wife, especially if the issue was children, it was less acceptable in other countries.

Isaiah shook his head. "That is not our plan. Caring for the two we have is hard enough." He chuckled.

After an hour and a half, they needed to get all the gifts wrapped and ready for Moses to return on the bus.

"Of all the things I've done on this trip home, this time with you may have meant the most to me," Isaiah said as he shook Moses's hand. "I hope you can consider me your brother."

"Thank you," Moses said. "I'm glad to know you better, too, Isaiah. Travel safely."

On the bus, staring out the window, Moses contemplated the last few days with Isaiah . He realized he did not know much about the many IDP camps in the north of Uganda. What had Isaiah's mother endured? What had happened to the sister that died before Awach? How badly was his other sister burned in the hut fire? Where did his father go? He'd always considered the Ugandans who'd been in the camps to have had an easy time during the war. Especially compared to Dan and him, and, he could finally admit, his own mother. Talking to Isaiah had helped Moses see how much they had in common. Isaiah might not have been exposed to the horror and violence of the bush, but he had also grown up without a father. He'd also lost his home and been abandoned by his mother, for reasons he may never understand, and he'd also lost siblings and friends to horrific tragedies. The difference was that despite all his hardships, Moses had always had Dan, whereas Isaiah had been completely alone. The longer Moses imagined Isaiah's experiences, the more he realized how grateful he was to have grown up with his brother Dan at his side. He would not have traded places with Isaiah. Not for anything.

26

October 2018—Gulu

Agnes had not seen Beatrice in the almost ten months since the wedding. Their phone conversations had become shorter and more stilted, and her calls to Beatrice went unanswered more often than not. Agnes chalked it up to the stress of medical school and, she hoped, the pleasures of being newly married, but underneath, she worried.

Beatrice had slept beside her in the same bed since birth so there was a part in her body that had been shaped to fit around her daughter, and now it was empty. All things felt different, somehow, than when Beatrice had first moved to Kampala for school. Was it she who had changed, or Agnes herself?

Agnes felt excited as she and Grace boarded the bus to Kampala. After lots of back-and-forth about the scheduling, it had been decided: on Independence Day, October 19, Agnes and Grace would have dinner with David and Beatrice at their apartment. Then they'd spend the night at Aiko's house, which had a spare bedroom.

The bus ride, though long, was uneventful.

At the crowded depot, David appeared out of the sea of bodies, his white skin very visible. "Mama-Agnes! Grace! Welcome to Kampala." He hugged them. "I have a taxi waiting for us."

They rode through the busy streets to a neighborhood near Makerere. He told them funny stories about the high school students to whom he was teaching English, and Grace chatted to him about the new missionaries and her own classes at school. David paid the taxi driver, then unlocked the front door of their apartment building and led them up three flights of stairs.

Inside their apartment, Agnes was surprised by how *American* it all looked. There was a sofa and a television in the living area, with photographs of David and Beatrice at their wedding hung on the wall. A small, round wooden table anchored four wooden chairs, and the small kitchen had an oven/stovetop and a sink. Cooking smells wafted from the kitchen: fish stew, Agnes thought, and perhaps . . . cookies?

David stepped into the kitchen and began stirring something in a pot. Agnes and Grace exchanged glances, smiling. How wonderful it was to see a man cooking.

"Where's Beatrice?" Grace asked brightly.

David stirred a moment longer before looking up. "She is finishing up studying at the library," he said. "She'll be home soon."

Agnes and Grace had traveled more than eight hours by bus, and Beatrice couldn't be bothered to come home to greet them?

Before Agnes could respond to this hurtful news, David said, "Come, would you like to see our wedding album?"

He got Agnes and Grace settled on the sofa and handed them a large, heavy book with hard covers. On the front was a huge picture of David and Beatrice in their wedding finery, gazing into each other's eyes. The words *Our Wedding* were blazoned along the bottom in white looping script. Grace cradled the huge book in her lap and turned the pages slowly.

All the photos showed David and Beatrice, with hardly any shots of their families or friends. Agnes began to feel uncomfortable. For such a long time, she had defined herself as a mother. The only thing that had mattered in the world was survival: her own survival, and her daughters'. She had agonized over how to keep them all safe, well-fed, and learning the right things so they could have good lives and be useful to the Lord.

Beatrice had wanted to be a doctor since she was perhaps eight or nine, coming home one day from school and announcing her intention to go to medical school. She had not wavered in her ambition since then. Agnes was proud of her. But now the pride was marbled with something else. Judgment, perhaps. For although she was fond of David, and although she remained steadfast to her own pronouncement that David needed a loving family, she still wondered whether this hasty marriage, at such a young age, was in her daughter's best interests.

Still, they were here now. Beatrice and David had been married before the Lord, and Agnes would have to trust that God knew what He was doing.

David's phone rang, and he went to the kitchen to pick it up. "Hi Bea," he said brightly. Then Agnes saw his face fall. "What do you mean?" he asked. He sounded angry. Agnes and Grace exchanged another look. Agnes had never heard David speak that way before, to anyone.

David went into the bedroom and closed the door. They could hear the anger in his tone, as he said, "Your mother and your sister have traveled all this way to see *you!*"

Agnes's heart sank. Did this mean that Beatrice was not coming home? And was David about to morph into his father before their very eyes? The tension was thick as she and Grace sat together in silence.

"Bea, I don't care how much you need to study. You're being selfish." David's voice was clear even through the closed door. "Think of how disappointed they'll be."

Another long moment passed, and David opened the door to the bedroom. There were bright red spots on his cheeks and his hair was standing up, as if he'd been raking through it. "Mama-Agnes, Grace," he said, his voice tight. "I am so very sorry. Beatrice says that she is . . . 'stuck' at the library studying, and will not be home for dinner."

Agnes felt as though someone had punched her in the stomach. Her own daughter would not see her. After she and Grace had traveled all this way. *What had she done wrong? Why,* she wondered, *was Beatrice angry at her?*

Grace looked like she might cry. Agnes put an arm around her. David was still breathing hard. "I do not understand why Beatrice is behaving this way," he said, "and I told her so."

He strode into the kitchen and began to bring bowls of food out and set them on the table.

Agnes took some deep breaths and tried to come back into her body. The sting of Beatrice's rejection was raw.

"I am terribly sorry," David said. "I would understand if you'd like to go to Aiko's house. But if you'd like to stay for dinner," he looked back at Agnes shyly, "I would love your company."

Agnes considered at that moment that David might be lonely. He was living in a foreign country, and he no longer had the built-in and enforced community of a Mormon mission. His companion was now Beatrice, and she was out going to class and studying at all hours of the day.

With a deep breath, Agnes straightened her spine. "Of course, we will stay for dinner, David. You are part of our family, and we are so grateful to you for welcoming us into your home."

They sat around the table, as David served fish stew with vegetables. Agnes praised his cooking and asked questions about his new job. She squeezed Grace's hand under the table where he couldn't see, and conducted herself like the loving mother she tried so hard to be.

But underneath it all, the pain of her daughter's absence burned.

27

"I don't know where I went so wrong, Aiko," Agnes wailed. "What have I done to make her disrespect me so?" Agnes was sitting on Aiko's couch with a cup of tea, her overnight bag stowed in the guest bedroom. Grace was down the hall hanging out with Adela.

Aiko was silent for a long time. Agnes took deep breaths, did her mindfulness exercises, and drank her tea. Being with her friend was soothing.

"I do not think you have done anything wrong, Agnes," Aiko finally said. "But I do have an idea of what might be going on with Beatrice. Would you like to hear it?"

"Yes," she said emphatically.

"You have told me of the trauma you experienced in the bush," Aiko said. "And I suspect that Beatrice has trauma from the bush, as well."

Agnes furrowed her brow. "Beatrice was so young," she said. "She has very few memories of that time. She was not stolen from her home or raped as a young girl."

"She was six when you escaped. Is that right?"

"Six, almost seven," Agnes said, nodding again, grateful for the warm mug of tea in her hands. She was safe here with Aiko.

"Six year olds remember more than you think. And even if she doesn't have conscious memories, her body will remember being unsafe. There is interesting research now showing that children's nervous systems wire in safety or danger from infancy."

Agnes felt her eyes widening. Carefully, she set her tea down on the low table in front of the couch. "Are you telling me that after everything I did to keep my daughters safe in the bush, that because I gave birth to them as a young, frightened girl, that *they* have trauma?" She felt suddenly desperate, like an animal trying to claw its way out of a cage.

"It's okay, Agnes." Aiko moved to sit next to her on the couch. "You are safe." They sat like that for some minutes, and then Aiko continued. "None of what happened to your daughters is your fault. You kept them as safe as they could. And yes, of course they have trauma. Grace, too. And in Beatrice's case, I wonder if she has suppressed the trauma for so long that now it is bubbling up, and she's directing that as anger toward you."

Agnes felt her throat thicken, thinking of her loyal, brave Beatrice being angry at her. "I did the best I could," she whispered. "I tried to be the best mother I could."

Aiko continued rubbing her back. "Of course you did."
They sat like that for a long time.

••••••

In the morning when Agnes came into the kitchen, Grace was chatting with Aiko.

"I had that assault by Mr. Carson when I was 13," Grace was saying. "I think that was traumatic. He didn't rape me, but he tried. Do you think that was trauma? I have not enjoyed literature since, Aiko. I wish I loved it like I used to. Is that because I don't talk about what happened to me?"

Agnes was surprised Grace was talking about this, as she hadn't heard her mention Carson in a long time.

"It could be," Aiko said to Grace. "Sometimes when we are trying to get over a bad thing that happened to us, it is good to just face it—walk right into it and find out that it can't hurt us anymore."

Grace nodded. "Good morning, Mama," she said. "Adela and I are going to walk to Acacia Mall and see some of Adela's friends from school."

"Be safe," Agnes said, taking a seat at the kitchen table, across from Aiko.

"There is something I wanted to ask you, Agnes," Aiko said. "But I wonder if you feel strong enough this morning. I do not want to upset you."

Agnes's stomach clenched a little. "Is it more about Beatrice?"

"No. It is about a project I am undertaking, which I would like your support on."

Agnes sat a little straighter, flattered that Aiko would consider her support valuable. "Of course. What is it?"

"You know that my life is dedicated to treating women who have been victims of physical violence, and you know I prefer to serve in places where little to no medical help is available. I've told you that in Utah I oversaw a hospital unit that treated girls who became pregnant so young that their bodies were not ready to deliver a baby, and girls and women who had been victims of violent rape and who suffered from badly damaged organs and genitals as a result. The more I did this work, the more I wanted to train others to do it, and to branch out to where it is most needed. Sadly, the places that need this service most are in Uganda and the DRC."

Agnes sighed. "It doesn't surprise me, but that is certainly not a distinction I wish for Uganda."

Aiko nodded. "This is why I came here. Bjorn can always find work, but I knew it would be hard to find a place where there was respect for doctors and nurses who did gynecological surgeries and then helped women see themselves as whole again and ready to return to their lives. I got a teaching job at Makerere and set up a specialized training clinic. I was able to get in touch with the famous Dr. Denis Mukwege in the South Kivu part of the DRC, in a place called Bukavu. He is a gynecological surgeon, and his work is well-known."

"Yes, yes," Agnes nodded. "Bukavu is far from Gulu, but I have heard of him."

"I have been studying this problem and discerning where I can best help. In the DRC, the war zones are very spread out. While Dr. Mukwege's hospital serves many women, there is still a greater need than they can meet. I have decided to build a smaller clinic, far north of his Panzi Hospital. I visited Dr. Mukwege, and have been working with him for two years, and he has advised me on how to proceed. I'm ready to build a clinic that performs these surgeries while also training more doctors in these procedures."

"God is with you, Aiko," Agnes whispered. Chills claimed her body, as she imagined the difference Aiko could make in so many lives. "I have heard about women who go there, and they could not afford the surgeries. But they got them for free."

"Yes, Agnes." Aiko smiled. "I intend to make surgeries free in the clinic I build." With that, she pulled a fat folder out of a drawer and showed Agnes some drawings of a simple plastered brick building with a wide veranda marked Waiting Area. "This," said Aiko, "is the clinic I intend to build next year in a place called Dungu. It is a small city 25 hours north of Bukavu, just west of the Garamba Forest."

Agnes's entire body stiffened. *Aba Camp is about 100 miles from a small city called Dungu.* Peter's voice at the Inn, from all those months ago, came back to her now. She could smell the dust and the musty paper map on which, together, they had traced her long journey home from the bush to Gulu. "Why are you telling me this?" she asked. She could feel the red dirt beneath her feet, the weight of Grace on her back, Beatrice's small hand in hers.

"Because, Agnes, I hope you might accompany me. To Dungu."

Agnes took deep breaths. "Why would you want me there?" she whispered.

"As a survivor of the type of trauma the clinic would treat, you would serve as an advisor, a consultant . . . you know, as someone who understands the challenges. And since some people west of the Garamba Forest speak only Acholi, you would translate." Aiko put her hand over Agnes's hand on the table. She waited.

I can't go back I can't go back I can't go back. Agnes's body began trembling. *Agnes had put Grace and then Beatrice to sleep in their tiny hut in Aba Camp. She was eating an extra portion of rice in the dark when she'd overheard two soldiers talking outside.* "Kony intends to lead us through Garamba, all the way to the Central African Republic."

That was the moment, Agnes suddenly realized. She had never pinpointed it before. But that was the exact moment, when she'd overheard the soldier say that Kony intended to take them all the way to CAR, that she'd decided to escape.

Garamba represented, for her, the point of no return.

And Aiko was asking her to return to it.

Aiko patted her hand. "Take your time, my friend. You can absolutely tell me no."

Agnes knew she had a choice, and having a choice felt good.

・・・・・・

In the van David had hired for their long ride home to Gulu, Grace slept most of the time. But Agnes was very much awake, thinking about that mass of land located in the northeast region of the DRC, near the borders of Uganda and South Sudan, and spreading into the Chinko Nature Reserve in eastern CAR. Working at the Inn, Agnes had trained herself to answer questions from tourists traveling there, often to meet with officials from other countries who were trying to protect the area environmentally. She had seen guidebooks describe Garamba Forest as a "breathtakingly wondrous land," home to "many rare mammals and birds," and a well-preserved place of almost "unrivaled solitude." A recognized UNESCO World Heritage Site, it was known now as ground zero in the elephant poaching wars, having once been home to 22,000 elephants, with fewer than 2,000 remaining.

But for Agnes, this place meant something very different. This was a place of danger for all the abducted boys and girls—like herself—who had been forced to trample along innumerable trails in a vast habitat with no way out.

When the van driver stopped for gas and a snack, Agnes reminded herself that even if Kony was still alive, he was far, far away now. She crossed her wrists tight in front of her chest and held herself. But she could not erase from her mind a recent speculation that if Kony did ever return, he would use the road that runs from Faradje, through Garamba to Dungu.

Sleepy Grace got out of the van and leaned on Agnes, who hugged her shoulders and smiled. "Have we crossed the Nile yet?" Grace asked.

"No, but it's near," Agnes said. "You can smell it in the air when we get closer. I love how fresh it feels."

When they climbed back in the van, Agnes told the driver that they would roll down the windows when they came to the bridge, as it was such an invigorating part of the trip on Gulu Road. He said he always did the same and was happy to slow down, letting the sound of the crashing waterfalls soothe them all. "It reminds me of God," he said. Agnes admitted that was true for her too.

●●●●●●

Grace went right back to sleep when they got home to Gulu, so Agnes took her phone outside into the night and called Aiko. She closed her eyes as the phone rang. She could not imagine subjecting herself to a voluntary visit to Dungu. Almost more than any other spot, the deep, dark, hot, dense forest held so much fear for her. No matter how much she loved Aiko, she could not go with her to open this clinic. She could not go back to the point of no return. Aiko would understand, this was not a good idea.

But when Aiko answered the phone, Agnes's words did not match her thoughts. Instead, she said, clearly, "Aiko, I have made my decision. I need to go exactly there. When do you plan to go to Dungu?"

Aiko said the trip was planned for January.

28

October 2018—Kampala

David and Beatrice never fought. They said over and over to one another how compatible they were, despite their vastly different backgrounds. They had spent the year before their marriage talking by phone across a great distance, sharing every feeling and impulse that came up in each of them, and they had come to know one another deeply. They were meant to be together. Their marriage in the temple had stamped their union for all eternity, with the promise that their lives would be ever entwined in perfect harmony.

Yet, David had expressed discomfort with the way Beatrice imposed the Gulu wedding party on her family. He was concerned she had been insensitive to them, especially Moses. David also thought Beatrice had been excessive in her criticism of Agnes at the Utah wedding, particularly when she spoke angrily about her mother giving a talk about abuse. But on the night after Mama-

Agnes and Grace had left without seeing Beatrice at all, he and Agnes had their first *real* argument.

"Honestly, Bea," he said, when she arrived home from the library at nearly midnight. "I don't care how much it drives you crazy that your mother is praised for being a hero of the LRA war. The fact is, she was astonishingly brave and strong to have dragged you and your sister out of captivity, and you have to be big enough to allow her some space in your life! All of us have to put up with a little bit of what drives us crazy, because we love, and are grateful for, the people who drive us crazy. Your mother came all the way from Gulu just to see you! Because she loves you!"

"Stop right there," Beatrice said. "Stop now. You do not understand." She blew out a breath through her nose, like a bull. "My mother, the great Adong Agnes, not only told me her story every day of my life, but everyone around me told that story too. Every. Single. Day." She clapped her hands on the beat of those three words. "That was all we meant to people. My mother was the amazing survivor of three hideous husbands, the child-mother who escaped from Joseph Kony and his rebel camp, the brave survivor who left the terrible Impenetrable Forest in the DRC, the most dangerous place on earth. She alone carried my little sister on her back and dragged her seven-year-old daughter all the way home to Gulu, to save our lives and to provide us the chance to enjoy a life of privilege, to allow me the chance to become a doctor. Everything I got was because she had sacrificed herself to bestow it on me, with no help from anyone, and certainly, not because I was special in my own right.

I was always just more proof of my mother's greatness. Everything I have become is used as evidence that *she* is astonishing. I'm sorry if it offends your sense of what a good daughter should be, but I am tired of being nothing more than proof of my mother's glory. I'm sick of it!"

David did not back down. He had heard this rant before, and he had grown tired of Bea's dramatic representation of how burdened she had been by her mother's legacy. "No, you stop it, Bea," he said firmly. "You are being unreasonable and narcissistic. This is not only about you and your tender feelings. This is about you making a plan to see your mother and sister and then standing them up! It was rude and disrespectful."

"Well, *something* has to be about me," Beatrice shot back. "Otherwise, I will always simply be an appendage of my mother's, proof that she came back from that war a great person. Not only a *great* person. The *greatest* person."

"You are being extreme," David replied. "You get so undone over anything that has to do with your mother, and you exaggerate! She does not expect you to be forever attached to her and her story. She wants you to be happy. She wants it as much as you do. She wants you to be independent and accomplish things on your own. She believes in you. She's interested in our life here, and how you are doing at school, and I don't think it's not too much to give her just a little credit for devoting her life to you and your sister."

"You have no idea," Beatrice's eyes narrowed as she accused him. "No idea what it is like to be her daughter. You talk about her devoting her life to me? Well, I've devoted my life to *her*. I have taken care of her my whole life."

"Bea, be reasonable."

"When we escaped from Kony, I was the one who ran along beside her at a speed impossible for a little girl, for fear of being killed if I couldn't keep up with her. When she got lost over and over again, it was me who pushed her on. And when she collapsed, and gave out . . . Have you any idea what that felt like for me? I was seven years old!"

Tears welled in Beatrice's eyes, but she fought them.

"We were there, beside some road, in a place I'd never been, trying to keep my baby sister alive, and my mother was unconscious. Can you imagine how that felt? I remember that! I remember it like it was yesterday. Me beside my mother on some dusty red road all alone, knowing there were strange soldiers nearby. Men who were ready to kill us."

"I didn't know—" David began.

"No, you didn't know, since I've never told you. Or anybody else, for that matter. I have never wanted to be that girl. So fixated on my experience of war that everybody would feel sorry for me, or admire me and think I was some kind of superhero."

She wiped her cheeks and continued, as if she couldn't hold the words back now even if she'd wanted to.

"I don't remember the camp. I barely remember the forest. I've tried—but I have no clue what happened to me there—but I do remember the escape that Mama talks too much about. I was there, and it was *horrible*! I remember an old woman who fed us when we were too hungry and too exhausted to go further. She was scary looking with wild hair, and I thought she was going to kill us, but she didn't. She turned into an *angel*. She had a basket of corn meal in a hut behind the one where she slept. The meal was old, but it was still good. She put some in a pot, and she had water. It was *pure water*, and clean. She made a fire and cooked the *posho* for us. It was the most delicious meal I had ever tasted. We ate a lot, and she was kind and allowed us to sleep there after eating. We felt safe with her and, for the first time in ages, we slept for the whole night."

David reached for her hand, but she pulled away.

"In the morning my mother said we had to run again. I wanted to stay with the old woman and felt so angry that my mother made us leave. If we had stayed, David, we could have saved her. But, *no,* my mother took us away and we ran again. My stomach soon hurt because of all the food I'd eaten and I began to cry. My mother yelled at me and *threatened to beat me*. She said she knew where we were going, but then she *got us lost again*. We walked and ran all day, until we came across the soldiers. They were in a truck, passing by on the main road. My mother said they were *good soldiers*, and they would *save us*. She made us run after their truck, but it was going too fast, back to where we had already been. I told her that, but *she wouldn't listen to me*. We lost them but we still ran. All day and night, we ran. We kept going until dawn until we smelled smoke. We followed the smoke and Mama said the old woman was cooking for the soldiers and we could eat again. We were near where she lived and wanted more food. I wanted to throw myself into the woman's arms and stay with her there where we were safe and fed. But when we finally got back to the old woman's hut, where we'd woken up the day before, we found her, dead. *She was covered in blood.* The soldiers my mother was so certain would save us had raped her, and left her naked from the waist down. I remember all the blood."

"Bea, I'm so sorry," David said, threatening tears of his own now.

"My mother started screaming. That dear old woman who'd fed us had been brutally attacked and killed, and her house was *burning*. All that remained were black sticks and straw. They'd even burned the hut where the posho had been. She had blood on her face, too, and her legs and all over. They had cut her neck and there was blood on the ground. My mother had promised they were safe. She'd told me the soldiers were *our friends*. She'd said they were good soldiers, but *she lied*, David. She lied!"

David shook his head, listening.

"Mama tried to find some corn meal to take with us. It was burnt, but she took some anyway, and we ran the other way. Grace was crying, but we ran and ran back to where we had come from. We went all day and didn't eat, and my mother screamed and *screamed*. Then she fell down beside a big road, and took Grace off her back, and she went to sleep. I tried to wake her, but she wouldn't get up. *She just slept and left me alone.* Grace started to wander off and it was *me* who kept her safe. All day my mother just slept. She would not wake up. She refused. *She left me.* She left Grace. *She pretended to die.* She just gave up, David! Do you hear me?"

Beatrice now stood in the middle of their little living room with her fists clenched beside her hips, determined that her husband see things the way she remembered them. He had to understand why she could not continue to center her mother's suffering in her own life. To understand that Agnes's heroism was not the whole story. "Do you hear me, David?"

He nodded.

"My mother pretended to die! She left me with my sister, in a place where I had never been. *I was alone,* and Grace cried and cried." Beatrice closed her eyes and swayed back and forth in the middle of the room, her hands still squeezed in fists with her knuckles turning white.

David put his arms around her, and held her to his body.

Finally, Beatrice began to relax and she sobbed against his shoulder. "We were there all night. The next day more soldiers came to kill us. My mother did not protect us. *She was not a hero!*"

David stepped back and let his hands slide down Beatrice's arms. He held her steady at arm's length, letting his calm presence reassure his wife.

"What happened then, Bea?" He prompted her gently, as if he understood she needed to get this story out of herself, once and for all. "What did the soldiers do to you?"

The tension softened from Beatrice's shoulders. "They were different soldiers than the ones we'd seen before. They had a bigger truck. But I was still certain we were about to die, the same way the old woman had. My mother did nothing, as these big men came for us. They had guns and wore uniforms. They said they were taking us somewhere safe, but I didn't believe them. I was terrified. They forced me and Grace into the back of a big truck, and put our mother beside us on the floor. They did not speak our language."

"And then what?" David asked quietly.

"They thought my mother was dead, but they took her too. Even in the truck, she still would not wake up. She wouldn't even tell them where to take us. She never told them where Gulu was. She just laid there in the truck. Not speaking, not taking care of Grace. It was *me* who did. I saved her. I saved Grace. My mother was useless. Do you hear me, David Murdock?"

She screamed his name, pulled out of his arms, and sobbed. She did not know how to make him understand how painful these memories were for her, how much their survival had depended on *her*, not just her mother. In her frustration and anguish, Beatrice lifted her fists up to her husband and beat on his chest.

"Bea." David's voice was soft. "Beatrice," he said. "I love you. You are safe now. I will always take care of you."

━━━━━━

With David's arms around her, Beatrice was calm. It was cool in the room, and he covered her with a blanket. They were together and alone and Beatrice began to drift off to sleep, safe in David's embrace. She slept deeply and when she did occasionally surface, he would still be there. She felt so tired she didn't care what day it was. She set no alarm. She just slept. When she felt him move and try to get up, she tightened her hold on him and clung on to him.

At some point she allowed him to unwrap himself and leave the bed. Through a haze of exhaustion Beatrice tracked her beloved David through the house, dimly aware of him in the bathroom. Pouring water into a glass. Speaking quietly into his phone, canceling appointments he had for the day and the next day, too. The familiar flick of the light switches and the firm click of the lock on the front door. His soft tread through the apartment and back to the bedroom. The drop of his clothes onto the floor and the movement of the mattress as he lay beside her again. The even rhythm of his breathing as he joined her in sleep. When she awoke in the dark, she touched his face, tenderly and carefully, before moving closer and going to sleep again.

What felt like days later, Beatrice lay quietly for a long time and sensed David emerge from his slumber alongside her.

"Bea?" David's voice was thick with sleep, but he pulled himself up on the pillow beside her. "I am glad you know I will never leave you. I will always be here. I am glad you know that, Bea."

"I am glad you call me Bea," she said. "Only you get to call me that. It is your name for me. Stay here."

"I won't leave," he said.

For a long time, they sat together in the darkness, until David asked, "Do you want to tell me more?"

Beatrice's voice still carried the emotion from the night before. "I will not become my mother. I refuse."

"That's fine, Bea. You are your own person."

"David, she is not the only one in Gulu who suffered in the war. Everyone did. Do you get it? Everyone did. Remember when Moses told you that? Everyone, he said. All of Gulu was at war. All the women in our compound suffered. All the people at church. In the North the war was everywhere. But others don't need to talk about it all the time. They hold their suffering inside of them and go on. Only my mother tells people. She has to tell our bishop. She has to tell Molly and Sunday. She has to tell others," Beatrice's voice grew stronger as she continued. "She wails and cries and screams in the night. I have to calm her and get her to go see Okot James. I call him and ask him to come help her. You don't know what she is like, David, when she has to talk about it. She tells us awful details. She tells us about her husbands and what they did to her. She says how terrible men are. She only knew bad men in the bush, and she remembers all of them. I hated those stories from the time I was so young when we still lived in our hut. I hated it when she went on and on in the night. She wouldn't listen when we begged her to stop. We hated it."

"I'm so sorry, Bea," David said. It was getting light, and he asked her if she wanted juice or toast.

Beatrice listened to him moving through the kitchen, opening and closing cupboards and the fridge. He brought her a fried egg on toast, orange juice, and hot sweet tea with milk, then sat next to her on the bed and reminded her of her classes.

"I'm not going," she said. "I'm staying home today." She sipped her juice ever so slowly and started again. "David, here in Kampala is the only place where she never tells her story. She is Acholi, and people here aren't interested in her suffering. Down here they are sick of hearing about the Acholi's war. She knows it. That's why we have to stay here. I'm safe here."

Beatrice sat up straighter and pulled the blanket closer to her chin, gripped in tight fists.

David sat beside her and covered himself, lying close to her. She felt his eyes on her and settled into her safe place. Together with David in their own apartment.

"Do you know how angry I was when she came to Utah?" Beatrice asked. "When she brought her story there, of all places." Beatrice's body grew tense once more and another sob rose in her throat. "There was my Acholi mother. In Utah. In a place where no one had to know, but she always has to be that suffering mother, the poor traumatized survivor that everyone admires."

David listened and loved her.

"And then, the day after our wedding day, she was off to some church, expecting your mother and everyone to go there and hear her tell her story again? Who does that? David? Who? Only my mother. She came to Utah for *our wedding*, and she turned it into *another place to tell her story*. Everyone there now knows about Gulu, but they believe that of all the people in Gulu, Adong Agnes suffered the most. They don't know that every woman was raped. They think only she had to fear for her life every day. They think only she had to watch her friends die in childbirth after being beaten. Childbirth, David. I have heard about the birth of my brothers a hundred times, and how my mama suffered. There was another one, you know. He died. She suffered three times with those boys. Twice with me and Grace. All women have pain in childbirth, but to my mother, only she had pain.

Do you know that I feared for my life and hers and my sister's? Do you know I just waited to be shot or raped or run over by a truck?"

Beatrice could not stop. No, she didn't want her phone. No, she didn't care what was going on in her class today. No, she didn't care who she had promised to share her notes with.

"Text them back, David, and say tomorrow." Then it was "No, No, No! Everything is no, today."

David brought her more tea with milk. He made it special. It was called African tea. It was about Africa. No, not only Acholi. She did not want things that were only Acholi. She didn't want to use her name, Aber. "I am Beatrice Murdock." David's name, she explained, was a better name for her because it disclosed nothing of her origins in Gulu.

David had some work calls in the afternoon, but he canceled everything, saying his wife was ill. He made some soup. It was a gray day outside, but it did not rain. Everything inside their bubble seemed to move in slow motion. At just past 4 p.m., Beatrice talked about the old woman again. The one who had been raped and had her throat cut by the soldiers. She revisited the horrifying details of the attack as if only by describing them could she finally purge them from her mind.

"Her legs were splayed apart, and there was blood on each leg and on her dead body." Beatrice could picture it in her mind as if she was back there again. She had never told anyone. To be her only lover and friend, her husband had to know her secrets. Here they were. *It was time.* And now he would know not to try to force her mother on her when Beatrice felt safe in Kampala, away from her.

"When I first came to medical school, David," Beatrice began. "I told a few people, including my professors, that I was from Gulu. The first thing anyone asked me was always about the war. As if that was the only interesting thing about me. After that I began to say I was from the North. I did not want to be asked my story. I never wanted to tell it! And I won't, David. All you have heard from me today is a secret that only we share. Promise me you won't tell anyone. Promise?"

"Of course, my love," David said. "You and all your secrets are safe with me."

David thought Bea might drop off to sleep again after such an emotionally exhausting release, but her hands had not let go of the blanket under her chin and her eyes continued to flash as though behind them she was reenacting scenes of her tortured life. With her eyes wild and distant, he decided not to interrupt what appeared to be harrowing moments that absorbed her full attention. For hours, he watched for a signal that her focus had shifted back to the present moment. Only then did he offer a soft intrusion. "Bea, would you like to change out of your nightgown, Sweetheart? Wash your beautiful face and freshen up?"

Bea almost smiled at him, and for the first time since the night before, she appeared to have returned from being "away." She nodded, then dragged herself out of bed and shut herself in the bathroom. She took a while, which David intuited was a good thing, but he somehow knew there was more to come.

When Bea finally emerged, she was naked. "I want to make love," she said. "Now."

Walking almost defiantly to their bed, she instructed David to undress and join her.

David removed his clothes, as directed.

"You know, David, the only battle I've ever won with my mom is with sex," Bea explained. "She hated anything to do with sex, so she wanted me to feel that way too. She told Grace and me every night, year after year, how terrible and awful sex was. She told us every detail about Samson's body, how his penis looked and how he'd stabbed her with it and made her faint from the pain. She told us where he had hair and where he didn't and how he smelled after sex. We heard about George, too, and even Peter Okello, but Samson's ghost inhabited our hut and then our house. A constant reminder that sex was awful. Something we should never do."

David listened, climbing under the covers as Bea joined him there and continued her story. "It bothered her when Dan and Dora made lots of noise when they made love. Grace and I were curious, but not Mama-Agnes. She loved them, but she was relieved when they moved farther away so we didn't have to listen to the sounds of passion anymore. She was probably glad Moses was laid up for such a long time too, so he and Mercy could not have sex."

She rolled her fingers along David's arm and softened her voice. "When we told her we wanted to marry, I truly believe the thing that bothered her most was that we would eventually have sex. She couldn't bear the idea of me undressing you, seeing you naked, and, God forbid, wanting you. One of the great pleasures during my first term here at Makerere was that I got to talk to you on the phone, night after night, about making love to you. We talked for hours about what we were going to do with and for each other. Remember?"

David smiled. "I remember."

"And for the first few months, I'd imagine we would do those things and make my mother watch us. I know, I know . . . but a part of me wanted to punish her for all she'd told us. For making me fear sex. I wanted to make her scream in pain from watching me fuck!"

She kissed David's neck, and he released a moan of pleasure.

But Bea still wasn't through. "David. Please understand. It's not about punishing her anymore. I want you to know this. For the first few months it was . . . it was all about revenge. But after a while I started loving the idea and could imagine us just making each other happy in bed. I had to learn to banish my mama from our bedroom! To release all that shame she had shackled me with."

He pulled her body closer to his, the two of them tangled together as one now.

"Now when we have sex—when we get such wonderful pleasure from love-making over and over—it's as though I have won at least one battle against her. It's the one place in my life where I've shrunk her to a proper size for a mother. Having sex all the time reminds me that I can be my own self—at least in this way. Now . . . come do what you do so well to me."

And for the whole night and morning of the third day, she could not get enough.

29

November 2018—Gulu

Grace knew there was something wrong the moment her mother answered the phone.

"It can't be," her mother whispered.

"What?" Grace said, nearing the phone. "What is it?"

Agnes shook her head, then put her mobile on speaker phone. "Grace is here with me, Isaiah. Tell us everything."

"Bad news, Grace," Isaiah said. "Peggy has uterine cancer."

Grace felt her chest squeeze. She wished that Beatrice was here, the one with the most medical knowledge in the family. She would know what questions to ask, how serious things were.

But Beatrice was in Kampala. Distant in more ways than one. She and Mama-Agnes were colder than ever toward each other, ever since the wedding and then the night when Beatrice had not come home from the library to see them.

"Her doctor has outlined a regimen," Isaiah was saying. "She's already had one surgery. But it didn't remove enough of the tumor. It . . . it is very serious." His voice broke, and Grace and Agnes looked at each other, their eyes wide and sad.

Peggy got on the phone. "Sorry to be a downer," she said, trying to keep a lighthearted note to her voice. "I wanted you to know, of course, and I needed to hear your voices and know you are praying."

After the call ended, a heavy silence fell on the house. Yellow light filtered in from the trees in the compound, and Mama-Agnes looked defeated.

Then, Grace felt herself stand a little taller. "Mama," she said. "I've thought of a way I can help. I'd can go to Seattle to care for Winnie and Aggie. I can help with the cooking too," she said, getting inspired as the idea took shape, "I could even take a college class."

Her mother fell into a chair outside the open door and rubbed a finger along her forehead. "Go to America?"

Grace nodded. "I know you don't like it when I speak of this, but Aiko and I—well, she thinks I should study literature. She knows about getting visas for students. And now might be as good a time as any to apply to university in the States. I could be a good auntie, and a student, in Seattle." She paused, waiting for a reaction. And when she got none, Grace continued. "Isaiah has done so much for our family. He *is* family. I want to help. This is my chance."

Grace watched her mother closely. She'd known how hard it had been to watch her girls grow up in an unpredictable world, one where dangerous men like Mr. Carson and Martin Mortenson lurked, and accidents happened at every turn. But no amount of control could have stopped Peggy from getting cancer. Sometimes, life was just that.

"You don't have to protect me any longer, Mama," Grace said with affection, taking her mother's shaking hand. "I can take care of myself. And I can take care of others, too."

At this, her mother stood and threw her arms around Grace. The surprising gesture almost knocked Grace over.

"Mama?"

"Just be careful, my baby. I feel I've lost your sister." She shuddered. "I can't lose you too."

━━━━━━

The logistics for Grace to go to Seattle quickly fell into place. Isaiah and Peggy were overjoyed and grateful that Grace would come to stay with them for a year. Everyone at their church was proud of Grace and gave her small gifts for Isaiah's family. Aiko helped Grace arrange her student visa in collaboration with Peggy's sister-in-law, Rita, who was an aggressive feminist lawyer. She prided herself in taking on women's cases and causes, and she was altogether delighted to help our her husband's sister by getting their Ugandan nanny into a local university.

Rita had all kinds of connections and helped Grace send in her paperwork to the University of Washington.

She only had to do a little string-pulling to get past the requirement of a transcript from Grace's very sloppy school administration, but she did it with enthusiasm and in the process invested herself in the opportunity this would offer Grace. She had heard of her from Isaiah, who had been hired right out of Brigham Young University–Idaho as a computer programmer, in her husband Eric's successful company, and had been impressed with his skill. Plus, while Eric and Riata weren't religious, they had become close as couples, and they were enormously fond of Isaiah.

Agnes was grateful that she had raised such a kind and responsible daughter.

But November was coming to an end, and as Grace's departure drew nearer, Agnes found the clarity and resolve she had enjoyed about going to Dungu unraveling. Small responsibilities felt overwhelming. She would start a small task and it would end in frustration, and some nights were as bad as they had been a decade earlier, with bad dreams waking her in the night.

Agnes was especially haunted by the many babies she'd seen killed in the bush. A rebel soldier grabbed one infant boy from his mother's clutches and smashed his head against a tree. When the baby howled, the soldier smashed him even harder against the same tree and silenced him forever. But in the new nightmares, Agnes was the wailing mother, crumpled on her knees until the soldier kicked her into a standing position and threatened to smash her head, too. That sound. The baby's scream. And then the blood on the ground around him as he lay silenced in the brush. It would never leave her.

How could she have said yes to Aiko's invitation to help her set up a clinic in Dungu? Could she have avoided all this by simply saying no?

And then there was Beatrice. Agnes hadn't heard a word from her older daughter since the ignored visit. She told herself to enjoy knowing her daughter was happily married and safe, and to relish watching her sons grow into their adult lives. But she worried more about her evasive daughter than she did about heading into the Impenetrable Forest.

●●●●●●

On a Sunday in late November, a few weeks before Grace was due to leave for America, Aiko drove up to Gulu to talk to Agnes about the trip to Dungu. She arrived midday, and the first thing she reminded Agnes was that the place they were going was safer than other parts of the DRC. "Some foreign NGOs are concentrated in Dungu for other purposes, and, as a result of an earlier Ebola threat, they will have their own medical personnel there. Increased foreign presence usually discourages activity by armed rebel groups, including any reconstructed LRA. Since conflict has been constant in the eastern DRC, there is no way to guarantee safety. But then, that is why doctors are needed there. We'll stay in a place that offers the safest possible conditions. And we'll keep the trip short, just a few days."

Agnes nodded, determined to overcome her fears and help her friend.

"You have told me your story, Agnes," Aiko said. "And I want to repay you for that trust you showed me, by telling you mine." She blew out a breath. "It starts with my grandmother. Do you know much about the Americans and Japanese fighting in World War II?"

Agnes shook her head. "I only know the part of World War II when Britain sent Ugandans to fight for Europe in India."

"Japan and the US were enemies in that war. It was a bloody, long, mean war," said Aiko. "The US dropped the two biggest bombs ever on Japan, and Japan lost the war. Then lots of American soldiers went to Japan for the Occupation, to make sure that Japanese people stayed beaten down. And as often happens, soldiers found girls and got them pregnant. Many Japanese girls were raped, and many died in childbirth."

Agnes's stomach tightened. How many girls have suffered such brutalities, all around the world?

"Some American soldiers brought their Japanese women home. My grandmother was one of these war brides. Since most Americans still regarded any Japanese person as 'the enemy,' she was shunned."

Agnes tried to imagine being forced to go to another country with Peter after the war, a country where she knew no one and didn't speak the language.

"My grandmother was named Kiyoko. And her husband was from Hawaii, so he took her there. It wasn't a state, yet, but it was a territory of the US," Aiko continued in a rush, as if she had stored up this story for a long time, waiting for a chance to tell it. "Kiyoko's husband,

Randall, made lots of money. But he was a terrible abuser. This man beat Kiyoko every day and night. He broke her bones and almost blinded her."

Agnes shuddered. He sounded like her first husband, Samson.

"When they had a son, called Ricky, Kiyoko hoped her husband would find joy, but he didn't. War does terrible things to many people's minds," said Aiko. "Like here in Gulu, some there were called 'war-crazy.' And Randall turned his war-craziness on Kiyoko and their son."

Agnes had never seen Aiko so upset before. Such a strong little woman with so much confidence in life, and yet she wept as she told this story. Agnes listened with a compassionate ear, honored that such a well-educated person would share such a personal story. Now she knew why Aiko needed her to travel with her. She needed Agnes because the work was as important to her as it was to Aiko. Because they both wanted to convert generations of women's pain into something positive.

"Kiyoko finally got away and married a widowed Japanese pharmacist. They had two daughters and moved to Utah, where they became Mormons. My mother was one of those daughters, and Kiyoko told her about her abuse every day. After Grandma Kiyoko died, my mother would say when she did something that was a pleasure, 'I'm doing this for my mother, Kiyoko!' Growing up my mother told me and my sister about our grandmother, too. And when we did good things, she always said, 'You are doing this for Kiyoko, and she would be so happy that she brought you to a better life.' Agnes, there are so many bad things that go on in the world, and so many people who suffer and die, many of them women and girls. And I just decided that I will help as many as I can."

Aiko used the corner of her sleeve to wipe her tears. She took a sip of water from the plastic cup Agnes had given her and said, "My mother carries in her the trauma and deep sadness that her mother experienced, and she says she will carry it to her grave. And in some ways, I believe that my sister and I carry it, too. We carry it in our bones. And this is why I do this work, Agnes. I believe I carry my grandmother's trauma. And I must turn all that hurt into action, to support other women who have been the victims of violence."

30

December 2018—Gulu and Dungu

Moses had offered to drive Grace to the airport in Entebbe, so early in the morning the three of them walked to the Seed Store, where the truck was parked. The sky was a very pale blue and Gulu was quieter than usual. Once there, Agnes hugged Grace very hard and reminded her that Isaiah would pick her up when she arrived.

"Remember to keep your phone charged," Agnes said. "And let me know when you've landed in Brussels and in Chicago and, finally, in Seattle. I will track your plane on the computer at the Inn. Molly showed me how to do that."

She could feel Grace smile a little into her shoulder. "Okay, Mama. I will."

Pastor arrived not long after Moses and Grace drove away. Agnes followed him inside where they talked about Grace's trip, then about Dan's work at the clinic with Dr. Bjorn, and about Pastor's business.

"You know, Agnes," Pastor said thoughtfully. "I wonder if now is a good time."

"A good time for what?" She was trying to stay present in the conversation but felt distracted by all the emotions of the day.

"To get things moving in earnest, on our shelter. We have the land, and I have been gaining the trust of the people who have been squatting on it. I have a feeling now is the time to do this."

Something struck a chord in Agnes's heart. She had been feeling unsettled about the upcoming year without Grace, wondering what would occupy her time when she returned from Dungu. "This shelter has been a dream for so long," Agnes admitted. "It is something fresh to think about. Something new and important."

"So, you have that feeling too?" Pastor smiled. "Like a new day is dawning?

She thought about it. "Perhaps it's because I am going to Dungu. I'm hoping this trip will clear some things out of my head. It is like the shadows know that their time is limited—that the light is coming. Is that what you mean?"

Pastor smiled. "Yes. That is exactly what I mean."

"Speaking of light coming, Pastor, I have something ask you," Agnes said, with more affection than she had ever spoken to him with before. Of course she could speak like this now that she was quite sure her suspicions were true. She'd long assumed Pastor was gay, and she hoped he trusted her enough to confide in her.

"When we were in an airport in America, we met a group of travelers who were going to a wedding too. Like us. Only they were going to the wedding of two of the men. They were going to a gay wedding. It's normal there," she said. "Legal."

Pastor looked shocked.

"When I said I wasn't sure there were as many gay men in Uganda as there were in the USA, they said they were sure there were just as many here as anywhere. They told me to think about all the men I knew who were not married to a woman and didn't seem interested in ever marrying. They said our laws here probably make them afraid to tell anyone. Pastor, I thought of you. And I hope you don't mind me asking, but, Pastor, are you gay?"

Pastor Emanuel's look of shock turned to a warm look of relief. "Agnes, it sounds like we have lots to talk about when you are back from Dungu."

January 2019

It had been a few weeks since Grace's departure, and Agnes talked to her every Sunday. Peggy's treatment was going well. And Grace was about to start two classes at the University of Washington. The third week of January had arrived quickly, and Agnes readied herself for the trip to Dungu.

She packed a small zipper bag with a change of clothes, which in itself felt odd. She'd had nothing to pack when she was with the LRA in the bush. Soldiers had occasionally stolen used American clothes from some village market and distributed them in a camp. Women and children had been allocated dresses or skirts and T-shirts.

Kony made them burn any T-shirts that had sexy pictures on them. Rebels usually got uniforms from somewhere in Sudan, and Kony had insisted they be kept clean, which meant the women were forever washing them. Clothes were another kind of burden.

Carrying even her small bag was a reminder that she was not the young girl she had been when she was forced to walk that terrain while wearing rags.

Aiko soon arrived to pick up Agnes, and they set out when the sun was high. The friendly driver and small SUV were another reminder that it was truly 2019, not 1990 or even 2005. There was air conditioning, should they need it. Aiko gave her a blue neck pillow, and Agnes was so comfortable she actually dozed off.

In only four hours, they arrived in Arua, which had become as modern as Gulu. Aiko and Agnes checked into a small hotel on the Uganda side of the border. This relieved Agnes. She remembered the last time she had crossed the border into the DRC and how she'd feared she might never make her way home. And since they'd heard rumors of recent thefts by bandits inside the forest, Agnes was pleased to avoid it after dark.

At dinner in the hotel's restaurant, they heard about the two refugee settlements near Arua. "I'd like to visit them if we have time," Agnes said. "I think I could learn something about the shelter project Pastor and I are planning near Kitgum. We do not have to stay long."

"Yes," Aiko said. "We can visit Rhino Camp in the morning."

Sharing a room with Aiko, Agnes slept deeply that night. A welcome surprise.

●●●●●●

Rhino Camp was closest to Arua, with Bidi Bidi another thirty miles down the road. At the entrance to Rhino Camp, Aiko showed the men in uniform a card from the hospital proving that she was a doctor. The men waved the car in, and they drove around.

Seeing refugees who had fled for their lives reminded Agnes that she was not one of them. She could see herself in them, and felt great compassion, but she was visiting the camps as an observer. She was no longer in flight.

There were *so many* people. A man they spoke to from the UN said that last January 2018, the Rhino Settlement had registered 123,243 refugees, mostly South Sudanese. This, she learned, was more than three times the number in the Palabek settlement near Kitgum, where Pastor had bought land for "their" shelter. And Bidi Bidi down the road was even larger.

Agnes was impressed by one woman who walked by with a big baby on her back and two more children hanging on to her tattered purple dress. She was a testimony to the fact that, when in danger, most people found ways to survive. Agnes recognized the look of resilience in this woman's eyes. She tipped her head at the woman, hoping she understood that as a gesture of admiration.

Bidi Bidi was huge, but they drove slowly around, and then went on toward the border.

●●●●●●

"It made me laugh, Aiko," Agnes said when they were back on the road. "This morning when the man at the front desk of the Inn asked where we were going. You told him Dungu. Did you see how startled he was?" Agnes laughed, and so did Aiko. "People are surprised by you, my friend. You are a small woman, and they do not expect you to be so bold. When they talk to you, they get humble."

Aiko laid a hand over Agnes's in the backseat. "It happens all the time," she said. "And I feel the same way about you, my friend. You are stronger than you know."

Agnes smiled and looked out the window.

They arrived at Faradje in the DRC well into the afternoon and drove through the forest without any problems. When they stopped to buy a Fanta and cookies, people were chatting and laughing and going about regular life. There were two exquisite hotels in the Forest for those wanting a relaxing tropical place to dine and watch animals come to the pool outside their windows. These tourist attractions countered the dark history of the place, and made it all seem like a dream to Agnes. They reached Dungu by 6 p.m., but they had lost an hour to the time zone change. No one had known about time zones when she had been in Garamba before. Another sign that times were changing, and that the past was in the past.

Several convents in the area had been forced to close because marauding gangs of militia "as bad as Kony's LRA" had terrorized Dungu for years. The soldiers had attacked and brutalized nuns. But in the last five years, a few convents had been rebuilt enough to open as small inns where the surviving nuns now cooked and served simple dishes. So that was where Agnes and Aiko stayed the night.

The first morning in Dungu, Aiko got down to business and showed herself even more remarkable to Agnes's eyes. It was in the way she carried herself, Agnes thought. She became no longer just Agnes's friend, but a renowned doctor and someone accustomed to leading.

Aiko had booked a "conference room" at the convent's inn where she met with different members of her medical team who had gathered there from other places in the DRC. These men and women showed her great respect, as well as gratitude that she was going to make this clinic happen. Agnes, who had purchased a small notebook to record her observations (and also to feel part of the team), was introduced as Aiko's "colleague" and friend, and this made her feel immensely proud.

The main team included five women doctors, all Congolese. All spoke French as their first language, but they used English for Aiko's and Agnes's sake. Three would work at the Dungu clinic when it opened, and the other two were from Dr. Mukwege's Panzi Hospital and were there to advise.

They talked in detail about how many operating rooms they would have and how long particular surgeries would take. Sometimes Agnes felt a little lost, and it must have shown on her face because the doctor next to her would lean over and explain to her in layman's terms what they were talking about. It was difficult for Agnes when they spoke of situations where the patient was found to be too damaged for surgery. Many of the cases she could imagine all too vividly. She remembered girls whom LRA soldiers had gang raped and ravaged and left lying on the ground in front of family members who were helpless to do anything but beg for their own lives. Or old women, like the one who had fed her and her girls when she was making her escape, only to be gang raped by Ugandan army soldiers hours after they had eaten the food she'd prepared for them. As the doctors described the worst-case scenarios, Agnes took notes to keep herself grounded in the present moment.

She learned a lot. And the most important thing, she reflected, was this idea of a *team*. The women doctors each knew a lot, and as they talked through different problems and situations, they each added to each other's points and built up everyone's knowledge. Agnes had feared starting the shelter because she'd worried she didn't know enough. But now, she understood that she did not need to know *everything*. She just needed to have a team in place that could problem-solve whatever situations would arise. And that, she thought, was revolutionary.

●●●●●●

That evening they enjoyed the best meal Agnes had eaten in a long time: fish from the Dungu and Kibali Rivers that people around here bragged about. One of the nuns who was serving them told them a story. In 1942, a Belgian colonial administrator was given the task of building a bridge across the Dungu River. Instead of building a two-lane bridge as ordered, he built a one-lane bridge. With the remaining bricks he built a medieval-style castle with 40 rooms between the Dungu and Kibali rivers. The castle is almost destroyed today, but what is left of it towers over several small grass thatched huts in the tropical forest area. Other run-down ruins dot the area, making Dungu look like a place where people have run off. The nuns told the doctors that some months many UN soldiers come there as part of the United Nations Organization Mission in the DRC, which used the French acronym MONUSCO. "You'll want to meet with the leader and alert them about the clinic you're building," the nun suggested.

Their driver drove them around the town a little bit to a very grand Catholic church. Aiko had arranged to meet with Sister Angelique Namaika, a member of the Augustine Sisters. These nuns confirmed that violence was never far away, which helped convince Aiko that her mission here was of tremendous value.

The second day they met with the architect. He praised Aiko's plans as simple and straightforward and said it would not be a big deal to complete the structure, especially since they were starting with an older building that had a firm foundation, despite being very run down. He recommended a short wall around the building, not so much to keep raiders out, since if someone wanted to get in, they could. But to provide a space around the building that was part of the clinic waiting area, and yet not actually inside of it.

Aiko liked this idea and decided to call it a courtyard for crowd control, for when many women came at once. "It would also be helpful to have a room inside for triage," where, according to Aiko, "brief examinations could be done to decide the seriousness of wounds, so that those in need of emergency intervention could be seen quickly." Others might have to wait for hours, or even days.

Once he understood, the architect changed his plans and enlarged the waiting area and added an overhanging roof in case of intense heat or rain.

On the last day of the trip, Aiko told Agnes of an abandoned village where a handful of Acholi women were reportedly living. "Could we visit on our way home," Aiko asked.

Agnes felt anxious, not knowing what to expect, but more so because this was her part in the effort, and she wanted to do it well.

They packed their things in the SUV, then drove eight miles back inside the forest. They had been given directions to the place, which had once been a village. Their driver pulled up to a ruined circle of six dilapidated huts. The place felt abandoned. The air was heavy with a smell of rot and a palpable sense of hopelessness. The grass thatch roofs had not been replaced in at least ten years. They no longer kept out the rain and probably had rats living in them. There was a pitifully neglected latrine with sun-dried waste around it. Agnes shielded her eyes and saw in the distance a bent-over couple digging in the small field behind the huts.

Agnes walked slowly through the camp . . . she could not call it a village, and honestly it was worse than the LRA camps she had lived in during all her time in the bush. Over the next two hours she found and spoke to nine people. All of them seemed afraid of her, though she spoke gently and insisted that Aiko and the driver stay back by the car.

They appeared dazed from the inert lives they had maintained. They kept talking about thousands of displaced people they believed were still roaming this part of the DRC, hiding from Kony. And they seemed to believe, if they stayed hidden here, they would not be attacked.

She spoke gently of options that might be better than the life they were leading: they could go to one of the refugee camps on the border, or come to Gulu with Agnes to seek out their families, or even go to St. Monica's Tailoring School, which had famously taken in returnees after the peace. She tried telling them about Gulu today (most of them seemed to be from Gulu), but the more Agnes talked to them, the more they seemed to distrust her. They had no faith that going "home" might improve their lot, and they showed no interest in leaving. They said that no one had harmed them in eleven years (since they had fled the 2008 Christmas Massacre perpetrated by Kony after the peace), so why not stay there? They were so weary and wan, and Agnes was reminded vividly of the years she'd spent roadside on the blue tarp, when she could barely move or speak or do anything but sell paper beads.

In the last hut, a woman was barely able to walk. Her son was fourteen and badly maimed; his face was scarred, and his ears had been cut off some time ago. She pleaded with Agnes not to harm him. He didn't speak but made grunting sounds and held the sides of his head where his ears had been.

Agnes wished she could convince them that there was more to life than this. But no one could heal by being forced. Still, she tried to remember how the missionaries had helped her to move ahead.

After some hours Agnes returned to Aiko. "I feel great compassion for these people. I have given them options and given them the chance to choose. I'd like to help in some way. But I can't fix their circumstances."

Aiko praised her compassion, and affirmed that these people were not Agnes's dependents. Agnes must not feel obligated to rescue them. "I find that I do my best work when I feel called," said Aiko. "I think we all do. If you ever feel called to come back here and do more, you know where to find them."

Agnes called Sister Rosemary, who ran St. Monica's. Even she said she only took women who came willingly. "I have rules here they must abide by," Rosemary reminded Agnes.

Where would she take these women if they came to Gulu? "Aiko, I know the challenges of finding the way home, as well as the despair of being rejected. I would do them a disservice if I convinced them to come to Gulu only to have them suffer more."

The woman from the last hut hobbled toward the car, towing her maimed son by the hand. She asked more about the offer to be taken to St. Monica's. Aiko and Agnes agreed to take her, and she appeared ready to join them. Then, suddenly, she turned back and shooed them away. "No," she said. "I'll stay here."

"Do any of the others want to come?" asked Agnes, one last time, as she followed the woman back toward her filthy hut.

"No," said the woman. "They want to chase you away. And they will do it. They are mean like that."

So Agnes and Aiko waved good-bye and got in the SUV. Agnes was conscious of the odor she carried with her and remembered it from her own smells long ago. She longed for a wash and her own house.

She suddenly felt very tired, and she dozed for the rest of the ride through the Garamba Forest.

••••••

The next day after she had gotten home and washed her clothes and her body and settled back into her house, Agnes called Grace on WhatsApp and told her all about the trip. Agnes could tell that Grace was proud of her for going to Dungu and for being part of Aiko's team.

Agnes tried to explain that the Acholi women had shown her what she no longer was.

Grace said, "But, Mama, we already knew that a long time ago."

"Let us just say that they reminded me," said Agnes. "Sometimes learning something once is not enough."

Part IV

31

January 2019—Gulu

When Pastor's name crossed Agnes's phone screen, her heart lurched. Although it had been three years since Moses's accident, she still associated her friend calling her unexpectedly with bad news. "Hello, Pastor," she said. "Is everything okay?"

"Yes, Agnes. Everything is good. Would you like to drive up to Kitgum with me to visit our land?"

"Our land?"

"The land for our shelter, Agnes. We've always said: shared hope, shared vision, shared land."

Agnes smiled. "I have all day."

••••••

Heading north along the road to Kitgum to see their land, Agnes reviewed the notebook she had begun keeping in Dungu. Since returning from the trip with Aiko, she had written down more thoughts, questions, and plans for the shelter she'd dreamed of building with Pastor someday. And she had begun to write down observations of healing steps that she thought might be useful to others. She saw herself giving a woman in need the kind of help she had been given. Writing those ideas down in her notebook had made her feel different. Like a leader.

Pastor drove for an hour or so, passing more and more pedestrians on both sides of the road. Dozens of men and women, with huge bundles on their heads, traipsed along, some quite quickly. Agnes had an impulse to offer a ride to a few of them, but that always caused a jam with lots of people clambering to climb in. She would not do that today. But when Pastor stopped behind a big truck for a minute, she did roll down the window and hand a small bottle of water to one woman who looked especially weary.

"It looks so different from what I remember," she said. "There are so many people walking, either up to Kitgum or back to Gulu. Is it always like this?"

"It is, Agnes," Pastor responded. "They say there are 45,000 refugees at Palabek, but they can hardly know, since people come and go. And many Ugandans claim to be refugees so they can get the welcome package from the UNHCR. It's a wonder the United Nations High Commission on Refugees has not run out of these. People either survive off those packages for a few days or sell them. In Uganda alone thousands of South Sudanese have crossed that border since their civil war heated up."

"I read that the population of Kitgum more than quadrupled," Agnes said, noting the flood of refugees that had crossed from South Sudan.

Pastor nodded. "Kitgum has gone from a dusty farmers' market town of 40,000 people to a bustling place with more than 200,000. Now it has shops, cafes, and gasoline stations for the unceasing line of trucks going in and out of Palabek and South Sudan. The border is quite open. I feel excited when I drive this road now," Pastor said. "I used to feel so hopeless and tired. There were so many people, so much need. It used to wear me down. But now I know we are going to help, Agnes. Even in a small way, we will make a difference."

"Did I tell you about Rhino Camp?" she asked. "It was bigger than Palabek. And Bidi Bidi was huge! I saw women there trying to pull themselves together, to become self-sufficient."

"Yes. I'm glad you got to visit. We should go to Palabek together soon. We can meet some useful contacts and see how things are organized there." He hummed a little, beating out a rhythm on the steering wheel. Then he asked, "What will you teach the women who come to us?"

Agnes wondered if he'd been reading her mind, as she'd just been thinking about that. "I've been keeping notes," she said, tapping her notebook. "About things that have helped me. But I worry that I don't know how to teach people."

Pastor chuckled. "Of course you do, Agnes. You have taught everything to your very able children, and to others in the compound. You tell people at the Inn all about Gulu and the history of the war. And you give advice to tourists. What do you mean you don't know how to teach?"

Agnes was quite stunned, but when she thought of herself in each of these circumstances, she realized she did indeed do this every day. "I guess you're right. I just have to organize it so that women who are in such a bad state can understand what to do first, second, third, and so on. Trauma makes it hard to think clearly."

"It helps, of course, that you have been through what they have, and can instruct them from a place of deep experience," he reminded her.

Maybe, all that 'deep experience' in the bush could be useful at last.

Pastor went on, "Just look at yourself and ask: *What have I done for myself that got me from that blue tarp beside a road in 2005 to where I am today?* Turn your answer into a plan for the women who come to Eve's Shelter."

"Is that what you will call it?" asked Agnes, startled. "Eve's Shelter?"

"I have been calling it that in my mind," Pastor admitted. "You told me years ago that you talked to a mother-spirit called Eve when you were at your most desperate. You said she was a strong, compassionate spirit who watched over you and the other child mothers. Since our goal is to offer that compassion and strength to women, I thought it might be fitting. What do you think?"

"Some Christians say Eve was the first sinner," Agnes said hesitantly.

"She helped you, and you convinced others to lean on her, so I presume you will convince more people now. You are persuasive, Agnes." He smiled again.

Agnes was warming to the purpose of the day. "You are right, Pastor. Certainly, when I think of a safe and protective place for women, I see Eve standing in the trees, with her arms out, ready to hold them with their babies," said Agnes. "One day, when the shelter is ready, we can feel if the name fits. It does sound right today."

Pastor turned right off Kitgum Road, and they bumped down a long red clay track. "'One day' may be sooner than you think."

• • • • • •

Agnes's eyes widened as they passed a row of trees and drove up to a construction site. Pastor turned off the engine and hopped out of the truck. Pointing in one direction he said, "The long, low buildings will be staff housing." In another direction he pointed out where the school would be. "And there are the first huts," Pastor said, turning Agnes's attention well beyond the school to ten huts with metal roofs, each painted and clean.

"Pastor! You have been busy!" Agnes put her hands to her face in both disbelief and excitement. "At Beatrice's party you told me there were issues with squatters. I had not imagined that you had resolved those and made so much progress in only a year!"

A stoic woman came out to greet them. "I am Atim Stella Angela," she announced. A small boy of about ten years of age ran behind her shouting, "Pastor, Pastor, come and see the school!"

Pastor smiled. "That's Hero," he said to Agnes. "I hired him to help clear the land for the construction."

Clearly eager to show them the progress that had been made, Hero led them to the school, which had a few walls built and benches stacked to one side. Agnes could not believe her eyes.

Pastor walked her through each section of the land, using his hands to sketch where he thought they could develop future buildings. They ended the tour at the shelter area, a big structure that could be seen from the road. One sturdy wall was already up. "Look here. I don't think we want full walls around the rest. What do you think?" Pastor asked.

The big shelter looked like it would easily hold more than 100 people seated at tables, and would have many purposes. The floor needed to be flat, so plastic chairs and tables could be easily moved around. Without tables, more could fit. Here they could hold meetings, in small or large groups. They could also meet outside, past the shelter and down toward where more huts were going to be.

Agnes had questions. But first they had to decide what to call the big structure. On a rough blueprint it was called "Main Dining Area," but because it had no walls, the workers were calling it the "Gazebo." They all seemed to favor that name, and Agnes thought it sounded cheery, unlike what buildings were called in the big camps. That's how it got its name.

As they stood at the center of the Gazebo, Agnes asked if they could kneel in prayer and thank God. "Of course. Let's take turns in saying what we want to say," said Pastor.

And so, they praised the Lord and petitioned Him for guidance. Even Pastor prayed.

When they stood up again, Pastor stretched his arms overhead and said, "Let's go look at the staff housing." They began to walk down the path from the Gazebo when Agnes stopped suddenly.

"Pastor," she said. "How have you been paying for all of this?"

"I have been saving up for this, Agnes. This is as important to me as my business, so I followed the same process. I decided what each thing would cost and, as I could afford it, I bought it. The land was cheap, and I did all the paperwork with the national land office and have obtained a solid legal title for it."

"This has been all bought by you," said Agnes. She felt very upset. "If you pay for it, then it is yours."

"Nonsense," Pastor replied. "I had an ideal I wanted to achieve. Since before I went to that awful Bible school, I have wanted to help people. But it wasn't until I watched you go through your healing journey that I could truly envision what my work in the world would be. Before I knew you, I lived with memories of what my older brothers did to our own sister and mother, and my imaginings of what they did to their 'wives' in the bush. This is for those women, as well as for you and the other child mothers." Pastor's voice had grown in volume and passion.

Agnes thought for a moment. "But what do I have to contribute, really? You have given all this money. I have given nothing."

Pastor stopped walking. "Agnes. The experience you bring is as valuable as anything I have paid for."

"Do you honestly feel that way?"

He turned and looked into her eyes. "You are an example of what is possible, Agnes. You will be a light to the women who come here. You will give them hope."

She felt then that God was speaking directly to her heart, calling her to her mission through Pastor's words. She straightened her spine, thinking. "Thank you, Pastor. And, going forward, we will need funding for staff and operations and things like that. I will talk to Aiko. She will know of some funding sources we can apply for." She let her mind wander over the people she knew. "And I will speak to Okot James," she added. "The Mormon church may be willing to support this work."

Pastor smiled a proud smile. "And there are other grants available, too. I've already applied for a grant to get generators. We'll figure it out together, Agnes."

He showed her inside the staff's living quarters and suggested that the eight permanent staff members would include himself and Agnes, a cook and a helper, a nurse, a teacher, and two security guards to start. There was apartment space for each, plus a bonus space for volunteers. "You and I can split our time between here and Gulu," Pastor explained. "But it's important to have living space here, I think, for when we can't travel back and forth in one day."

Last, he showed her the ten huts close up, expecting they would need more. Beyond them, newly cleared fields were already growing with corn, beans, sim sim, and greens. The place had a well-kept yet unfinished feel. "We inherited gardens from squatters who had been good farmers. I paid them more than I paid the owner of this land. It surprised them when I offered them money, as they were not owners and we both knew that, but they had been hoping someone would buy the land and they would have just enough to go live in Kitgum."

Agnes smiled. "I am sure they were very grateful, my friend."

One of the workers began to ask questions about the Gazebo. Pastor followed the man back to the construction site, and Agnes stood in the center of the ten huts, lifting her face to the sky. She thought of her conversation with Okot James just five years ago about agency. How people can make things happen if they choose their goals wisely, then think of the steps they have to take to get there, and move forward one step at a time. This project had gone from being a wish to a plan, which she shared with a person she trusted, and now their plan was becoming a real-life project that would be the result of good choices made and followed. She had become a woman with agency.

• • • • • •

When they climbed into the truck to drive back to Gulu, Agnes took one last look at Eve's Shelter and smiled. The future looked bright.

Pastor put the truck into gear, and they began bumping along the red clay track toward Kitgum Road. "I have been thinking of your role as the director," he said. "And of myself as the manager. What do you think?"

"Adong Agnes, director of Eve's Shelter?" She smiled at the sound of it.

"It sounds just right," he said, and it was done.

They rode in silence for a few minutes and then Pastor said, "Let's talk more about staffing. We both have to feel good about each hire, as we will be working with them closely."

"Of course." She nodded.

"I have been thinking of Vivian for our nurse," he said. "She used to work at Lacor Hospital."

Agnes nodded again, remembering Vivian from Gulu.

"And I think Jonathan would fit in well as our teacher," Pastor said.

Suddenly, the atmosphere in the truck's cab changed.

"Why don't you tell me all about Jonathan," Agnes said, calmly. "Don't you think it is time?"

Pastor remained quiet. He adjusted the windows and drank some water. "So . . . you know?"

"I know only the foundation," she said carefully. "And it is up to you how much you want to tell me, but remember the way we have always been with each other. It is like when you told me you were Samson's brother. You were meant to be different from him. That is how you were born. But once you thought I would figure it out, you told me directly. I think it was good that you told me, and I did not have to guess and wonder."

"How did you know about Jonathan?" asked Pastor. "Who told you?"

"Pastor, I am not a worldly woman, and you are right to assume that I would be the last to know, but I do work at the Inn and people come from everywhere, and they talk about life in the world. And I have Isaiah and Grace in Seattle, and America is good about these things. I have David and Beatrice in Kampala. And I told you about the gay men at the airport in America. Remember I told you that I thought of you when they told me that many, many men want to live with other men but in places where it is illegal they can't tell? Right then I knew. No one told me, but I thought of how I've heard you speak of Jonathan, and I just knew."

"Is it obvious?" Pastor asked, his voice revealing his concern.

Agnes shook her head. "I know how dangerous it is to be gay in Uganda. Isaiah said it right, when he told me that he thought you were gay. He said, 'It is our honor to protect Pastor. His secret has to be our secret. We are a family.'"

Pastor gripped the wheel. "He said that?"

This time, Agnes nodded. "You have watched over me and my children all these years, doing so much for my sons. I want to do the same for you, Pastor. You are safe with me."

Pastor swallowed hard and was quiet for a long time. Finally, he said, "Jonathan and I have spent twenty years hiding our secret. We know it is almost as dangerous to those who know we're gay and would support us, as it is for us. We have had to be discreet. We know we will have to be careful, but I promise you, we know every precaution to protect ourselves, and we will keep you and the shelter safe too."

"I know you will," she said.

"Please understand, Agnes, we want to be together out here. We will not live together, of course, but he will be the head teacher and will have his own apartment, and we will be able to see one another every day that I'm here."

"Then you must, of course," Agnes replied. "But for now, will you tell me about him?"

Pastor took some deep breaths and slowed the truck. They approached a little market, with tires hanging outside a wooden garage. He pulled up and called out to the proprietor. "Do you serve Fanta?"

The man nodded and pointed to a small wobbly table with a faded vinyl cloth over it, and two rickety chairs. He and Agnes left the truck as the man brought out paper napkins and metal spoons. Agnes sat down and said, "I'd love a Fanta, and some cake." They made sure the table was out of the sun, which was beginning to sink in the western sky. Pastor ordered tea and cake and peanuts, and they smiled at each other, acknowledging their deep connection.

"Jonathan is a good man," he began. "He's been a teacher in Lira, fifty miles from here, for nearly ten years, and he loves his work. Before that, he was a pastor, like I tried to be. We met at the Bible School during the war. He was able to do that for a decade before he started teaching children. We used to say that we both enjoyed watching things grow. He, children. Me, seeds. He has been building the school at the shelter on Saturdays and

Sundays. I hope that is fine with you, Agnes. I believe you will accept him and want him to stay."

"I will and I do," she said reassuringly. "Seldom do so many things in one's life all seem in harmony with the Heavens. You know, in the Bible, Jonathan was known for his loyalty."

Pastor nodded.

They sat together and ate their cake as the sun set behind them.

32

February 2019—Kitgum

Agnes and Pastor headed again toward Kitgum, but today they did not turn off on the road that led to the shelter. They wanted to poke around Kitgum, then visit Palabek.

Agnes knew about the thousands of South Sudanese refugees that had been coming across the Uganda border for years. The number had increased in the last five years as a more savage civil war spread inside South Sudan. The Ugandan government had been very welcoming, allowing refugees to move not only into camps along the border between the two countries, but to travel—when they were able—through any camp or settlement, and then on into the local Ugandan towns and villages where they might find work, purchase land, and become permanent residents. This put them in competition with local people, so the Ugandan government's promise had potentially violent consequences.

Women were the most vulnerable, of course, arriving sick, battered, hungry, raped, and encumbered with children. How to help these women become able? How to prepare them to find land or a job or a sustainable way to survive?

This was where Agnes came in.

She knew she was being called to the border, and she imagined encountering women there just like her younger self. She wanted to ask them, "How can I help you become able?"

······

As though her body remembered before her mind understood, Agnes's heart drummed faster when she saw a road sign for Lamwo. She distinctly remembered crossing a border up here in the year before she'd escaped from Aba Camp. However, she had either never known or had forgotten the name of the crossing point until Peter had told her that Kony's soldiers and their families had crossed at a place called Ngom-oromo border post, in Lamwo. She'd never returned, of course, but the sign indicated that she was headed to this post again, all these years later.

According to Peter, this border crossing was the precise place north of Kitgum, where she'd been pushed with over 70 others, maybe by Peter himself, in a forced march out of Uganda and across the South Sudan border to get up to Juba, and then down to Aba Camp. She had stumbled along, not knowing where she was going, back then. She now wondered what it looked like and whether she'd recognize anything. Back then, she recalled hearing the name Lubanga Tek. She'd learned from Peter that it was a place nearby.

"Are we headed to Ngom-oromo or Lamwo, to see the refugees at that border crossing?" she asked Pastor.

"Near there," he replied. "Palabek and the refugee offices are about 50 miles west. Do you want to see Ngom-oromo?"

"Not today." Agnes shook her head. "We will be up here again. I just can't help but wonder about these places that were part of my past."

Pastor nodded.

"When we are seeking to help others to heal, we are led to them by our own wounds. I have wounds that are connected to the border crossing at Ngom-oromo. I am drawn to this border by those memories, and I understand more clearly now," Agnes explained. "Let's focus on Kitgum and Palabek. I have never been there, as far as I know. I was so young."

They stopped briefly at an office in dusty Kitgum, which was on the verge of turning from a large village to a town. Pastor had visited before and followed the signs to Palabek Refugee Settlement area.

Clerks in the office confirmed official estimates that this area had nearly 60,000 refugees from Sudan. "Most are Acholi speakers," one said. "They move most easily into the settlement and then into the towns. They have a language advantage, providing they survive what they had to do to get out of their own country to begin with."

Another noted, "Acholis had oft been subjected to discrimination and vile persecution in Sudan, compounding their suffering and lack of a secure place to live. The Ugandan government could not provide any protective police to safeguard the new arrivals."

Agnes understood the fear of being pursued through the bush by armed enemies, and what it was like to be threatened and beaten with no protection around. She dared to look into a few drawn faces and speculate on the life story each woman had.

The youngest and strongest of the refugees would head beyond Kitgum to the towns in Pader and Gulu districts. Some had relatives back in Sudan that could send money to invest in various business ventures in Uganda, and many of the most well-off Sudanese actually drove growth in towns like Gulu. Agnes had seen the mechanics garages they'd set up to fix bodas and cars. The new restaurants they invested in. The barber shops and hair salons they opened around town. Sometimes they competed with local Gulu residents, but more often they served other Sudanese. Ideally, they melted together. Things were not always prosperous for them, but it was a start.

Around, in front of, and behind these stronger and younger Sudanese, were those weak and ignored refugees, just trying to keep up. Many gave up along the way, or left parts of their families behind. Some arrived at the border and simply collapsed into Uganda. Pastor and Agnes drove slowly along a main drive toward the marked national boundary. These were "their people."

These border-crossers were the enemy of the poorest Ugandans, since the incoming Sudanese had become poorer, unskilled, and hungry, and had nothing to lose by picking a fight. Naturally, the local poor dreaded another conflict in this place, where Kony's war had ended nearly twenty years ago. No wonder tension brewed between the Ugandans and the immigrants.

The Settlement road northwest was not tarred and even in this dry month it was not in good shape. Repairs had been attempted, but with more refugees arriving all the time, heavy trucks traveled the road daily. The terrain was grimy and parched, in contrast to the more verdant areas around the shelter site.

In the distance, clumps of people were squatting among tall grasses as Pastor drove toward Palabek. From each rise in the road, Agnes could see scattered huts and temporary dwellings made of tarps spread over sticks. The legs and feet of the occupants huddled together inside these strange structures made any onlooker curious as to what on earth they could be doing in such confined spaces. In some, people lay on mats and slept curled up like snails. Clothes that had been washed were spread all over some fields, evidence that people were trying to care for their basic needs, even in these impossible circumstances. It looked stark and forbidding, to say the least.

Agnes took in all of it. Had she lived like this when she'd traveled with Kony? These circumstances looked far worse than what she remembered, but she knew this *was* how it had been. Like her former self, these people out here among the grasses, were barely hanging on.

A mile or so into the Palabek settlement, they approached a string of sprawling roadside makeshift villages that included three trading centers. It was impossible to tell who were Sudanese and who were Ugandans pretending to be refugees so that they could be fed and protected for a short time and given a few supplies to later sell in the marketplaces.

A few of the more able refugees had put together sturdier huts, similar to the traditional Acholi huts around Gulu. Every few miles Agnes and Pastor would notice great piles of bricks covered in blue tarp, which seemed to be available for refugees who had staked out a claim of land somewhere in the sprawl. Maybe they were being baked and stacked by some entrepreneurial person.

The bricks matched the rusty red color of the road, a tone that was characteristic of the area, where low plastered buildings were mostly that same familiar color, sometimes painted over in yellow or orange. Some held food shops, and others sold miscellaneous basics. There was a petrol station and a garage with men working inside, and nearby, another shop offering tire repair.

They drove past these market areas and at least ten NGOs before spotting a small office marked, "Reception-Palabek."

Refugees who had crossed nearby could register and be supported for at least two weeks. They were screened and separated if they had a communicable disease. They were fed and given a "settlement kit" by UNHCR. The kit was supposed to offer everything necessary to survive in this new land for a short time. Once they had their package, each person was encouraged to find a small plot and squat on it. While the area looked crowded to Agnes, they were told that there was still space farther along the border, where patchy grasslands stretched for miles to the east and west.

"This land does not seem at all welcoming," Agnes observed. "It's so arid. How can people expect to grow anything here?"

"Yet more and more Sudanese arrive every day, hoping to find a spot to live among the wild grass and dry brush." Pastor pointed into the distance. "There used to be trees up here some years back, but most have been cut down to provide firewood for cooking or keeping warm at night, or to warm water to wash clothes."

Here and there, remnants of the green forest growth, usually away from roads or well-used tracks, still bore witness to the richness of the fertile Ugandan soil. And while the quality of most land they could see didn't seem worth contention, here and there people squabbled over some choice piece of Ugandan land. Good soil gave them hope.

"It's hard to believe we are only 60 miles from Gulu," Agnes said. "And yet, a world apart."

Soon, they came across a few large tents that seemed to be for official purposes. People sitting at tables with papers and laptops seemed to be keeping track of who came in and what they needed. They passed various NGO offices—International Rescue Committee, World Food Organization, and Food for the Hungry. African Women Rising also had an office in Gulu and although Agnes knew some of the women in this office, she didn't stop to talk.

When they encountered health stops, they stopped to leave their names and phone numbers, explaining that if women arrived that seemed particularly traumatized, they could refer them to Eve's Shelter, down the Kitgum/Gulu Road. They explained that their shelter had been approved as a partner by the UNHCR and was ready to receive anyone needing their services.

Agnes and Pastor were surprised that Ugandans who were not refugees were entitled to use these clinics, but they did know that the towns between Palabek and Gulu did not have good health services. One clinic called Jerusalem, funded by the EU, had a long line and looked accommodating. In fact, it looked so well-equipped that Agnes felt self-conscious representing a place that might not ever be up to par. But Pastor told her to forget her self-doubt and think of what she knew she could offer. They were told by the official at the reception office to expect calls about placing some women identified as having high needs.

"When can you start receiving residents?" he asked, noting that someone had already come to inspect their site.

"Two weeks," Pastor replied.

Agnes was wary about inviting people while the facilities were still under construction. She turned to interrupt Pastor, then saw a young woman with a baby on her back and a child by the hand. She was clearly unwell and struggled to move with the clinic line. Her baby looked far too thin and quiet.

"Three weeks," she said, smiling at Pastor. "Let us know when you have some women for us. We can take up to four the first week of March, and when they are settled we will let you know how many more we can take."

"The rains usually come in March, you know," the official said. "Transport gets very difficult with the mud and humidity. Then, only the most desperate find their way."

"Then we will be ready by the first of March," Agnes confirmed.

They shook hands with one another.

・・・・・・

Agnes was especially interested in getting a good look at how a big kitchen tent worked. About two hours before serving food, the tent's side flaps were down and everything seemed closed up tight, but now it bustled with activity. Cooks worked over stoves with fires under large pots of rice, cornmeal posho, and soup. She watched how they organized the ingredients and who was cooking what, and how the people were being served. Astonishingly, some people appeared to be making this whole system work for them and would live to tell of it. They arrived in droves, greeting one another with smiles and a wave.

After watching hundreds line up in the tent to receive their afternoon meal, Agnes and Pastor were reminded of why they were doing what they were doing, and with a clearer idea of who they would be serving.

Watching one family walk by, Agnes turned to Pastor and said, "We underestimated how many children would be here!"

Pastor smiled. "I was thinking the same thing."

Agnes added, "We'll have to expand the school, and we will need larger huts so that the women can keep their children with them."

Not far from the food tent, children kicked things around where the grass had been cleared or trampled. It wasn't a proper ball, but it was something that could be tossed, and caught, and kicked, and cheered for. Little children mimicked bigger ones. Life found a way to go on, slowly, plodding. Agnes found herself alternately filled with hope and overwhelmed by the sheer size of the need.

Passing the UNHCR Reception building, Agnes and Pastor saw four women sitting on the ground near the door, possibly waiting to be processed into the holding area. They each seemed too dazed to move on, and Agnes looked away because she could not yet offer them help. She remembered how people had looked away from her during those aimless years when she had sat on the side of the road after leaving her father's village. She wanted to reassure each one of these women that there was life beyond this temporary sojourn, in this place between before and next.

Agnes spoke to a woman working in a prefabricated office building with the World Vision logo on the side, which Agnes recognized. She had friends at World Vision, a major NGO, that had worked in Gulu since she'd arrived back from the bush, and she trusted their ethics. The people there likewise trusted Agnes and were pleased to learn she was opening a shelter in support of this work. She asked them more intentionally now about their work and what facilitators of women's groups did to encourage new arrivals. Agnes took notes. Their ideas left her optimistic about inviting people to come to the shelter as soon as possible.

Back in the truck, they turned on to the main road that led out of the official settlement area. After driving a short while, Pastor stopped the truck. The two looked back at where they'd spent the better part of their day, trying to process the weight of what they were about to take on by opening this shelter. In all directions, men and women continued going about their business, moving almost in slow motion through the camp. The energy was subdued and quiet, creating a dream-like quality to this place. And yet, they worked as if they fully expected to live another day. Among all the suffering, these refugees had found a way to hold on to hope.

While Palabek was one of the smaller refugee settlements along the Uganda border, even here, what struck Agnes, was the sheer number of people needing assistance, the crowds stretching as far as they could see. Who, of all these people, would end up at Eve's Shelter? And where would they be in ten years' time?

●●●●●●

As delighted as Agnes was in the promise their shelter held, and how spacious it had seemed when Pastor had shown her around the plot, having visited Palabek, she knew that within weeks of Eve's Shelter coming alive to its purpose, it would be too small. There were just so many women and children in need. The numbers seemed limitless!

Agnes had once said that there would be no accommodations at the shelter for women to make permanent homes there, or even long-term ones. Their place was designed for temporary support. She now understood that the women would probably not be able to move on as quickly as she and Pastor had speculated. None who came would be a quick fix. The shelter would offer a drop in the bucket for meeting their many needs, but it would serve some, and Agnes was as aware as any, that to save one mother on the run, was of great worth.

Seeing the shelter, then driving up to Kitgum, then Palabek, had opened Agnes's mind fully to the task ahead. This had been an eye-opening reminder of her original dream. Why had she waited so long to get up to the shelter site? Why had she delayed the finishing touches? They needed to hurry and get on with this essential work. She chastised herself for being absorbed with trivial problems, then determined to focus on the birth of new things.

She had prayed each day for what was ahead. She still thought of Peggy, Isaiah, and Grace, and all the children, and she had a part in every prayer preserved for those around her in her compound, and in her children's families. But her heart was now full of expectations for the shelter, and she asked her Heavenly Father to turn His attention to things there.

• • • • • •

Before March came, Agnes had instructed the day workers Pastor had hired to build ten more huts. Unlike the first ten huts, which were small, these were medium-sized, appropriate for mothers with more than two children. Each would have four plastic chairs outside, and a grate for a cooking pit outside the entrance. Benches inside would serve as seats during the day, and beds at night. It was faster to affix metal roofs than thatched ones.

Pastor promised to return to Palabek when the designated NGO that did most of the screening called to say they had identified some apparently traumatized women in severe need of extra services and assigned them to Eve's Shelter. By now he and Agnes had expanded enough to accommodate up to twelve women, but it was hard to keep count, as sometimes a woman would cross into Palabek, register, and get an ID card, and then be told where to settle temporarily until she could see her way clear to move on into Uganda. Sometimes the woman might have more children, or a sister, or be traveling with someone else who is not assigned. Instead of one woman, Pastor would sometimes get four people. A quota for twelve had to remain flexible.

On March 1, 2019, he transferred a family to the shelter and the following day, two women arrived in a World Vision van and were dropped off with their children. One woman was extremely quiet with blank eyes. After Agnes registered her and discovered her name was Alice, Agnes led Alice to a hut and explained that it would be her home for at least three months. The woman looked briefly into Agnes's eyes, but otherwise, she was without expression.

Alice had been given a settlement package of a jerry can and a mat and a few other things, but somehow she had forgotten where she'd left them. How long had she been in Palabek? Alice just stared when Agnes asked these questions; she seemed to have no idea. The ID said she spoke Acholi, and some English, but it was not apparent that she understood either. Agnes left her to sleep on her mat in her hut and covered her with a blanket. She doubted Alice would sleep, but she wanted her to know this was a safe place.

When the cooks served plates of posho and soup with fish for some of the staff, Agnes went and collected Alice from her hut. She guided her by the arm to the Gazebo and to a table, where she placed a plate in front of her, with flat bread to eat with. Alice seemed unaware of the food at first, but Agnes let her sit with it for an hour, until Alice dipped her bread into the soup and took some bites. Slowly she began to eat.

"She ate enough to live another day," Agnes observed to one of the cooks. "Just let her be." She recalled the barracks in Parongo, and how they told her she had been there at least a week without knowing it. They said she had eaten, too, but Agnes had no recollection of any of it. She had lived a full life since, so she knew Alice could do this, too.

The other woman who had arrived was Apiyo Irene. She had a baby and two children about seven and four, all girls. She apologized to Agnes for being there. She did not want to be any trouble, but she had no choice, she said. She repeated this over and over, along with the fact that she was hungry. It took Apiyo Irene no time at all to set herself up in her hut, and then she was ready to eat and feed her three children until they were full, with second helpings of posho and soup. She found the fish and fed it to the baby. Her eyes darted from the children to the other things in and around the shelter. She was anxious.

Agnes talked to her and held the baby, while Irene washed up the little girls. None of them seemed particularly healthy, although a doctor at the Palabek entry point had checked the family for serious diseases. They just needed care. More healthy food and safety.

Apiyo Irene told Agnes her brief story. A now common tale.

"Too bad, too bad," she said. "The boys are gone." Her sons had been taken before she'd left her village. She'd been told they were forced to become soldiers, though Irene was sure they were dead. "Such good boys," she repeated. "Too bad, too bad." She said she wished she'd left the baby with her mother, as she was too big to carry all the miles to get here. She was not yet a year old.

She told the same story again as Agnes listened. The girls joined her on the part where they all repeated, "Too bad, too bad." In a kind of chant.

From what Agnes could tell, the boys had been taken some time ago. Maybe over a year or two. It wasn't clear. It didn't need to be for now. There would be people at the shelter to listen to Irene, as many times as she needed to tell her tale.

Agnes wasn't sure, of course, about Irene's future, but she knew not to predetermine the small woman's destiny. She wondered if perhaps, Irene may become a strong teacher. Anges was not sure why that occurred to her. Something about how animated Irene was. She walked the girls over to where the school was shaping up and promised them that a teacher had been hired and would move here in a week. "His name is Mr. Jonathan," she said.

Hero, when he wasn't clearing more land, was teaching Atim Stella's boys, who had become very helpful children. Irene's daughters had healthy curiosities, but were not eager to join. They would soon, Agnes thought. Especially the younger girl, also named Grace.

Agnes did not immediately evaluate the third woman, nor her child.

Four more mothers and twelve more children arrived by week's end. With Hero's help, Agnes had things moving along. She had hired two cooks from Gulu, who were hard working and pleasant. She had instructed them a little in the appropriate ways to behave around women, so freshly traumatized, and they understood. One was old enough to have his own experience of surviving bad things. Hero was the runner. He did every errand that Agnes imagined and thanked her when she thanked him. He was obsessively obedient and observant.

Agnes made a list of the helpers she needed for the following week.

Pastor would be back at Eve's Shelter by nightfall, bringing three more guards he'd hired. He assured Agnes that he had known two for some time and trusted them. Two had guarded the Seed Store and other businesses in Gulu, and the third one was willing to learn. He had warned them to absolutely leave the women alone.

Agnes went home to Gulu the next day with lists flying around in her head. She needed sewing machines and women who could teach sewing. She needed clothes for all the new refugees, and plastic washing buckets and bowls. She knew how many flip flops she needed and for whom. She smiled. This was her work, her calling.

She wrote down in her notebook what each next step would be. There would be order at the shelter, so that each person could remember where things were kept and not be surprised or lose things. It had to be a place to rearrange their minds from escape-mode to recovery-mode. She and Pastor made large posters for the Gazebo and attached them to the pillars that held up the roof so they could be easily seen. For those who did not read, they explained them as a beginning literacy lesson and Agnes led groups to discuss every item on the posters.

On a poster with the heading ALWAYS, she listed things the women should do every day:

- Always go for water.
- Always keep your hut clean.
- Always make sure you know where your children are.
- Always wash your clothes when they are dirty.
- Always take your plates and forks to the dishwashing area after you and your children eat.
- Always report to Director Agnes if you have a fever.

This was the partial list. It was important, but so was the list headed, "NEVER."

- Never hit anyone.
- Never steal other people's buckets or jerry cans or clothes.
- Never forget to tell the Director or the Manager if something of yours is stolen.
- Never tell lies about anyone.
- Never hide food in your hut that spoils.

They reviewed the posters every day and Agnes would begin by asking, "Why is this rule important to all of us?" Sometimes they added new rules.

When the women were accustomed to the routine, Agnes had determined that savings and loan and computation skills could begin. This was to help the women feel less vulnerable to being cheated when they went outside. This had been found to be very important, as refugees were often vulnerable to thieves and felt stupid if they made mistakes with small amounts of money.

There was time set each day to quietly mingle. There were short quiet times where nothing was expected of the women except for them to be cooperative and to begin to imagine doing something new. While trauma had left some with no emotional stability to even attempt these things, Agnes knew that soon they would be stabilized enough to do what she had begun so many years ago.

The borehole was working well, and water had remained clean and steady. Pastor had constructed a protective fence around the whole perimeter of Eve's Shelter. They now had electricity and soon would have internet access. Mothers were beginning to notice these things, as were their children. Three mothers and five of the older children began to use computers that were donated from downtown Gulu businesses. Some mothers kept a watchful eye on their own children, and others seemed to feel relaxed enough with this new place, with its fence and kind people, to ignore them. Bigger kids began to care for littler ones. People stayed clean and became better nourished. The shelter was working.

With Moses running the Seed Store and calling Pastor with reports two or three times a day, Pastor was content to stay all night and day at the shelter, and Agnes had started to stay over most nights. It made sense not to make the long journey back and forth every day, especially after dark.

Every few days Pastor or Agnes got a call from World Vision or the UNHCR coordinator asking if they could take more women and children. Huts could go up in a couple of days, although they did need the mortar between the bricks to dry hard and to prepare roofs to be affixed. Pastor had been able to get fourteen more metal roofs and, using some refugee volunteers and workers from Gulu, they built three circles of huts for sleeping, with a couple for cooking. This was in addition to the ten thatched ones they had built before they opened, and the larger ones they'd built at the end of February. In such a short time, they had gone from a dream they'd sketched on paper, to a small shelter with a few huts, to a bustling community with an entire staff serving the needs of many women and children. Eve's Shetler was quickly becoming something more along the lines of a small village.

First, Pastor and one of his builders drew more circles on the ground where the walls would be erected. Following this template, the volunteers dug a trough the width of the bricks, and then had the bricks from Gulu carefully dumped near where the huts would be built. For people who had lived for so long without these important materials, the abundant bricks and mortar seemed like a king's ransom.

When they saw the materials, the refugees were glad to help build more huts. With everyone's contribution, it took less than a week to get the newer huts built. Most of the women knew how to build the huts, although traditionally it was men who built them, and women wove the grass thatch for roofs. Some of the older boys moved into the role of placing the bricks neatly in rows, rising out of the shallow circular trenches. They were probably from families that had once lived with men among them and knew the roles. But other boys seemed oblivious, since the social structures where they grew up had been blown apart by war.

Agnes and Pastor talked every day about their limits.

"How many could actually live here safely?" they asked one another.

They did not want to make a dangerous, overcrowded place. They knew that the many IDP camps which had been built during the war were notorious for overcrowding and filth because of a lack of systems to handle garbage and human waste. They had already built two larger latrines far away from the huts and the school, and would build two more, unless the UNHCR and another aid agency could donate some composting toilets that were increasingly popular in the aid communities. Many people who were given access to them in camps didn't use them as they were so unusual, but this contained space was an ideal place for a trial.

More women were coming.

33

May 2019—Kitgum

In May, Agnes received a call asking if they could take two more women, each with infants, and she said yes, then informed the World Vision representative that Eve's Shelter was full for the time being. They had reached their first quota of 25 women, with a total of 55 children. Agnes felt herself stretching into new capacities of leadership.

When the World Vision van arrived, the two climbed out. Brenda held a tiny, hungry baby named Beatrice. Agnes felt a big ball of emotion in her chest when she heard this name, as she did Brenda's intake and Vivian, the nurse, checked Brenda and the baby. Both seemed healthy, although Brenda complained of cracked and bleeding nipples and was having pain while nursing. Baby Beatrice though, seemed to be eating well and gaining weight.

Magda, half-fell out of the van. She had two children with her, as well as five-week-old baby Hope, whom she had apparently given birth to and cared for while literally running for her life. Vivian immediately noted that Magda had a breast infection and was still bleeding vaginally although the five weeks had gone by since her delivery. Despite her suffering, Magda was a big, strong, charismatic woman, and Agnes liked her right away.

Agnes kept watch over the two new arrivals and was having concerns about Brenda. Brenda was alternatingly very possessive with Beatrice, and then very neglectful, putting her in a basket in her hut and leaving her alone there while she cried. One minute, she would complain loudly about her breasts hurting from bleeding and clogged nipples and recurring malaise that was hard to explain. And the next minute she would get almost giddy playing with someone else's child. She was young. Too young. Agnes and Vivian put her near more attentive mothers whenever they could. They hoped if Brenda could observe attentive mothering, she would learn.

Magda tended to her children and fed her baby regularly, all while telling jokes and generally being a wholesome light for everyone. The other women took a shine to her and helped her with meals. Soon, Brenda switched huts to be closer to Magda. She seemed to look up to her and want to be around her. Hut switching wasn't allowed, and Agnes was planning to move Brenda back to her original spot, but when she saw how often Brenda and baby Beatrice were outside Magda's hut, she wondered if Magda would be a good role model. But she worried about the dynamic, too, as it seemed that Brenda wanted to be mothered by Magda as much as she wanted to be a mother like her.

All in all, Agnes was surprised when Vivian found her in the Gazebo two mornings later and said in a low voice, so as not to startle any of the other women, that Magda needed to be taken to hospital right away. "I did not know how bad her infection had gotten," Vivian said. "Her fevers have been getting worse. She is very, very sick."

Pastor and drove Vivian, Magda, and baby Hope to the main hospital in Gulu where, thankfully, Magda's life was saved.

A few hours later, Agnes heard screaming from one of the huts. She ran down the hill to find Brenda and baby Beatrice both in distress. Agnes took the baby from Brenda and saw at once that Beatrice's tiny feet had been badly burned.

First things first: Agnes gave the baby to one of the trainers and told her to quickly dip the baby's feet in cool water, and to ask one of the security guards to drive her and Brenda's baby to the closest clinic in Kitgum. Agnes trusted Hero to accompany them and report back on what she needed.

Agnes then pieced together the rest of the story: Magda, it seemed, had been nursing baby Beatrice for Brenda for two whole days, and Brenda's milk had all but dried up. When baby Beatrice had cried for milk and Magda was gone to the hospital, Brenda refused to feed her, and then when the baby would not stop crying, the young mother burned her baby's feet on the fire and threatened to throw the infant into the flames. One of the other mothers stopped her.

Agnes put Brenda in her hut with another one of the trainers and called Pastor to discuss the situation. He suggested they call Moses and ask him to bring Justine, Agnes's neighbor, to care for baby Beatrice until Brenda was well enough to care for her. After debating whether to call the police about Brenda, they decided to see if a hospital in Kitgum would treat her for mental illness.

A week went by, and Magda returned to the shelter after having her cervix cauterized and being treated for a severe uterine infection. Now that she was healthier, it became even more apparent what a natural leader she was. She sang to the women, and told stories, and listened as they told their stories.

When Brenda was sent from the hospital to jail for harming her baby, Justine begged to continue caring for baby Beatrice. Agnes agreed, offering her a small stipend, knowing that her daughter had recently lost her job at a hotel. Justine's three granddaughters were a big help too, and Agnes trusted they would be the ideal family to love little Beatrice back to health.

But just when Agnes thought everything was working out well, she was notified that Brenda had intentionally starved herself to death in the jail. Agnes became so emotional that she told Pastor he needed to take over the shelter alone. "I can't do this," she said. "I was wrong to pretend I could."

He put a hand on her shoulder. "Agnes," he said. "You are doing a remarkable thing. It is very hard to care for people who are so traumatized. I know you must feel very upset about Brenda and baby Beatrice. Why don't you go home for a week to have a rest?"

Agnes could see the wisdom in this. When she was at home in her own house, going about her regular routine, she felt more grounded. And she knew that this would have to be a regular pattern: to stay at the shelter and work hard for the women who needed her, and to come home regularly to rest and be renewed.

34

July 2019—Kampala

Agnes' daughter (now preferring the name Bea) was mostly at peace in her new life, despite the nagging sense of loss and grief and anger in the hole where her mother's presence had been her whole life. Until . . . she became pregnant. Despite careful use of birth control, the pregnancy test showed positive, sending her into a spiraling state of anguish as she ranted to David about what an awful time it was for them to have a baby. That she could not take care of a baby. That David had no idea what to do with a child.

"Men never do. Truly! Show me one," she demanded. She felt out of control and terrified.

She missed classes and cursed and swore. She convinced herself that somehow her mother was to blame for the pregnancy, insisting that Agnes made her pregnant through some dark means. She told David she wanted an abortion, "I'll call Aiko and ask her how to do it. Aiko knows about such things."

Aiko urged her to take things slowly.

Sturdy David proved himself almost unflappable. He had a long phone conversation with Aiko and Bjorn, while Bea listened from the sofa. They were sympathetic and explained that what Bea was going through was normal, especially given all the recent research about intergenerational trauma. They recommended some good online articles, which David read while his wife rested.

"The science of epigenetics, literally, 'above the gene,' proposes that we pass along more than DNA in our genes. It suggests that our genes can carry memories of trauma experienced by our ancestors and can influence how we react to trauma and stress."

David called Aiko again the next morning. "How can I help her? I have to get her help," David said. He explained that Bea believed her mother had cursed her with the pregnancy, and that he feared she might be a danger to herself.

"There are many good specialists in Uganda who have expertise in trauma and how to treat it. In the meantime, stay with Bea and get her to walk outside. Speak lovingly about the baby," Aiko advised. "This isn't to shame her for thinking about an abortion. It is for her to see something possible and real in the future that is a pleasure if she chooses to keep the child. She might want an abortion only because she believes the alternative will result in a terrible life for her or the baby. Stress the fact that she has all the care she needs for a successful birth if that is what she chooses, and that it is not a threat to her health or her future if she does."

David would do anything he could, but he was scared and wrestled with his own morality. "I always thought I was against abortion," he explained to Aiko, "but if that is what Bea needs, and if she continues to threaten that she will find a way to give herself one if I won't help her, then I will obviously help her."

After some consideration, David showed Bea what he'd learned online about epigenetics. She listened to her husband's calm voice: "It makes sense, doesn't it? It says here that the children of holocaust survivors experience trauma generations after their grandparents suffered. Given your childhood and your mother's childhood, it's likely you were primed for this."

Bea read the online research with the same verve she attacked all her other medical research, skeptically but thoughtfully. She became her own patient and agreed to meet with the local therapist Aiko had suggested.

••••••

In November, Agnes's phone vibrated in her palm, and her eldest daughter's name flashed onto the screen. Rather than asking about Gulu or indicating an interest in how her mother and the family were doing, or even sharing a few happy details about her life as a promising professional, or a wife, Bea launched into an announcement.

"Mama-Agnes, I have something to tell you that is upsetting me and David. I'm not calling to ask for your advice, and I do not want you to worry or try to help. It is something that we will handle, but I just thought you should know," she said.

"What is it?" Agnes asked in the moment between the warning and the report.

"I'm expecting a baby. I am three months pregnant," Beatrice blurted into the phone. "It was an accident. We didn't want a baby, but we can handle this, Mama. Please just let us handle this." Bea raised her voice, sounding firm, but distressed.

Agnes intuited that the substance of her motherly response to this news, and her tone, would be scrutinized, so she paused before carefully responding. "My dearest Beatrice, motherhood is such a blessing! Having a baby and raising her will be your greatest joy, as you have been mine."

Beatrice sighed. "Of course, Mama, we know that and will welcome whatever baby God sends us, but it's not what we wanted. We have been so careful to use birth control. We'd planned to wait another few years before we started our family. The timing is so inconvenient."

Her daughter's offhand remark landed as a blow to Agnes, and she felt the breath sucked out of her. *How could Beatrice describe pregnancy as "inconvenient" to her, of all people?!* Agnes had had no choice in whether she wanted to become pregnant or not, in whether she was ready to become a mother or not. It was thrust upon her without her consent. And when other war "brides" had killed their newborns, Agnes had taken it upon herself to be the best mother she could be under the impossible circumstances. *Inconvenient?!* Agnes recoiled from this casual dismissal of pregnancy. Bea understood, better than anyone, the way her mother's children had come into the world and the centrality of her role as the bearer, rescuer, nurturer, and encourager of her offspring.

Despite her daughter's request for her to stay out of it, Agnes could not hold her tongue. "*Inconvenient?*" her voice pitched into an injured wail.

Bea did not soften. Instead, she countered with another punishing rebuke. "Mama, I don't have the life you have, and I don't want your life. I intend to live my life differently. Bringing a child into the world right now will mess up a lot of things for me. I don't expect you to understand, but will you please not judge me? You are always judging me. I will never be as heroic as you are!"

Agnes was dumbstruck. Beatrice's distant behavior had been hard to understand for some time now, but her child had *never* voiced such a stinging criticism. Agnes hung up the call with tears in her eyes, not so much in anger but in bewilderment over how to respond to this damning chastisement. Her mind ran toward that familiar whirling numbness. Somehow, the fact that this blow was so immediate, and not a memory from the past, kept Agnes from becoming entirely overwhelmed. Still, she didn't move for about an hour. A neighbor returning empty detergent bottles shook her temporarily into activity, but Agnes soon sunk back to her stunned state where she remained into the evening and long after the compound was silent. She had been through much worse than this and had survived, and she had come to a place where she thought of herself as a nearly-healed woman. Agnes had changed. She felt confident and brave in the world. She spoke up to strangers who wronged her or wronged others. She'd held others up through illness and the loss of loved ones. She was competent in her work at the shelter, remaining steady and constant. Surely she had battled her share of storms even as she expected to withstand future ones. So . . . how strange that this single remark from her daughter could be so devastating.

Though it was not the appropriate time of day for washing clothes, Agnes decided she needed some brisk, physical work to shake her back to stability. It worked. After an hour of carrying water to her wash tub and scrubbing a few dresses and hanging them on the clothesline, Agnes drank fresh water, and retired to the bedroom. She knew not to stay there, as the empty bedding was a powerful reminder of the two girls who were no longer there.

Had either of those beautiful gifts been an inconvenience in any way? Agnes could not comprehend describing her children this way. Motherhood had been hard, but her daughters had been her greatest blessing. She turned from the room and carried her Bible to the table, where she would read the scriptures, but that was perilous, too. That room and that table was where Beatrice and David had told her their intentions, which had seemed to be the beginning of the unraveling of her relationship with Beatrice.

Agnes sat and folded her arms on the table, unwilling to leave her house and stir anyone to inquire of her well-being. Finally, her head still reeling, she lay her face on her arms and, there, in the quietest, loneliest hours of the night, she slept.

As the morning dawned, she roused herself and went to her mat with the understanding that this reality was now hers. By tomorrow she would be, by all outward appearances, back to normal, but this contempt from her treasured child had changed her. She wasn't certain how; she only knew she would be different from now on.

∙∙∙∙∙∙

David's face was lit up. "You did it, Bea," he said.

"I feel like I just broke my mother's heart," Bea responded, expecting no praise for what she had done, even as she felt it was a big step in asserting her independence in her relationship with her mother.

"You were clear about how you're feeling," he said. "It's important not to keep holding all the pain inside of you. Speaking freely will allow you and your mother to move forward, in time."

They sat together and replayed what was just said on the phone to Agnes, and what they had both said to each other after. Bea wanted reassurance. Was David just being kind to her? She did not want to be placated. She recoiled from the image of herself as David's troubled wife.

David smiled, "I mean it, Bea. I am proud of you."

"I guess you're right. My mother deserves a more honest daughter than I have been. Maybe honesty is good, even when it hurts."

David smiled affectionately at Bea. "Like the day you told her we were going to get married, no matter what. I remember it so well."

She remembered the evening too, and that it had been the right thing to be firm about. "When something is right, we have to step up and say so," she said, still seeking assurance that her dear husband was on her side.

He was. He held her as they stood in the middle of their little Kampala home, and she felt the anxiety lift from her body. She'd spent a lifetime lying about how she felt. Especially to her mother. It was endless and demanding work. She had tried so hard for so long. A weariness crept over her, and she went back to bed.

•••••••

After the blow of her conversation with Beatrice, Agnes took four days off from the demands of the shelter to spend time in her home. The days ahead looked too empty, so she offered herself to Sunday and Molly for a few extra shifts at the Inn. She'd kept up two days most weeks, as she needed the familiarity of her old routine. It helped to keep her mind occupied but did not ask too much. Late the second night, while Molly and Sunday hosted an AA meeting, Agnes received an unexpected phone call.

"Hello, is this Agnes Adong in Gulu? This is Marian. Marian Mortenson, the one in Utah with the bashed in head. Remember me?"

"Of course, Marian, how are you?" Agnes was surprised to hear the American woman's voice and perplexed about why she would be calling.

"Is this a good time?" Marian went on.

"Yes, Sister Mortenson. Yes, of course."

"Good. I called you as I have complicated things to discuss."

"But first, how is your head?" Agnes asked.

Marian glossed over Agnes's concern. "I still get bad headaches, but the rest of me feels a whole lot better as I have a very public protective order to keep Martin away now. I'm safe for the first time in all my married life. And he even spent a couple of nights in jail for what he did to me, which felt really good. I've learned that even the worst of abusers rarely even serve a day, but he has. The old devil," she replied bluntly. "I want to talk to you," Marian went on. "I have a real purpose for this call, but it was too hard to put in an email. I know you must be very busy with all you have to do, but I think you are the only one who can give me the assistance I need."

Agnes's curiosity grew. "What can I do?"

"Well, I know you're in the church, but I don't know if you fully understand what it's like to live almost right under the same roof as the Brethren out here."

"I am not sure what the Brethren is," Agnes replied.

"Oh, I mean The Twelve—the Mormon men who run the church. This includes the Prophet. They make all the policies. Well, the PR department has a big say, too, but no one admits that." Marian spoke quickly and with confidence, explaining that after word had gotten out that her husband, who was a leader in the church, had been abusing her for years and no one had done anything to protect her, the *New York Times* had written an article about it.

"It was a big deal, Agnes," Marian said. "The article trashed the church for the way it ignores women's pain. The story was a huge embarrassment for the church. Sister Adong, you were in the article too! Talking about the abuse of women in Africa and in Utah. The story caught fire, or as we say, it went viral. You know, like a virus—it spread." Marian was almost shouting over the phone now.

"Oh, that is too bad." Agnes could not tell by the woman's tone, whether Sister Marian was pleased or unhappy about the story.

"No, no. It's a good thing," Marian continued to shout, and Agnes gathered that the volume of her voice indicated excitement, not anger. "That's what I am calling you about. You see, the church was talking all about supporting refugees three years ago. Mostly in Europe or the US. They talked quite a bit about how we were all once refugees in America, and how we should have sympathy for refugees and help them all we can. This was in 2016."

Agnes was nodding again. Since Uganda had lots of refugees, the local Mormons had been glad to hear of their church's commitment to this issue. "And it is in the Bible, too, in Matthew," Agnes offered, still unable to connect Marian's story with the PR department and now with refugees. She wondered where this was going.

"Yes, precisely," Marian shouted into the phone. "And since the church has been falling over themselves to make up for how they failed to protect me in the past, they've offered to donate $500,000 for a project of my choice. A project that would specifically help women who were victims of violence. But they strongly suggested that I consider a project focused on refugees in Africa! Just like that. They asked if I could find a way to make good use of that money and that's why I am calling you, Agnes Adong."

Five hundred thousand dollars. Agnes had to sound the numbers out in her head and then write them down on the message pad that lay next to the phone at the Inn's reception desk. Had Marian Mortenson really just offered her this huge sum of money? To help women refugees in Africa?

"Hello? Agnes?" Marian's voice arrived full and impatient. "Are you still there?"

"Yes, I am," Agnes replied quickly, "Thank you, Sister Mortenson," she said eagerly. "What can I do to help?"

"Well, first of all, you can stop calling me that," Marian said. "I don't like my husband's name."

"Of course," Agnes said, her brain buzzing with excitement. She could not wait to tell Pastor about this miracle!

"Well, suddenly everyone around here has become an expert on refugees in Africa. Seems they all want to be my partner and come to Africa with me. They told me about all the refugees they knew and how their favorite programs could benefit from this money. But, I told them, No. I said, I am going to go to Gulu to talk to my friend Agnes Adong. Are you doing the work you talked about with refugees from Sudan?"

"Yes," Agnes said. "It's actually South Sudan, just across our border. I have a new shelter there that we are busy building up. We have already begun to welcome women and their families. It's called Eve's Shelter."

"Perfect," Marian crowed. "That's exactly what I hoped to hear. I know and trust you, and I want to send this money to your organization. Are you happy to let the church say they donated it?"

"I would be very happy with that. This will be a huge help. I need to speak to my partner, Pastor Emanuel. He is the manager of Eve's Shelter, and I am the executive director."

"Is he a good man?" Marian asked, and Agnes heard a note of caution in her voice. A familiar concern among women who'd had bad experiences with men. "It is specifically a women's refugee center, right?"

"Yes, and Pastor is wonderful. Very hard working. In fact he lives out at the shelter most of the time. He has provided trucks and equipment for building, and so much more than I could ever have done without him."

"That's good, Agnes." Marian's voice softened. "I have learned a lot this year, but I admit that I don't know where to begin. I know whatever you are doing is the right thing."

"It is the right thing, Marian," Agnes confirmed. "I know that God approves of it."

Marian responded. "My plan was to come and work beside you, but I am not yet steady enough. It makes me mad, but I still get bad headaches and have blackouts. It will be a while before I am able to participate, but at least the money can start to work for you in the meantime."

"Are you sure you want to give it all to us?"

"Yes, I'm sure, Agnes Adong. I can have the church cut the check to you this week."

"Someday you must come to see the shelter, Marian. You will love it," Agnes concluded.

As soon as Marian had hung up the phone, Agnes called Pastor at Eve's Shelter. They celebrated Marian's offer, and discussed how the donation would help them enlarge their estimates of how many women and children they could take in. It was beyond their wildest dreams.

●●●●●●

Bea had spent a pleasant hour on the phone with her sister as Grace asked questions about life in Kampala and filled Bea in on her time in Seattle.

"Moses and Mercy are building a real house," Grace told her, but made no mention of Mama-Agnes, and Bea did not mention her pregnancy. She had not yet decided how she was going to proceed and, for the moment, she preferred the feeling that she was in control.

"I can't wait to see you when you come home for Christmas," Bea said, and she actually meant it. But by nightfall, the anxiety muddled her mind again as she stormed through the apartment, repeating her convictions that she did not want a baby. That she could not take care of a baby. That she would be a terrible mother. That David was inadequate to take care of a baby. That the baby would die. That any baby she had would die. God knew she would be a bad mother, so why didn't he let her baby die now? Surely her mother had lied to God and told Him to make this baby in her womb. Why did her mother always make bad things happen to her?

Why? Why? Why?

35

July 2019—Kitgum

Agnes was pleased to be included in the list of professionals who received a *Dungu Newsletter*, the official updates from Aiko about the clinic in Dungu. It made her feel like one of the team and reminded her that these impressive people considered her a serious professional woman. A contemporary. This helped bolster her confidence at Eve's Shelter in times when she questioned her leadership. Plus, Agnes was genuinely interested in what went on at Dungu. After all, she had been there in the beginning.

Aiko's *July Update* informed them that the clinic was nearly finished and that Aiko had hired a psychiatrist who specialized in trauma. This was considered an essential service since all patients at the clinic suffered from trauma to their minds and hearts and souls, as well as their battered bodies.

Dr. Berniss Kabongo, Agnes read in Aiko's report, "had a background working with not only those with recent traumatic experiences, but also with those for whom trauma was compounded by it being passed on from previous family members and from lives immersed in communities of violence and war." The doctor had published a paper in a Paris medical journal on "Intergenerational Trauma and Epigenetic Transmission: Understanding adverse childhood experiences."

Fascinated, Agnes searched for more articles about the subject. While intergenerational trauma explained why so many young people behaved as if they'd been in the war when they had not, it could also make mothers of affected children feel even worse about their parenting, as they came to believe that their own trauma had harmed their children. Agnes could think of a few women who'd had worse experiences trying to put themselves back together after a trauma-filled life, and how they worried they'd made their daughters fearful of everything without even knowing they were doing it. She thought of her own children, and her understanding of how she'd harmed Beatrice and Grace, because she was still affected by trauma.

She knew that many of her friends, Molly and Aiko included, had praised her in the past for the work she'd done on herself and on mothering her children well, but Agnes considered herself an honest woman, and she knew the truth. Being a mother was her most important task, it was the first calling God gave her, and it was where she had failed the most. The proof was right in front of her.

Her own daughter, Beatrice, had condemned her and cut her out of her life. That was all the evidence she needed that she had passed her trauma on to her children, new proof that her sons, and her daughters, had all been robbed of their real joy in life, because she was their traumatized mother.

Agnes worried especially about Beatrice. Even more than Moses, who basked in the love he now enjoyed from Mercy, Moz, and Peace. If only Beatrice would give her mother another chance. All these years, the girls had been Agnes's central concern. But still her efforts had miscarried.

Agnes wondered what Dr. Kabongo would recommend to the mothers that would come to her seeking advice, and if she should travel to Dungu herself and ask how to change? If Aiko knew how important this was, Agnes was sure she would reach out to Beatrice, who was obviously suffering. She resolved to call Aiko.

······

"Aiko," Agnes said into her phone. "I was so interested to read about the new doctor you found for the Dungu clinic. I admire how thorough you have been in building your team. You have located such fine women for Dungu, and I am honored to know them."

"Thank you, Agnes," Aiko said. "I hope Dr. Kabongo will teach us all something. I am sure I will learn things from her both as a doctor and as a mother, who comes from a lineage where at least one of the women suffered real trauma. One that I know of but, who knows, perhaps there are others in past generations who had their own burden to carry. They are surely part of me, too. I give them credit for inspiring me all these years later, to turn my attention to others who might need my help."

"I had not thought of it like that," Agnes replied, encouraged by Aiko's words.

"I presume, Agnes, that it is your legacy of suffering in the bush that guides you in your work on the shelter you are building, right?"

It took Agnes a little while to absorb what Dr. Aiko was suggesting. She had not heard this idea before, but she liked the thought that both good and bad could have come out of her suffering. "It must be so," she said quietly, turning the idea over in her mind. "If we pass on the trauma we inherited, surely we also pass on the desire we have to help others survive it."

"Exactly," Aiko said.

"I wish it would guide me to do something to lift up Beatrice. I'm so worried about her, Aiko. She has not spoken to me except to let me know she is pregnant, and since then, nothing. Have you seen her?"

"I have," Aiko said. "I think she is still working on becoming whoever she was meant to be."

"I hope she is happy in Kampala," Agnes said, wishing she knew how to ask Aiko to pass on any news of Beatrice, regardless of how insignificant it might be. It had not been that long ago that Agnes had known everything about her daughter, and now . . . nothing. It embarrassed her to lean on Aiko in this way, especially since Aiko had praised her for being a good mother, but as she chewed on the information Aiko had included about Dr. Kabongo, she built up the courage to ask, "Do you think I could learn something from the psychiatrist, if I met with her?"

"I am sure you could, and surely you have a lot to teach her as well, Agnes. You've lived a life that teaches lessons. We are all still learning about trauma in families and in communities. We teach each other."

Agnes found this a comforting thought, as it implied that there was still time to learn and do better. She wished she could ask Beatrice what would help her do better.

As if reading her thoughts, Aiko continued, "I hope that someday you and Beatrice can teach us all something about what it has been like for the two of you to live through your trauma and healing. Since you have both thought seriously about all the tough questions that have to be faced in a family of survivors, you would be the ideal people to address this."

"It's nice to think it can be so," Agnes said. But still she yearned for a word from her child.

······

Grace sounded cheerful and normal whenever she called Agnes for advice or to chat about her Seattle life. Agnes loved hearing every detail, more so since Beatrice had become so silent. With each interaction, Grace sounded more and more mature, but she never suggested that her adulthood meant she felt less dear to her mother.

"Thank you, Grace," Agnes wrote in each text she sent, grateful when they ended their calls, that there wasn't a hint of anxiety, or the kind of fears and upset that Agnes associated with trauma. Was it possible, she wondered, to pass on trauma to one child and not another?

One evening, Agnes received an email from Diana Nielsen, with whom she had shared some of her dismay about Beatrice. Diana wrote that it was completely normal for girls to pull away from their mothers if they had been very close, but her response only convinced Agnes that this was an American pattern. Diana could not possibly imagine how close she and Beatrice had been. After all, in America, mothers and daughters don't sleep in the same bed until the girls marry. Beatrice had been right beside Agnes—always—until now.

36

December 2019—Seattle

Grace sat alone in a Seattle Starbucks sipping a peppermint mocha. It was very cold outside—at least, cold to Grace at 40° F—and rainy and gray, as usual. She seldom enjoyed such solitude and took the time to reflect on her time in America. It had been a full year, and Grace wondered what part of her experience she would share with her mother when she went home. Surely not most of it, although she did not like to be dishonest. Had she told her mother about Reggie? About Sylvie and Cassie? How about Jamie? Maybe not him. Grace allowed herself to drift into the memories of those first days in this new city, when everything had felt strange. She'd taken small steps toward acclimating to this totally new place.

When she'd arrived in Seattle, Peggy was undergoing heavy-duty chemotherapy for her uterine cancer, and the chance she might die was real. The gregarious, optimistic Isaiah had become a different man, having been greatly altered by his wife's illness. Grace pledged herself to contribute something valuable to the family and to the lives of Winnie and little Agnes. She had experience with children, and enjoyed reading to them, playing with them, and being a kind auntie. Isaiah asked that Grace speak to the children mostly in Acholi, both as a comfort to him and so they would learn a little of the language. He was easy to live with, but sadness hung in every room of the house.

Rita, Peggy's sister-in-law, had been a huge help and supported Grace's transition to university and life in Seattle. She'd registered Grace in one class for the spring semester, and then two classes for the summer. While the commute to the University of Washington was challenging at first, Grace mastered it and welcomed the chance to wander around the big city. Within three weeks of starting school, she had made two friends—an enthusiastic young woman from Jamaica named Sylvie, who loved English literature too, and her buddy, a blonde Irish girl named Cassie, who had a Tanzanian grandmother and was a physics major.

Grace emailed her mother often and called her on WhatsApp weekly. Mama-Agnes offered insights into Isaiah's challenges and shared some of the content of the sporadic emails he sent to her in Gulu. His emails were often written in the middle of long solitary nights when Isaiah needed to spill out his grief and his fear of losing his wife and raising two children alone. He imagined what life would be like living with sorrow, which took him right back to his childhood in Gulu. He wrote many words meditating on the losses suffered by fathers and mothers in Gulu, where he recalled no escape from everyday sadness. What would he do if Peggy died? Could he go on? How did people survive this kind of decimation of one's world?

Agnes filled Grace in on what was going on in Gulu and made clear how grateful she was that although Grace was thousands of miles away, they still communicated regularly. "I'm so proud of you, my child, that you are so capable," Agnes had written in her last email.

In the weeks before she'd left Gulu, Grace had initiated online English literacy lessons for Moses, and she was pleased he'd stuck with it and kept up a pretty good email communication while she had been away. Moses did not provide much detail, but she knew the broad parameters of his life with Mercy and the kids.

Most of all, Grace texted Agnes with encouraging messages full of exclamation points and emojis. But the thing Grace missed most was hearing from Beatrice, and she wondered if her sister ever missed her too.

······

Reading novels by Jane Austen, Charles Dickens, Henry James, and Thomas Hardy had become an additional joy in Grace's life. The Brontë sisters, which she had read in Uganda, thrilled her again, along with Shakespeare. Grace remembered how she became almost giddy with excitement when she read the syllabus for her new college and bought the books with Rita. It didn't take her long to realize she had lots of pages ahead of her, but she threw herself into this new adventure, delighted that she could talk about it with Sylvie and others in her class.

She was not as academically equipped for her course as some students, but she improved quickly and her professor spent time helping her. Class discussions were a treat, and she was lucky that being Ugandan was considered an asset to the class, along with her accent and frequent blunders in American English. And because Isaiah was paying her what felt like a *staggering* amount of money, she did not have to worry about how much things cost. That kind of financial freedom made her feel light and free.

Throughout her stay, Grace remained conscientious about her commitment to Isaiah's family. She was careful about time and responsibilities. She adored Winnie and he loved her back, which was a wonderful feeling, and she was working on Little Agnes, who was more challenging.

Isaiah had hired a housekeeper/nanny/home health aide who was responsible for running Winnie back and forth to kindergarten and to his numerous school-related activities. She also did a good deal of nursing care for Peggy, as well as the cooking and cleaning. That left three-year-old Agnes for Grace to look after during the day, plus Winnie when his school activities were done.

Grace relished her responsibilities with the children. She sang to them and played finger games with their little hands. Little Agnes was more demanding than Grace had expected, and her relations with her didn't go so smoothly. Grace quickly learned that American children were more demanding in general than the children she had known at home. Still, she hung in there, and never let her failures with this girl child undermine her pledge to support this family. Grace found Isaiah's kids a pleasure, but soon found she was eager to get them to sleep so she could get back to reading. She was obsessed.

That is, until she had her first encounters with a very flirtatious guy in her class named Jamie. He was shockingly handsome and made no secret about his interest in the new girl, "Grace, from Africa." This was a surprise—an unexpected bit of bliss. Being African did not seem to exclude her from friendly banter between boys and girls where there was clearly a sexual undercurrent, and it didn't ever feel dangerous. Grace was fascinated, and she liked it.

She had wondered if she was supposed to tell Isaiah about Jamie. Or perhaps Rita? Or—her mother. She decided she would tell Isaiah if he asked, and of course, Rita. But she was quite sure that she should not mention this to her mother. Grace hoped her mother had been better lately, but she did not want to test the idea by sharing any tidbit that might trigger another spiral of worry for Agnes.

As Grace discovered her new sexier self in Seattle, the amount of time she spent thinking about Jamie—at school, on her way home, on a weekend—made her realize that this subject was becoming a bit of a preoccupation. Apart from Jamie and her lovely college friends, Grace also had a group of cheerful LDS friends from all over the country. Even a few from foreign countries. They met on Sundays, and Grace enjoyed the gatherings that the ward set up to facilitate romances. Yes, that ward was specifically for Young Single Adults (YSA). That was its purpose—approved flirting. Still, Grace could not tell her mother. Agnes would not understand.

Grace was finding an easy rhythm to her days when, along came an even more appealing guy, one who swept into her life and challenged, at the very least, her time management efforts. Reggie was a little older and she thought of him as a more reflective guy compared to her playful personality. He was part Jamaican, with a New York American mother, and spent his days studying at a near-by computer school. Grace was taken off guard and quickly lost interest in Jamie. Reggie presented a world of new possibilities.

Reggie returned Grace's interest and was soon racing across town to meet her after classes. He would ride the monorail and a streetcar, just to sit with Grace as she made her way to and from home. She lost track of all the things she'd worked so hard to keep under control.

Isaiah sensed what was happening, and they had a good talk about her social life and dating. Grace had every intention of taking his advice, but Reggie was a distraction.

Isaiah was fair and never made her feel guilty. "I simply ask that you tell me when you have to be late." Then, one evening, he said, "Ask him to pick you up at the house, so I can meet him."

Grace arranged the introduction. She and Reggie went to a movie, and he took her home on a bus. Isaiah was waiting and Grace told Reggie good night as he gave her a quick kiss at the door.

She couldn't wait to see him again.

There was a next time, and a next time after that. She found Reggie so easy to talk to. He had been raised by religious people, too. "I understand you, Grace. We come from similar people. I know you are a special girl, and I like you very much."

When Reggie kissed her properly the first time, like she'd seen in the movies, Grace was surprised to discover that she was not the least bit afraid. In fact, she wished he would kiss her more, and as time went on, she began to wish he would kiss her in different ways. Ways that went beyond the gentle kisses he left her with at the door, or in the back of the monorail.

One Saturday night Grace proposed a new plan for the evening. "Isaiah is taking the children out. Let's go back to the house and be there alone—just the two of us. We can watch TV and hang out."

Hanging out alone offered so many opportunities to kiss much more deeply than they had done before, and it was quite wonderful—even more wonderful than Grace had secretly imagined. Except that things didn't go far enough for her. Within an hour, Grace was wrapped all around Reggie, who was initially tentative and careful, but then more obliging, and soon took the role of the experienced lover. He had his careful hands up under her sweater, moving enthusiastically around her breasts, with Grace guiding him the best she could to any hard-to-reach places. She was without caution, until Reggie shook his head with a gentle smile. "Gracie, don't forget your commitments to your mother and to your family of Mormons. And to God."

Grace felt her blood rise. She wanted Reggie to undress her, and she wanted to undress him. She tried to go ahead, but Reggie backed off again.

"Come on, Gracie," he said, more firmly this time. "You have told me too much about yourself to go down this path."

He gave her a good, warm last kiss, buttoned up the Levi's Grace had managed to get inside, and moved slowly but deliberately away from her. Then he smiled and left.

Grace was not sure if she was mad, insulted, grateful, or just disappointed. She was definitely confused. This was not what she'd expected from a man. She called and tried to arrange for another rendezvous, which Reggie made a polite excuse for. Grace became obsessive. She practically stopped attending her much-loved lit class, and plotted ways to get Reggie to come to Isaiah's house while the kids napped.

Finally, Grace's determination and organization prevailed. She figured out a way to skip the Mormon YSA Ward on Sundays, and persuaded Reggie to come to the house while Isaiah was at church with his children and Peggy was asleep in her bedroom. Her persistence and enthusiasm worked its magic on this fine young man, and soon Reggie and Grace were enjoying passionate sex, every Sunday. Reggie was not only willing by now, but prepared for Grace's set ups with packages of condoms. He always arrived on time and eager.

But much to Grace's annoyance, Reggie kept raising concerns about where this was leading. "What about your description of your family as the most solid Mormon family in Gulu? What about your description of your mother as the most religious Latter-day Saint in Uganda?"

"I know you're a good man and you're only thinking about me, Reggie, but I can make my own mind up about these things," Grace argued. "This is what I want."

But Reggie knew this path would not serve either of them well in the long run. One Sunday afternoon, while Grace described her romantic plan for them to get married and have babies, Reggie pushed himself to the side of the couch and held his hands for her to stop.

"We can't play games with our lives, Grace. I am in love with you, but this is not the time for making such disruptive plans. I know how committed you are to your family. I know how much you need to excel at school and finish university. I know you have serious things to accomplish, and they can't be served by us being irresponsible." He touched his hand to her face. "Please, Grace, we need to be very careful, so we don't make silly mistakes." He smiled at her lovingly, and reassuringly. "Please understand that I'm pulling back for your own good."

But when he expressed his worry, Grace turned punitive. She threatened to sleep with Jamie. She made other loose threats, and seemed clueless as to where this behavior could lead her.

"What you don't understand, Grace, is there is no safety net waiting for you if you fall. Can you see that? If you get pregnant, you don't have the kind of parachute rich kids have here. A well-off American girl has a team of wealthy family members, well trained at erasing the obvious—and ready to provide her with a new start. If something happened to you, where would you turn? If you get yourself pregnant, or flunk out of school, who would pick you up and start you over?" He took her hand

and squeezed, making sure she understood how earnest he was.

But Grace would not listen. She shook off his hand and became resentful. She had not had an easy life. She had earned this kind of pleasure. She was determined to get what she wanted in America.

In anger, she broke up with Reggie, and she was not kind about it. She said he was weak and not a real man.

Reggie expressed his sadness at Grace's decision but told her that he knew her well enough by now to give up. "You are strong, Grace, but naïve. You seem determined to head down the path to self-destruction. It seems to me that getting out of your way is the best way I can help you."

So, Reggie stepped out of Grace's life.

Certain that she was exercising her own freedom, Grace put Reggie to the back of her mind. She was soon back to chasing Jamie, skipping classes, missing babysitting, and heading for a fall.

She was a little surprised when her two closest friends didn't side with her.

"All women have a right to live their own lives and make their own choices," Sylvie said. "Without other people imposing old-fashioned values on them. But I'm telling you from experience, that there's a difference between you as an African and the Americans you have met so far."

"Sylvie's right," Cassie chimed in. "You only have a few chances to make good, Gracie."

Grace was blessed to have found these girlfriends, as they each had at least one poor parent who had given their all to their children. A parent they had, at times, resented but who had taught them good lessons. Supporting one another, Sylvie and Cassie weighed in on Grace.

"First, you need to go to a clinic and get reliable birth control," Cassie said. "Second, you need to get back to studying and not flunk your first university class in Seattle."

"Think of your mother," Sylvie said.

"You carry on like this, Grace, and it will kill her," Cassie added.

From somewhere down deep, Grace turned hostile. "I've given up too much because I am Agnes's daughter. I won't give up anymore. It is so hard to be the daughter of someone who needs so much for so long. I'm done." Grace walked away from her friends, and then she cried like she had not cried in years.

By the next week, Grace had fallen behind on her schoolwork and had missed a call from her mother. To make things worse, she was having a weird pain when she peed. Frightened, she called Rita, who told her to meet her at the campus clinic right away.

Rita gave her a hug and marched her straight into an exam room and requested a pregnancy test, and a full panel of STI tests, including one for HIV.

Grace was frightened.

"How long have you been seeing this young man?" Rita asked.

"A few months," Grace answered in a small voice.

"Let me guess," Rita said. "You're having sex and always use protection, except for that one time."

Grace nodded miserably.

Rita put both hands on Grace's shoulders. "How is your semester going?"

Grace admitted in a small voice that she was behind.

"If you go back to Uganda with a poor letter grade from an American university, it will ruin your chances for a scholarship," Rita said gently.

A medical tech came in, gave Grace a cup to pee in, and said the phlebotomist would come to take blood. Grace submitted to the testing meekly, and when they'd finished, Rita bought her a coffee at Starbucks. "How can I undo what I've done?" Grace asked.

Rita smiled. "Go home and study. Show up for the children. And call me when your test results come in. It should only take a day or two."

Grace spent those two days alternating between terror (what if she *was* pregnant? Or had HIV?) and absolute focus on her responsibilities.

When the test results hit her inbox two days later, she was immensely relieved that she was positive only for chlamydia. The doctor had prescribed antibiotics; she could pick them up at the pharmacy and that would be that.

She called Rita and cried with relief.

That Sunday Grace went back to her YSA ward and made an appointment with the bishop, whom she scarcely knew, to talk about "some stuff." He was cheerfully willing to find a time that fit her schedule, and Grace was reminded of Okot James and how he had seemed to practically give his life over for the people in the Gulu Ward. How many times had he made himself available to listen to Agnes go over and over her trauma from the past? This bishop here had four kids and a job and commuted a long way to the church. How many other young men and women took his time to confess their indiscretions, and their endless excuses for them, and cried in his office over their inability to stop having sex? And yet, he was "called," and he had accepted, and he was only in year two of what she suddenly saw as a four-year sentence. She decided to be brief when she went to talk to him and to think in advance of her own way forward. Beginning with studying those fabulous books from the library. Reading the writers she so admired. Some of them made more sense to her now, as she had taken her version of roads the characters had traveled.

She'd didn't tell the bishop everything, undoubtedly to his relief, and he kindly recommended "a path to repentance," giving her a calling to minister to another young woman in the ward whose sister had cancer and needed some "compassionate service." Grace got the point of all this. She visited the sister, liked her, and visited again. This new LDS friend told her she was trying to decide whether to go on a mission. Had Grace considered that? No, admitted Grace, it had never occurred to her. But what an idea. This exciting new thought took over the spot in her brain that she'd reserved for Reggie and Jamie. It was a loss in some ways, but a relief in others. A big relief.

Later, sitting alone at Starbucks, Grace thought back on those weeks of real fear of being pregnant or having HIV. What had she been thinking?! Her friends had been right. She did only have one shot to make a good life for herself. She wouldn't be foolish again and risk ruining this opportunity she'd been given.

She tapped her phone screen and checked the time. She was looking forward to hearing her mother's voice and felt an excited anticipation for the phone to ring. The Starbucks was filling up as she took a sip of her mocha. After everything she'd been through, Grace was grateful for what she'd achieved since arriving in Seattle. Under the circumstances, she was thrilled when she managed to squeak by with a C+ in English literature from a very reputable university in Seattle, Washington, in the USA. She could claim credit for teaching Winnie, and hopefully Agnes, a bit of Acholi and some songs that would last for a lifetime in their sponge-like brains. She'd also managed, just barely, to not disappoint her kind and generous uncle, who was struggling so much to regain his footing during his wife's illness. Her biggest regret was that she had not been close to Peggy, as she was often off limits because of her compromised immune system from the chemo, but Grace admired her aunt even more for what she had learned by living in her home.

A young couple pushed through the door into the Starbucks. They stood close together, touching easily as they decided on their order, bright wedding rings on each of their hands. Grace's thoughts turned to Beatrice. The last time she'd seen her sister had been at her wedding almost two years ago. That seemed so very strange, given that they had spent every day of their lives together before that. She wondered if they would ever be close again.

After considering the bishop's suggestion, Grace had told Isaiah that she was considering a mission. He sighed. "Well," he said, "a mission can be a wonderful thing. It doesn't solve all problems. But your age is a very tumultuous period in every person's life. A mission offers two years for you to leave "the world" behind and concentrate on purer things. Think and pray about it. It might be just what you need."

As Uncle Isaiah said all these wise and kind things, Grace wondered if he knew about what she had been doing. Had he just kept quiet to avoid a fissure in their relationship? He made it clear that he cared about her and that he expected her to do what she promised while also enjoying her year in Seattle. Grace was not yet old enough to go on a mission for the church. She needed another semester, if Isaiah would have her, which he would. And he would tell her again about how the chance to go on a mission in 2008 had opened the world to him. "We all have different paths in life, don't we, Grace?" he'd said, lovingly.

She smiled and nodded, sure that she and Rita and God knew she did not have a single regret for the zig-zag path she had taken to get to where she was now.

Grace had taken two summer courses, and two in the fall, and from reading about life in the wonderful novels she had been assigned, she decided that she wanted to write someday. She had stories inside her about lovemaking, and loyalty, and race in America, and life in Uganda, and a whole lot about what it was like to try to raise a particularly spirited little girl. In America they called little girls like Agnes Christina Odeki "a pistol," or even "destined for greatness." In Uganda, little Agnes would have been beaten until she started to obey. Another big difference in culture.

Her phone buzzed once on the table and Grace snatched it up. Her mother's voice at last.

"I love you, Grace," Agnes said in greeting, and launched immediately into the conversation. "You'll be home in just ten days."

37

December 2019—Kampala

Moses secured Grace's suitcases in the truck so no one would steal them, then got into the cab next to his sister. Grace beamed, grateful her brother had come such a long way to welcome her home at the airport rather than having her hire a driver to bring her to Gulu. "I'm looking forward to seeing the shelter, and celebrating Christmas there," Grace said. "When is the party?"

Moses knew the dates and was proud to advise Grace on the plans. "But listen, Gracie," he said, his voice turning serious. "While we are so close to Kampala, I want to go see Beatrice and David."

Grace was silent. Was he serious? Did he remember what had happened when she and Mama-Agnes had come to Kampala to see her older sister? "She shuts me out," Grace said, horrified to feel a lump rising in her throat.

"I want to apologize to her," Moses said. "If we just arrive there, do you really think they will not open the door?"

"Maybe," said Grace. "Or David might let us in, and then Beatrice might leave."

"I think David would be glad to see us," Moses said. "I want to tell Beatrice that I forgive her for inviting Okello Peter to Gulu last New Year's. I've been thinking about how angry I was. I was so furious at Okello Peter, I was on fire. And then I was furious at Beatrice for trying to pretend he was a good person, a decent man. I was angry for months. But, Grace, I have come to realize that everyone has a bad story in Gulu. Some are worse than others, but for nearly everyone in the war, there is a bad story. I've been thinking about how some of us have to lead the way in putting the bad stories away. I have carried a stone in my heart for a year. Longer even. Mercy is the one who tells me to throw it away. She says that's what Jesus expects of us."

"It sounds like you've been going to church." Grace knew that he and Mercy liked their priest very much and had become very religious. She also knew, after talking a lot to Isaiah about such things, that many people became very religious after trauma.

"Yes," said Moses. "Father Luke's ministry is about bringing an end to the war in people's hearts. He begins each mass with *Luke 6:3: Judge not, and ye shall not be judged: condemn not, and ye shall not be condemned: forgive, and ye shall be forgiven*. There was a man in our church whose heart was hard, and he said he would never forgive the man who took his mother's life. And Grace, this man suffered every sickness. Father Luke said he suffered because he could not forgive his enemy. But one day the sick man took up his bed and laid it out on the altar and forgave the killer, and Grace, the man was lifted up in front of us. We all saw it. He kissed the ring of Father Luke, and Father said that the man was forgiven and could go on his way in peace. He was made whole. I saw it, my sister. He forgave, and he was made well."

"Moses, you are a sincere Christian," said Grace. "And you're right. You have a message to give Beatrice. I'll go with you." She looked out the window and steeled herself for an awkward encounter.

Moses pulled the truck up in front of the building where Beatrice and David had their apartment. "That is their living room window," said Grace, pointing up three floors. "I'm going to text her to say we're here and give her a little warning." Then she collected herself.

"I will lead the way and knock. I'll bet she welcomes us," said Moses.

Before he even knocked, Beatrice was above them on the stairs, smiling, and telling them to come in. She hugged both of them, and so did David, although he looked a bit apprehensive. "I'm so happy you're home, Grace," Beatrice said. "You must be so tired from the long trip. I hope you'll stay here tonight."

It was strange for Grace to see Beatrice with a rounded belly. She found herself picturing what Beatrice and David's baby would be like.

Beatrice asked her lots of questions about Seattle, and asked Moses about Mercy and Moz and Peace. It felt almost normal, Grace thought with relief. No one mentioned their mother or the shelter.

"I felt quite sick, at first," said Beatrice when Grace asked how her pregnancy was going. "I thought morning sickness was only something Americans got. It was pretty hard to live with the first three months, but the next few months have been fine. I'm due in April. Here people talk about it and don't try to pretend they aren't pregnant like they do in Gulu." She laughed. "Some strangers even ask me when I'm due."

"Beatrice, I have something to say to you." Moses shifted forward so that he was perched on the front of the gray-green sofa and stretched out his hands across the low wooden coffee table. As Beatrice reached for his hands and smiled cautiously, he began. "Beatrice, when you brought Okello Peter to Gulu for your wedding party, I was so angry at him and at you that I wished evil on both of you. After you left, and much of the past two years, I held on to those very bad feelings. But, my sister, I have had a change of heart. I have accepted Christ Jesus as my Savior. I have laid my anger on the altar and my anger is gone. I have forgiven you, and I beg you to forgive me for the anger that I held for you. I am truly sorry for judging you and for carrying dark thoughts for so long."

With these words, Moses leaned across the low table and kissed her hands in his. She looked stunned. David's expression was as eloquent as if he had spoken, and what it said was, *I didn't think he had this in him.*

Grace felt warm as she thought of how angry her brother had been when his leg was first broken.

Beatrice stood and met Moses at the end of the table, embracing him, as both released their pent-up tears. "Moses, it is I who should beg your forgiveness for not taking into consideration your feelings when I organized that party. I was thoughtless, and I am sorry for what I put you through. But I did not make the effort you have made to acknowledge my wrongdoing. You are the bigger person."

"That was powerful, Moses," said David sincerely, shaking his brother-in-law's hand. "And now I'll make sandwiches to eat before we go to bed."

There was a silence as each looked at the other with curiosity and amazement.

"I'm sure you remember, Grace, that David does most of the cooking," said Beatrice, in the only allusion to the visit the year before when she had snubbed Grace and Mama-Agnes. "Come with me and we'll get some blankets for you two to sleep on. You can argue over who gets the sofa and who gets the floor."

◼◦◦◦◦◦◦◼

Moses was not comfortable in the modern kitchen they had here. So, he looked about the room and took in what hung on the walls and how the chairs were neither plastic nor the large wooden ones that seemed to dominate the modest homes in Gulu. He wondered if the preference for bigness had to do with the fact that chairs were usually where a respected elder sat, or an adult with a few children hanging out on a knee or lap. He preferred the small, soft chairs across the coffee table that had bright pillows on them.

He and Mercy were building their first house, and it was the first time he had ever thought about the things that go into a home. He would like some of those soft chairs, he thought, and a sofa like Beatrice's. He had already picked out a ceiling light for their house, with two bulbs, and he was glad his choice was not far from what Beatrice and David had here. He had even chosen a dimmer switch.

Then he was drawn to the framed photos on the walls, of different sizes and in interesting groups. He looked at photos from the wedding in Utah, and realized he hadn't been interested in those before. That made sense. He was not ready then, and his mother wasn't ready to show them either. But here there was a fine picture of Agnes. Beatrice did not hate her mother after all, perhaps. This photo captured Agnes's warmest features—her bright, always flashing eyes, her raised brows and her smile, with her slightly open mouth ready to speak. His mother was not a quiet woman. While she was neither loud nor abrasive, she was rarely silent. He had resented this for so long. Now he was grateful for the permission it gave him to speak and grow into his words.

As his curious eyes moved around the room, he found pictures of himself: Moses, the good father, in his cast and out of it; Moses with pregnant Mercy and then with her and Moz and baby Peace. Most were of Peace wrapped around Mercy, but he looked a moment longer at a new favorite one—one where he had Peace on his shoulders with her grabbing his hair, and Moz standing proudly at his side, with Mercy on his other. "We love that picture of you, Moses," said Beatrice as she returned with the blankets. "Since we are not coming home for Christmas, I'd like to give you your Christmas present now. We had that same photo enlarged and framed." She handed him an unwrapped box and he took it with both hands, with gratitude.

●●●●●●

In the morning David made them all eggs and toast, and Grace enjoyed a cup of coffee, joking about how much she'd come to rely on coffee in America. "As a strong Mormon, Isaiah didn't have it in the house, so I had to drink it at the university. When I get home I will go by Mama's rules and drink that tea of hers," she pledged, hoping that mentioning "Mama's rules" didn't sound like a jab. And then, before they knew it, they were hugging goodbye and climbing back into the truck.

As Moses drove onto the Kampala-Gulu Highway, he and Grace chatted about Seattle, and Moses was aware of how much he had changed. Driving a truck had once been about being alone and venting his anger at life and God. But four years after his accident, driving a truck had become a place where he showed off his healed femur and his full strength. He now realized that driving a truck allowed him to share long conversations with his sister. He laughed at himself. Ten years ago, he had never thought about the joy of a conversation. Even five years ago, conversation was a threat and he counted on the truck to block out anyone who might try to start one. But now, he routinely planned his days and weeks around when he might get to drive someone he cared for, especially, if he could ask them about life's joys and sorrows and tell them his.

"How is Moz's Acholi coming along? Does he still get picked on by bigger kids?" asked Grace.

"He speaks better now. The kids used to be mean, but their cruelty only forced him to learn quickly. Now there is another new boy who can't speak Acholi, and they are all mean to him."

"Do you go to the Inn with Moz and do homework on the computers?" Grace went on.

"Yes. Sometimes more than twice a week. Since Moz is teaching me to read English and speak and write it better, we both look up things that help us. Pastor says I speak it pretty well, but I want to improve," replied Moses proudly. "It's bad because I never went to school, Grace. But you know that. You have always understood that. Sometimes in the store I can't understand a customer and I feel stupid." He hoped Grace would stay home awhile because he learned things from her. And he now hoped he might be the person to help his mother and Beatrice reconcile, although he knew it might be after the baby came. He would pray to know how to be an instrument for peace in his family.

Grace asked about Molly and Sunday, and Moses became very animated as he gave examples of their generosity and encouragement. "No wonder Mama knows so much about the world, Grace," he said. "You can get educated by being at a computer. And do you know what? People come from everywhere and ask where Mama-Agnes is. How did she get famous?"

Grace smiled. "Isaiah says such nice things about her, too. He says she saved him from being just another lost war victim. He gave a talk in church about her. You know that part of Matthew 5 that people quote? '*Ye are the light of the world. A city that is set on a hill cannot be hidden. Neither do men light a candle, and put it under a bushel, but on a candlestick; and it giveth light unto all that are in the house. Let your light so shine before men, that they may see your good works, and glorify your Father which is in heaven.*'"

Moses nodded.

"Isaiah tells his children that their grandma in Africa is like a light that shines in the darkness. He means it. We're lucky, Moses, to have her."

"You're right, Grace. We are."

"I just hope Beatrice comes around, soon. She didn't make any promises, but she did remind me to call Mama-Agnes last night, to tell her not to worry because we were staying over."

"Yes," Moses said. "So maybe she thinks about Mama, deep in her heart."

Grace took out her phone to text Mama-Agnes. *Dear Mama, we are almost home. Expect us around noon. Moses is a good driver. If you are at home, I will see you midday. If you are at the shelter, maybe Moses can take me there to see you. We have not crossed the Nile yet. It will be good to be home in Gulu.*

38

December 20, 2019

Agnes, Grace, and Pastor bumped along the lane to the shelter. Agnes was excited for Grace to see everything and meet everyone. So when she saw Hero scrambling toward the truck with a look of terror on his face, her heart lurched and she steeled herself for a disaster. "Hurry Mama-Agnes," he pleaded.

She told Pastor to show Grace around and she followed Hero to the birthing hut, where a young woman, Anna, was screaming in labor. Magda and Vivian were doing their best to push Anna's baby back into her uterus, since the child was breech and delivering him without turning him would be too much for the mother's birth canal.

"This baby is . . . huge," panted Magda. She and Vivian exchanged a look that said, *Can we save them both?* They might both die, Agnes realized, and her heart sank like a stone.

She leaned in to relieve Magda, who'd been sitting on an overturned yellow bucket between Anna's knees. Magda showed Agnes how to press on Anna's lower belly to try to encourage the baby to back up inside.

Vivian swiped away the sweat on her forehead with her wrist, then held a whispered consultation with Magda in the corner of the hut. They came back to the laboring mother, Agnes, and two other women who were helping Anna count her breaths, their faces grim. "We must try to turn the baby," Vivian said. "Agnes, could you ask the security guards if they can find some gin?"

Agnes sent Hero, who was hovering outside the birthing hut, and he ran off like the wind, returning five minutes later clutching two plastic packets of gin with foil tops.

Vivian explained, murmuring softly, what they were about to do. "This is going to hurt, Anna," she said, "but it is the best chance to save you and the baby."

Anna nodded, her eyes clenched tight as tears ran in tracks down the sides of her face. Magda peeled back the foil on a packet of gin and lifted it to Anna's lips and she drank—one, two, three good swallows, then offered her the second packet. Her body relaxed noticeably, and Vivian nodded to Magda, who held Anna tight while Vivian reached up inside the woman's body with one hand and pressed on her abdomen with the other.

Anna screamed and screamed, but about fifteen minutes later (with the help of the rest of the gin), Vivian delivered a baby boy who immediately began squalling. All the women around them in the hut sighed together with relief.

When Agnes left the birthing hut to find Grace, she found a huddle of women standing a short distance away. All of them were pregnant, she realized. There were nine pregnant women at the shelter right now, or rather eight, Agnes mentally corrected herself, since Anna's baby had just been delivered.

One of the women stepped forward. "Mama-Agnes," she said, "we all want Vivian and Magda to be at our births."

They crowded around her then, and each woman had a story of a birth she had witnessed, either at Palabek or on the road or back home, where the laboring mother had not had the safety and the attendance that was offered here. Agnes promised that they would have the best care the shelter could offer.

She quickly found Grace and Pastor outside the Gazebo and spoke to Pastor. "I was thinking," she said, and he smiled at that. She had gotten more bold with her ideas since starting the shelter. "Let's inform Palabek that we specialize in supporting pregnant mothers. We have good care here, better than what they can offer in many other places."

"I'll call our contact at the UNHCR office at Palabek and ask him to update our policies," Pastor said.

"And we should probably have a midwife on staff, too, to help Vivian," Agnes said, thinking. "*I wonder how we can find one.*"

"I'll reach out to *Medecins sans Frontieres* in Palabek to see if they have any applicants who are trained as midwives."

Agnes smiled. "Thank you."

He bobbed his head and grinned. "My pleasure, Director."

She laughed and walked on, sharing scattered thoughts with Grace. A woman in labor needed special care and understanding, she explained. Grace knew that Beatrice was on her mother's mind . . . Beatrice, who would have all the support she needed during her labor and delivery. It would certainly be a far cry from Agnes crouching in a dark hut, chomping down hard on a stick as her friend Nancy had helped her deliver Moses. "I hope my daughter is surrounded by doctors and midwives when she's ready," she whispered. She envisioned them gathered around Beatrice's bed, encouraging her and getting her anything she needed. David would be solicitous and attentive. Agnes had already watched him exhaust himself when he was trying to help her with anything. Cooking. Arranging her schedule. Making their apartment neat for guests. Sacrificing his work (which Agnes always forgot he had) for her work. Yes, he would be best. When she complained, he would never say what others might say. *Stop complaining. I have better things to do with my time than to listen to you complain.* These familiar words came so quickly to mind that it shamed her. Yes. She had said those words to her daughters countless times; she had taught them never to complain when they were little girls, just as she had been taught to never cry in the bush.

They walked silently, as Agnes tried to remember what her girls had done when she'd said that. It was a long time ago. If Grace had a complaint, she would tell it to anyone in the compound, or at church; she was as carefree with her complaints as she was with her compliments. Beatrice was different. She knew not to bring them to her mother, but she seldom took them elsewhere.

Agnes wondered now what it had cost Beatrice to hold those complaints inside. And she wondered if she could be a better mother to the young women at the shelter.

Grace hugged her as they entered Agnes's little apartment and asked about the laboring woman. Agnes told her everything that had transpired, as they sat down in the white plastic chairs. They took some deep breaths together like they used to do after a nightmare. When they finished, Grace was smiling.

"You did it, Mama-Agnes," she said. "May I pray for you?"

What a beautiful daughter I have raised, Agnes thought, her heart swelling with pride and gratitude. Grace prayed for God's blessing over the shelter, over the women in residence as they healed from their trauma, and over the staff who were helping them. "May your servants here at Eve's Shelter be blessed with a peace passing understanding," Grace prayed, and Agnes felt that peace spreading through her.

······

The next morning marked one week until Christmas, and there were many preparations to be made. Agnes and Pastor led a staff meeting to walk everyone through the upcoming special events and to discuss any problems that were brewing.

"First is the paper bead necklaces," Agnes said. She explained that every woman was making a necklace, and on December 23, they would each draw a name from a hat and give the necklace to that person. "It will make everyone feel remembered."

"Does anyone need help making their necklaces?" Grace asked.

Agnes smiled. "Yes. Let's check in with everyone during bead-making time."

She consulted her notebook. "Magda is organizing a live nativity and will work with the children to practice that for Christmas Eve. Finally, on Christmas Day Father Luke will come from St. Barnabas in Gulu to say Mass here in the Gazebo, and afterward we will eat a special meal together. We will also distribute T-shirts at that time."

Agnes flipped back a few pages in her notebook and explained that the women had voted about what would be printed on the shirts. "We had two sayings for them to chose from: *'To Heal It, You Have to Feel It'*—which a few preferred—and the winning option, *'Everybody Has a Story'*. The T-shirts will be red, and they should arrive in the next few days. We've ordered enough for everyone."

Moving down her list, she reminded the staff to make sure everyone was showing up for the special activities. Changes in the daily schedule often led to some women and children feeling confused or overwhelmed, so she reminded everyone to report any extreme behavior. "Disassociation," she said, ticking off the behaviors on her fingers. "Confusion about who they are or who their children are; accusations; erratic or violent behavior . . .

check with me or Pastor or Jonathan if you see any of these."

They went around the table and each staff member shared a "win" they'd seen that week—a woman making a breakthrough or changing her behavior—as well as anyone they were concerned about. Agnes made a note that there was some concern about Gladys, who had been stealing washtubs again; Irene, who was behaving as though she had lost touch with the present; and Gloria, who had wanted the other T-shirt saying.

Agnes ended the meeting and reflected how glad she was that there had been almost fifteen years between her own trauma and opening the shelter. It was difficult for anyone to work with sad people every day, but she was so grateful to work alongside a team of such dedicated people and to witness moments of deep joy, too. Even with all the complexity, there was something about this hallowed place that gave back to her. She gave and gave to it; and in turn, it gave her wisdom, power, and strength.

She had prepared a lifetime for this.

─────

Grace had vague but happy memories of being with her mother and sister in a safe place, on the roadside, watching her mother learn to make paper bead necklaces. The beads themselves were so beautiful, and she remembered her mother's excitement when she was able to sell her first necklace to a tourist. The beads, somehow, had become a symbol for Grace of the magic of resilience.

And so she didn't really believe the cautionary tales from the staff meeting that the paper bead necklaces could cause conflict at the shelter... until she saw it firsthand.

The bead making had begun in November, so some women had already made a necklace or two for themselves. But that morning, when the trainers reminded them that they must each make a necklace to give away on Christmas Eve, and that they would each draw a name out of a pot that would direct them whom to give it to, there was an instant uproar.

Women shouted that the trainers were being coercive; one person yelled that she didn't like so-and-so and would never give a necklace to her; another insisted that she should be able to keep all the necklaces she made for herself and her daughters; still another was arguing that these shouldn't be permanent gifts. Grace was astonished at the turmoil and ruefully told her mother later that she had thought they were all being dramatic.

Agnes sensed that all this rage was a stand-in for anger at something else—something bigger than a paper necklace, but something so deep inside each woman that she was afraid to acknowledge it was even there. "Let them argue over this," Agnes advised the trainers. "Unless they are hurting each other seriously, let them be angry. After Christmas we can talk about what they are really angry at. They will need to do that."

So, Grace took a deep breath each morning before beadmaking and waded into the chaos. Grace could see the best in almost everyone and tried to treat each one accordingly. She held her expectations high and slowly, the women seemed to calm down. Inwardly, she marveled at her mother's leadership. Every decision was carefully considered, and nothing was the result of thoughtlessness.

* * *

Agnes and Grace had taken to going for a walk together each evening after dinner. Grace told her more stories about Seattle, and Agnes shared more stories about the shelter. It was so good to be together again.

"Mama," Grace said as they walked in the soft twilight. "Are there any women who can't get better?"

"Yes," Agnes said immediately. "It is very difficult. But there are women whom we cannot help. There was a woman called Faith who came about three months ago. She was smart and educated, but she was forever stealing from the other women, and she was very aggressive when Pastor and I tried to work with her. We put her on a daily reporting routine, and we both encouraged her to stop stealing. But she became hostile to me, and then she accused Pastor of inappropriate behavior."

"No!" Grace said, shocked. She knew Pastor would never, ever do such a thing.

"Yes. We tried rewards and we tried loss of privileges, but we could not help her shift her behavior. So, Pastor took her back to Palabek. We heard later that the UNHCR officials had to call the local police on her because she had kicked down another family's tent. She begged to come back to the shelter, but we held firm. She simply could not be trusted. And to help her all the time would have required one of us to ignore so many others."

Grace absorbed all of this. "What is the difference," she said, "between someone like Faith and someone like Magda? Both educated. Both went through terrible experiences. But Faith can't let herself be helped and Magda... is Magda."

Agnes knew what she meant. Every day she marveled that Magda was so steady. And she had a sense of humor, which was sorely missing out here. "I wonder about this all the time, Grace. How do some people recover each time they face what seems to be unbearable, while others cannot reassemble themselves? I don't know the answer. But when I asked Magda about it, she said, 'All I can say is what is *usually true* and so I expect it with everyone new. If you teach people that they are resilient, and that thinking of joyful things will make their way easier, soon they will get it, and then they will teach it back to you.'"

Grace smiled. "I like that, Mama."

••••••

The T-shirts arrived a few days before Christmas and were distributed according to strict rules. Only those older than 16 would receive a T-shirt, and the shirts could not be exchanged or given away, as this often resulted in fights later. If the T-shirt did not fit, a person could go to their trainer to exchange for a different size. Agnes had learned the hard way that making rules about every little thing went a long way toward harmony.

But she had grown more worried about Gloria, who had become more and more sullen as the T-shirts were handed out. She pouted and suffered and complained all that day and into the next, and she seemed to be leading a small group in a revolt against the whole process. So when Agnes saw Gloria outside her office the next morning, she was worried.

But Gloria was very self-possessed, and she began to negotiate. She would promise to stop being angry, starting fights, and stealing, if Agnes would promise that the T-shirt saying Gloria had wanted ('*To Heal It, You Have to Feel It*') could be ordered for later in the spring. Amazed that Gloria was presenting this very reasoned argument, Agnes agreed.

There were still some minor complaints and criticisms from Gloria's group as the women wore their '*Everybody Has a Story*' shirts, but Agnes reminded herself it was simply another exercise in learning to live in harmony with those who are different.

※※※※※

On Christmas Day Agnes was delighted to welcome her family to the shelter. Grace was already there, of course; but Moses and Mercy, and Dan and Dora, and all the children came to celebrate with them too. Beatrice and David did not come, but this did not surprise Agnes, even if it did sting. She wondered if her relationship with her oldest daughter would ever improve. But she was determined not to let Beatrice's choice ruin her mood.

Father Luke was as charismatic as Moses had promised, engaging the crowd during his homily and keeping the hymns rather short. He said a blessing over the whole shelter and all the people in it, and then he left.

Agnes looked around to give Moses a thumbs up. She knew he would be proud and pleased that his recommendation had gone over so well. But although she looked and looked, Agnes did not see Moses. She saw Mercy and Peace, who was usually at his side, but not her son.

A terrible feeling came over Agnes. She felt sick and desperate, without quite knowing why. She paused to decide in what direction she should begin to look. And in a weird way, she thought to look around for Gloria. Gloria had been on good behavior and had neither stolen anything nor started any fights. But she wasn't anywhere in the Gazebo now, as everyone lined up to fill their plates with Christmas dinner.

Agnes stumbled out of the Gazebo and ran toward Gloria's hut. As she got nearer, a breathless Moz sprinted toward her. Her sense of foreboding increased, and she slowed down and held out her arms to him. But he ran by and shouted, "No, Mama-Agnes, don't go! Turn back. Please turn back. Papa told me to get Grace. He doesn't want you, Mama-Agnes!"

Why Grace? Why not Pastor? Why not Mercy? Agnes kept running toward Gloria's hut, and outside it she found Moses. He was seated in the plastic chair with his face in his hands. "I'm sorry. I'm sorry," he said, rocking back and forth.

"You pig!" Gloria screamed from inside. She came out of the hut, disheveled and naked from the waist up. "You scum! You dirty bastard!" Her voice was hoarse as she screamed. "You vile man, I should have killed you!" She saw Agnes and her eyes narrowed meanly and she said, "This rotten beast raped me, or at least he tried! I fought him off. He's a killer, this one."

"Get more clothes on!" Agnes barked. "You are safe with me here." She knew immediately what had happened: Gloria had upped the ante today. She had gone after something far more valuable than a jerry can or a wash tub. She had gone after Mercy's husband.

When Gloria came out wearing the new T-shirt, Agnes took a deep breath. "Gloria, what happened? How did Moses even find his way down here?"

Gloria yelled for several minutes, accusing Moses of a hundred crimes. He did not defend himself but sat crying in his chair. Then all at once, Gloria's posture sagged. "It's not him. It's me. It's all my fault." She went inside the dark hut and threw herself on her mat and cried.

Agnes went inside and sat on the floor near her.

"I saw him with his wife and his children, and they looked so happy. I don't have children. They're gone. I asked him to make a baby with me. I begged him." Gloria cried. "I am not worth saving. I lie and steal. I will never change." She covered her head with a blanket.

Agnes heard voices outside the hut, and Magda came in to sit with Gloria. "Everyone is worth saving," Agnes said quietly. "And everyone can change if they decide to."

She went outside. Moses was still sitting in the chair, crying. "Moses, what happened?"

"I didn't rape her, but I may have had sex with her, if it weren't for Moz coming in. Where is he?" Moses asked, looking around.

Just then, Moz returned, leading Grace and Mercy and Peace.

Agnes sighed. It was now a family affair. She had expected drama from the shelter guests, but not from her own family.

Moz saw that Moses was crying and stood stock-still for a long moment. Then he threw himself at his mother in terror. "Mama, don't take us away! Mama, he didn't fuck her. I was here. He didn't fuck her, Mama-Mercy. I know, I was right here."

The eleven-year-old child they all knew as gentle, tender, and full of love went wild with heartbreaking grief, kicking and screaming. "She is evil! That woman is of the devil. Mama, don't leave Moses. Mama, we love him. Mama, he's my Papa."

Moz finally dissolved completely into tears, climbed into Moses's lap, and wrapped his arms around his father's neck. He wept and wept. "Papa, don't go with that bitch-woman. Don't ever leave us. Mama won't leave you. I know she won't."

Agnes stepped forward and rubbed Moz's back. Gradually, his sobs turned to snuffles and he began to calm down. Agnes explained to Mercy what had happened.

Gloria reappeared in her doorway with Magda at her side. Agnes braced herself for a fight, but none came. Mercy looked at Gloria and smiled. "Thank you for your honesty," she said. No doubt she was remembering so many women in similar circumstances back home, or maybe even personal experiences from her own traumatic past.

She handed Peace to Grace, then walked forward and put a hand on Moses's shoulder and another hand on Moz's. She closed her eyes, then turned to Agnes. "Mama," she said in a strong voice. "This is because of me. My womb is dead. I can bear no more children to bless our home. God has punished me, and when we prayed He told us to have faith in the Holy Bible. It will lead us back to Him. Psalm 127 says: *'Behold, children are a heritage from the LORD, the fruit of the womb a reward. Like arrows in the hand of a warrior are the children of one's youth. Blessed is the man who fills his quiver with them!'*"

Moses cleared his throat and opened his eyes. "I didn't rape her, Mercy, but I confess my sin. I promised that you would select our second wife. Without you choosing, I was going in there to make a baby with her until Moz showed up and stopped me. I'm so sorry, Mercy. I'm so sorry, Moz."

Mercy uttered a brief prayer in French, then looked at the family around her. "My husband is a man of God. Do not persecute him. The Bible told us to do this. I prayed that Jesus would bless us. I prayed for your forbearance. Is that the proper word in English?"

Agnes thought of the verse from 1 Corinthians 7:14: *For the unbelieving husband is sanctified by the wife, and the unbelieving wife is sanctified by the husband: else were your children unclean; but now are they holy.* "But now they are holy," she said. It was not her place to disagree with Moses and Mercy. "You have my blessing if you decide to take a second wife, Moses. It is not my business," Agnes said, softly but clearly. "But it cannot be a woman from Eve's Shelter."

Moses nodded.

"They are finding their way, Mama," said Grace quietly, as Mercy and Moses and Moz huddled together.

"If I grant some space for independent opinions among these mothers, I need to remember to grant space to my own children," Agnes said softly. "I know he has thought a lot about this, and he and Mercy are of one mind. Having you here, Grace, has kept me thinking about whether I am proud of my judgments or not. I am so glad you have come home. I am glad you haven't changed how you think about important things."

She squeezed her daughter's hand, and with tears in her eyes, she went back into the hut to console Gloria, and tell her she was a loveable, good person, who almost lost her way, but didn't. And there was always tomorrow.

"Thank you, Mama-Agnes," said Gloria. "And I mean it. I will stop stealing."

From the Gazebo the sound of singing drifted toward them on the evening breeze.

Silent night, holy night
All is calm, all is bright . . .

Agnes thought of a quote that Grace had told her, which she'd heard form Isaiah's sister-in-law Rita. "All I require of a religion is that it be tolerant of those who do not agree with it." This is their religion.

39

April 2020

A week before her due date, on April 14, 2020, Beatrice woke in the middle of the night when a pain surged through her abdomen. She smiled. Could baby Emma be coming?

"David," she whispered. "Wake up. Wake up. I think I might have had a contraction."

For the next few hours, they tried timing the contractions, but they were irregular. Aiko had advised her to labor at home for as long as possible, and to stay active while she could, so in the morning Beatrice and David walked slowly down the street and David got some breakfast at a street cart. But after just a few blocks Beatrice doubled over and moaned and they walked slowly back to their apartment.

All that day at home in their apartment she labored, until around 2 in the afternoon, when she gasped that it was time to go to the hospital. She was admitted and her doctor was pleased that her cervix was dilated to six centimeters. "Great work, Bea!" the doctor said. "Keep laboring, and I'll be back to check on you soon."

The nurse helped her bounce on a giant ball and walk small circles around the hospital room, then checked Beatrice's cervix again a few hours later: still six centimeters.

The doctor returned. "The baby isn't descending," she said briskly, "but that's not unusual for a first baby. Plus, she's pretty big. But there are no indications for a Cesarean section, so we'll carry on."

Beatrice drank some apple juice but then threw it all up. The pain was worse than she had anticipated. The nurse checked again, and active labor had stalled. Hours passed and Beatrice had been in labor for almost twenty-four hours, but the doctors said now it was 'unproductive labor'—that the baby was not close to being born, though her heart rate was steady, so she was not distressed.

Beatrice, however, was distressed. David was beside her, of course, and his mother Sandy had flown in from Utah as the due date drew near, so she was there too. The doctor suggested an epidural to help manage the pain. "Sometimes an epidural can also relax the body, which allows the cervix to open," she said.

Beatrice had wanted to have a drug-free childbirth. She had simply assumed it would be possible. Her mother had given birth to five babies in the bush without drugs or medical personnel or even a sterile room. Surely Beatrice could give birth in a safe, comfortable hospital!

But she couldn't. Why had no one told her that labor would be this bad? Hours and hours went by, and nothing seemed to happen except more and more pain. *Where was her mother?* She clenched David's hand and screamed with her next contraction. "Call my mother," she gasped suddenly. "I need her. Get her here. Please, David."

It was very early in the morning, and Beatrice had been in labor more than 27 hours. David's eyes widened, but he motioned for Sandy to take over holding Beatrice's hand and coaching her on her breathing as he stepped into the hallway and called Agnes. He explained what was happening. "Beatrice is safe," he said, "and so is the baby. But the labor is not progressing, and she is frightened. She wants you here. Can you come?"

David knew it was a long trip.

"Of course," Agnes said. "Moses will drive me. I will let you know when we have left."

Hours and hours went by. The labor progressed very slowly. Beatrice was so tired and in so much pain she could barely see or hear. Finally, around 11 the next morning, after 32 hours of labor, she decided to get an epidural.

Sweet relief washed over her, and she fell asleep for about thirty minutes. When she woke up, the nurse was checking her again. "Good girl," the nurse said. "You're fully dilated. It's time to start pushing, Beatrice. I'll get the doctor."

Relieved to hear the end was in sight, Beatrice pushed on her back for fifteen minutes, then on her side with pillows propping her up, then on her other side. After two hours of pushing and straining, the baby was still not even crowning. Beatrice cried and cried with frustration and exhaustion. Sandy and David looked at each other, helpless.

And then Agnes walked into the room.

"Mama!" Beatrice gasped, tears rolling down her cheeks. "Mama! I can't do this. I'm too tired. I can't do it, Mama."

Agnes came to Beatrice's side and gripped her hand. "Listen to me, my daughter. You can. You are strong. So strong, my Aber Beatrice." Agnes hummed a song under her breath. "You kept me going on our long walk, when we were escaping the bush. You kept your sister safe when I was too sick to go on. You helped us find our way home."

Beatrice nodded, her eyes locked on her mother's.

"Listen to me, Beatrice. We are going to call the baby by name. This is what my friend Nancy did for me in the bush, when I was giving birth to Moses. I was thirteen years old and so frightened. But Nancy whispered to me: *Tell Moses you will stand beside him always, as God has chosen him for important work. Tell Moses God has a plan for him. Tell him over and over until he hears you.*"

Beatrice nodded, her eyes wide and frightened, then a look of resolve coming into them.

"Let's do it, Bea," David said gently. "Let's call baby Emma by name."

"No," Beatrice said, her teeth clenched as she pushed through a contraction. "It's not Emma." Her eyes closed and she pushed and strained, then gasped, "Her name is Eve. The baby's name is Eve."

David nodded and gripped Bea's hand tighter. "Eve, we love you. Eve, come on, baby."

Beatrice nodded too. "Eve, my beautiful daughter, it is time to be born. God has a plan for you, Eve. God has a plan for you." She cried and pushed.

"Good," the doctor said. "The baby is crowning."

Beatrice called for baby Eve, and pushed, and called, and pushed, and slowly, slowly, Eve came into the world. The doctor lifted the baby onto Beatrice's chest, and Beatrice held her and sobbed with relief.

An hour or so later, after the cord had been cut and the baby checked and weighed, the nurse helped Beatrice get Eve latched onto her breast. "Mama," Beatrice said, and Agnes came and stood next to her.

"I am sorry, Mama, that it took me so long to forgive you," Beatrice said, her voice thick. "I had to process so much, and it was very painful. But I am so grateful to you." She cried. "So grateful that you came when I needed you."

"I love you, my daughter," Agnes said. "I always will. No matter what."

Beatrice looked up at her mother. "This is Eve Adong Murdock."

Tears glistened in her mother's eyes. "After me?"

"You brought her here, Mama. You brought us all here."

Epilogue

Kampala—2025

"Look out the window, Eve," said David, beckoning enthusiastically. "You can wave to Mommy-Bea, Mama-Agnes, and Auntie Grace as they head to Entebbe."

"Bye, Bye," Eve cheered as the women returned her waves with excited smiles.

"They will pick up Mama-Aiko, too," David added, explaining again that the women were all going to fly on a big airplane to France. "I'm so glad Gracie could go with them to this special conference. She will take lots of pictures when the others are giving their talks."

"Is that why Auntie Grace gave me this new puzzle? So I can find it on this map?" asked five-year-old Eve, returning to the coffee table where Grace had started her off on a child's map of the world. She'd even stuck a little red dot on Paris so Little Eve could see where they had all gone in such a whirl of excitement, telling her young niece, "That's a very pretty city where we are going."

> **INTERNATIONAL CONFERENCE**
>
> *Breaking the Cycle of Intergenerational Trauma*
> *After Persistent War*
> L'Institut de Psychologie, Paris, France
>
> **CONVENER**
> Dr. Aiko Yamada,
> Makerere University and
> University of Utah, USA
>
> **PRESENTERS**
> Dr. Berniss Kabongo,
> L'Institut de Psychologie, Paris and
> L'université de Kisangani, DRC
>
> Dr. Beatrice Murdock,
> Makerere University, Kampala, Uganda
>
> **DISCUSSANT**
> Adong Agnes,
> Director, Eve's Shelter,
> Gulu, Uganda

Bea had spoken regularly about this opportunity to present findings from her own research on intergenerational trauma, and she would be presenting alongside her esteemed colleague from DRC and France who was already an expert in the field. It had been Dr. Aiko's idea for them to present together, and to have her as the convener when they presented. And then, of course, to have Bea's mother be a discussant made perfect sense. After all, she could represent practitioners who work where their applied theories were especially relevant. "They will sell recordings of each session, and I'll get one for you," Bea had promised as she kissed David good-bye.

"While you work on your puzzle, Daddy's going to make a frame," David said, eager to hang the conference invitation on the wall along with the notification that Bea's and Dr. Kabongo's papers had been accepted. "We'll surprise your mother when she comes home. She'll love that!"

THE END

Author's Note

Fall 2024

This book is a work of fiction, but the story is true and the characters are real; true and real in the sense that women like the ones I portray live today in Gulu, the city in Northern Uganda that was the epicenter of the war that Joseph Kony perpetrated on his Acholi people in the name of God. These women all tell similar stories about themselves, stories that share so many details with my characters that I do not believe anyone in Gulu would accuse me of exaggeration or dramatic enhancement. However, I have not tried to replicate any one particular person's biography. I have worked hard to make Agnes's story different enough that no one from Gulu who reads this will try to find herself or himself in the book. I do this to respect the privacy of any particular person who shared a personal story.

What was most important to me was to tell the story of a formerly abducted child mother who returns home to post-war Gulu after being held in captivity by Kony's

Lord's Resistance Army (LRA) since childhood, only to find herself unwelcome. She would then have to make her way in this unfriendly environment, often with children of her own, with little local support and no western outsider telling her how to heal and how to build a life for herself. I tell it this way because this was the typical homecoming experience of most child mothers. I did make Agnes exceptionally diligent and creative as she tries to find her footing after returning home, and I did give her some extra good luck in the form of kind friends, but mostly I tried to make her an ordinary daughter of Gulu. Like so many thousands of others born there and abducted in their youth and kept in captivity for a decade or more, she would be recognizable to anyone there that read her story here. She could be real.

I also hoped to provide more detail about the history of the war in the northern part of Uganda that lasted from 1986 to 2006, with occasional skirmishes after the fragile ceasefire was established. The fighting between Kony's LRA and the people around him was most intense during those twenty bitter years, and touched the lives of everyone in that region in many violent and awful ways. His male captives, often young boys, were abducted from their homes, then armed and trained as soldiers, while many of the female captives were handed to violent officers as their wives. These captives were expected to bear children as soon as they were able, despite many of them still being children themselves.

The experiences here are ones that thousands of Acholi women share. Many of these women either walked across the countryside to find their families if they could,

Author's Note

or were picked up by a truck and deposited at one of several designated meeting sites where they were promised their family members would be there to meet them (many never did). I received invaluable help from mothers who survived these experiences of escaping and remember vividly the scenes of not being welcomed home.

I've approached this task with great humility, as I am fully aware that I am an older North American woman with various kinds of privilege and a full life doing other things. My life is very different from my character, Adong Agnes, and from the lives of the women I know in Uganda on whom she is modeled. Frankly, I had never imagined I'd write a novel about child mothers in Northern Uganda. My path to this goal was not direct.

I trained as a political scientist in the 1960s at the Fletcher School of Law and Diplomacy in Medford, Massachusetts, and had presumed I would be a diplomat. I was waylaid from my path in the mid-60s, when I became involved in the Civil Rights Movement, the Anti-War Movement, and then the Women's Movement—all of which engaged thousands of activists that I lived among. The energy for these campaigns was wild and fierce and converged geographically, but also emotionally, for me, around Cambridge, MA. I took time off from my diplomatic career ambitions to accept a teaching job that I expected to be temporary. I taught courses in comparative politics, but also on public policy, and international law and human rights. I soon gravitated to teaching women's studies and focused on how public policy impacts women's lives. I would go on to teach for forty-seven years at Suffolk University. I never regretted this decision.

Around this time, I also joined a collective of women scholars I met at my church, who were looking into the history of women members of the Church of Jesus Christ of Latter-day Saints. I developed a fascination with the ways in which women build communities of mutual support when in dangerous situations: birthing babies, educating children, educating themselves, and pursuing political power to ensure gender equity and human rights. In the 1970s I followed the organizing of a global women's movement through the U.N. and aspired to attend the First World Conference on the Status of Women when it convened in Mexico City, Mexico coinciding with the 1975 International Women's Year. Between 1972 and 1982, I also bore four children of my own. Becoming a mother sharpened my empathy for and sense of connectedness with women everywhere and strengthened my determination to confront discrimination against women around the world and to protect women and children from violence.

In 1985, I had the opportunity to spend three weeks in Nairobi, Kenya, at the Third World Conference on the Status of Women. At least sixteen thousand women attended the conference in various capacities, committing to appraise the achievements of the U.N. Decade for Women (1976–1985), and to set goals for women into the next decade. These U.N. conferences helped combine the intellectual with the practical parts of life for literally millions of women and brought women from different parts of the world together for the first time.

Much later, when I went to Dakar, Senegal as the Dean of the Senegal campus of Suffolk University, I was motivated to find on-the-ground situations in an African country, where I could help to improve the lives of women already helping one another with limited resources. It was this intention that led to my trip to Uganda in 2009.

Around the same time, in 2008, I taught a particularly large class on African politics. Several of those students requested that I teach an advanced course on African politics, with a focus on assessing the progress, or lack thereof, in post-conflict situations. They showed a particular curiosity in studying the rehabilitation of soldiers—including child soldiers—and the reactivation of political activity and social infrastructure building, and also the long-lasting challenges of nation-building in places where divisions ran deep. I saw this as an opportunity for the students to go on a month-long trip to Africa where we could study alongside African students and instructors. We chose Uganda, and in spring 2009, twenty-three students and I left for Kampala. There we met not only academics, but also members of Parliament and leaders in other sectors in the country. As the war with the LRA in the north had recently achieved a ceasefire, there was a kind of excitement and optimism about the future, and our meetings with Ugandans were particularly candid and open. Malia Everette, from AltruVista in CA, arranged for some local people to talk with us about Kony's rise to power, how he created the Lord's Resistance Army, and his tactics and practices for the twenty years he ravaged the area north of a branch of the Nile that runs west to east across the small Central African country. We returned home inspired and motivated to come up with ideas for starting innovative non-profits that would contribute to Uganda's recovery.

I returned to Uganda the following year with a group of ten women, some of whom had experience in counseling. We introduced ourselves to a parish in Gulu, where we bought bricks and built eight huts for people identified as the most vulnerable. Each of the ten of us spent time with at least one woman identified as a child mother, and asked what she considered her biggest personal need and the biggest need for the community. The women spoke of housing, land, and a safe place to stay, a job, literacy training, and school fees for their children. Noticeably, each also spoke about getting help with nightmares and fears and memories of captivity. When we used the term 'trauma,' they rejected it at first, but when we were able to engage them in conversation about it, most agreed they needed help overcoming exactly that.

The first time I attended a church service in Gulu the pastor switched from English to Acholi and almost everyone in the congregation folded their hands up against their chests and rocked back and forth, nodding their heads in unison. They began to hum together and sustained a sound of collective grieving for some time. A Ugandan man leaned forward from his seat behind me to say, "You do understand, don't you Mama, that everyone up here has PTSD."

Over the years that followed, as I became more deeply acquainted with those who lived in and around Gulu, I would find his statement to be true. Trauma hangs in the air. Even when sitting among young mothers nursing sleeping babies under a tree while their older children laugh and play nearby, one has the sense that an unexpected loud noise or the approach of strange men could quickly turn the scene to chaos. Fear and tension rests just beneath the surface of the everyday. It is this undertone that inspired me to tell the world the stories from this place. I wanted to learn as much as I could about the internal lives of child mothers, and what I could not learn and never experience first-hand, I wanted to envision in as informed a way as possible. I hope I have not done any disservice.

My husband, Jim Coleman, my daughter, Eliza, my first cousin, Kathleen Sorenson from Salt Lake City, as well as two friends, Eden Williams and Linda Taylor, and several others, committed ourselves to building a center in Gulu where, in a safe atmosphere, we could offer courses in literacy and job training, and leadership training in borrowing money and repaying small loans. There were other non-profit organizations that arrived when we did, all offering a variety of essential services. But more and more, we heard the request for an organization that would help the local women better manage their nightmares and irritability, and what gradually emerged as a call for ways to respond to trauma. The words we all used were not easily translated, but the women persisted, and we tried to be good listeners. As I'd learned on a previous visit, the Ugandan war survivors were very sensitive to any indication that we thought they suffered from mental health problems. Gradually, we understood they wanted activities that could lead them down the path of healing from the deep trauma of war and sexual violence they had suffered during their captivity. We began a program offering a variety of ways to support the women who came seeking support in healing from trauma. We listened to many discussions among mostly young women with children, who had spent time living with the LRA in the bush, as they expressed what they believed they could accomplish if this kind of trauma work was made available to them.

I am proud of what I consider the successes that grew out of our good listening skills. An example was when we bought land from a group of older mothers from the war and built a building on the land. The land was sacred to the women who had bravely kept it and raised crops on it during the war, and we were fortunate that James Latigo, our friend and the first man I ever met in Gulu in 2009, was able to convince them to sell it to us. My daughter Eliza had worked hard to raise the money for that land purchase and its successful development meant a lot to her and to us. However, before we could begin construction, our Country Director, Alal Single-Dora, insisted we build a wall around the property. At first we did not understand the importance of this wall, but at the insistence of the local women, we agreed, and it was built. Our organization grew, and as more and more women came to access services there, we realized that for traumatized women, safety is the first need. Building a wall around the place they would gather signaled to them that we heard their expressed needs. Once the wall was up, things progressed quickly.

Overcoming the multiple challenges of fundraising, identifying, and hiring local Ugandans, and becoming legally incorporated in both Uganda and the U.S. we successfully established a non-governmental organization called THRIVE-Gulu. Several of the staff are themselves formerly abducted women and men, and some worked with the agencies that located families for returnees after the war. We were lucky to hire Alal Single-Dora as our very able Country Director in Gulu. Alal had worked at both World Vision–Uganda Children of War Rehabilitation Center and also Gulu Support the Children Organization (GUSCO) for the final years of the war. She had also managed a triage process for women who had been returned to Gulu from Kony LRA camps or from Internally Displaced People's camps (IDPs), assessing those who were critically emotionally disabled, and working to promote their well-being through psycho-social support, leadership building, literacy education, and peacebuilding. Alal's intimate knowledge of the magnitude of the challenge helped THRIVE develop several programs that consistently provided what assessment teams found to be the most helpful and appreciated capacity-building and skill-teaching curricula for hundreds of people each year. Our organization has grown to become an established NGO that began with private funding from family, friends, and other good-hearted people, and went on to be supported by grants from large international aid agencies. However, we have maintained our independence, and involve our Gulu-based Ugandan Country Director and her staff in all the decisions we make around how best to serve those healing from trauma. This remains at the heart of what we do: support mostly women and their families as they heal from the trauma caused by war and sexual violence during the LRA war, and from the continuing gender-based violence that is perpetrated on so many women in the post-war world.

My husband, Jim and I dedicated a good part of our lives after 2010 working to be effective and creative in our efforts to aid in what continues to be a major challenge for thousands of survivors in Northern Uganda. After Jim's death in 2013, I continued to manage the NGO from my home in Boston, MA in the U.S., doing what I could to encourage ever more effective programs in group counseling and individual therapy, to supplement the other programs we have at the THRIVE Center. I was blessed to attract the volunteer service of Mike Bello, who, as Board Chair, took THRIVE to a higher level, and managed the hiring of Mick Hirsch, a wonderful American man of many talents and past experience working with refugees and trauma recovery. Along with other dedicated Board members we have continued to help thousands of mostly women. We've offered training in avoiding gender-based violence (GBV) as well as in pregnancy prevention, and the other programs that we started when we established ourselves in Gulu. We have managed to expand our services to South Sudan in the Palabek Refugee Community and to Odek, the small home village of the notorious criminal, Joseph Kony, himself.

As expected, different therapeutic techniques have had varying degrees of effectiveness with different women. At one point, we employed video interviews with child mothers about their life experiences. We hoped to use the videos in therapy groups, including those that encourage storytelling and narrative therapies. These interviews, and ten years working with the women who have come and gone through THRIVE-Gulu, suggested to me that a wonderful way for us to help may be to encourage women to write their own stories. Several of us hoped we could assist in the writing of memoirs and journals where the women could express what happened to them, and how they have rebuilt their lives. Professor Erin Baines from British Columbia, Canada, is well-known in Gulu for establishing the Justice and Reconciliation Project that helps honor and "document and promote survivor-centered approaches to justice and social repair since 2004." She successfully collaborated with a child mother in writing her autobiography. The book, *I am Evelyn Amony: Reclaiming my life from the Lord's Resistance Army* (edited with an introduction by Erin Baines, University of Wisconsin Press, 2015), has been published and released around the world. I found their success inspiring and would have loved to help others achieve something similar, but the logistical challenges have discouraged me from continuing with this ambitious project. These challenges, coupled with the Covid pandemic, have complicated plans to travel back and forth to Gulu and meet with the women there.

Without easy access to fulfilling this hope, I decided to write this novel myself. I believe the book communicates to readers what a child mother from Gulu would want the world to know about her life in the LRA and after. I believe it shows the struggles of surviving abduction, the abhorrent abuse and violence that followed, and a rocky return to a home where she was not only unwelcome but, in many cases punished for having been kidnapped, as if it had been her choice to go over to Kony's side. I relied on my ten years of traveling back and forth to Gulu, and on my ongoing phone and email communication with child mothers. Whenever I ask a question, the women and men I reach out to have quickly and thoroughly responded. Whenever I needed pictures to supplement what I was hearing, people have been eager to provide them. Phillip Odiambo has been particularly helpful in sending photographs of places I have not visited, and James Latigo has shared invaluable information with me as he has documented the life experiences of so many survivors over the years.

Writing this book has been a challenge, but it has also been a deeply joyful experience. Coming to know and respect the women I have met in Northern Uganda has enriched my life considerably. Each woman had her own unique experience during the war, and I have been fortunate to witness the profound specialness in each individual's way of working on her healing. That is the main message I hope this book conveys: People in Gulu who have been working on recovering from the war experience have mostly welcomed advice, support, and help from outsiders whom they trust and who have come there for that purpose. But what I appreciate more now than ever before, is that each person there has had to heal herself. Too often those of us in the West focus on what outside NGOs or individual aid-workers do for people in Africa. We give credit to Westerners for being the saviors, the healers and educators of the Ugandans, or Liberians, or Sierra Leoneans, or South Africans, or Rwandans, when in fact, we are at best adjuncts to the process we watch unfolding when we are lucky enough to be trusted.

Hilary Mantel wrote a magnificent historical saga of the rise and fall of Thomas Cromwell in the court of Henry

Author's Note

VIII in Tudor England. Commenting on her process when writing historical fiction she said, "I had a kind of greed for knowing more of what I had not seen before." When asked what motivated her to dig deeply into the history of extended families in the 16th Century, she said, "Historical fiction comes out of greed for experience. 'Violent curiosity drives us on, takes us far from our time, far from our shore, and often beyond our compass.'" (*Why We Read Historical Fiction*, Gramercy Books). She went on to remark that with historical fiction, the writer can bring a nearly inaccessible cast of characters from a nearly inaccessible place and pull them into our close and present moment. Careful, solid history writing does not speculate carelessly, and it does not explore the minds and hearts of people only to exploit them. The opportunity to bring history to life in a sensitive manner is reserved for the truly curious and humble.

As I spent more and more time among the healing women, I felt the greed Mantel describes to know more, but I was also grateful for the privilege I was given. I wrote this book to put my life in the service of their beautiful stories. I hope I have done them justice.

······

I dedicated this book to two child mothers in Uganda that I met the first time I went there. Lucy Aol and Rose Aber.

One came with an impressive group of nuns from Gulu that worked at St. Monica's Girls' Tailoring School that had harbored hundreds of young people during the war and kept them from abduction and fed them a meal a day. Its founder and director, Sister Rosemary Nyirumbe, later celebrated as Time Magazine's Woman of the Year, confirmed what I knew. Before she left Gulu she said, "You have a charism. Don't resist it." I didn't know the term, but as I explored it, I did what she told me to do, and what this calling laid out for me.

The other came with a powerful woman lawyer and activist, Lina Zedriga Waru Abuku that I had met when she received a Certificate in Women and Public Policy from J.F. Kennedy School at Harvard University in Boston where I live. As a Ugandan woman who had been part of innumerable activities and organizations committed to empowering women in her country and in all of Africa, she had been a presenter at a conference organized by Ambassador Swanee Hunt, the founder of the Women and Public Policy Program. She was instrumental in helping lay out a plan for our initial activities in Gulu and literally drove me there in her car when I went there for the first time and met the wonderful Beads of Hope women.

On several occasions we were graced with the presence and encouragement of Betty Bigombe, who has held countless positions in Gulu, and in the Ugandan National Government, in the World Bank, and in the Ugandan Parliament. And she was the first person to famously dare to go into the forest in the North to engage Joseph Kony in an effort to bring about a cease fire in the war. She has mediated untold numbers of conflicts on the Continent in her many capacities. She closely and actively advised us as we began our work there. She is held in such esteem, and many credit her with ending the war.

Acknowledgments

Elie Wiesel said, "Why were human beings created? Because God loves stories."

Each person's story *is* sacred. It must be listened to, heard, remembered, and revered. When I listened to child soldiers and formerly abducted girls from Gulu tell their own fresh, raw stories on my first visits to Uganda, they took my breath away. I felt entrusted and responsible and morally required to let these young people know that I was truly listening. I said to them, "You matter." And the more I heard, the more I knew, I had to amplify what I was told. I knew I could not take them in all alone, and share them with the world, so I relied on others. I want to acknowledge the help that came from so many.

Sister Rosemary Nyirumbe, with her entourage of nuns from St. Monica's Girls Tailoring School, had saved thousands of kids from the Lord's Resistance Army, and she traveled seven hours to Uganda's capital to educate me and my students from Suffolk University about this hideous war that was slowly ending. She brought nine young survivors that shared tales of battlefields, forced marches, and rebel camps.

Lina Zedriga, an outspoken Ugandan lawyer who spoke at Harvard, and stayed in our home, spent hours teaching me about young women in Gulu and led a hut-making trip I organized for women to go build shelters in Gulu. One woman in particular from that trip, **Linda Taylor,** went back five times to help with reusable menstrual kits and formed strong bonds with several women.

My husband, **Jim Coleman,** loved Gulu, too, and took on most of the work of building out THRIVE-Gulu and focusing its mission, for five years. It was one of the best things we did together and was a shared passion. It was when he suddenly died and I retired from university teaching, that I began to write this book. I know he would be pleased.

I found various ways to record and collect some stories, but I found no one in those years able to write a personal history. My daughter, **Eliza,** and my son, **Nate,** were among those that helped video women telling stories. "Someday," we said. **Eliza** also raised money to buy the land for our THRIVE-Gulu Center and build the wall around it. She was invaluable and so loving that it helped me believe we could stay there and help.

My cousin, **Kathleen Sorenson,** was the first donor to THRIVE-Gulu and has continued to be its major funder. She went to Gulu and helped build trust with people there, as she is a beautiful communicator. When people there said, "Now we know what a donor looks like," I had to tell them that not all are so lovely and kind as she is.

Eden Williams from Boston is my former student who helped organize the initial trip to Uganda and went on to be on the Board of Directors for THRIVE-Gulu for more than a decade. His love for people there has earned him such deep respect from so many that he could find out anything I needed to know when I wrote this book. He is deeply connected to the Acholi culture and encouraged me from the beginning and organized Gulu readers to comment on the story as it evolved.

Over eight years, I spoke with others that were part of Uganda history and taught me things about women in the war that I needed to know. I acknowledge their role in helping me shape this novel. **Betty Bigombe** is from Gulu herself and was the first person brave enough to go meet Kony in the bush to try to negotiate a peace in 1994. Kony refused her initiative, and she took various positions in the Uganda national government but stayed devoted to peace. She remains a major figure in the peacekeeping and conflict resolution world. She helped me early on to understand life particularly for young women in the North of Uganda.

Patrick Lumumba Oola, a young, returned child soldier who worked as an intern in the Gulu municipal offices, showed me all around his city and was our first employee at the THRIVE. He went on to be elected mayor of Gulu and owns a seed store and seems to know everyone. He is a master at connecting people to one another. He became a close friend, and introduced us to **Doral Alal Single**, who has been our Country Director.

A wonderfully helpful person I met on my first visit to Gulu is **James Ojera Latigo,** who has conducted considerable research on Northern Uganda, with an emphasis on traditional practices in the Acholi Region. James has been part of multiple efforts to record memories of the war and to document post-conflict rebuilding. He not only wrote about Reconciliation efforts, but he also led many himself, and is an expert on lives lived and lost in Internally Displaced Persons camps in Northern Uganda. He is also a leader in the Church of Jesus Christ of Latter-day Saints in Uganda and introduced me to many other members so I could see the role the church in Gulu played in their lives, which informed my novel.

When I worked on the first drafts of this book, **Michael** and **Brandilyn Tyler** listened endlessly to my efforts to shape the plot. The fact that **Michael** had been a missionary in Gulu somehow made me see how my characters could be almost real.

Since I went to Gulu less often during Covid, I had to depend on my dear friends in Gulu to fill in the many things I still did not know about the lives they had lived during and after the war. **Lucy Aol** and **Rose Aber** were the most forthcoming with their tales of abduction and escape and recovery in a fractured community where others were healing at the same time and often engaged in undermining behaviors. They answered hundreds of questions about relationships among people who were often compromised in the war and are now neighbors, as well as about parenting styles and sewing school uniforms and helping children learn to read at schools that are resource poor. I am intimately close to them and to their children, some of whom have also shared things with me that helped me write this book. I thank them all: **Vicky, Mugisha, Dorah, Mercy, Winnie, Judy Pearl, Eden Bright, Nathaniel Mark.** Each of them brought a different perspective that enriched my novel. For example, they pushed me to consider what it means for some children to know and interact with their fathers, while others long to identify a father but know he is their mother's rapist and kidnapper. They continue to teach me about interactions among family members when violence and secrets are part of their stories.

Another close friend who supported my work from Gulu is **Phillip Odiambo,** who agreed to scout out places across northern Uganda and to photograph and describe and explain their importance in the war's history. It is through him that I "saw" Palabek and came to understand the lives of refugees along the border with South Sudan. He commented extensively on the manuscript and checked for errors. Several other people from Gulu read a late manuscript of this book and were willing to participate on a panel to discuss it and help me improve parts. **Muhamad Gadafi** and "**Big Emmy**" helped organize those discussion groups.

I've always loved good fiction, and I am particularly drawn to historical fiction, but I had never written any fiction myself. **Brooke Adams Law** was my first editor and she had to begin with such basic guidance and learning assignments that I give her high praise for gently but sensibly moving towards draft after draft of a very rapidly changing manuscript. She was so orderly and loving, as well as cheerful and encouraging. She loved my characters, and I appreciated her affection for the story I wanted to tell. Brooke suggested I bring in another editor, and that's when **Rachel Rueckert** jumped in and did a brilliant reorganizing of the whole book, breaking through some literary barriers for me before she sent me off to find a totally new editor. With no guidance I took a chance and connected with **Julie P. Cantrell**, who was so quick and careful and helpful that I felt lifted up by her editing and final polish

I've had some serious health crises during the years I wrote this book, and my friend **Linda Andrews** has assisted in making my life easier. She helped me with the technology I needed to use when sending things to readers and editors.

I'm blessed to have my family living close to me in Boston. There have been weeks when I barely spoke to any of them because I was working on the book. I thank them all for being happy for me and never acting like they thought I was doing something impossible for an 82-year-old mom. In addition to **Eliza** and **Nate**, **Aaron** and **Leni** (who also went to Gulu and taught a workshop) and **Ben**, and Liza's husband **Peter** and Nate's husband **Ami**, have also taken my writing seriously and have encouraged me. It's amazing how important that has been to push me over the finish line. Sometimes a visit from my grandchildren—**Kyle, Sofia, Jovan,** and **Bourne** and **Bodie**—was what I needed, and they came through. **Jovan** even stopped by my place to play Chopin when I was discouraged.

JUDY DUSHKU is an American academic who taught at Suffolk University in Boston for 47 years, a humanitarian who established an NGO that works to improve mental health in Uganda, and a writer best known for her contributions to the Mormon feminist journal *Exponent II*, which she cofounded. She is an active member of the Church of Jesus Christ of Latter-day Saints and was Boston Stake Relief Society president. Her husband Jim Coleman died in 2013, but she lives near her 4 children and several grandchildren in Watertown, MA.

Made in the USA
Middletown, DE
02 March 2025